"You and ole 'Squirrel Tooth' do bear a striking resemblance."

Kathleen squirmed against Sage, unwilling to wage a full-fledged battle again. "She's at least ten years my senior and missing half a dozen teeth."

"So you saw the resemblance on the wanted poster as well?"

She could hear his smirk. How dare he assume she was some lowlife? Some ugly old woman of such ill repute that she was wanted dead or alive. She lifted one leg and drove the heel of her boot into his shin.

His arm came across her chest, pinning her to him. "Damn. You're a hellion. If I weren't . . ."

He stopped abruptly. She wondered why. Then she heard the voices. Still far off, she couldn't discern the words, only the feelings. They were rough and unforgiving. They put a fear in her greater than any the dirty cowboy had. She pulled her head away from his chest in a effort to hear better.

He slid out from under her and turned over. She lay under him now, cocooned by his body. The only thing that prevented her from being crushed was the strength of his left arm, which supported his weight.

She set her head back down and opened her eyes to find she was staring into his, inches away. They were pale blue. Liquid blue and there was question and humor in them. The whole situation was so . . . so intimate.

The Wild
IRISH WEST

JOAN AVERY

LEISURE BOOKS NEW YORK CITY

A LEISURE BOOK®

February 2003

Published by

Dorchester Publishing Co., Inc.
276 Fifth Avenue
New York, NY 10001

ISBN 0-8439-5145-1

The name "Leisure Books" and the stylized "L" with design are
trademarks of Dorchester Publishing Co., Inc.

Printed in the United States of America.

Visit us on the web at www.dorchesterpub.com.

For Gail Oust,
a great friend and fellow writer
who never lost faith in me.
This one's for you.

The Wild
IRISH WEST

Chapter One

Deadwood, South Dakota 1876

"Aaauuck! Let go of me yeh fiend!" Kathleen Callahan pulled against the metal handcuff.

"So I'm a fiend, am I? Well, if you don't stop fidgeting, you'll have my wrist worn clean through."

"Yer wrist! What about mine? Look!" She held up her shackled appendage.

"Frankly, I don't give a rat's ass. You should be grateful you're here with me and not stuck in Deadwood's jail."

"Grateful! Grateful! Yeh . . ." Several choice words crossed her mind. She stared at the dirty cowboy. His calm demeanor did more to irritate her than the rocks that tore her soft kid boots and made every step excruciating. She was gasping for air after their long run. She looked up. Before

1

her the terrain rose rapidly into the Black Hills. What did he think she was, a mountain goat?

"I'll be grateful when yeh're hanged. That's when I'll be grateful," she finally shouted.

They had to be caught soon. A man with a woman handcuffed to him was no match for a posse on horseback, and this dirty scoundrel certainly deserved whatever punishment was in store for him. She had heard he'd shot a man dead with barely a word exchanged between them.

"Hurry up. Stop dawdling."

As he dragged her reluctantly along, she searched behind them for someone to save her. There was no sign of a posse, and Deadwood was now barely a dot on the horizon. How could a posse have missed them on the long flat stretch? Still studying the horizon, she issued an ultimatum. "Yeh'll not be convincin' me to go a step farther if yeh don't slow your pace."

"I'm afraid Miss . . . ?"

Kathleen gasped as she bumped into the man. He had stopped and turned. She stood nose to chest with him, unaware that the peacock feather in her perky green bonnet was dancing before his face. He was one of the tallest men she had ever seen. Well over six foot. Six-foot-four maybe. Standing within inches of him, her eyes had trouble focusing. She stared uncomfortably at his middle shirt button, which needed to be stitched on properly. She looked up, way up, to his tanned and bearded face.

"Me name is Callahan, sir. That it is, and proud of it I am."

"Well, Miss Callahan, the charming brogue won't help you one bit. The sheriff believes you're the notorious 'Squirrel Tooth' Sally, wanted for bank robbery in three states. They're after you as much as me, my dear Miss Callahan.

And they won't hesitate to shoot first and ask questions afterward."

For the first time since this latest disaster had begun, a wave of fear coursed through Kathleen's four-foot-ten-inch frame. "Well, since yeh put it that way, I'll be following along until we can get these things off." She held up her handcuffed wrist, only to have it jerked back down abruptly.

"Ouch, yeh're hurting me. Yeh certainly are no gentleman." She turned away from him in a small act of defiance before she continued. "In Boston . . ."

A dirty hand clapped over her mouth without warning. "Shhh . . . quiet."

She shook her head furiously to rid herself of his hold. He jerked her down behind a small outcropping of rock and held her tighter. She could hardly breathe.

She'd had enough. She bit down as hard as she could into the callused flesh that smelled of tobacco and whiskey.

"Damn!" It was an irritated whisper. He yanked his fingers away but caught her hair and pulled her back until she lay in his arms. "And you, Miss Callahan, are no lady! So if we are to have an understanding, it will be that you do what I say when I say. Do you understand?"

Kathleen doggedly refused to shake her head in acceptance of his ludicrous demand.

"Let me put it another way. That posse you've been hoping for has flanked us in that gully, and they're nearly on us." His left hand now circled her throat. He whispered in her ear, his breath raising goose flesh on her arms. "Now, I'll explain this one more time, and I want you to listen very closely. Those men on horseback out there—I don't want them to find me. Every moment I spend dragging you along makes it more likely they will. Unfortunately, our separation

3

would require your dismemberment or some other bodily rearrangement. Right now I am still reluctant to resort to this method. But believe me, if you don't shut up and do as I say, I won't be responsible for my actions. Is that clear?"

This time Kathleen shook her head in the affirmative.

"Good."

She felt him expel a relieved breath. It seemed out of character for a cowboy who had killed a man in cold blood in Deadwood and just threatened to do the same to her.

"I don't think they've seen us yet." He added as he lay back and skidded along the dirt and down into a three-foot wash below the rocky overhang. Kathleen was carried along on top of him like a bird on a tortoise's back. She felt ridiculous.

She knew she should be quiet and not aggravate the man further, but as her father used to say, "Kathleen, me dear, yeh run off at the mouth somethin' fierce." Besides, she was curious.

Undaunted she blurted out, "You don't sound like a cowboy."

He shifted under her, then brought his right hand slightly around her to allow her to rest her raw wrist at her waist. "And what does a cowboy sound like?"

She had the uncomfortable feeling he was smiling.

"You know." Kathleen lowered her voice into a gruff imitation, "Howdy partner. Let's round up da cattle and head for some grub. Cattle thieves are so thick 'round here y'ud think they had a bill of sale on the whole damn country."

She could feel the laugh in his chest rumbling against her back long before she heard it.

It irritated her. He was making her feel like a fool. She was mortified. "If yeh don't stop laughin', they'll find us for sure," she snapped.

4

"My dear, Miss Callahan, I believe you have been reading too many dime novels."

"I do *not* read dime novels." Her whispered hiss would have been enough to intimidate even the most dauntless Boston fop. "I read literature, if you have a clue as to what that might be."

"Let me guess, Miss Callahan. *The Iliad*. Perhaps in the original Greek? No. No. Ibsen's *Peer Gynt*. Too grim I'll wager. I've got it. It's Alcott's *Little Women* when you're not reading dime novels."

Kathleen colored. He had come too close to the truth.

"You should try the works of Bret Harte if you like the West, Miss Callahan."

"Stop it!"

"Stop what?"

What was it she wanted him to stop? She wasn't quite sure. She threw out a quick response. "Stop calling me Miss Callahan."

"What would you prefer I call you? 'Squirrel Tooth'?"

She fought against him, trying to worm her way out of their snug hideaway. He brought his left arm around her as well. When she realized it was useless, she lay back against his chest. "I am not 'Squirrel Tooth' whoever you said. I am certainly *not* a criminal like you." She could feel his chest move in an easy rhythm, his warm breath on the back of her neck.

"It's not often they see a woman dressed in such a fancy frock out here. It must have attracted a good deal of attention. That, and the fact that you and ole 'Squirrel Tooth' do bear a striking resemblance."

Kate squirmed against him, unwilling to wage a full-fledged battle again. "How dare you. She's at least ten years my senior and missing half a dozen teeth."

5

Joan Avery

"So you saw the resemblance in the wanted poster as well?"

She could hear his smirk. How dare he assume she was some lowlife. Some ugly old woman of such ill repute that she was wanted dead or alive. She lifted one leg and drove the heel of her boot into his shin.

His arm came across her chest pinning her to him. "Damn. You're a hellion. If I weren't . . .

He stopped abruptly. She wondered why. Then she heard the voices. Still far off, she couldn't discern the words, only the feelings. They were rough and unforgiving. They put a fear in her greater than any the dirty cowboy had. She pulled her head away from his chest in an effort to hear better. The feather on her hat dusted the rocky face above them and dirt fell like snow.

"I'm going to sneeze," she warned.

He slid out from under her and turned over. She lay under him now, cocooned by his body. The only thing preventing her from being crushed was the strength of his left arm that supported his weight.

Her sneeze found the curly hairs above the open neck of his flannel shirt.

She set her head back down and opened her eyes to find she was staring into his, inches away. They were pale blue. Liquid blue and there was question and humor in them. The whole situation was so . . . so intimate it was ridiculous, but she had little time to consider her plight.

The voices had grown much closer. The words suddenly distinguishable.

"Where the hell they go?"

"Maybe they went north to Spearfish."

"Damn, Otto, yer so stupid. If ye'd noticed they was amissin' earlier, we'd a found 'em by now. Now they're in the rocks and hills, there'll be no trail."

"Maybe they didn't go into the hills."

"Aw, shuddup. They're a might brighter than you. Them hills could hide an elephant if'n there was one 'round here. I'll wire the railhead at Cheyenne. Chances are that's where they'll be aheadin'."

Kathleen waited. The horse's hooves grew fainter and fainter. When she could no longer hear anyone, she kneed the cowboy in the groin in a single swift move. "Get off me, you oaf!"

She heard the man's hissed intake of breath. She'd hit her mark.

"Shit!" He rolled away from her, his free hand cradling his damaged goods.

His handcuffed hand flipped her over and left her face-down in the dirt just outside the alcove. She attempted to rise to her hands and knees, but despite his pain the cowboy kept her down with a jerk. She lay quietly, her forehead against the fine grit and pine needles on the ground, and prayed she had not gone too far. He had no weapons. His gun and knife had been taken away when he was arrested, but he could still strangle her . . . or crush her head with rock.

That would be the ultimate irony, to die out here, in the middle of no man's land. Her body left to the elements to be eaten by . . . She wouldn't think of such things. She had survived the embarrassment of her marriage to Bret Merriweather, his deception, theft and desertion. She would survive this too. Never again would she trust a man. Never again would a man get the better of her.

"Listen you evil little leprechaun, if you try that stunt

again, I'm not going to be held responsible for my actions. Do you understand me?"

Kathleen lifted her head just enough to nod. Then she set her forehead back on the ground, relieved.

For the first time since her wedding day, she felt tears well up in her eyes. The moisture ran down her cheeks until small drops soaked the ground. Her self-pity was short-lived.

He made a strange noise—half-choke, half-snort. He was laughing! She swore he was laughing.

"Pray tell me, Miss Callahan, where you learned that little move?"

She shook her head, rocking her forehead against the ground. Then to her surprise, she began to laugh. Perhaps it was hysteria, but she didn't care. For the first time in over a month she was laughing, and it felt good.

It was more than a minute before she could compose herself enough to speak. Her earlier sad tears were masked now with tears of laughter. "I had no brothers. There was just me and me Da, so I learned to defend meself."

"Do you always learn so well?"

She lifted her head and looked over at him. He was up on his side facing her, his head resting on his left hand.

"That I do, sir."

"I'll remember that." His smile warmed her.

He rose to a sitting position and extended a hand to her. Together they struggled to a standing position. Kathleen looked up with new interest at the tall man. His hair was unshorn, almost to his shoulders. It hadn't seen a barber or a washing for a very long time. He had a beard. It was scruffy and lighter than his hair. His hair was the color of the fresh Irish peat, black and dense. It was matted and tangled, and his beard was no better.

He resembled the drunkards who wandered the streets

of Boston begging for a nickel for their next beer, and he smelled about as bad. She hoped he carried no vermin, but she suspected the worst. No doubt they had spread to her by now. Just the thought made her whole body itch. But he didn't speak like a drunkard . . . or a cowboy.

"What will they do if they find us?"

"Hang us, I suspect."

"Surely, they'll give us a trial first?"

He shook his head. "I wouldn't bet on it, sprite."

"Don't call me sprite."

"You don't like it?" He faked surprise.

"Yeh don't talk like a cowboy at all."

He laughed. "No I suppose I don't. But then you don't talk like a notorious bank robber."

"I told you before, I'm *not* a bank robber."

"Then who are you? And what the heck are you doing in the middle of nowhere with me?"

"Yeh know how I came to be with you," she replied indignantly, then added, "I hope that deputy yeh hit didn't die."

"Deputies have notoriously hard heads, Miss Callahan. It's a fact of the West."

"Don't be that way."

"What way?"

"Superior."

"Why not?"

"Because yeh're nothin' but a dirty cowboy."

"And you are?"

"I'm . . ." She lifted her head high and threw back her shoulders. Unbeknownst to her, her hat was now awkwardly tottering on the side of her disheveled red curls. "I am a member of Boston society."

"A slip of an Irish girl like you? Unless the Boston Brahmins

9

have changed in the last five years, I think there's a better chance of me getting into heaven than you getting into Boston society."

"Me husband is the son of one of the most respected members of Boston's elite."

"So it's the Irish Mr. Callahan that's the prince of Boston. Things have indeed changed for the better."

She looked down at the ground. "He's not Irish. His name isn't Callahan. It's Merriweather. Bret Merriweather." She looked up and saw a brief glimpse of curiosity shadow his eyes.

"Well, Mrs. Merriweather." He bowed at the waist mockingly. "The pleasure is mine, I assure you." He took her captive hand and raised it. She could feel the pressure of his rough lips through the soft kid of her gloves.

"And where is Mr. Merriweather that he lets his wife wander the Wild West unescorted and tempting a fate much worse than any that could await her in Boston?"

"He's . . . He's . . . I just missed him in Deadwood. He was there on some business. But now he's gone on . . . on to Cheyenne. That's where I was headin'. I was inquirin' at the saloon for a stage when the sheriff . . ." She let her voice trail off. There was no use retelling the embarrassing story of her arrest. She would have proven her identity and been on her way by now if this man hadn't decided to escape after they were handcuffed together for a trip to the circuit judge in Rapid City.

"Cheyenne it is then."

"But they'll be lookin' for us in Cheyenne."

"As you said, all the better for you if we're caught."

"Not if I'm shot first."

"Well, I'll make sure we're not caught then."

"But . . ." There was something frustrating about the

man's logic. He could take her words and twist them until she didn't know whether to agree or disagree with him.

"That's not what I meant."

"Well, when you decide what you meant, let me know. Until then, it seems we're on a chase. You for your husband and me for a man who owes me."

"What does he owe you, this man? Money?"

His features darkened, and she felt fear once more as he answered. "His life."

Chapter Two

"Stop. You have to stop. Mister . . ." Kathleen was barely able to get the words out, she was so winded. Her fine kid boots were badly scuffed. The green taffeta traveling dress and its many petticoats were torn with hemlines sagging and lace trailing behind her. Her arm ached as the man climbed before her, dragging her behind, leaving her barely enough time to scramble after.

"This is madness. I don't even know what to call yeh."

The man didn't turn as he grabbed her wrist and hoisted her up once more, this time onto a flat protuberance.

"Sage."

She labored for breath. "Sage?"

He had finally stopped. She stood on the rocky platform nearly doubled over as she fought to regain a normal breathing pattern. When she finally was able to straighten, she looked at him in confusion.

He spoke distractedly. "Sage Duross. You asked my name. It's Sage Duross."

Kathleen repeated the name. "Sage. *Sage* Duross." Then she began to laugh. "So yeh've stepped from the pages of a dime novel after all." She saw her words sting, but kept on. "St. Sage, as I remember, was the patron saint of sagebrush was he not? No doubt yer parents saw him as protection from all the dangerous bushes rollin' about the range. He's done well by you, I see nary a brush bite on yeh, Sage. A prayer of thanksgivin' then to St. Sage." She clasped her small hands together in mock supplication.

He stood glaring at her. "It's getting dark. We'd better find a place to settle for the night." He jerked her hands apart with a tug on the handcuffs.

"Ouch!"

"Behave yourself, *'Squirrel Tooth.'* "

She glared back.

Trailing after him, she was caught up with other more disturbing worries. *Dark Night. Just the two of them.* Kathleen hadn't thought much beyond her aching feet and raw wrist, let alone contemplate what the future might hold.

Now, in the chill of early evening, other concerns began to make themselves known as well. They stood on the edge of a small glade. Against the far side, a sheer wall of rock edged the area. Down it ran a foot-wide band of water, making her aware of her thirst and the more disturbing need to alleviate the discomfort from her morning intake of liquids.

She looked desperately around. Behind and below them was the blackness of the dense pine forest they had climbed through all afternoon. Beyond that, almost a thousand feet below them, were the plains. The featureless flatlands stretched for miles into the horizon. In the receding light they almost looked like a glass-smooth lake.

Water! All these thoughts of water. She had to do something—and fast, or she would embarrass herself for sure.

"Sage?"

"Yes?" He lifted an eyebrow warily, as if waiting for the next onslaught of abuse.

"I . . ." He looked even more puzzled when she couldn't quite find the words to make her awkward request.

"Spit it out, woman. You certainly haven't been shy about expressing yourself. So what is it you want?"

"We've climbed nearly all day. An' that without nary a drop of food or water. Now there be bodily needs to be met."

"Yes, I know. You're hungry." He turned and pulled her forward into the small glen. "We'll forage for food as soon as we've built some kind of shelter."

"Ah man, yer dense as a ham hock, that yeh are. I need to relieve meself. Can I be more plain?"

He stopped in his tracks. Obviously it hadn't crossed his mind.

"Well then be about it, woman."

She held up her shackled wrist. "Well, what about these then?"

"For goodness sake, you Irish madwoman. If I couldn't remove them when our lives were at stake how do you think I can now?"

"But . . . ?"

"You've got good wits. Figure it out. Figure it out!" he shouted.

"Well, there's certainly no reason to be short-tempered about it," she snapped back.

She looked around the small clearing. To one side stood

a particularly large black pine. Its girth was just what she needed.

She pulled him over to the tree. "Wait right here."

She stretched out her arm to keep him on one side of the tree as she sought the opposite side. Unfortunately, her arm barely made it around a quarter of the trunk's circumference.

Her mouth formed a small moue. This wouldn't do.

"Sage?" At least he had the decency to be looking the other way. "Could you be so kind as to extend your arm a wee bit this way?"

He did as she asked, and his long reach got her to the far side of the tree. Her free hand struggled with her petticoats. She had thought herself wise not to have embarked on her journey from Boston wearing a crinoline. It was a blessing in disguise. In the long climb they had just made, the cumbersome garment would have hindered her and probably aggravated her captor to a point she didn't like to dwell on. But now the weight of her five petticoats was an impossible burden with only one free hand. To be so close and yet not be able . . . She was growing more desperate as the falling water gurgled and splashed into a small pool not ten feet away.

"Ye'll have to step closer and lower yerself as well. But mind to keep yer back to me."

She waited patiently.

He didn't move.

She continued to wait.

Finally, he went down on one knee next to the pine.

The saints be praised! She could now use her cuffed hand. She crouched slightly, then reached under the layers of petticoats to get a good grip before hauling them up nearly to her waist. His hand! She had forgotten about his hand! She

15

felt it brush against her upper thigh. It sent a frisson of something she had never felt before shooting through her. She
forced herself to ignore the unfamiliar sensation and con-
centrate on her more pressing problem. Within moments
her relief was accomplished.

She came rather shamefacedly from behind the tree.

"And . . . ?" he questioned.

She looked at him puzzled. "Thank you."

"You're welcome. Now . . . ?"

It took her a second before she understood what he was
trying to say. Then she couldn't restrain herself. "Yeh've got
good wits about yeh, lad. Figure it out. Figure it out!"

His look of disgust made her smile. But she wasn't smiling
for long. She was back against the tree—this time on the
front side.

Sage stared down at the button fly of his worn twill pants,
then at his arm stretched halfway around the tree. Damn
the woman. *Figure it out*, she said. Well, he wasn't going to
stand here like some idiot for the sake of her delicate feelings. He came out from behind the tree and with both hands
began to unbutton his trousers. When he looked up, he
noticed the red-haired she-devil's eyes were as big as his
mother's dishes and her pale skin had just about reached
the brilliant hue of her hair before she turned away. Com-
pleting his task, he turned and soaked the stately pine.

"Good! Now let's find something to eat."

What had he gotten himself into? he wondered. What was
he going to do with this banshee? She had no business being with him, and yet he couldn't risk her returning to Deadwood.

Her color had dulled to the warmth of a summer sunset,
and her green eyes showed just a tinge of shyness. *Shy*. It
was not a word he would have initially thought of upon

meeting Miss Kathleen Callahan. Fiery, passionate, aggravating, intriguing perhaps, but not shy.

Now that they were well away from Deadwood, he thought about freeing her. But the hint of vulnerability he saw in her eyes told him he couldn't abandon her in the wilderness of the Black Hills.

"Lift your skirts," he demanded.

Her eyes were huge again, but this time her face had drained of all color.

"Damn it, woman. Lift your skirts."

She looked like a fawn separated from its mother and about to be eaten by a mountain lion. What did she think he was going to do?

"Don't yeh even think it," she said between clenched teeth.

"I don't have time for this foolishness." He swooped her up in his arms and carried her over beside the small pool, where he plopped her on a moss patch and lifted her skirts above her ankles.

As fast as he raised her skirts she shoved them down. Up. Down. Up. Down.

"For God's sake, woman, lift your skirts. What do you think I'm going to do?" How could he be such a dolt? One look told him what she thought he was capable of.

"I'm not after your virtue, you hellion. I can't imagine anyone who would want to bed such a perverse woman. I need a piece of your petticoat if we're to eat tonight."

She stared at him as if digesting what he had just said. Still looking slightly suspicious, she bent and raised the hem of her skirt slightly to reveal her petticoats.

Not too delicately, he sorted through the mass of fabric. Finding what he wanted, he raised the chosen petticoat and used his teeth to rip into the fabric. All the undergarments

17

were of fine quality, he noticed, and they all smelled of lilac, despite the day's activities. He also couldn't help but notice her ankles and the delicate line of her calf as it slipped under the disheveled mass of fabric.

Once he had made a tear in the material, he ripped off several lengths.

He was aware of her curiosity as he separated each strip into three and began to plait the thin linen strips until he had a lightweight lariat.

He set the lariat aside and, rising to his knees, cupped his hands and drank from the small pool. Before long he was joined by Kathleen. He watched her reflection in the water. She rinsed her face and ran her wet hands behind her neck and down the front vee of her dress, letting the moisture drip between her breasts. He averted his gaze.

His thirst satisfied, he suddenly realized how hungry he was.

"Come on, '*Squirrel Tooth*.' "

"Don't," she retorted.

Despite his verbal jab, something in him made him pause and offer a hand to the hellion.

"Give me your hat." He noticed that the item in question, now crushed and forlorn, was teetering precariously atop her brilliant red curls.

"What are you going to do?"

"I'm going to 'rustle us up some grub.' As a good cowboy would put it."

He rigged the small lariat into a noose-like circle, before spreading it into a large oval beside the pool of water. Then, taking the peacock feather from her hat he stuck it into the ground inside the trap.

"Yeh think the wee animals are that witless, do yeh?"

He didn't honor her jibe with an answer. Instead he

slowly backed up, the end of the lariat in his hand, until they could sit partially hidden beside a large pine tree.

He was exhausted. He prayed she would just sit silently for a moment. No such luck.

"And . . . ?" she questioned.

"We wait . . . quietly."

"But I'm hungry."

He closed his eyes and let his head fall back against the tree. With his free hand he massaged his closed lids in an effort to release some tension. It did no good.

He couldn't help himself. "Tell the waiter to bring you something light, then. Tea perhaps, with some small cucumber sandwiches. Alas," he put the back of his hand to his forehead in a mocking gesture, "it is too late for tea. I fear you will have to wait, madame, until I can catch and gut a damn rabbit."

"There's no need to be mocking and nasty about it."

"There's no need?"

She must have known that she had overstepped her bounds because she shrank back in anticipation of the verbal drubbing she was about to receive. He wasn't going to disappoint her. She aggravated him more than any woman he had ever known.

"I'm stuck here handcuffed to a Celtic *she-beast* who not only has slowed my escape to a crawl but now expects to be waited on hand and foot."

"That wasn't what . . ." she protested.

"In case you haven't noticed, my dear Miss Callahan, you are not in Boston. We are in the middle of the Black Hills, a week's walk from Cheyenne, with only the clothes on our backs. And once the sun sets, it gets damn cold up here this time of year."

He saw a shiver run through her. "Yeh're right. I shouldn't

be complainin'." She looked appropriately contrite.

"Where are your clothes anyway?" he demanded.

"With my valise at the train station in Deadwood."

"Great!"

"I know they'll not do me a bit of good there. But how was I t'know that I'd be arrested an' hauled off like some criminal?"

She had a point there, he conceded. He was too tired to battle further. "Try to get some rest."

She nodded and a section of red curls escaped to fall over her face. He took his free hand and tucked them behind her ear. "You can rest on my shoulder if you want." Even to him it sounded like a grudging concession.

She bobbed her chin again, but he noticed she did not take advantage of his offer.

He continued to lean against the tree, feeling the rough bark underneath his scalp. *What the hell was he going to do?*

He awoke with a start. It was almost dark. He must have been asleep for a half hour or more. The banshee was asleep too. She had crumpled over onto him. Carefully he let her down onto his lap. He looked at his manacled hand and then at hers, resting on her midriff. He was too tired to worry about propriety. He placed his hand next to hers. He could feel her breathing, slow and easy. With his free hand, he gently brushed stray curls away from her face.

He didn't know how old she was, but asleep in his lap she almost appeared to be a child. If he didn't know better, he would have felt very protective of her. The truth be known, he did feel very protective of her, despite her feisty temperament and air of invincibility.

What had possessed her to go traipsing across the West

alone? What kind of man—of husband—would allow his wife to do so? However much of a shrew she was, she didn't deserve to be left on her own out here.

A last ray of sunlight snuck through the pine trees leaving a golden band of light across her face. He knew he shouldn't, but he couldn't resist a touch. Her skin was as smooth and downy soft as a rose petal. He saw a hint of freckles across the bridge of her nose and the top of each cheek.

He felt a hand grip his heart until he could hardly breathe. An image of his wife Victoria lying in his lap under the big oak seared his brain.

He had to stop his thoughts from going there. He lay his head back against the tree and closed his eyes. With his free hand he pushed back his tangled hair. His head came forward, then went back against the tree. Forward and back. Forward and back. He needed to beat down the feelings that were still so raw they threatened to overwhelm him.

Victoria . . . Victoria.

He looked down at Kathleen Callahan. She was as out of place in this scenario as Victoria had been on their homestead.

Although Victoria had never reproached him for dragging her thousands of miles to the hardships of the plains, never mentioned the elegant life she had led in New York, he had reproached himself every day since her death.

You are my life, my darling. I want nothing more, she had said. And he never doubted that she meant it. It was an undying testament of her faith in him, and he had let her down just like he had his brother. If he had not let Jimmy out of his sight, Morse and his men would never have baited the sixteen-year-old out to the old mine. Never have beaten

21

him . . . The picture of the boy's mangled body at the bottom of the shaft took what little hope he had left.

Edward "Sage" Duross closed his eyes once more as if this simple act could obliterate the image of his dead brother and wife from his mind.

Mercifully, a rustle distracted him. He turned his head to peer around the tree. A large rabbit had approached the snare trap. No animal had shown enough curiosity to come close until now.

The wary animal came to the lariat and, sniffing it curiously, looked as if he might not venture any farther. But then the rabbit saw the peacock feather. *Witless creature,* she had said. A smile crossed Sage's lips. He willed the rabbit forward across the line that would mean dinner. *Come on, little fella. Come on.*

The rabbit hesitated, then took a small hop away from the trap.

"Shit! Come on. We need this," Sage whispered.

The animal seemed to heed his words. It turned back and took a single hop into the noose.

"Yes!" He jerked the thin lariat and caught the animal by two legs.

"What!" Kathleen gasped, awakened by the sudden movement.

A grinning Sage looked down at her. "Dinner is served, madame."

Chapter Three

It was the best meal she had ever tasted. She had tried not to watch as Sage gutted and skinned the rabbit. She was afraid she wouldn't be able to eat it. But the smell as it roasted on a stick over the small fire eliminated any qualms she might have had.

"Are you finished?" Sage asked.

"Yes, thank you."

"Let's wash up then."

Kathleen didn't like having to come to a mutual agreement on everything they did. She had never depended on a man in her life—except once—and she wasn't about to repeat that mistake. No, trusting a man never came to any good in her experience. She had counted on Bret Merriweather to get her a place in Boston Society, and look where that had left her. One hundred thousand dollars poorer for starts. The laughingstock of Boston as well. When

23

she caught him and that slut mistress of his, Elizabeth Milgrim, there would be hell to pay. Deserted on her wedding night. Left standing in her Parisian negligee. She'd been mortified. The fact that he had cleaned out her bank account only compounded the pain.

"What's the matter? You don't want to wash up?"

"No. No, of course I do."

Even after she answered, he continued to stare at her. "Where were you just now?" It almost sounded like he cared.

"Someplace I never want to go again."

They rose. Again he offered her his hand. It was the second time he had done so since they stopped. She was surprised he even knew how. But perhaps she was being too harsh on the man. He was a strange one, Sage Duross, that was for sure. He still made no sense to her. One minute yelling at her, the next . . . She remembered the way he had pushed back her hair. He wasn't at all awkward. It was as if he'd done it often. It puzzled her and made her more curious.

"Did yeh indeed kill that man in Deadwood?"

They were on their knees at the small pool. He was rinsing off his face, but stopped abruptly. He didn't look at her. He just stared at his reflection in the water. She didn't think he was going to answer.

"Yes."

Something in her sank when he answered. She wondered if she had been hoping he would deny it.

"They said not a one knew why yeh did such a thing. Yeh barely talked to the man, they said."

"The man I killed knew why I did it. That was enough for me."

Sage Duross had turned hard again. It had happened in an instant, and it frightened her.

"But aren't yeh afraid of dying yerself if they catch yeh?"

"I'm only afraid I'll die before I kill Morse Templeton."

Kathleen knew better than to ask anything more. A closed look had shadowed the man's face.

It took Sage Duross a long moment to come back to the present. He was lost in thought somewhere outside of these hills, far away from her. Finally she saw his face relax before he turned to her.

"We'd better get going on that shelter before we lose any more light."

She accompanied him as he broke low-hanging pine branches. When he had enough he took them back to the mossy clearing and built a small lean-to. He used a tall pine to back the small structure and the fire in front to add warmth. She shuddered suddenly.

"Are you cold."

"No."

"You will be before the night is out. It's going to get nippy."

She scrunched up her nose, but couldn't find the words to ask the question that had pestered her since dinner. The shelter was barely large enough to hold one person.

She rubbed her sore wrist.

"Let me see your wrist."

"No,'tis fine."

"Show it to me."

" 'Tis fine, I say."

He didn't ask her again. He reached out and, taking her manacled wrist, lifted it closer to the fire.

"Come here." He led her to the pool of water and sat down, bringing her with him. Without asking, he lifted her

25

Joan Avery

skirts and ripped a new piece of soft cotton from one of her petticoats. He pushed the handcuff up her slender arm and, dipping the fabric in the cool water, began to clean the rough raw skin. When he was done, he wrapped the cloth gently around her wrist, tied it in place and slid the cuff back down.

"I'm sorry."

She just shrugged, then lowered her head. Suddenly she was exhausted.

"Tired?" he inquired.

She looked back up. The firelight was reflected in his light eyes. She felt as if he was asking more than what he voiced. He was asking for her forgiveness, but how could she forgive this man who could murder in cold blood? Before she could answer her own question, he spoke again.

"I think we'd better get some rest. We still have a long way ahead of us." He rose and then offered her his hand. Together they walked to the small shelter. He must have felt her hesitation.

"Surely, Mrs. Merriweather, you're aware a man and woman can sleep innocently together."

She wasn't sure of anything. She hadn't been sure what to expect even on her wedding night. Her mother had died at her birth, and her father had never discussed any of the delicacies of life with her before his death. For some reason, tonight, she could remember only one thing he had told her. *If yeh ever find a man who can shut yeh up, Kate me dear, marry him quick 'cause there'll be but one in a million that can manage that.* It was a strange thing to remember out here in the middle of nowhere.

Sage Duross lowered himself down and into the shelter. Kathleen was forced to follow. The handcuffs made everything awkward. It quickly became obvious that there was

26

only one comfortable way they could sleep and still both be under the pine canopy. They would have to nestle together like two spoons. She delayed as long as she could, playing out every possible sleeping arrangement in her mind. Head to toe, toe to head, side to side, front to front, back to back. None of them offered any hope of rest. Finally, she gave up and lay down with her back to him. He stretched out his handcuffed right arm. She lay her head on it, and he curled it around her until she could rest her matching handcuffed left hand comfortably across her stomach.

"Are you all right?"

She nodded. It was peculiar to be in a man's arms. Any man's. Bret had never held her. Never kissed anything but her hand. She'd attributed it to Boston propriety. It should have been a warning.

"Sage?"

"Yes." His breath moved the fine hairs on the back of her neck. She felt her arms prickle with gooseflesh at the sensation.

"Did you mean it when yeh said no man would want to bed a perverse woman like me?"

"The perverse part? Yes."

Kathleen felt her heart sink. She was hopeless it seemed.

"About the other . . ." he continued, "some men have been known to do foolish things for love."

"Have you ever done anything foolish for love?"

She waited.

Finally, he answered. It came as a whisper.

"Yes."

A great weight lifted off Kathleen, and she fell asleep almost immediately.

*   *   *

Sage Duross felt Kathleen's breathing slow and her body relax. What the hell was she asking that for? What if he'd been the kind of man who would see it as an invitation? She was so naive it was almost laughable. Where the hell was her husband?

He could smell her. Lavender and fine French soap. He had been right. She could not be left unprotected. He bent his head until he could touch her hair with his forehead and have its strands caress his cheeks. His cuffed hand fell forward until it brushed her breasts. He closed his eyes and told himself he was a fool. She was no safer with him than with any other man. He moved slightly forward until he could feel her entire length. He felt his body respond to her. He hadn't had a woman in over two years. Not since Victoria had died. He closed his eyes and inhaled the woman in his arms. Then he smiled at the thought of the fight he'd have on his hands if he tried anything.

Kathleen awoke with a start. The sun was just up. She lay very still, her heart beating rapidly as she tried to remember where she was.

It all came back rapidly, too rapidly. Without turning she had no way of knowing whether Sage Duross was asleep or awake. Only his relaxed breathing led her to believe he was still asleep.

He had moved closer to her during the night, folding around her until she felt perfectly protected. It was a strange feeling, considering who and what he was. She could feel his even breath on the back of her hair. The flannel-shirted arm that served as her pillow was muscled and sinewy. His strength and his size should have made her fear for her well-being, but they didn't. Last night only confirmed what she had known all along. He would not hurt her. But last night

28

had taught her a lesson as well. She would never hurt him. Never turn him in to the authorities. It was against everything she had been taught by the nuns; and yet she knew, at some deeper level, it was the right thing to do.

She shifted her weight and felt him move at the disturbance.

"Are you awake?" she whispered.

"No," came the whispered response.

She smiled and was content to lie there awhile longer.

Sage dug into the hot ashes and removed several strips of rabbit he had stored there for the night, hoping the smell of the charcoal would mask the scent of the meat from any wild animals. He offered a piece to Kathleen. "Here take it. And don't turn your little nose up at it. You need to eat it. I'm not about to carry you all the way to Cheyenne."

"If yeh want me to eat this, let me at least wash the ash off."

"All right. All right." He reluctantly followed her to the pond. She crouched and brought him down with her. His cuffed hand moved with her every gesture. She was like an old Irish washerwoman about her laundry. He smiled at the thought.

"What in the divil's name are yeh smiling about?" She had not turned, and for a moment he felt like a guilty child.

"What makes you think I'm smiling?"

"Your reflection in the water, that's what. And don't deny it."

"The smile was about nothing."

"I would think a man in yer straits wouldn't have cause to smile."

"Perhaps you're right. I apologize for smiling."

29

She turned to him with a dazzling smile lighting her own face. "Apology accepted then."

"Here." She offered him a piece of the newly laundered meat.

He watched her curiously as she ripped off a section of her petticoat and carefully wrapped the remaining dry meat in it.

"Shall we have a picnic later?"

"By all means a picnic, madame." He rose and taking her hand kissed it. He was surprised to see her blush.

He then helped her to her feet and smothered what remained of the hot ash. He looked up and studied the terrain. They were still several days from Cheyenne, and the climbing would only get more difficult. Soon he would have to make a decision.

"Can we not stop soon?" Kathleen's feet hurt worse than yesterday. She had not removed her boots in over twenty-four hours and was desperate for some relief. The hills had only gotten more rugged. They were moving through a small glade at the moment, and she wanted nothing better than to plop down and never move again.

His response was not the one she wanted to hear. "There's water up ahead. I want to get to it before we stop."

She knew better than to press her demands.

It took them ten more agonizing minutes to reach the small waterfall and stream.

Kathleen sat down on a large rock in the sun and began to unbutton her shoes the best she could without a hook. Each small button only frustrated her further until she was near tears with pain and frustration.

"By the holy saints!" She stamped her feet on the ground in defeat as tears welled up in her eyes. The pain of this ill-thought-out move only added to her temper. "How can yeh expect me to walk one step farther? Me feet feel like they're nothin' but raw meat in a grinder."

"A gentlewomanly comment."

She looked up at him, her anger peaking. "If yeh remember, this was not intended to be an adventure tour for me. I was just mindin' me own business when you dropped by to drag me off into this folly."

"Folly, is it?"

"Yes, a folly. And a damned foolish folly at that."

"*Tsk, tsk,*" he admonished. "Redundant and blasphemous. How unlike a Boston Society woman we are this morning, *'Squirrel Tooth.'* "

"I wish I were 'Squirrel Tooth' right now. I'd ... I'd ..." She shook her head as the tears came rolling down her cheeks.

"Here." He knelt beside her and started to work on the unfinished buttons. When he had completed one shoe, he slipped it off. Her stocking was bloodied. He reached up under her petticoats.

She was too tired to object as he removed her stocking, rolling it down from above her knee. When he got to her ankle, he stopped. He raised her dress and tore a section from her already well-used petticoat.

She had stopped crying, intrigued by what he was going to do. He reached over and soaked the strip in the small stream, then pressed the wet cloth to her foot to loosen the dried and caked blood until the stocking could be removed without causing her any further pain.

"We're going to have to do something about this. We have at least four more days of walking before we reach Cheyenne."

She moaned. She couldn't go another minute let alone four days.

"Let me see your other foot."

She offered him her other shoe. He proceeded to unbutton the second boot and remove it. This foot hadn't suffered quite as much. She was very aware this time as his hands moved up her leg searching for the garter that held the top of her stocking. He moved with a certain assurance. It was not the first time he had removed a woman's stockings, she grudgingly concluded. But then what did she expect? No doubt he spent many hours in the brothels that seemed to dominate every town west of the Mississippi. At least in Boston the whorehouses were out of sight and not blatantly placed in the respectable parts of town.

The sensuous feel of his hands as they slid back down her leg made her wonder what he did in those houses of disrepute. And the wondering gave her the strangest sensation. She suddenly felt warm. She felt flushed. Perhaps it was the warmth of the day. But the sun did not explain the peculiar feelings she had still lower. Feelings she couldn't really put into words.

"This foot doesn't look nearly as bad. Let me clean them both up, and I'll try to make some kind of bandage for the worst places to take the pressure off until they can heal."

Obviously no similar thoughts stirred in him. He was very matter of fact, as if he often found himself stripping a woman of her undergarments. She was in grave danger of making a fool of herself.

"It makes no matter. I'll happily take care of it. Thank yeh kindly, though."

"Don't be a fool, woman. I have more experience in these things than you."

"I am not a fool!" She could feel her blush darken.

"All right, '*Squirrel Tooth,*' you're not a fool. But hand-cuffed to me, you're in an awkward position to do anything about these feet. Get down off your high horse for a moment and just let me do it."

She didn't answer and he went on with his task, gently cleaning her feet and then wrapping them with pieces of the petticoat. He restored her stockings, rolling them only midway up her calves before hesitating and then stopping abruptly.

Quickly he took her shackled wrist. He inspected it carefully. It, too, was chafed and raw above the bandage he had placed there the night before.

"Give me a hairpin," he demanded.

"What?"

"Give me a hairpin."

She used her free hand to loosen a hairpin and offered it to him, curious as to what he was about to do next.

He stuck the pin into her cuff and with a quick flip of the wrist released the manacle. He repeated the action on his own wrist. The handcuffs fell to the ground with a metallic clang.

Kathleen sat dumbfounded, staring at the means of her torture for the past two days.

"Yeh could've done that anytime yeh wanted then? Flip, flip and they're off?"

He shrugged. It wasn't a conciliatory move.

"Yeh could have done that anytime! And yeh wait until I'm broken and bleedin' to borrow a hairpin and flip yer wrist." She demonstrated his action in a pique.

"There's no need to get in a high dudgeon about it."

Kathleen Callahan rose, all four feet ten inches of her, fire in her eyes and color in her cheeks, and Sage Duross knew his troubles were only beginning.

33

Chapter Four

"Yeh bastard. Yeh evil divil bastard."

"My, my. Such vulgarity from a Boston Society woman. You're sounding more like ole 'Squirrel Tooth' every day."

"I'll kill yeh. I'll kill yeh with me own bare hands." With this promise, Kathleen began pummeling Sage Duross with her small fists.

"You hellion. I've half a mind to turn you in for the reward, *'Squirrel Tooth.'* "

"Yeh wouldn't dare!"

"Don't be so sure."

Kathleen glared. She had stopped thrashing, but rising up on her tiptoes she delivered a slap to his face that echoed back from the hills around them.

Sage had had enough of her antics. He placed a hand on each of her upper arms and raised her up, trussed in his grasp, until she was eye to eye with him. "Listen to me. Yes,

I could have released you at any time. But can you swear to me you wouldn't have turned back to Deadwood and pointed out my path to the sheriff? He would have certainly appreciated the help and probably would have been more than happy to listen to your little story of mistaken identity."

He waited for a response.

Kathleen was eager to deny his accusation. But something Catholic in her wouldn't let her lie. "And wouldn't yeh have deserved whatever punishment they had in store for yeh. I'll bet me blinkin' bloomers yeh would."

"You don't know what you're talking about, so I'd shut up, if I were you."

"Shut up?" she protested. "I should shut up?"

He dropped her so abruptly she toppled over sideways, knocking the wind out of her and successfully silencing her.

"Quiet at last, are you?"

Kathleen's eyes watered with pain and anger. Not yet having her breath, she was unable to respond to the arrogant man.

"What are we going to do now?" she finally gasped.

"We? I thought now that you're free you'd be hightailing it back to Deadwood just as fast as your little feet could take you."

"Yeh know well enough that I couldn't find me way back even if I wanted to."

"You don't want to go back then?"

He was doing it again. Twisting her words all around until he had completely changed her meaning.

"That's not what I meant."

"Well then, I bid you adieu and good riddance. I believe Deadwood is that way." He extended a finger in a north-westerly direction. "But if you change your mind. I'm head-

35

ing that way." Again the irritating finger. "That is, if you choose to accompany me."

"Accompany yeh? Accompany yeh! Yeh think this is some Sunday excursion I can go or stay makes no never mind?"

"You can come with me, or you can go back on your own." His voice lowered, and suddenly he became very serious. "I've never forced a woman to do anything in my life, and I'm not about to start now."

There was something very reassuring about his words and suddenly very seductive at the same time. It made Kathleen wonder what he did with a woman who came willingly.

He stood staring at her, awaiting her response. She was sorely tempted to stay behind to prove a point. It had always worked with her father. Her da had always capitulated in the face of one of her temper tantrums. But this man was not her da and she was not convinced that he would care if he left her behind. Padrig Callahan may have raised a stubborn daughter, but he had not raised a stupid one. Kathleen knew her chance of successfully retracing their steps was almost nil.

"Well?" he demanded.

With as much dignity as she could muster, she answered: "I'll go with yeh only as far as Cheyenne. Then yeh're on yer own. I hope to never see yeh again in me life."

"Good. Then it's settled."

She was a little irked by his easy acceptance of her demands.

"Yes, settled," she murmured. She looked up at the imposing granite hills ahead and prayed to the saints for strength.

* * *

Kathleen Callahan was struggling, but Sage knew the stubborn Irish hellion would rather die than say a word to him.

They had almost reached the top of the ridge of hills. Around them the black humps of mountains rolled down to the plains like the backs of great whales lounging in the sea. Ahead they still had a difficult climb.

"Give me your hand."

She looked at him suspiciously. What the heck did she think he was going to do, bite her?

"It's getting steeper, I thought you might use some help."

She didn't answer him, but took the hand he offered.

"How're your feet."

"Fine."

They weren't fine, and he knew it. On level surfaces she walked with an odd tilting gait, and when she was required to master any actual climbing, her mouth made what at first was a most attractive little moue, but with every step it become more and more of a pained grimace.

He wanted to put still more distance between them and Deadwood's sheriff, but he knew Kathleen Callahan was moving ahead on sheer grit, and he gave her credit for having guts. He knew few women who could have accomplished the climb of these last two days. She couldn't go on much longer without collapsing. Although the makeshift bandages on her feet seemed to have helped, he knew they could do nothing for her aching muscles.

He was increasingly aware of the fact that she would never make it to Cheyenne on foot. She was a city girl, and even a woman acclimated to the hills would have found it difficult. There was only one solution he could think of, short of abandoning her in the wilderness. Instead of walking along the top of the ridge, they would have to go down the far side of the hills and catch the Deadwood-to-Cheyenne stage.

Even as he thought about the idea, he knew it was a foolish one. No doubt the sheriff had warned the stage-coach drivers to be on the lookout for a murderer and a bank robber. But then he wasn't the typical murderer, and Kathleen Callahan certainly wasn't your typical bank rob-ber. If he gave the idea a little thought, maybe they could pull it off.

"We'll be stopping soon," he said. "I know of a cave not far from here. We can spend the night there. It'll offer more protection than we had last night. There's water. Really quite luxurious accommodations." He smiled at the weary Kathleen and got no response, not even one of her typically snide remarks. It was the surest sign she was exhausted, he thought with bitter humor.

"Well what do you think?"

It was a peculiar question. What did he expect her to say?

"It's nice." It did have some advantages over the night before.

There was a small clearing like their previous campsite, but there was also a pool of water formed by a stream. Pine trees lined the clearing with an occasional aspen inter-spersed. The aspens had already begun to change, their leaves showing amber with the cooler fall weather.

"If I remember correctly, there's a good size cave over here." Sage pulled back some shrubs growing against a rocky face, revealing the entrance. "Yes!"

"How did you know that all this was here?" Kathleen let her curiosity overcome her stubborn reluctance to talk.

"My brother and I used to trek back through these hills for some peace and quiet after the cattle drives. It kept him out of trouble." Again he seemed to drift off. Somber and thoughtful.

He released the small lariat from his belt, where he had placed it after using it the day before. "I'm going to go and try to get us something to eat."

The peacock feather, her hat for that matter, were nowhere in sight. She groaned. Her fair skin had suffered the past day and a half. She knew the freckles she hated must have sprouted on her face like so many sunflowers in a field.

"What's the matter?"

"Me hat."

"Where is it?"

"I must have left it behind."

"Tough luck. I can't be responsible for your things and mine."

"Yer things! What, pray tell me, are yer things?" She surveyed the clothes on his back.

"This?" He held up the small lariat.

"Very funny. Yeh compare that bit of me petticoat to me fried skin. I need me hat."

"Too late. You already look a bit pock-marked. Besides, that hat was nothing more than a feather holder."

"But it was . . ."

"Was what?" he asked.

French was what she wanted to answer. But under the circumstances it sounded so petty and trivial.

"It was *some* protection," she declared.

"I'm off to find us something to eat. You might consider cleaning yourself up a bit. I won't return for an hour or so." With that he headed off into the trees.

Had he just ordered her to clean up? The nerve of the man.

She *was* hot and dirty. She looked at the pool of cool water and was sorely tempted. But if she didn't want to re-dress in wet clothes, she'd have to strip naked to enjoy the beckoning liquid. Naked. She looked around her. Sage was gone. He'd said an hour. She didn't know if she trusted him, but he hadn't lied to her yet. She suddenly realized he hadn't told her much of the truth either.

She unbuttoned the top of her dress. With a quick glance around, she undid the bodice and released her skirt. She let the green taffeta slip to the ground. She was left in her camisole, drawers and petticoats. Once more she gave a furtive look. If she was going to do this, she'd better do it quickly. To waste time was to risk being naked when Sage returned.

She sat down and removed her shoes and hose. Her feet were no worse, thank goodness. She untied her camisole and petticoats and stood up, leaving her underclothes in a white pile. She hurried across the ten or so feet and lowered herself into the cool water. It was colder than she antici-pated. She hesitated for a moment. The alternative was to continue standing there stark naked. She held her breath and waded in. It wasn't deep, but since she was under five feet, the water came breast-high, completely covering the important parts. This was good. She turned back to face the bank and felt her body shiver all over.

Quickly, she splashed some water on her face. She rubbed her hands up and down her arms, grateful for the cleansing effect of the cold water. Suddenly something brushed up against her foot. Something moving and slimy.

"Eeeeeeeeek!" She took a quick step back only to sink completely underwater.

She came up sputtering. She had been standing on a rocky ledge, and that single ill-taken step had caused her to lose her balance, dunking her. She thrashed and gasped as she fought to regain her footing. When she finally stood the water was nearly to her chin. She moved back up onto the rocky platform she had first occupied, and shook her soaked head. She let out a moan.

Her hair! She had no comb, nothing with which to untangle it. It would wind up tight as springs, forming an ugly matted mess. She would look like a drowned retriever.

"Jesus, Mary and Joseph. Is there much else yeh can do wrong, Kathleen?" she berated herself.

Suddenly she heard Sage returning. He must have heard her shriek.

She scurried out of the water, picked up the pile of taffeta and linen on the run and headed for the far side of the clearing. Quickly, she sorted through the garments, throwing some over the green bushes nearby as she did. She grabbed her camisole and drawers. Every piece resisted her frantic urgings, clinging instead to her wet body. Just as she slipped on the bodice of her dress, she heard Sage enter the clearing. She turned her back and quickly did up the buttons.

"What the hell was that?"

Kathleen stepped from behind a tree.

"What would that be, yeh're talkin' about?"

"I thought I heard a scream."

"I think yer imaginin' things"

Sage looked skeptical.

She waited to see if he would pursue the matter.

"You look like a drowned cat. Are you sure you're all right?"

Kathleen pulled at her hair self-consciously. "Yes, yes of course I am."

41

He studied her for a long time before letting his line of questioning go.

"I've caught us a dandy dinner, *'Squirrel Tooth.'* "

Kathleen sighed with relief.

"Look here." He held up a ball of fur.

"What is it?" Kathleen queried.

"A yellow-bellied marmot."

"Oh." She was less than enthusiastic, but she wasn't about to complain, no matter how unappetizing the dead animal looked. She was hungry, and the rabbit he had fixed before had turned out to be quite good. What difference was there between one furry animal and another? she rationalized.

"Go collect some dry tinder and wood while I get this ready." Once again he held up the dead thing for her approval. She hurried away, unwilling to contemplate what must be done to the creature to make it edible.

When she returned, her arms full of kindling, he had skinned and gutted the animal. It was even more unappetizing than before. Sage set to work starting a fire while she sat quietly on a small boulder to one side of the pool. She tried not to look at the carcass that was to be their dinner.

How in heaven's name had she gotten herself into such a ridiculous position? Just wait until she caught her scoundrel of a husband. Bret Merriweather would pay for all this.

She shifted uncomfortably on the rock. Her underclothes were feeling uncomfortable and scratchy.

"I've been thinking." Sage spoke between puffs on the glowing tinder as he bent to start the fire.

"Been thinkin', have yeh? Congratulations."

Sage glared at her.

"I'm sorry." And she realized she was.

He seemed mollified. "We're still a long way from Cheyenne. I thought we might go down the far side of these hills and catch the Deadwood-to-Cheyenne stage."

"Are yeh daft man?"

"No, I'm not daft, as you put it."

She had irritated him again. It wasn't her intent. "They'll catch yeh sure as the sun rises."

"Well, that shouldn't concern you, should it?"

The man was stubborn. That was for sure. She had to stop him from risking his life for her. She shifted uncomfortably again. Her skin was hot, and her clothes seemed to irritate every inch they covered.

"Did yeh think that maybe *I'd* not want to be caught." She waited to see if he got her drift. When he seemed puzzled, she continued. "I don't have time to explain to any dullard who c'not see that I'm not that . . . that . . . *other woman.*"

"You mean ole 'Squirrel Tooth'?" He smiled.

She ground her teeth. Here she was trying to help him, and he continued to find pleasure in goading her. She would not reward him with a response.

"You'll never make it to Cheyenne," he stated matter of factly.

"Did yeh ever think I'd make it this far?" she demanded.

"No, I didn't."

"Well?"

"Well, what? Do you understand what I'm saying, Kathleen? Even an experienced mountain woman would have a hard time. We've barely covered twenty miles, and there's at least ten times that far to go."

He had called her Kathleen.

"Do you understand me?" he demanded again. "Look at your shoes. They're not meant for this rugged terrain. *They* certainly won't make it."

She looked at her shoes. Suddenly her ankles itched. She reached down and scratched them, but it only got worse.

"We're catching the Deadwood-to-Cheyenne stagecoach and that's final."

"But . . ." She scratched her arm, distracted by the itching once again.

"For Pete's sake, woman, what's the matter with you? You've been fidgeting like a roped calf."

"There's nothing the matter." She rubbed her stomach.

"What are you scratching at?"

"I don't know. All of a sudden me body itches everywhere." As if to confirm her statement, she began to itch as many places as she could reach.

"Where have you been?"

"Here of course. D'yeh think I've been traipsin' out to do me shoppin'?"

"Where here?"

"I took me bath, and then I went over there to dress." She pointed to the group of bushes.

Sage rose from the small fire and walked over to where Kathleen had dressed.

"Here? Were you here?"

"Yes."

"Were you naked?"

"I don't think that's any of yer business."

"For God's sake woman, were you naked?"

"That's where I got dressed." She was aggravated with him now.

"Come here."

She rose, still scratching, and crossed the clearing to him.

"Show me your hands."

She did as he demanded. He turned them palm down.

"Shit!"

"What is it?" She was more than alarmed.

"Take off your clothes!"

Kathleen stood stunned.

"Did you hear me? I said to take off your clothes."

Chapter Five

"How dare yeh!"

Sage had to smile. She was ready to fight him tooth and nail. Pity the man who tried to get into this woman's britches.

"You've been in poison ivy, and if you don't get out of those clothes and wash, you'll be more miserable than you ever imagined."

She eyed him suspiciously. "I've seen no ivy, poison or otherwise."

"Those bushes over there. The ones I assume you threw your clothes on while changing. They have poison ivy growing all over them. It'll make your skin break out in blisters. The more you itch the worse you'll make it. And as long as you've got the oil on your skin, you can keep spreading it."

"What am I t'do then?"

He could tell she was using all her restraint not to scratch.

46

"You'll have to get out of all your clothes. Go back in the water and wash yourself and your clothes thoroughly."

"All me clothes?"

"Every stitch."

"And then?"

"And then *what?*" What the hell was her problem? he wondered.

She continued to stand there with a suspicious look in her beautiful green eyes. "Just what will you be doin' while I'm naked as a jaybird?"

"I'm not a Peeping Tom. If that's what you're insinuating."

"Of course, I know yer name's not Tom," she mumbled under her breath.

He shook his head, exasperated. "I'm going off to find something for the rash. I thought I saw some jewelweed— some orange touch-me-nots—over on the ridge. We can use their juice. It'll help with the itching. I'll yell before I come back."

Her eyes were still leery. He didn't have a clue as to her problem now.

"But . . ." She hesitated.

"But what? Spit it out, woman. I don't have all day."

He had angered her for sure. She bristled. "Am I to wear me soakin' clothes then? I'll surely catch me death if I have to wear them all night."

"If it pleases the missus, I'll order something up from Worth's of London for the evening. Formal? Do you think?"

"Stop it." She stamped her foot. Then she had to bend over and scratch her ankle.

"Stop itching. Here." He began to unbutton his shirt. He noticed that she watched him in fascination. With the last button complete, he stripped the flannel off and offered it

47

to her. He was tempted to smile. She looked absolutely appalled.

"Not good enough. Well then . . ." He began to pull the shirt back on.

"No. I'll take it." She held out her hand.

He dropped the flannel onto the ground before her. "Better not touch it until you've bathed. Your hands will be covered with resin."

He turned to go, calling out behind him. "Take your time and do a thorough job."

With his back to her he allowed himself a broad smile.

Sage ground the jewelweed between two flat rocks. This woman was going to be the death of him yet. He had to admit it would be an interesting way to go.

She had looked like a half-drowned dog. Her hair all matted and tangled. Scratching like a flea-infested mutt. Why did he find it charming? Even her feisty spirit had its appeal.

He knew he was right about the stagecoach. But she was right too. A man and a woman alone on the road, miles from civilization. They would be suspicious under ideal circumstances. And there was no doubt in his mind that Sheriff Davis in Deadwood had wired the stagecoach company. The drivers would all be on the lookout for them. He would have to think of a way.

He could always pull a tree stump over to block the road. When the coach stopped Kathleen could ask for assistance. They wouldn't refuse to take her even if they were suspicious. He'd leave it up to her to fabricate a story. With her female wits he was sure she'd finagle her way on board.

When she reached Cheyenne, "Squirrel Tooth" could straighten out the mixup easily enough. It was the obvious solution to the problem. He'd be free of her and could make better time.

He picked up the stone that held the crushed weed and its juices and headed back toward the clearing. Somehow the thought of being free of Kathleen Callahan didn't bring him as much joy as he thought it would.

She was sitting cross-legged on a rock, squeezing the last of the water out of her dress. His shirt was huge on her. She had rolled up the cuffs until they reached her elbows. The cloth draped around her, covering everything including her legs. Her hair was newly wet. He had the urge to help her untangle it. In fact, he had the urge to do more than untangle her hair, but he quickly drove the thoughts from his mind.

"Did you get everything done?"

"Aye."

"You'd better get this juice on you. Cover every inch of yourself, even areas that haven't broken out yet. It should save you from the worst of it. Use the cave." He nodded in the direction of the opening. "I'll lay your things out to dry and start dinner." He watched her walk off, the tails of his shirt brushing between her legs. He would have to watch himself very carefully or he could do something he would regret.

The marmot was almost done. He had rigged a skewer held up by two Y-shaped branches. He had managed to keep the meat turning so that it had browned nicely. It had been almost an hour and a half since he last saw Kathleen. He was tempted to go and check on her, but he didn't dare trust himself.

"Sage?"

He was startled from his thoughts. "Yes?"

"I need yer help."

He stood and turned to face her. What he saw stunned him.

The light from the fire gave off a warm golden glow. Kathleen Callahan stood bathed in it. He knew now what she had been doing for such a long time. She had used her fingers to comb her hair. It had dried into a nimbus of spun sugar. Each strand danced in the firelight, translucent and ethereal. He had never before seen such a delicious riot of titian curls. He studied her face.

Funny, he hadn't noticed that her pale skin had become the color of honey. He remembered touching it when she was sleeping. Now, he envisioned running a finger across the freckles that dotted the bridge of her nose and the tops of her cheeks . . . cradling her beautiful face in his hand and burying his fingers in her glorious hair . . . pulling her forward to kiss her. . . . His body tightened. Need coursed through him.

"Please, Sage. I've done as yeh said but I c'not reach me back."

She held up the rock with the jewelweed. He took it.

She turned around and, unbuttoning two buttons of the shirt, let it slip down her back until it draped low, almost past her waist. He wanted to refuse to touch her. But she wouldn't understand. He needed to do this for her.

She picked up her hair and let it drape forward over one shoulder. The rash wasn't as bad as he feared. There was some redness where the straps of her camisole had lain and more near her waist, but the great expanse of her back was the color of Dresden porcelain. Smooth and unmarred.

He moistened his hand with the liquid. He started high on her neck and ran his hand slowly down it to her shoulder. He let it rest a moment, then moved down. The tips of his fingers unintentionally brushed the fullness of her breast under her arm. He felt her shudder. He continued until he cupped a part of her small waist in his palm. He paused. Neither one said a word. He leaned in toward her. She still smelled slightly of lavender. He wanted to slip his hand around to her belly and move still lower.

"Yeh best do the other side." Her voice was deeper than usual.

The other side? Was it an invitation? Of course not, he warned himself. His body was tense. He moved quickly to moisten his hand again. He hurriedly ran it down the left side of her back. Once more down the center. Then he turned and almost ran to the water where he washed his hands with concentrated effort.

Kathleen watched the firelight on Sage's bare back. It played out the sculptured lines of muscle and sinew. She felt drowned in him. In the touch of his hand and the smell of his shirt and the warmth of his bare chest against her back. What was wrong with her? She had said something and now he had grown distant just when she had wanted him closer. When he touched her, she had felt stirrings deep inside. What was it that she wanted? What was it that was so elusive?

"The meat is done." He rose and came back to the fire. He busied himself with the meat, offering her a piece without ever looking up at her.

They ate in silence . . . a long interminable silence.

"You'd best get some sleep. You can use the cave. I'll sleep out here."

Kathleen rose and headed for the shelter. Finding a leafy spot just inside, she lay down. What had she said? What had she done? Why was he so cold?

She curled up into a ball, tucking her feet into the large shirt. It smelled like Sage. She remembered sleeping in the warmth of his arms. Despite her best efforts, tears welled up in her eyes. Nothing was going as she had planned. Nothing at all. She had always been so practical, so sure of herself. Even when Bret Merriweather had abandoned her, she had known what she would do. But now things were all confused. Now feelings, illogical unbidden feelings had risen up to confuse her. She squeezed her eyes tightly shut to rid herself of them, and a single tear rolled down her cheek.

"Here are your things. You'd best get them on." Sage stood over her, a look of disapproval on his face.

"I will." The sun was well up, she had slept late.

She watched Sage walk away. The arrival of the sun had done nothing to thaw his chill. She had done something wrong, said something wrong. Of this she was sure. She just couldn't figure out what it was.

She rose, stiff from the cold and the hard ground. It was difficult to dress. The unforgiving fabric brushed against the rash on her skin and made it itch again. The juice had helped. The rash had not spread and what there was of it seemed less irritated. Still, as she took a step forward and the clothing moved against her, she knew a day's walk would leave her in desperate straits. But she wouldn't say anything to him. She had her pride. Stubborn pride her father had called it.

Outside, he was stooped over the fire. He had already caught some kind of a bird, for it sizzled over the fire. She felt like she had not eaten in days.

"It smells delicious, that it does." She offered a smile.

All she got in response was a grunt.

"I wish t'thank yeh for the weed, the . . ." She searched

for the name of the plant. "What did yeh say it was called?"

"Jewelweed. Genus *Impatiens capensis*. Or the orange touch-me-not as it's commonly known."

He was being arrogant again. She sensed it was intentional, meant to drive her away. But all it did was make her more curious. Who was this man? He was no common cowboy.

"Yes. The impatient cap 'n sis."

He looked up at her. He was smiling. She was thrilled.

"That's *Impatiens capensis*."

Whatever, she thought to herself. It didn't matter. The only thing that really mattered was that he was smiling again. She returned the smile.

"Yeh've been up and about early, have yeh. It smells delicious. May I?"

He nodded and she pulled off a leg section.

"I've decided we'll spend the day here resting."

Kathleen didn't like the idea of him changing plans for her.

" 'Tis foolish to waste time. I'm perfectly fine. There's no need. Really there isn't." Then as if to remind her of her lie, her midsection demanded scratching.

"Mmmm. 'Tis good. 'Tis really *very* good," she said with a mouth full of bird. With the words came a surreptitious rub or two across the stomach, but the itching only made it worse.

"Are you all right?"

"Yes, of course. There's just a wee bit of a tinglin', if yeh know what I mean."

"You want to scratch it like hell, don't you?"

She laughed. "Yes."

"I like to hear you laugh." He looked at her all queer.

She didn't know what to say. She liked to hear him laugh

too. She liked to see him smile. Most of all she liked him to touch her.

"No, not that way!" Sage yelled.

"Well, which way then?"

Sage and Kathleen sat on large rocks across from each other around the small pond. Sage had rigged some fishing hooks out of barbs from a wolfberry bush, and lines from the fine lace of Kathleen's petticoat. Instead of a feather, Sage had used small pieces of the green taffeta as a lure.

The sun was warm, and for the first time in the past two days they could relax. Kathleen had re-applied the jewelweed, and the rash had diminished considerably. It was a small miracle in her estimation.

"Hold the line taught. Like this." Sage demonstrated his technique.

"Like this?" She imitated, pulling up a little of the slack on the lace line.

"No, no," he answered, disgusted. He set his makeshift fishing gear aside and came over to where she sat.

"If we were lucky enough to have a fish bite the darn thing, you'd lose him for sure." He sat down beside her. "Pull up a little."

Kathleen did as he said.

"Now move your hand up and down ever so slightly."

Kathleen pulled her hand up and down.

"I said *slightly*. You look like you're milking a cow." He got up and sat behind her. He moved his arms into position around her until he could hold her two hands in his. "Like this. Do you feel that?"

Yes. She felt it indeed. His arms around her. His breath moving tendrils of her hair.

"Move your hands out farther over the water."

54

She moved her hands away from her.

"How d'ye say I was t'do it then?"

He leaned in to reach her outstretched hands. His head was beside hers, his chest against her back. She closed her eyes as he moved her hands up and down. Up and down. The rhythm was soothing and then more than soothing. She could feel his breath across her ear. Curiously, it raised the fine hairs on her arms. Up and down. Just a small movement. His hands cradled hers, and their warmth made her own moist. Up and down. Up and down. He ran his thumb along hers almost absentmindedly. She felt safe here in his arms. At the same time she felt strangely ill at ease. The speed of the movement had increased. Up and down. Up and down. Unbidden, unwilling, unstoppable. His breathing grew more rapid and ragged. Her own had almost stopped. Kathleen closed her eyes. She could feel him. Smell him. Touch him. She was lost in him, but still she wanted something more.

"I think you have it now." He pulled away, and she almost fell backward he moved so abruptly.

She looked up at him. Her eyes asked the question her lips could not.

"No, Kathleen."

No what? She didn't even know for sure what she was asking of him, but he seemed to know and had delivered his answer.

"I'm going for a walk. I'll be back before dark." He left, walking into the woods.

She sat for a long time staring into the water. Nothing intimate had ever occurred between Bret Merriweather and herself. She remembered the humiliation of her wedding night. She had been prepared for anything but Bret's cruel words. "My dear Kathleen, you don't think I married you for your looks or place in Society do you? Dear girl, you are so innocent, I almost feel guilty." Bret had had a mistress. Everyone in Boston knew about Elizabeth Milgrim. Elegant and refined, she was everything Kate wasn't. And everyone knew about Bret. The one hundred thousand dollars he had taken from Kathleen's bank account hadn't hurt her as much as the fact that he had managed to dupe her while all of Boston looked on without saying a word.

Boston Society had no place for the unsophisticated daughter of an Irishman who made his money in the slaughterhouses that kept meat on their table. She was an outsider and always would be.

Bret had called her innocent. He was being kind. She had been stupid. She wouldn't be again. She had been a bad judge of character once. She wouldn't let herself be again. Sage Duross was an admitted murderer. She must get away from him, away from this place. She had strayed from her purpose. And Sage Duross had been her main distraction. She needed to find Bret, get her money, and get control of her life once again.

Sage was still shaken by the incident at the pond. Things had gotten out of control. While Kathleen Callahan may not have known what was happening, he certainly knew better. He became aroused just thinking about it. Damn her. Why had she been so compliant? She had not drawn back. He wondered what kind of lover she would be. Would she bring to lovemaking the boundless energy and wonderful humor she possessed in abundance? He warned himself to stop, but he couldn't. He had had too much of her already. The feel of a single tendril of her hair. The softness of her skin. The smoothness of her neck and back as his hand slid down. The tease of her breast as it slipped past his fingertips.

The roll of her hips and the promise of magical things hidden there.

Putting her on the stage to Cheyenne would be the best thing he could do for her.

He looked up. The sun was low. He headed back.

"Ahhhh! Oh Lord help me! Oh no . . . Oh no!"

This time he was sure about the screams. He ran into the clearing just in time to see Kathleen scurrying from the underbrush. She held her dress up above her bare ankles. She was shoeless.

"What is it this time?"

"Oh, me God. I've been bitten by a viper." Her voice trembled with terror. Her bright eyes were awash in tears.

"A viper, is it?"

"Oh, I'm t'die here in this wilderness. T'die. Jesus, Mary and Joseph, I pray to see me past this trial. Don't let me die here. Not here, not now." Her voice rose almost to a shriek with panic.

"Let me see." Sage ordered the distraught Kathleen. "Sit down." He pointed to a rock.

"I'm t'die here. It's too cruel. I don't want t'die. Not here. Not now." She shook her head vehemently, upsetting a tumble of red curls.

"Be quiet, woman, and let me see! Sit down." He took Kathleen by the shoulders and guided her to the rock, forcing her into a sitting position. He knelt and lifted her skirts. "Where do you think you were bitten?"

"On me ankle. Me right ankle," she sobbed.

He lifted her ankle to get a closer look. She strained to see as well.

The outside was perfectly fine. He turned to examine the inside.

Two small puncture wounds bled red. He suddenly felt

57

ill. He didn't even have a knife to open the wound. The venom was spreading even now. What would he tell her? He had seen burly men die of a snakebite under the best medical care.

He doubted the petite Kathleen Callahan would survive the night.

Chapter Six

"What is it?" she demanded. " 'Tis a poison viper that bit me. I know it!" She was beginning to lose control.

"Kathleen, be quiet!"

She was stunned by the harshness of his command. Tears welled up in her eyes.

"Getting upset won't help. You need to keep still until I can find something to open the wound and try to suck out some of the venom."

" 'Tis indeed a snake bite then?" she whispered, as if whispering the truth would make it somehow less frightening.

"Yes, it's a snake bite."

"Poisonous?"

"Yes."

"Perhaps yer wrong," she whispered hopefully. "How can y'tell these things?"

He seemed reluctant to answer.

" 'Tis all right. Yeh can answer me."

"These two puncture marks here. They're fang marks. Only poisonous snakes make them."

"I see." Her quiet response only underscored her stark fear.

He studied her. It was as if he were assessing her strength. She could survive this. She *would* survive this. He needn't look at her that way.

Suddenly he picked her up. She felt very small, very vulnerable in his arms. He took her to the cave and laid her down.

"Lie still."

She lay there, her mind swirling with so many thoughts. Suddenly Bret and his mistress—the whole incident in Boston—seemed no longer important. "Jesus, if Yeh only let me live I promise . . ." What could she promise Him?

She could donate even more to St. Patrick's.

No. Money did not seem the right thing to offer.

She could become a nun!

No, she thought. Death was probably a better choice.

She was distracted by Sage's return. He had the barb from their fish lines. He knelt at her feet. "This will hurt."

She nodded.

He raised her skirt above her ankle and gently turned her foot outward to expose the two puncture wounds.

"Ohhhh." It was almost a gasp. Still, she tried not to move as he used the barb to slash her skin.

Again, the searing pain. She clenched her jaw, unwilling to make another sound. Again and again the stabbing ache came, until finally it was over. He bent over and she could feel his mouth on her wounds. She watched, eerily fascinated, as he drew out the venom and then spit the bloody poison onto the ground.

"I'm going to build a small fire here at the mouth of the cave. You'll need the warmth. I'll collect some kindling. Will you be all right?"

"Yes." She answered without thinking. But when he began to walk away she almost panicked. She wanted to call him back. She didn't want to be alone. She had learned that you can be alone even when there are many people around you, even a fiancé. Why was it that with Sage she never felt alone? She closed her eyes, wishing him back, but suddenly she very, very tired.

"Damn!" Sage stumbled over a stump. It was dark. Only a sliver of moon lit the rough terrain. He had an armful of wood as he headed back to the clearing and the cave.

He stopped and his head dropped. "Damn!"

He'd seen men die before. It wasn't unusual to lose men on cattle drives—to stampedes and illness, to brawls and accidents. He had lost friends, men he had known for years. But he never felt like this about those men.

Why did losing this slip of a woman, a woman he had known barely two days, make his insides feel like they were being ripped out all over again? It was the same helpless feeling as when Victoria . . .

"Damn!" He raised his head and continued on.

He found Kathleen asleep. That was probably best.

Her leg was still weeping blood. That was probably good too.

He set about building a new fire at the cave's entrance. Even as he worked, he couldn't help looking over at her. In the dim moonlight that penetrated the clearing she looked very pale . . . and very beautiful. She rested on her back, one arm lying above her head cushioned by her flaming curls, the other across her breasts. In the darkness, the green of her dress had taken on the ominous color of black. It was as if the tender tableau had been bled of color.

He blew on the tinder, encouraging the small flame to grow. It licked at the wood, then spread. He blew again and the fire grew. He added larger and larger kindling until the fire began to give off heat and light. The firelight gave her cheeks a flush and returned her dress to its original color. He fed the fire still more wood and blew again, nurturing it as if it might somehow restore Kathleen Callahan's health as it had her color.

He looked over to her. She slowly opened her eyes. "I'm afraid."

"Yes, I know."

"Will yeh hold me?"

Sage rose and went to her. Lying down beside her, he took her in his arms. "You should try to sleep." He kissed the top of her head without thinking. He felt her body relax.

"Talk to me."

He smiled softly as he rose to one elbow. "What should I talk to you about?"

"Have yeh ever been in love?"

He paused, frightened by his own memories. It was a long time before he answered her. "Yes."

"I think that's what I'll miss most of all. Never havin' been in love."

"What about your husband?"

She shook her head and didn't answer his question. Instead, she pursued his past. "Where is she now, the woman you loved?"

"Gone."

There was silence for a while. Then Kathleen spoke

again. "To another place? To another man? Is that what makes yeh so bitter, then?"

"No, she died."

"Yeh should be happy then."

Sage looked at the Irish lunatic in disbelief. "Happy? You think I should be happy?"

"Because she's happy in heaven with God. And she wants you to be happy here."

The sprite meant every word of it. He grew thoughtful. "I wish I had your faith, Kathleen."

He ran a hand through his shoulder-length hair, pushing it back, and stared into nothingness. Kathleen lay her palm against the softness of his beard. She drew his attention back to her.

"Me da always told me when I missed me ma that she was standin' in heaven holdin' God's hand and smilin' down on me. And that if I closed me eyes and stood very still I could feel her smile warmin' me."

"Your da must love you very much."

"That he did. He's gone now t'be with me ma." Kathleen became thoughtful, then her face scrunched up. "I must say that I was not always fond of his love, especially when it was a paddle to me behind."

Sage laughed.

"Close your eyes, Sage Duross," Kathleen commanded.

Sage closed his eyes and lay his cheek into her hand. "They're closed."

"What was the woman's name?"

"You mean my wife?"

"Your wife, was it?"

"Yes, my wife. Her name was Victoria."

"Can you see her? It's Victoria and she's smilin' down at yeh. Can yeh feel her smile warmin' your heart and your

63

soul, so that yeh know she's all right and that yeh're goin' to be all right as well?"

Strangely, Sage could see Victoria. Her favorite blue dress. Her dark hair blowing in the wind. Her broad smile and the twinkle in her eye that spelled mischief. He hadn't been able to think of her this way since she died. Suddenly, he did feel warmer.

"Yes, Kathleen, I believe I do."

He opened his eyes and looked down into trusting green ones. This slip of a girl had given him a great gift. If she only knew.

Kathleen was smiling up at him. "Yeh see then, everything's going to be fine."

Despite his fears, he couldn't help smiling back at her. "Yes, everything is going to be fine."

She nestled into him, talking to his chest.

"Why did yeh kill that man in Deadwood?"

Involuntarily he held his breath. He might have known she wasn't about to let him off easily. And in light of her dire straits he wasn't about to deny her. She deserved more.

"He had killed someone . . . someone I loved."

"Victoria?"

She deserved an honest answer. "No. *I* killed Victoria."

Now it was her easy breathing that had stopped. He could feel her turn away from his chest slightly to stare up at him again. His eyes were focused on the roof of the cave. He dared not look down. He didn't want to see the trust seeping away.

"What do yeh mean, yeh killed her?"

Yes, it was the truth. He had never admitted it to anyone but himself.

"My pride took her away from her family and friends, away from her comfortable life in New York. I dragged her halfway across the West . . ." His voice broke with emotion, and it was a second before he could continue. ". . . to sit and watch her die needlessly because I couldn't afford a doctor."

"Surely, yeh cannot blame yerself for that?"

He looked down at her. "I'm not as forgiving as you, Kathleen."

"But yeh don't understand, I'm not at all forgivin'. Me da used t'say it would be me downfall. I think perhaps he was right."

Sage pushed her hair away from her face. "I don't think he was right. You've forgiven me."

"Who did he kill, this man in Deadwood?"

"He killed my brother. My sixteen-year-old brother. He and Morse Templeton and some others baited Jimmy and lured him away from Cheyenne. Then they beat him to death to get even for my firing them. They left him in the bottom of a mine shaft up in the hills. It took me two days to find him and when I did . . ." He couldn't relive it. Not now with a dying woman in his arms.

" 'Tis not murder then."

"Tell that to Sheriff Davis."

" 'Tis justice. God's justice."

"Administered by a less than perfect man."

"There's nought of us that's perfect, y'know."

"But some of us are less perfect than others."

"Me da used t'say I was anything but the perfect, dutiful daughter. We used to get in such rows. He'd yell and I'd yell. 'Ye'll be the death of me yet, child,' he'd say. But he loved me jist the same. I knew that."

"I'll bet you were an obstinate child."

"I'd not like t'think of meself that way. Opinionated perhaps. A bit strong-willed."

Sage laughed. "A *bit* strong-willed?"

"A tad?" she responded, smiling.

"You're an Irish banshee sent to bring men to their ruin."

"Yeh think so, do yeh?"

"Look what you've done to me."

"What have I done to yeh?"

What had she done to him, indeed. Made him laugh for starts. He couldn't remember the last time he'd laughed. He'd laughed more in the last two days than he'd laughed in the previous two years.

She'd given him hope. Hope that life with all its joys could still be attained, at least by some.

And most importantly, she had enabled him to remember his beloved Victoria without pain.

She'd lifted the weight of the last two years off his shoulders, even if it was only temporarily.

"You've nearly done me in. That's what you've done to me, Kathleen Callahan."

"You're a might fit-lookin' man for bein' done in."

"Fit, eh?"

"Yes, fit and handsome."

He laughed. "Handsome, you say?"

"Well, if yeh cleaned yerself up a bit, I bet yeh'd be a fine handsome man."

He looked down at her. She was perspiring. He brushed the damp hair back off her face. "And you're a beautiful woman."

"Do yeh think so?" she queried with a child's innocence.

Sage realized she really had no idea how beautiful she was. In the firelight, her eyes bright, her skin moist—almost translucent—her hair brilliant, she looked like a Titian goddess.

"Yes, I think so. You are one of the most beautiful women I've ever met."

"If I keep me mouth shut."

He smiled. "No, even with your mouth open."

"Yeh think I'm beautiful?"

"Yes."

She curled into him again. Sage felt her shiver. The fever was starting.

"Sage." She looked back up at him. He could see droplets of sweat running down the open neckline of her dress.

"Would yeh kiss me?"

"Kiss you?"

"Could yeh pretend yeh loved me and kiss me?"

It wouldn't be hard to pretend he loved this Irish hellion.

"I know it would not be an easy thing for yeh to do. But I don't want t'die . . ." Her eyes shone with unshed tears. "I don't want t'die without knowin' what it would feel like."

He brushed her hair back from her damp forehead once more, and with his thumb he wiped away a tear. Then he bent and touched his lips to hers. He kissed her gently at first. When she did not push him away, he buried his hand in her hair and deepened the kiss. He pulled back slowly, kissing her brow and her eyelids as he did.

With her eyes still closed Kathleen lowered her head against his chest. Within moments she was asleep.

Chapter Seven

Kathleen awoke with a start. She wasn't dead. In fact, she felt quite fine. Sage was nowhere to be seen.

She pinched herself to make sure she wasn't dreaming, then sat up tentatively. She took a deep breath.

There was no question about it. She was still alive. She lifted her skirt to look at her ankle. It was covered with some dried blood, but it was neither swollen nor discolored.

Sage's shadow suddenly filled the cave entrance.

"Do you see what I have here?" he said.

"I c'not see. Yeh've the light to yer back. What is it?"

"It's your snake." The clang of metal hitting metal rang in her ears as a small trap landed practically in her lap.

"Well there's no need for yeh to be nasty about it." Kathleen was hot with indignation. " 'Twas not me that said it was a snake bite. Puncture wounds yeh said. Poison.

68

Fangs." She held two fingers up to her mouth to demonstrate the fangs.

The gesture irritated Sage. "It wasn't *me* who came running from the woods screaming that I'd been bit by a viper. You never actually saw the snake did you?"

"Not exactly."

"Well if you'd taken a moment, instead of getting hysterical, we could have saved ourselves both a lot of . . ."

"A lot of what?"

"Foolishness."

"Foolishness? I'm lying here thinkin' I'm dyin' and yeh call it foolishness?"

"You didn't die though, did you?"

"No thanks t'yeh. Yeh've probably scarred me ankle for life."

"Let me apologize for trying to save your life, madame." He bowed low.

"Always puttin' on the airs, y'are. I accept yer apology." She sniffed.

Sage shook his head in disbelief. She accepted his apology! He was about to say more, but then thought better of it. "Let's go. If we're going to get you on that Cheyenne stage, we'll have to get out of these hills by sundown."

"What d'yeh mean, get *me* on that stage. Yeh're not comin'?"

"No. Now let's go."

Kathleen grabbed her hose and jerked them on, forcing her toe through one. "By the saints, yeh'd think he was countin' on me dyin'."

Sage stalked off to the far side of the clearing. Minutes passed. What was taking the woman so long? She was impossible. Absolutely impossible!

The thought of the last ten hours they had spent together was painful. She had gotten him to admit things about Victoria that he'd never shared with anyone before. His soul still felt raw from baring so much of himself. But there was something even more disturbing about last night. He hadn't thought of Victoria without pain for so long that he had thought it was impossible to do otherwise, and yet this sparkling Irish twit had given him a moment's peace for the first time since his wife's death. It was something even Jimmy's concern couldn't accomplish.

And Jimmy. Why had he told her about his brother? He had killed a man in Deadwood who well deserved it. He would kill Morse Templeton too. Nothing this wisp of a woman said would dissuade him.

Of himself, of his own fate, he barely gave a thought. It didn't matter what happened to him. He fully expected to be hanged for the killings. He had accepted the fact that he had no future. So once he put Kathleen Callahan on the stage to Cheyenne that would be the end of it.

Besides, she was married.

But married to someone who didn't love her? Why then was she chasing him all over the West? Did she love him that desperately? What hold did this man have over her?

"All right, I'm ready." Kathleen came hobbling out of the cave, scratching at her stomach.

"Do your feet still hurt?"

"No, me feet don't hurt, thank yeh kindly. But me body still itches like the bejeezuz."

"Better that than dead," he said with some sarcasm.

She glared at him, ready for a fight.

"Let's go then if we're going." He turned and stalked off, but she was faster. She passed him in a huff. He watched her march off into the woods. He had to grudgingly admit that she was certainly one of a kind.

Kathleen barged ahead. She could hardly keep from blushing at the thought of what had happened between her and the man. Why had she asked him to kiss her? He probably thought she was some loose woman, some harlot. If he tried to take advantage of her she'd be ready, she swore.

But the mere thought of their kiss left her warm all over. It had been exquisite. Everything she had dreamed of and more.

The perfect moment to die.

Unfortunately here she was, scratching like an old dog, stumbling down over rocks and hills.

She had not anticipated the climb down would be harder than the climb up. Half the time she had to make her way down backward. Sage had gotten ahead of her. He barely looked back to see if she was keeping up.

He was a strange man. One minute she was sure he liked her, if only just a little, and the next he was yelling at her. She knew she irritated people, but for some reason she didn't want to aggravate Sage. It was not that she was afraid of him. She didn't think she had ever really been afraid of him. She had seen through his rough facade almost immediately. He was hurting, and she thought she understood hurt. But having him angry with her was upsetting.

It was well after noon when midway down a rocky incline her foot slipped. She abruptly ended up in a pile of petticoats and taffeta about six feet below where she had been moments before. Her backside hurt.

With the racket, Sage finally stopped.

"Are you all right?"

"Yes, thank yeh, sir. I am perfectly fine." But when she

tried to get up, she fell back in a dusty heap.

He moved back up to her and held out a hand. She took it reluctantly.

"Do you need to rest?"

"I need somethin' to eat, if I'm to keep up with yeh."

"We can't afford to stop now. The Deadwood-to-Cheyenne stage only runs twice a week. It leaves Deadwood on Mondays and Thursdays. By my count, today's Thursday. The stage should pass down below early tomorrow after stopping for the night at old Farley's place. That means we have to be out of these hills by the end of the day. We've a good six hours until sundown. We'd best make use of it."

"Yeh expect me to go on without a bit o'nourishment. Without a drop o' water? Yeh were in such a state, in such a hurry t'leave, I didn't even have time t'take a sip."

"I didn't stop you."

"No, but yeh ran off so fast, like a bull in heat, I was afraid I'd lose yeh."

"A bull in heat?" He raised an eyebrow.

Kathleen realized she had chosen her simile poorly. She could feel herself color from her toes to her head. Damn the man. Why couldn't he have let it pass?

"Yeh know what I mean."

"I'm not sure I do. Perhaps you could go into a little more detail."

"No. I won't, and no gentleman would pursue it any further." Kathleen studied her boots.

"I don't remember being accused of being a gentleman. A murderer perhaps. But not a gentleman."

"Well, yer not a cowboy." Kathleen pushed a sweaty strand of hair out of her eyes.

"Ergo, I must be a gentleman. Makes perfectly good sense to me." Sage shook his head in amusement.

He was toying with her. She hated it. "I don't want to talk about it anymore."

"Fine," he responded, running a hand through his hair. "But I was interested to hear that you were afraid of losing me."

She glared at him before stalking ahead down the next hill.

Kathleen was at the end of her endurance. She was hot, tired and sweaty. She must be a fine sight tramping down these hills in the middle of nowhere, her hat missing, her petticoats dangling, her shoes almost worn through. What story was he going to concoct to convince the driver to take her on? The man was an idiot, a bloomin' idiot. Still, his words haunted her. He wasn't going with her.

Was she afraid of losing him? No. She was certain about that. It's just that . . . However embarrassing last night's soul baring had been, she now thought she understood the man better. She was just concerned about him. He was going to put her on the stage, and what in the name of sweet Jesus was he going to do? Go off and kill another man? Get himself hanged? No God-fearin' Catholic girl could allow such an unjust thing to happen.

She waited a moment until he caught up with her. "I'm curious about this plan of yers. What is it exactly that yer goin' to tell the driver to convince 'im to pick me up?"

"I'm not going to tell him anything. You're going to be the one doing the talking."

"I am, am I? Well yeh'd better have a pretty good story, because I'm a terrible liar."

"Funny, *'Squirrel Tooth,'* that's something I thought you'd be good at."

They were fighting words. Kathleen had had enough. She stopped abruptly and turned on him. She dug her hands into her hips and planted her feet firmly on the ground. "I may be a lot of things, Sage Duross. Me da was not one to pass on pointin' out me shortcomings, but I am not a liar."

Kathleen was genuinely hurt. He had gone too far this time. Angrily she craned her neck to see his face. There was amusement in his light blue eyes. If he dared to smile, she'd . . . she'd . . .

The shadow of his face covered hers, and she felt his kiss ever so lightly on her lips.

"I'm sorry, 'Squirrel Tooth.' That was hitting below the belt."

She had been prepared for any response to her anger but this. It took a minute for the kiss to register. Then the impact was palpable. The softness of his lips brushing hers, his closeness made her shiver despite the heat. Just when she thought she had him figured out, he'd do something strange.

He was six steps ahead of her before she even knew it. He seemed to think nothing at all of the kiss as he blathered on. "I don't know what we'll tell the driver, but we can work it out."

"Work it out!" she yelled as she stumbled over a large rock in her pursuit of him, for some reason more aggravated than ever.

"Yes, work it out. You could tell him your horse went lame and you were left to walk." His long strides kept him just ahead no matter how fast she tried to walk.

"And where pray tell is me lame horse to be?"

"Then tell him you fell off a wagon." He gestured, indicating a less than gracious exit.

"Fell off a wagon! I'm to be such a bloomin' fool that I fall off wagons?"

"Well, you figure it out then." Again he was shaking his

head in disgust. She hated when he did that. Especially when she couldn't see his face.

"I've figured it out. I'm not goin' without yeh." She took a stance, arms akimbo. She wouldn't move another step without settling this matter.

Sage must have sensed that she had stopped again. He turned with a condescending smile on his lips. "That's very touching *darling,* but I think the two of us stumbling out of the hills together would more than pique their interest. Plus, I've no inclination to be hanged before I've finished my work."

She held her arms out in exasperation. "But after yer done killin' another man, yeh'll no doubt be happy to be hanged, eh?"

"I think happy might be an exaggeration. Content, perhaps."

"Yeh've completely lost yer wits then, man." She let her arms drop in disgust.

"I didn't expect you to understand. For that matter, you didn't figure into the scenario at all." He no longer smiled, but rubbed his scraggly beard thoughtfully.

This only exasperated Kathleen. "But I am part of your little unfoldin' drama now, and I deserve some consideration. Do yeh ever think of anyone but yerself in this little play yeh've written?"

"There's been no one else to think about." He looked away back up into the hills.

"Well there is now."

Sage stared at the inimitable Kathleen Callahan.

Someone else to think about. Hell, she was all he thought about anymore. This Irish witch was distracting him from what he had to do. With her stubborn ways and gutwrenching hold on life, she had pulled him back from the brink of despair. This chit of a woman, all bark and dander one minute, was perfectly happy to die with just a kiss from him. What kind of fool was *she?* And, more importantly, why did it matter so much?

"Your husband is probably in Cheyenne. You said you'd just missed him in Deadwood. He'll be able to settle things with the authorities on your mistaken identity."

"He won't be there."

"How can you be so sure?"

"I've lost too much time."

"What was your husband's business in Cheyenne?"

"The same as in Deadwood."

"The last I remember, you hadn't told me what he was doing in Deadwood."

"Business."

"What kind of business?"

"Business, business. It should make no never mind to yeh what his business is."

"No, you're right. It shouldn't matter to me. But you implied that I was to think about other people. And right now, you're the only other 'people' I have to think about."

"Well, stop yer thinkin' right now. 'Twon't do you a bit of good thinkin' about me and me troubles."

Troubles? So there was more to it than she was willing to admit.

"Troubles?" he questioned.

"Troubles catchin' me husband, that is."

He let it go. They had reached relatively flat ground, punctuated here and there by rocky outcroppings the size of small houses. At one point the stage road ran between the hills and one of these rocky outgrowths.

Sage studied the landscape and then walked over to the

barren remains of a fallen pine tree. "Help me with this." Sage grabbed one end of the dried trunk. "We need to drag it across the road."

Kathleen struggled with her end, half-carrying, half-pushing until the tree covered almost all of the road where it passed between a group of rocks and a sharp cliff-like approach to the hills.

The last rays of the sun softened the harsh landscape. Sage noticed it gave Kathleen Callahan an ethereal quality, tingeing her flesh and hair with its glorious auburn color. Making her flesh slick with sweat, imminently touchable.

But he was allowing himself to be distracted. There were only a few more minutes of daylight left. He sat down with his back to the largest rock and signaled Kathleen to do the same.

"What do we do now?" she asked as she crumpled to the ground.

"We wait."

Kathleen awoke disoriented. They were still sitting beside the rock. Sometime during the night Sage had put his arm around her. She reclined with her head against his chest. The first few buttons of his shirt were unbuttoned and the front lay partially open. She could feel the warmth of his skin against her cheek.

She remained perfectly still for a long moment, listening to his heart beat, unwilling to break the simple pleasure of it. Her right hand rested against his chest. She could feel the texture of its soft, dark hair beneath her fingers.

She moved her index finger ever so slightly. He didn't wake. Slowly, she splayed her fingers and rubbed her whole hand gently against his bare chest. The curls of hair tickled her palm, as soft as his beard had been. She had never touched a man like this before. It was a heady feeling.

She had never really wanted to touch her husband. She had never tried to fool herself. She did not love him. It was a marriage that would benefit them both. She would have gained the place in Boston Society her father always wanted for her. He would have her fortune.

Marital relations were inevitable. She wanted children. But these things were something one endured rather than enjoyed.

But this . . . this feeling was not unpleasant at all. Quite the contrary. The warm feeling building inside her frightened her a little. There was a growing need. She felt strange. Strange in a wonderful and unknown way.

She remembered when her da used to come home late sometimes, disheveled and smelling of perfume. He would be especially nice to her the next few days. She had always been curious, but knew better than to ask her da.

Now, she was sorely tempted to further her exploration. Sage Duross's chest was an unknown world to her. Broad and well muscled, it reflected the rest of him. His was the body of a man who worked outdoors long and hard. She smiled. It was a cowboy's chest. Dark curls spread across its upper width, then trailed down to his waistband tapering slightly as they reached his belt.

Kathleen blushed. Her hand still rested over Sage's heart. But just beyond it lay a chestnut nipple. She inched her hand forward. With her index finger she brushed the deep red tip. It was soft and warm. She brushed it again and ran her finger around the aureole. She watched, amazed, as the tip seemed to take on a life of its own, standing straight up as if at attention. The small move made her insides tighten. She touched the nipple ever so lightly. It was no longer soft. She ran her finger around its firmness. Circling slowly before brushing its tip again. She placed her hand over it. Excited and frightened by what she'd done.

"You don't have to stop." His voice was deep and raspy. He was awake. How long had he been awake?

Long enough. But she didn't want to stop. She was fascinated with the feel of him. She ran her palm over his chest until it brushed over his other nipple. It, too, stood erect at her caress.

She brushed it with her thumb and she heard him softly suck in his breath. It was an intoxicating feeling to have this much control over a man. She had never dreamed it possible.

She slid her hand down under his shirt, across his taut belly and back up. Once more she ran a finger across his nipple, once more around the dark ring that encircled it. She heard him moan softly. It excited her.

His hand came over hers. She felt him softly kiss the top of her head. His hand moved hers lower. Past his belly. Past his belt buckle.

She gasped. Her palm was filled with a bulging mass.

He shuddered, and she shivered in response. She should pull her hand away. It wasn't proper. It wasn't right.

She looked up and his mouth captured hers. Devoured hers. He kissed her lips, her cheeks, her eyes. She opened her mouth at the onslaught and he was inside of her, his tongue probing and searching. His right hand was buried in her hair holding her to him. His other hand kept her own palm on him, on his manhood swollen with desire. She was wilting under his onslaught, and she didn't care. She wanted to find out where this all led. What was it her body demanded? What satisfaction did it crave?

He laid her back onto the ground and she arched against him, needy, searching for something.

Then they heard it. The stage!

He pulled back. His eyes still hooded with passion.

"Remember what I told you."

He rose and helped her up. He was leaving. He was three steps away before she could speak

"No!" she blurted out. Her mind was in chaos. She searched for some excuse, anything to keep him near her.

He turned angrily. "Tell them your horse threw you," he commanded.

"No!" she shouted in defiance.

"What do you mean, 'no'?" His eyes were hard, determined.

"I don't want to go."

"You have to." It was an order that brooked no contradiction.

"I don't have t'do anything I don't wish, and I don't wish to leave without yeh."

He took the three steps back to her and grabbed her by the upper arms. "You have to!"

She looked up at him, pitting all her four-foot-ten-inch might against his towering authority. "I will not go without yeh. Yeh c'not make me. And that's final!"

Chapter Eight

"Ouch!" Kathleen winced as the stagecoach pitched in a large hole.

"Be quiet."

"But me bottom is as raw as a fresh piece of meat," Kathleen whispered harshly.

Sage was not sympathetic. "You could've been sitting inside comfortably, but no. . . . Here we are instead trussed up like a couple of carpetbags."

" 'Twas your idea."

"And not a very good one. You left me little choice with your hysteria."

"Hysteria! Is that what yer callin' it?"

"What, pray tell, would you call it?"

"Determination."

"Just shut up and be quiet," he grumbled dejectedly.

The Irish hellion had done it again. The damnable

woman had given him little choice. He couldn't leave her stranded in the middle of nowhere, and she'd never make the hundred or so miles to Cheyenne on foot.

When the stagecoach had stopped at the barricade, Sage had counted their blessings. There were only two passengers plus the driver and guard. And only a single trunk on the back.

They had stayed hidden until the last moment. As the stage pulled off, Sage had thrown Kathleen onto the back luggage platform, and then he had climbed on himself. He had quickly pulled the cowhide tarp down to cover them.

Amazingly, it had worked. Neither the driver nor the watchful guard had taken any notice.

Now they sat, as best they could, on a three-foot-long trunk. The trunk sat on the small slatted platform that protruded from the back of the coach. The cowhide tarp left them in the dark.

Every bump and lurch sent them tumbling into each other. It was utter chaos. The dust whirled up under the tarp like a miniature dust devil, making them both cough and gasp for air.

"I swear, I will never ride in one of these awful things again as long as I live."

"You've done this before?" Sage teased between coughs.

"Inside, yeh idiot. Inside. I thought it was bad inside one of these things, but this is . . . I c'not breathe."

Sage had to agree. They would suffocate at this rate. He had to do something. He leaned over and almost fell as the coach lurched.

Kathleen reached out and caught his belt. "What the devil do yeh think yer doin'?"

"I was attempting to keep us from suffocating."

Kathleen braced her small feet against the wooden slats

of the platform and took hold of his belt with both her hands. "If yer intent on killin' yerself, let me be of service."

Kathleen provided just enough counterweight to allow Sage to lean forward and grab the bottom of the tarp that covered them. Struggling as much against the jolting of the stagecoach as with the heavy tarp, he managed to fasten one side up, tying it with the rawhide strips intended for the purpose.

He moved to the other side. It was a delicate balancing act. He held on to the rawhide tie with his left hand as he fought with the tarp. It was several minutes before he got the second side secured. Just as a smile of accomplishment crossed his face, the stage careened wildly. Sage cursed as he slipped. Within seconds, he found himself half on, half off the small platform with only Kathleen Callahan preventing him from being thrown off the reeling vehicle. His right arm and leg dangled off the end of the platform as his torso balanced on the edge. Only the Irish sprite's hold on his belt kept him from a serious encounter with the hard ground spinning past at a dizzying rate.

"Pull me up."

"What d'ye think I'm tryin' to do? Yeh're the size of a full-grown cow. How am I to haul yeh up?" Kathleen clamped her jaw shut with the stress—her face now as red as her hair.

"We'll do it together." Sage forced his hand between the open boards of the luggage platform. "On three pull as hard as you can."

Kathleen nodded.

Sage raised his head.

"One, two, three . . ."

Kathleen groaned with the effort. Sage seemed to be making some progress. He was able to twist and get a second handhold. It seemed an eternity as he edged his torso completely back onto the small platform.

He lay facedown. His feet still hung off one side.

"You can let go now."

Red-faced, Kathleen realized she still had hold of his pants.

But they had succeeded.

Sage slowly drew his legs in and recovered a sitting position. They both took a deep breath.

"Is that better?"

"Yes."

They now could breathe, but their close brush with disaster prevented them from enjoying the slight victory. The coach still careened and lurched as the driver whipped the horses. A hundred miles a day, the coach drivers loved to brag. With a stop for fresh horses every twenty miles. There was still the chance they could be caught at one of the stops.

The stage moved across a dried riverbed. The washed-out gully grabbed at the coach, making it pitch violently.

Sage and Kathleen were being thrown about worse than ever.

"Ouch, me foot." Kathleen winced. Sage's foot came down on hers as he strove to regain his balance after one particularly nasty bump.

"If you're not quiet, the passengers will hear you and we'll be caught."

"Hear us over the din of the coach? Are yeh daft? I can barely hear meself talkin'."

"Have it your own way. Just make sure you attend my hanging."

Kathleen looked properly remorseful.

"Come here," Sage demanded.

"Here where?"

Sage pushed back on the trunk and opened his legs wide for support.

"Here." He indicated the small part of the trunk between his legs.

"I don't think so." Kathleen shook her head.

"Suit yourself."

With that, the stage hit a large rock. Kathleen went flying. Sage grabbed her arm, saving her from ending her journey prematurely.

"Here." He pointed to the trunk between his legs once more, still holding on to her upper arm.

Reluctantly Kathleen took her new seat. As she did, Sage's hands circled her small waist, safely securing her.

Neither spoke of what had happened earlier, before the stage's timely appearance. The incessant careening of the stage gave them enough to think about. Just staying on the blasted thing was a major accomplishment.

The minutes became hours. Sage's legs ached with the attempt to keep Kathleen from the worst of the jostling. But even the discomfort couldn't keep him from eventually dealing with what had happened.

He should have stopped her instead of encouraging her. It was obvious she didn't know what the hell she was doing when she had fondled him . . . or what reaction it might raise in him.

For a moment he wondered what it would be like to teach her. To show her what pleased a man. And please her in turn.

Funny that this chit, this Irish elf, should be the first woman since Victoria to summon these feelings. He hadn't frequented the brothels, as so many cowboys did. After Victoria, the thought of being with another woman, especially one who had to be paid, was repugnant.

He knew he was moving into dangerous territory, but they would be apart soon enough. Despite, or rather because of, the erratic movement of the stagecoach, he had become acutely aware of her presence in his arms.

His thoughts wandered. To have Kathleen Callahan in a soft bed, with crisp linen and the golden light of sunset. To explore and be explored. Her lips, her breasts, the back of her neck and her ears. The softness behind her elbows and knees.

He stopped himself. He was a fool. A damned fool!

He lay his head against the back wall of the coach and tried not to think anymore.

Kathleen felt ill, and it wasn't the swaying coach that had made her stomach rise to her throat. What had she done? She had acted like a wanton woman. What would her da have said?

And then when she could have left him—when he begged her to go—she had stubbornly refused. What was happening to her? None of it made sense in her head. But in her heart, she acknowledged, in her heart it seemed to all make sense.

She looked up. The stage had slowed. They must be approaching a stop. She nudged Sage.

"What?"

"Have you been sleeping?" She didn't wait for an answer. "The stage is slowin'. I think it's goin' to stop."

Sage picked her up and set her to one side. Quickly he released the straps that held up the luggage cover. He lowered himself beside her and held a finger to his lips. She nodded.

The stage rolled to a stop.

"Any trouble, Clem?"

"No. For a minute there I thought we might be in fer it. There was a tree down across the road. No mistake 'bout it—somebody'd put it there. But nobody gave us no trouble. Told Bert, here, that maybe ole 'Squirrel Tooth' Sally thought she'd do one last job before high-tailin' it outta here. But somethin' must have scared her off, 'cause there was no one to be seen."

"Well count yer lucky stars. 'Cause they ain't caught neither one of them outlaws. That cowpoke they got fer murder ain't been found neither."

"Well thanks fer the word. How's the road up ahead?"

"Should be fine all the way to Cheyenne. Have a good trip."

"See ya next week."

Kathleen groaned. The stage had started again. The thing was too damned efficient for her. Her backside hurt like the dickens. Why couldn't they have taken a few more minutes to change the horses? She would have loved just a minute or two more without being bumped and thrown around like a sack of potatoes.

Sage tied the tarp back up and teased. "Well, 'Squirrel Tooth,' seems you're still in as much demand as me."

"But yeh're the one they're eager to hang."

"Which brings us to another problem."

"*Another* problem?"

"Yes, I believe it's number four or five," Sage added.

"It seems mighty mean of yeh to be countin' them."

"I didn't have to start counting them until I met you. They seemed to have doubled and quadrupled since we've been together."

"Yeh cannot argue with fate."

"Fate, was it? Damned bad luck, I'd say."

"Well if it was such bad luck, why d'yeh stay? No one made yeh come with me."

Once again her logic failed him. "No one made me! I'm to forget that you stood there refusing to leave me."

Kathleen had the good sense to blush. "It wasn't you I was refusin' to leave."

"Who was it then?" His eyes squinted as he studied her.

"It wasn't a 'who.' "

He wasn't going to let the matter drop. "If it wasn't a who, what was it?"

"It was a matter of principle."

"And that principle was?" His eyebrows raised with the inquiry.

"I could not leave yeh to do somethin' yeh'd regret."

He shook his head in disbelief. She was going to make a career out of protecting him from himself. Well she'd better get over it.

He was suddenly very serious. "I am going to kill Morse Templeton. Whether I do it today or ten years from today, nothing will stop me. Do you understand, Kathleen? You cannot stop me."

He wanted to take her and shake her. "It's a debt I owe to my brother. A matter of honor." He did take her by her upper arms now. ". . . and they will hang me. Do you understand that? So any other foolishness you have in your head, get rid of it. It's too late, Kathleen, too late for me. I am beyond your redemption and forgiveness. Leave me, Kathleen. If you have any of the good sense your da gave you, leave me. Go find your husband. Have babies. Be happy."

Kathleen was angered by his words. "Me husband will

never make me happy. That is a lesson yeh've taught me, Sage Duross. And yeh never should have taught me that."

Sage couldn't answer her. She was right, of course. It had been unfair of him to offer her something he could not give.

Chapter Nine

Sage nudged the sleeping Kathleen.

She made a funny little snort. "What?"

"Shhh."

He lifted her and set her beside him on the trunk. "You snore like a sailor."

She gave him a belligerent look. He smiled and shook his head, his finger to his lips to silence her.

Kathleen was willing to be silenced when she realized that once more their pace had slowed.

It was dusk. To the west, the sun painted the sky with broad swaths of color—magenta and rose, violet and pink. The colors were at once vibrant and subtle, changing with every moment that passed. It was a living mural of such loveliness that it almost took Kathleen's breath away.

It struck her that she had barely noticed sunsets until she had come out west. In Boston they were too often hidden by grit or masked by tall buildings. When she returned to the East she would miss the sunsets.

A nudge from Sage brought her back. "What is it?" she whispered.

"I think they're stopping for the night. We need to get off." He peered around the corner of the stagecoach.

A day's worth of jostling had left Kathleen sore from head to foot. She wondered if her legs would even hold her.

Kathleen grabbed Sage's shirtsleeve as she leaned out to get a look herself. The horses had slowed to a walk as they made their way leisurely toward a small stand of trees and a simple wooden building. No doubt the coach stop. It seemed rather forlorn, but it was the first building they had seen since leaving Deadwood. Its meager amenities were suddenly so appealing that Kathleen fought the thought of turning herself in for a hot meal.

She felt Sage's arm around her waist. "Come on." He slid down off the trunk. They sat at the end of the platform their legs dangling off the end. She wanted to warn him about her shaky limbs, but before she could, he lurched forward. They hit the ground harder than she had expected, and her legs crumpled under her. Her unexpected dead weight toppled them both. She found herself sprawled on her back with Sage on top of her.

"Graceful as a gazelle, I see." He smiled. His face inches from hers.

"Well, if yeh had given me jist a bit of notice, I might have told yeh I didn't think it was a great idea."

"And you, I suppose, had a better one."

She didn't answer him. "Would yeh be so kind as to remove yerself from atop me? I'm squished. I can barely breath."

"Pardon me, madame. How ungracious of me." He

backed off to his knees and then rose to tower over her. He made a grand sweep with his arm before offering her his hand.

"Yeh think it's funny, do yeh. I'm starvin' and we're still in the middle of nowhere." She quickly dropped his hand once she was upright and swiped angrily at her dusty skirts, as upset by the feel of him on top of her as by his annoying sense of humor.

"We'd better get off the trail," he murmured.

She looked up, but he had already turned and started to move away without a backward glance for her well-being.

"I'm hungry!" she said, moving forward gingerly on her tingly legs. She gave a sidelong glance toward the wooden building, whose windows now shone with the warmth of lamplight. They reached a stand of trees, and she paused.

She watched enviously as the passengers alighted. No doubt there was a hot meal awaiting them inside.

Sage moved on toward a second stand of trees about a hundred yards from the building and its corrals. She dragged behind—sore, tired and hungry.

Most of all hungry.

Her stomach felt like it was eating itself. It growled so loudly that she was sure Sage would turn around, but he didn't. Only when he reached the small group of aspens and a comfortable-looking patch of grass did he turn to see if she was following.

He plopped down on the ground and lay back in the grass. She heard him mumble something appreciative of the non-moving bed.

She walked toward him, forming her argument for a hot meal as she did. "Sage?" She softened her voice, hoping she might win him over.

"Sage?" She spoke a little louder as she moved still closer.

Then she heard it. He was snoring! He had fallen asleep with no regard for her whatsoever. Damn him, she thought as she crumpled onto the grass beside him.

Sage awoke with a start. Something was wrong. Yet, as he lay there listening, he couldn't put his finger on what it was.

He rose on one elbow and looked around. He knew now what it was that had disturbed him. He had spent the better part of the week with the familiar sound of the Irish sprite's light snoring in his ear. Now, there was nothing. He rose cautiously to his feet. Perhaps she was behind a tree, re-lieving herself. "Kathleen?"

He waited. There was no response.

"Kathleen?"

Still no response. He went over his last few conscious moments. What had she said?

Shit! He looked toward the coach stop. *She was hungry!*

One guess as to where the Irish hellion had disappeared. He didn't much care if she were caught, he told himself. But if she were caught, he could get caught. And he still had to settle the score with Morse Templeton.

Grudgingly he rose and headed out into the darkness.

All seemed quiet. It was late. Kathleen had watched the moon climb slowly in the sky as Sage's even breathing drove her crazy. He slept like he hadn't a care in the world, and here she was almost dead with hunger.

With the moon full overhead, she'd had enough light to make out her surroundings. She had clung to the aspens and the pines as she worked herself toward the coach stop. The stage sat out in front of the rough-hewn building. The horses had been unhitched, and they stood with several others in the small corral. They appeared to have eaten their fill and now stood motionless except for the gentle back and forth movement of their tails. They resembled clock pendulums slowly marking the movement of time.

She had told herself not to rush. Rushing would only increase the risk of making a noise that would give her away. In front of her lay the last fifty feet. There was no protection. She would have to make a run for it. She looked up. The moon was about to disappear behind a large cloud.

"Jesus, Mary and Joseph protect me." She crossed herself and sprinted forward hiking her dress high above her ankles.

She reached the building panting. Her short breaths were as much the result of excitement as exertion.

She'd show Sage Duross a thing or two. She could take care of herself.

She placed her hands on the sill of the single window on this side of the building. She rose on her toes until she could see through the filthy glass. There seemed to be no one in sight. A door on the left lead to a back room. They must all be asleep.

Before her, the remnants of a meal lay on the rough-planked table. She felt saliva forming in her mouth as she noticed several untouched baking powder biscuits scattered among the plates that held uneaten beans. Her stomach growled. The beans, half-dried in their salt pork sauce, suddenly seemed far more attractive than she could ever have imagined.

To the right, she could see the door to the outside. A hefty board straddled its width. At each end it rested in daunting iron supports. It seemed impenetrable. There had to be a way. She studied the window. She pushed gently against it. It didn't budge. Then she remembered the one in the sheriff's office in Deadwood.

She removed a hairpin from her disheveled curls and began to pry at the edge of the opening. The window gave a little.

Yeh've got it now, girl. She smiled, pleased with herself. The window pushed out and was secured with a stick. She looked down. It was clear that a hairpin would not do the trick. She had to find something sturdier to pry it open.

She began a careful inspection of the grounds. One of the horses whinnied and she froze in place. She watched the building, terrified that someone had heard her. After a few seconds with no movement from the cabin she continued her search.

There was a second building, not much more than a shack, behind the main building. Carefully, she picked her way among the discarded harnesses and horseshoes. Her progress was excruciatingly slow. With every step there was a potential hazard and the possibility that she might make a sound that would wake those sleeping only a few feet away.

"Saints be praised!" she whispered and crossed herself in thanksgiving. She had reached the building, and the door was ajar.

The moon had reappeared, creating a slash of light across the dirt floor. An anvil dominated the room. That was good, it meant that there would be blacksmithing tools. Surely she could find something that would do the trick.

She took a step forward. "Oh, Jesus save me!" She clasped a hand over her mouth, startled by her own outburst.

There was someone else in the shack. She could see movement, a shadow against the back window. A man's hat.

"I don't mean to steal anything," she whispered to the figure, conveniently ignoring the fact that it was a lie. She backed toward the door. "I was just lookin' for a place to rest me head." Before she could get to the door. The hat lurched forward. She opened her mouth to scream. Then clamped it shut again as the hat tumbled to the floor and a large cat jumped nimbly behind it. As the huge calico passed her on the way to the door it stopped momentarily.

"Meow."

"Meow to yeh. Yeh nearly scared me t'death, yeh old pussy," she reprimanded the cat under her breath. Her heart still beat wildly in her chest. She tried to calm herself. It was clear she didn't have what it took to be an outlaw.

Still, she was determined. Her stomach growled loudly to reinforce her resolution. She searched as much by feel as anything and gratefully found a small rasp. It would work just fine.

Once more she took the torturous route back to the window. She inserted the metal tool in the crack and began to pry. The window opened fairly easily, and she smiled with satisfaction. This wasn't hard at all.

Well, Kathleen, yer hunger has really addled yer brain. She realized she had another problem. The window was too high for her to climb in.

Carefully she released the window and began a new search. This time she didn't have far to go. A hay bale lay at the rear corner of the building. She made her way to it and bent to pick it up. She almost fell over backward as its unexpected weight caused her feet to slip. The bale barely budged.

She kicked the hay in frustration. "Don't think yeh've got the better of me, yeh hunk o'hay!"

Taking a new approach, she began to push and drag the bale until she had it where she wanted it, under the window. She sat down on it for a moment, winded. She thought of Sage sleeping peacefully. Her Irish dander rose.

"I'll show yeh, Sage Duross." She swore under her breath.

She rose, pushed the hale bale on end and clambered up. Perfect! She pried open the window and forced her head and shoulders into the opening. Standing on her toes, she forced herself up still farther until she teetered on the sill—half in and half out of the building. Beneath her dangling feet, the hay bale plunked silently over on its side. She couldn't worry about that now.

She began to walk herself down the inside wall of the cabin below the window, grateful for the raised floor inside that cut the distance she had to maneuver. Her palms stung and her wrists nearly gave way as she hit the floor. She crumpled into a mass of green taffeta.

Me Gawd, Kathleen, yeh'll raise the dead, she berated herself.

She could barely breathe. She lay there in terror listening. Nothing.

Quickly, she gathered herself up and moved to the table. She pulled up the over skirt of her dress and made a small indentation where she plopped the biscuits one after the other, resisting the urge to stop and sample one.

After a longing glance at the leftover beans, she trotted back to the window. Tucking the hem of skirt into her waistband, she safely secured her horde. Quietly she opened the window and looked down. The drop on the outside was a little more daunting now that the toppled hay bale was half of its former height.

Still, she had made it in and she could make it out, especially with the promise of biscuits at the end of her escapade. She rose on her tiptoes and managed to get her lower chest onto the sill. Teetering precariously she rocked from side to side inching the top of her body out the window. When she reached her waist, she realized she had a problem.

The biscuits. She didn't want to crush them. The idea of presenting Sage Duross with beautiful intact biscuits was one she would not abandon. She'd have to roll to her side and work them over the windowsill before she dropped.

She leaned to the left and with her right hand began to work the bundle of her skirt and its precious contents upward. The open window rested on her head and moved haphazardly as she struggled. Her side ached with the pressure of the sill. It was turning out to be harder than she thought, but still she would not abandon the struggle. She'd show *him*.

She bent her head to tug at the reluctant fabric. She gave it one last effort.

Success!

She felt the weight of the skirt clear the sill.

Disaster!

She began to tumble out the window completely out of control. She put her hands out to break her fall.

The impact never came. Instead, she hung there dangling just above the hay bale. It took her a moment to realize what had happened. While one of her feet was free, the other shoe's buttons had caught on a nail protruding from the far edge of the sill. She hadn't noticed it on her way in. If she had, she might not be in her present predicament.

She felt like a fool, dangling like a cured piece of meat. To add insult to injury, the biscuits hung before her nose. They were so close she could smell them. Their proximity only aggravated her more.

The biscuits also prevented her from getting a clear view of her ensnared shoe. She angrily pushed aside her skirt and tried to get a better idea of how she might extricate herself. Blood was rushing to her head. Her free foot was in danger of hitting the window and breaking one of its panes. If that happened she knew it would be all over.

She fought to hook the toe of her free foot back over the sill to steady herself. On her first try she succeeded only in making herself sway wildly. She approached the task more gingerly. This time she succeeded.

Warily, she shifted her weight to this foot and tested the other. She moved it forward, then backward. To one side, then the other. She tried to lift it up, but the weight of her body was too much to overcome. Nothing seemed to free it. She tried to think.

She wasn't going to be caught this way. She had her pride. She'd happily break her neck before she'd let them find her this way.

Once again she shoved her skirt to one side and bent her head and rested the top of it against the rough exterior wall of the cabin. She'd have splinters in her hair.

At first the shadow that fell over her didn't register. The moon had been in and out of clouds all night. But as she studied her shoe above her, she slowly became aware that she was not alone. She pivoted her head on the rough-hewn planks of the cabin. Someone was there, standing no more than a few feet away.

She dropped her head. For the first time she regretted her impulsiveness. Tears began to sting her eyes. Whatever had happened to sensible Kathleen Callahan? Here she was, 'Squirrel Tooth' Sally strung up like a cured ham in the middle of nowhere. The humiliation of it all.

She had barely a moment to think further. The man grabbed her roughly by the waist and she heard the soft leather of her shoe rip as it was torn from the nail.

She would just have to explain to them calmly and rationally about the mistaken identity and then . . .

The breath was suddenly knocked out of her. Instead of being placed upright, she had been indecorously heaved over the man's shoulder.

"Well, well, well. What have you gone and gotten yourself into this time."

The man's voice was barely above a whisper, but she knew it well. Sage! If she weren't so upset about being man-handled, she might have been tempted to admit that she was almost happy to see him.

He had her at a distinct disadvantage. She was bouncing along staring at his back as he strode back across the open field to the protection of the aspens.

When they reached the clearing he plopped her down on her backside.

"What do you call that little stunt?"

"It wasn't a stunt. I was hungry."

"And you risked getting us both killed for what?"

Carefully she loosened her skirt hem from her waistband and unfolded the green taffeta. Kathleen looked horrified at the crushed and broken biscuits.

"Yeh dimwit. Yeh've squashed 'em after all the trouble I went to t'get 'em."

"What!" Sage thrust his hand into his hair. "You're worried about your precious biscuits when you could still be hanging by your toes back there. Is this the thanks I get for saving your pretty behind from who knows what?"

"Left to me own devices, I would've gotten meself free."

"You think so, do you? You were always delusional. Why should I think you've gained any wits at all these past few days!"

"Delusional? You think these are delusions?" She shoved a handful of the sorry biscuit remains into her mouth.

"They're delicious," she mumbled, her mouth full to overflowing. Even as she spoke, several crumbs escaped and tumbled down the front of her dress. "They're absolutely delicious.

"And don't think I'll be offerin' yeh any after the frightful way yeh've treated me."

Sage threw up his arms in frustration. There was no getting through to the little chit. She was beyond his help.

He turned and threw himself back down on the crushed grass that had been his bed. Kathleen hurled another handful of crumbs into her mouth.

They hardly exchanged a word the next morning. In the darkness just before dawn, they managed to regain their seating on the back of the stage without being detected. As the stage pulled out an icy silence settled in.

They passed another two stage stops and it was afternoon before Sage finally broke their long silence. "We're almost to Cheyenne. I want you to get off first. Then I'll know you're safe. Make your way into town by the main road. Tell them your horse threw you. Go to the sheriff and straighten out the whole mixup."

"But what about you?" The pleading look in her eyes startled him. He wasn't going to get caught up again. The little leprechaun wasn't going to make him change his mind.

"I'll get off a ways farther down."

Kathleen shook her head violently. The stage had not slowed. It still careened wildly. Her hands flailed about. "How d'yeh expect me to get off this blasted thing?"

What was wrong with the damned woman now? Obviously, the afternoon's ride had done little to improve her temper from last night.

"You're to jump! It's not hard!"

"Not hard! Yeh've got britches on and sturdy boots. I'm t'jump in me dress and petticoats?" She held up the remnants of her dress for his consideration.

"Kathleen, there's no other way."

"I'll just wait 'til it stops."

"No, you won't wait until it stops."

"I will." She had placed her hands on her hips. It was a bad sign. He had seen that move before and he was acutely aware that it hadn't ended well for him.

"You won't. If they find you on the stage, it will be harder on you."

"That's my choice."

"No, Kathleen. The choice is mine." Without warning he picked her up under her arms and leaned forward. She was now dangling over the rutted road. Her eyes were wide with disbelief. She cautiously squirmed in his grasp.

"Let me go," she demanded with a withering look. "Let me go. You wouldn't dare!" There was a challenge in her narrowed eyes. It was all Sage needed to make up his mind. He unceremoniously dropped her off the back of the stage.

Kathleen landed in a pile of dusty green taffeta. It took her a moment to catch her breath. Then she scrambled to her feet. She was yelling, but Sage couldn't hear over the rumble of the wheels. He was sure she wasn't sending her love. Her arms were flailing madly about her making vaguely threatening gestures.

Kathleen Callahan, he mused, was definitely not happy.

Chapter Ten

The stable owner studied Sage. "Nice boots."

"Thanks."

"Mexican?"

"Yes."

"Juarez?"

"No, Nuevo Laredo."

"Nice hand work. Give you five bucks for 'em."

"No thanks."

Sage knew he was taking a big risk, but the stable was always the quickest way to get information on who might be new in town.

"I'm looking for a man. Thought he might have brought his horse here to be stabled. Tall, maybe six foot. Dark hair and a mustache."

"Is he that cowpoke Sheriff Davis wants for murder over in Deadwood?"

"Yeh. He killed a friend of mine."

"Real sorry about that." The stable owner visibly relaxed and then warmed to the subject. "No, ain't seen no one like him 'round here. Heard he was with a woman, that 'Squirrel Tooth' Sally. They say she's an ornery one."

Sage saw an opportunity. "Ornery is being kind. Saw her once. Tall woman, missing most of her front teeth. Short hair. Dresses like a man. She was pistol-whippin' some cowpoke for callin' her 'dearie.' Wouldn't want to run into her."

"Yup, plenty of ornery men around. Don't need a mean-spirited woman."

"That's for sure. Haven't seen any strangers then?"

"Not here. But you might check with the sheriff. I know he's been looking for both them folk. If they got any sense, they've high-tailed it out of the territory by now."

"I imagine you're right."

"You can bet on it."

"Got a saloon in town?"

"Yup, got two. The Golden Eagle and Pearl's. Pearl's is just there." The man pointed to a drab-looking, unpainted wood building several hundred feet away. "The Golden Eagle is farther down, next to the train station. It's the fancy one. But if all you want is a good drink, I'd try Pearl's."

"Thanks."

"Don't mention it, mister."

Sage turned and walked out through the stable door.

The owner called after him. "Hope you find them folk."

"Yep, so do I."

"And remember, mister, if you ever want to sell those boots. I'll buy 'em."

"What d'yeh mean, I c'not send a telegram?" Kathleen was tired, dirty and out of sorts. She had trailed the stage into

104

Deadwood. It was early afternoon, and she hadn't eaten all day. "I am tellin' yeh. I will pay yeh as soon as I can send the telegram and get some money."

"Sorry, ma'am. Like I told you before, without no money you can't send no telegram."

"But d'ye not see the idiocy of this? If I c'not send the telegram, I c'not get the money. What exactly d'yeh expect me t'do?"

"I'm sorry, ma'am. Maybe you could go talk to the sheriff. He might be able to help."

The sheriff was the last person Kathleen wanted to talk to. She'd been humiliated enough for one day. Still she had to do something. She glanced around her.

Cheyenne was considerably larger than Deadwood, but then Deadwood had not been much more than a single street and a saloon. Cheyenne was a bustling metropolis by comparison. It had a main road with at least two side streets she could see. The railroad through the town was the obvious reason. *The railroad!*

She picked up her soiled taffeta dress and worked herself across the busy main street to the small yellow-planked train station. Every bone in her body ached as she stepped up onto the train platform. She dragged herself to the window.

"Good afternoon to yeh, sir." She smiled and hoped the clerk didn't notice her insincerity.

"Afternoon."

"I'm lookin' fer a man and a woman. It was my thought that they might 'ave purchased tickets from yeh." Or maybe not, she thought hopefully. She needed Bret and his paramour, Elizabeth Milgrim, to still be in town. That way Kathleen could demand her money back from Bret and be on her way back East in a matter of hours.

"I sell lots of tickets, ma'am." The clerk was staring at her.

It was making her uncomfortable. She must look a wreck. She patted down her dusty taffeta and pushed a stray tendril of red hair away from her face.

"They are from Boston, the two. He's about five-foot-eight with a thin, weasely face and pale hair the color of straw. The woman's blond as well. Stringy as an alley cat, with a nose that turns up at the end like turnip."

"Ah, you mean Mr. and Mrs. Merriweather."

"Mrs. Merriweather! Is that what she's callin' herself these days? Just wait 'til I get me hands on her little throat." The outburst left the clerk stupefied.

"They're in town then, waitin' fer the train?"

"No, ma'am. Mr. and Mrs. Merriweather caught the train yesterday. They've been gone . . ." He pulled out a pocket-watch and checked the time. ". . . a good eighteen hours now I'd say."

"Where were they headed . . . Mr. and Mrs. Merri-weather?"

"Why, all the way, ma'am. To San Francisco."

"What would be the fare, then, to San Francisco?"

"That'd be twenty dollars."

"When will the next train be by?"

"Not 'til later this afternoon. Round about three she usually pulls in. Of course if she's been delayed by . . ." The clerk droned on but Kathleen no longer cared.

Three o'clock. She had between now and three o'clock to get the train fare she needed. "By the saints," she swore under her breath, "I'm goin' to get that poor excuse for a man, if it's the last thing I do." She looked down Cheyenne's main street for inspiration. She wondered where Sage was. Lord knows he was infuriating. No doubt he'd get himself killed in the end. She was certainly better off without him, she told herself without much conviction.

The Wild Irish West

*   *   *

Sage weighed his options. If he went around asking too many questions the sheriff would surely want to make his acquaintance. He was thirsty. He fruitlessly patted his pockets. Sheriff Davis had taken every cent he had in Deadwood. Short of his boots, he had nothing to trade on but himself. Maybe that would be enough.

He made his way over to Pearl's. The town was quiet. It was early afternoon and most of the cowhands were no doubt still sleeping off the previous night's revelry. He pushed open the bar's swinging doors and took one step inside.

The place was empty. Besides the bartender, there was only one person in the bar. A woman.

"Howdy, stranger. What can I do for you?" The bartender seemed happy to see a customer.

"Well, I wish I could say a whiskey, but the world's not been too kind to me lately. So if you don't mind I thought I'd just come in out of the sun for awhile."

Sage stood at the oak bar, one foot on the rail, his elbows on the polished surface.

He saw the bartender give a look in the direction of the blonde in the corner. The woman had to be thirty-five, but she carried the years well. She was dressed quite elegantly in yellow satin except for her décolletage, which went farther down than propriety dictated, and the hemline that ended scandalously at her knee.

Sage smiled. Polite society would have been properly scandalized. She wore makeup, but it wasn't garish. He knew society women in New York who wore more, all the while claiming the blush on their cheeks was natural.

"You're a big one, ain't you?" The woman stepped from

107

the shadows. In the harsher light she showed a little more of her years.

"Yes, ma'am."

"Polite too. I like polite men." She signaled the bartender. "Abe, pour the man a drink."

The bartender scurried into action. "Yes, Miss Pearl." He poured a double whiskey into a glass and slid it to Sage.

Pearl sauntered over to the bar and signaled Abe again. A whiskey glass was set before her and quickly filled.

Sage saluted the woman with his glass. "Thank you, *Miss Pearl.*"

"The pleasure's all mine, you can bet on it." Pearl returned the gesture.

Sage took a swig of the whiskey. It was far from the best whiskey he'd ever tasted but at this particular moment it was nectar from the gods.

"New in town?" Pearl slid her glass down toward Sage and then followed it herself.

"I've been here before. Cattle drive."

"A cowboy, eh?"

Sage nodded.

"I like cowboys." Pearl indicated a table. "Why don't you sit for a bit?"

It was clear Pearl didn't intend for him to sit alone. As Sage took one of the wooden chairs at the table, Pearl took an adjoining one.

"You're not from 'round here." Pearl studied Sage.

"No, ma'am."

"Out East, I'd guess. Not Boston. New York?"

Sage raised a toast to her correct guess. "You're very good."

"I ought to be. Spent the last twenty years watching men coming and going in one flea-bitten town or another. I was from out East myself once, though you'd never know it now. Wasn't more than a girl when I left."

"You have the look of a woman who made the best of what she had and ended up on top in the end," Sage stated sincerely.

"If you call this the top." She raised her own glass to indicate the saloon.

"At least it's yours. You don't owe anyone for what you've done with your life."

"You don't look like the kind of man who'd owe anyone for his life either."

"I'm not." Sage stared at the whiskey in his tumbler and swirled the honeyed remains around slowly.

"You've got regrets, though. I can see 'em in your eyes."

"There are always regrets."

"Why don't you let Pearl make 'em go away, if only for a little while?"

Sage laughed kindly. "I told you, Pearl, I'm flat broke. Not a cent to my name." He splayed his hands. "Sorry."

"This one'd be on old Pearl." She studied him more closely.

Sage still stared at his drink. "That's a kind offer, Pearl. Kind indeed. But I think I'll have to pass."

"You've got a woman?"

"Had one. She died."

"No." Pearl rejected this idea. She took a moment to study him longer. "You've got a woman, cowboy. You may not know it yet, but you've got a woman."

Kathleen strode along the planked sidewalk of Cheyenne's main street. She was on a mission. She needed to find a mercantile, a dry goods store. There was a bank ahead of her and a dressmaker's shop. On the far side she saw a drugstore and the telegraph. A barbershop with its red-and-white pole graced the first corner. She stepped down into the dust and started across the side street.

"Hee awww!" The thunderous rattle of a freight wagon reverberated between buildings.

Kathleen looked up just in time. She stepped back and lost her balance. The huge iron-clad wheels missed her toes by inches.

"What the divil d'yeh think yer doin'!" she yelled after the driver. "Yeh almost killed me here!" She sat on the dusty road for a moment. No one came to her aid.

She struggled to her feet. Enough of this, she thought as she quickly made her way to the other side of the street. Once she stood safely again on the sidewalk, she brushed at her skirts. Every stroke left a new dusty handprint. She stomped her foot in frustration and looked up.

"Ah, Mother Mary, I thank yeh kindly." Before her was the very place she had been looking for. A sign in the window announced McCarty's General Store. It was large and appeared to be quite well stocked. Several gold watches lay in the window along with some frilly bonnets. It was more than what she had hoped for.

She made her way in. A small bell hung on the door tinkled to announce her arrival. A mother and her small daughter glanced up. Kathleen smiled. Protectively, the woman put an arm around the girl and took a step back.

Kathleen smoothed her hair and looked away from the twosome. A small mirror hung behind the counter.

Oh me God! Would the saints look at me. Kathleen couldn't believe her eyes. *I look like I've been attacked by a Bean-Sidhe. 'Tis no wonder they're all afeared.*

Still there was little she could do at the moment. She tucked several stray strands of hair behind her ears and patted at her dress, but the action only created a cloud of dust, and she began to sneeze.

The sneezing fit doubled her over. She had no handkerchief, no gloves. . . .

When she looked up a clerk was hurrying over to her.

"Is there something we can help you with ma'am?" He asked with disdain. His aloof attitude made her feel like the only thing he wanted to help with was getting her out of the store as quickly as possible.

"Yes, if yeh could be so kind as to call Mr. McCarty."

"Mr. McCarty?"

"I believe that is what I just said. He is the owner here, is he not?"

"Yes, ma'am."

"I wish to speak to him on a matter of some urgency so if yeh could . . ." She shooed him away with her hand just before she sneezed again.

The woman and her young daughter circumvented Kathleen, passing behind a large stack of flour sacks, to reach the door as quickly as possible.

Kathleen couldn't help herself. She stuck out her tongue at their retreating backs. When she turned back a rather imposing man stood behind the counter. Kathleen had the decency to blush—a condition that did not enhance her already questionable looks.

"Yes?"

"Mr. McCarty, I presume."

"Yes, McCarty's my name. And you'd be?"

"Kathleen Callahan, sir. It's a pleasure to meet yeh." She extended a dirty gloveless hand.

The storeowner glanced down and did not offer his own.

"Sir, me horse threw me just out of town"—she pointed

111

in the direction of the hills—"and ran off with all me wordly possessions."

"Your horse threw you, eh?" He looked at her taffeta dress. "Is that what the fashionable ladies are wearing on horseback now?"

"Me clothes . . . me clothes were all lost sir. In the river, sir. Crossing in a wagon. I had only the clothes on me back to me name."

"And some money to buy a horse?"

"The saints be praised, I did. And then, when the horse chose to go his own way, I lost what little money I had." She thought about crying but she was simply too exhausted, too angry to attempt such a ploy. "I've naught but this ring me dear grandmother gave me on her deathbed to call me own." She tugged at her wedding ring. It was a simple gold band set with a single good-sized emerald. The ring resisted her attempts to remove it. She tugged and pulled. Finally the ring came flying off onto the sawdust-covered floor.

"If ye'll excuse me for a moment." She held up a finger, then dived for the ground. Where had the darned thing gone?

"Is this what you're lookin' for?"

Kathleen looked up from her hands and knees. A rather large man stood holding her ring. It wasn't until she was back upright that her heart dropped. The man wore a shiny metal star on his vest.

"Sure, it is now. Thank yeh kindly, sheriff." Kathleen took the ring from the man's outstretched hand. She curtsied and smiled brightly and as innocently as she could manage.

She had not heard the sheriff come in. He must have been in the back room with the owner. How much of their conversation had he heard? Even she would never have believed her story.

The sheriff tipped his hat. "Sorry to hear about your troubles, ma'am."

" 'Tis nice of you to say that, sir." Kathleen dropped her head. She couldn't look at him, afraid to death she would betray some of her fear.

The sheriff seemed in no hurry to leave. "A young lady has to be very careful nowadays. Just a couple of days ago Sheriff Davis sent word to be on the lookout for a couple of outlaws. 'Squirrel Tooth' Sally was one of 'em."

Kathleen swallowed. "Jesus, Mary and Joseph protect me." She crossed herself. "I saw a poster of her once." Kathleen stuck out her upper teeth and clamped them firmly down over her lower lip. " 'Tis the reason they call her 'Squirrel Tooth,' yeh know."

The sheriff still studied her.

"Truly, me husband has sent for me. He's in San Francisco, and I'm t'join him. But now I need money fer the train. I thought perhaps, Mr. McCarty here . . ."

The sheriff seemed to have made up his mind about her. "Cheyenne's got plenty of 'fancy ladies' to go around, if you get my drift. So if I were you, I think moving on might be a wise thing to do."

How dare the man think she was a whore! She felt her ire rising. She tried to stay calm. It would be foolish to lose her temper when the man who could do her the most harm seemed about to leave.

"Do we understand each other, ma'am?"

"That we do, sir. That we do."

"Good day to you, Michael." The sheriff acknowledged the store owner with a tip of his hat.

"Have a good day, sheriff."

Kathleen's heart was beating like a trapped rabbit.

"Now what is it you have to sell me?"

Kathleen couldn't move she was still so upset by her close call.

"Ma'am you have something you wish to sell me?"

Kathleen turned to the storeowner. Her wedding ring lay in the palm of her hand. "This ring, sir. 'Tis gold, and that is an emerald. A fine, fine stone it is."

"An emerald, you say? We don't see much merchandise like this." He took the jewelry and inspected it more closely. He looked doubtful.

"On me mother's grave,'tis an emerald. One carat at that."

"Your grandmother no doubt told you that."

She would play along with their misconceptions. "Well, if I'm to be totally honest with yeh," she looked properly contrite, "I've had other occasions to, shall we say, 'loan' me ring out fer some cash in the past. I swear on me grandmother's grave 'tis a fine stone worth a fortune." This last part, at least, was the truth. Bret had paid over four hundred dollars for the ring. That was just over a month ago. A month! It seemed an eternity!

"Well." Michael McCarty studied the ring. He placed it on a scale and calculated its weight. "I'll give you twenty dollars for it."

"Twenty dollars!"

"I'm being generous with you. It's a tiny thing, and the gold isn't worth but half that."

"But the emerald!"

"I have only your word on that."

" 'Twas an heirloom. It's worth five times that!" Kathleen was fast losing her volatile temper.

"Ma'am, for all your Irish charms, I'm not a fool."

She bit her tongue to silence it until she calmed down. She forced a smile.

"And I don't take yeh fer one sir. But surely yeh've had

some experience with fine stones, even in this . . . place."
Kathleen caught herself. It would do her no good to belittle
the man's hometown however backward it seemed.

"I've seen an emerald or two in my day, even out here."
He raised an eyebrow. "But it's mighty interesting that a
woman of your obvious lack of means should have such
an expensive bauble. I don't party to stolen goods."

Kathleen realized she was in no position to argue. It might
mean a return of the sheriff. She extended her hand.

"Twenty dollars it is then."

Chapter Eleven

"Come in, purty lady. Come in."

Kathleen stood self-consciously on the rough-planked walkway outside the saloon. She let the double-bar doors she had been peeking through swing shut, blocking her from the man inside. A garish sign above proclaimed GOLDEN EAGLE SALOON in gold letters.

What had she been thinking looking in?

It was sounds of the poker game inside that had enticed her.

Poker—her one vice!

She had her father to blame for that. Even as a toddler at her father's knee, she had liked the laughter of the players, their exasperation and frustration. She remembered the pungent smell of cigars, the tang of beer, and the overwhelming male scent that had permeated the back parlor of their home.

As she grew, the uncertainty of a dealt hand, the subtle signals of the players, the skill of the play had captivated her. It was a study of human nature in all its nuances . . . and she adored it!

"Don't be shy there, missy. We're all real friendly here," someone encouraged from the other side of the swinging doors.

Kathleen looked at the twenty dollars in her hand.

It wouldn't pay for all she needed. New clothes. Train fare. Accommodations in San Francisco. She would have to telegraph Mr. Grunwald at the First National Bank in Boston for more funds. No doubt he would want an explanation of why she needed the additional money. The thought of humiliating herself yet again held no appeal.

She looked around. Where was Sage? Her heart dropped. He had not said he would see her in Cheyenne. Somehow she had just assumed . . .

She had been foolish to think that he would say goodbye. She was alone. On her own once again.

She looked down at the twenty dollars.

She'd do anything to avoid telegraphing that sourpuss Mr. Grunwald. She could hear him tut-tutting already.

"Well, welcome purty lady. Ain't you a handsome one. I knew you'd want to come in and meet us two gents."

Kathleen was almost swatted by the swinging doors as they shut behind her.

"Heck, Harry, I think someone forgot to feed her."

"She's a bit of a runt all right."

Kathleen's eyes finally adjusted to the dark room. The two men were at the long oak bar. They were laughing.

Their cowhide vests and dungarees proclaimed them cowboys. Their flannel shirts looked like they had been recently washed. Pomade slicked back recently cut hair.

117

"Listen, little lady, Lonny here and me are looking for a little dyversion, if ya get my drift. Been on the trail fer over three months and doggone but we need some good times."

Kathleen's mind was working frantically, but she could find nothing to say.

The taller one, Harry, spoke. "How about you and me have a little private party at that table over yonder."

"Come on, Harry. I saw her first."

"You can have her after me."

"But that's not fair."

"Hell, Lonny, yer face looks like the east end of a west-bound jackass. Ain't no lady going to cozy up to you first thing. She needs to be fine talked and brought along careful like if we don't mean to scare her off."

Kathleen stood mortified. Of course that's what they thought she was! Why would any respectable woman set foot in such a place. Why, in God's name, had she?

"Leave the lady alone, fellas."

Kathleen turned toward the voice.

"I've always found that cash entices more than pretty words or liquor. Ain't that right, ma'am?"

The speaker sat at a poker table with three other men. It was clear that he was having a run of luck. A stack of gold and silver coins glittered on the table in front of him.

"Funny yeh should mention money, sir." Kathleen finally mustered enough courage to speak. "Since it's money that really interests me at this moment."

The poker player smiled and signaled the man to his left. The cowboy got up from the table leaving a vacant chair.

"What is it you had in mind, sweetheart?" He indicated the vacated chair. "Get the lady a drink, Shorty. A whiskey."

"Thank yeh kindly, sir, but I really don't drink with strangers."

118

"What then do you do with strangers?"

She heard the snickers of the men behind her.

"Play cards," she stated emphatically.

"Cards it is then, my Irish beauty." The man once more indicated the empty seat. This time Kathleen moved slowly toward it and sat down.

"And the lady's preference is . . . ?"

"Draw poker, gentlemen, if yeh please."

"Draw poker it is then." The man with the black mustache nodded to the other players, then started the deal.

Kathleen laid her money on the table. She had a ten-dollar gold piece and ten silver dollars. She needed at least ten more dollars. With ten more dollars she wouldn't have to telegraph Boston. It would appear to all that nothing untoward had happened on her trek west.

But something had happened. She looked toward the saloon doors. She was a different woman than the one who had left Boston less than a month ago. A prayer crossed her lips. She prayed for the man who had changed everything. She prayed that he not be caught. She prayed that he not do anything else that would get him in trouble with the law, like kill Morse Templeton.

"What's your bet then?"

"I'll match yeh and raise yeh five dollars."

"Fold."

"Me too. It's gettin' too rich for my blood."

"Jack high flush." The player looked pleased.

"Full house." Kathleen resisted the urge to beam. In a little over an hour, she had doubled her money. It was time to quit.

She scooped in the coins. "I want to thank yeh, gentlemen. It's been a most pleasant game."

The men at the table looked expectantly at the dark-haired man who had invited her to play.

"It's too early to quit playing, darlin.' "

"But I've things t'do."

"You've got to give a man a chance to win back what he's lost."

"Yeh don't understand. I'm catchin' the train to San Francisco this afternoon and I must attend to a few matters before then."

"I understand you're not being at all friendly." His hand was on her wrist. He was hurting her. "I think these gentlemen agree, it would be mighty unfriendly of you to leave when we were just getting acquainted."

The speaker clearly dominated the room, but it wasn't respect that gave him his position of power. Kathleen suddenly realized it was fear. He smiled and his thin mustache made the smile suddenly sinister.

"One more game it is. But I must insist on goin' then. Surely yeh can understand?" Her eyes searched the saloon for support. There was none.

Kathleen rose and moved one seat farther away so that the two of them faced each other.

The man dealt two cards to determine the dealer. He had a queen. Kathleen, a seven. The man would deal.

He put in his ante—ten dollars!

Kathleen tried once more to withdraw. "I think the play is gettin' a little rich for me own blood as well."

"You said one more game. I thought I'd make it more interesting."

The look on her opponent's face told her she had to proceed whatever the outcome might be.

The first card was dealt. Kathleen picked it up. It was a

120

queen. The queen of spades. Her heart was pounding. She did not like the card. It was a bad omen.

She studied the dealer's hands. They were toughened by years on the trail. Her wrist still ached where he had grabbed it. No doubt she would have a bruise. She suspected she was not the first person this man had hurt.

She studied his deal. She could see nothing wrong. But she was not accustomed to playing with anyone who cheated. Her da's friends played for the pure joy of the game.

Her second card was placed facedown on the green felt. She picked it up—a two of hearts.

The occupants of the bar, Harry and Lonny, and the previous players all stood around the table cutting off any chance for a breath of fresh air. She felt trapped.

Her opponent smiled at her. It was more of a leer. "You and me could find a lot more interesting things to do than play cards, y'know."

"I don't know what yer referrin' to, sir."

He laughed.

It gave Kathleen a chill. They both knew what he was talking about. She kept her cards close to her chest, nestled in her hand, and she watched her opponent.

He dealt another round. She picked up her third card— the ten of hearts.

One of the man's hands disappeared for a moment under the table. Kathleen did not like it. She watched intensely. She didn't know how to challenge the man. Not here. Not now. She would have to rely on her wits and outplay him.

In quick succession the last two cards were dealt.

She looked at her hand. She had the queen of spades, the jack of spades, the ten of hearts, the ten of diamonds and the two of hearts.

Joan Avery

The chances of her getting a straight flush were dim. A pair of tens. She could work with that.

"Five dollars." Kathleen pushed five silver dollars into the center of the table.

"I'll see your five and raise you five." The dark-haired man smiled for no apparent reason other than to unsettle her.

"Five it is then." Kathleen saw all her previous winnings back on the table, in danger of being lost on a single hand.

"How many cards, Irish?"

"Three." Katherine kept her pair of tens, discarding the others.

"Three it is, pretty lady."

The man slowly dealt three cards on the table, leaning forward as he did. Kathleen could smell his breath, fetid with tobacco and whiskey.

He leered and she turned her head away from the man, away from the table.

"Two for the dealer."

Kathleen unfolded the cards in her hand like a delicate fan. First the pair of tens. Then a king and another king. She had two pair—king high. This was good. She held her breath and moved her thumb gently to reveal the last card. A ten! She had a full house. *Jesus, Mary and Joseph, thank ye.*

The dealer looked at her expectantly.

Kathleen said a quick novena and pushed a ten-dollar gold piece into the middle of the table. "Ten dollars."

"The lady is feeling lucky, boys. What do you think the chances are she's bluffing?"

"Call her on it, Morse. Go ahead call her."

"I'll do you one better." He lifted his whiskey glass and toasted his comrades at the bar. "I'll see you and raise you ten, sweetheart."

122

Kathleen thought her heart was about to explode in her throat. What had they called the man? *Morse*. She had never asked Sage what Morse Templeton looked like. Who was the man across from her?

"Well, Irish, what do you say. Have you got it in you?"

Kathleen could barely think. She had no options left. She pushed her last ten silver dollars into the pot.

"I'll call you." A full house. Kings high. Kathleen held her breath.

The man showed no expression for what seemed an eternity. Kathleen clung to a shred of hope.

Then the man slowly smiled. One by one he laid down his hand. Ten of spades, jack of spades . . .

"That c'not be."

"Don't get yourself all excited, Irish. I'm not through yet."

He continued to lay down his cards. Jack of spades. Queen of spades.

"Yeh've cheated me. Yeh've cheated me! That's what yeh've done!"

The man tilted his chair back and smiled.

"Cheated? How have I cheated you, pretty lady?"

"The jack of spades. The queen. They were my cards. I discarded them. Here . . ." She flipped over her discards on the green felt. Not one of the three cards were the ones she had discarded.

"But . . ."

"I think the lady is a little confused. A little too much whiskey, I'd say."

"How dare yeh! I haven't touched nary a drop! I'll get the sheriff, I will." It was an idle threat. The sheriff was the last one Kathleen wanted to see.

"Harry! Lonny! Fetch the sheriff for the leprechaun. You know I don't cheat, isn't that so, boys?"

The man turned on Kathleen. His eyes were hard, his tone vicious. "It'll be your word against ours, Irish. And they're not gonna take a harlot's word against ours."

Kathleen rose with as much dignity as she could muster. "I'm not a harlot."

She remembered what the sheriff had thought and her pale complexion suddenly colored.

Her opponent pushed his own chair back. For the first time Kathleen saw the gun he wore. He walked toward her, and she moved away. With each of his steps forward she took a step back, trying to work her way toward the door of the saloon. Suddenly she couldn't move any farther. She was pinned against a piano, which sat just inside the door. She had missed her mark by some six feet.

"Well, Irish, I'm not a hard man. How about I let you work for some of your losses—on your back."

Kathleen slapped the man across the face with all her strength. The imprint of her hand left a red welt. The man reacted faster than a snake. He grabbed her by the upper arms and threw her across the keys. Her head hit sharply against the raised back. She felt dizzy and nauseated.

"Don't you ever hit me, you slut. Do you understand?" He shook her violently. "I'm no two-bit cowboy who's too stupid to know your game. You can't play the innocent with me."

"I don't know what yer referrin' to."

"I'm referring to the fact that you thought I was an easy mark. Thought your fancy clothes and pretty face would keep me from seeing you cheat. Well I know a trick or two of my own."

"I wasn't cheatin'. How dare yeh! You were the one cheatin'. You took my cards and played them as your own."

"I don't know what you could be talking about."

"The jack and queen of spades. They were mine."

The man turned his head just enough to address the other men in the saloon.

"Did any of you gents see her cards?"

There was a murmur of "no"s.

The man turned back on Kathleen. "Morse Templeton one-upped you at your own game, didn't he, sweetheart?"

"No!" Kathleen could barely grasp the reality of what had happened. Of what was happening.

Morse Templeton! Sage's Morse Templeton!
The man who had killed Sage's brother in cold blood!

"No!" Kathleen barely got the denial out. The man clasped his foul mouth over hers. She was suffocating. She struggled to get away. He held her firm.

Kathleen bit down on his lip as hard as she'd ever bitten anything in her life.

"Gawd almighty!" The man stepped back, his hand to the gash she had inflicted in his upper lip. Blood seeped through his closed fingers.

Kathleen saw her chance. She kicked him in the groin, and he stumbled back. She dashed for the door. Once outside she lifted her skirts and ran faster than she ever had in her life.

What had she done? She had just lost forty dollars to Morse Templeton. Sage's Morse Templeton. As she ran her mind kept screaming her denial. No! It couldn't be. It mustn't be!

Chapter Twelve

Kathleen gasped. She doubled over in pain. She couldn't move a step farther. She'd die here on the dirty street. Crows would peck out her eyes. She'd be buried in some cowboy boot hill. And Bret Merriweather would get everything she owned!

Kathleen straightened. It would be a cold day in hell before she let that happen!

She looked behind her. Templeton was nowhere in sight. She plopped down on the boardwalk to ponder her fate. She was worse off than before. Once again she had no money and now she had nothing left to sell.

Suddenly behind her there were voices.

"I told you, cowboy, this one would be on me. An hour in bed with Pearl is not to be turned down lightly."

"Pearl, I think you've been out West way too long!" There was a man's laughter.

"Don't make up your mind too quick now. I got a soft bed and clean sheets. A bit better than a crib on the edge of town. I don't just give away my goods. I like the way you talk, mister. Makes me feel like a real lady, you know."

"Well, I'll think about your gracious offer, madame."

Think about her offer! How dare he!

Kathleen rose to her full four-foot-ten stature and barreled through the saloon's doors, red curls streaming behind her.

"Don't think too long!" she spit out.

Sage looked up dumbstruck.

Pearl smiled. "Ain't got no woman, eh?" She rose slowly from the table patting down her blond curls. "I suspect you and the little lady have some talking to do."

"I am not *little!*" Kathleen snapped.

"Gawd almighty. What's got your Irish dander up?" Sage signaled her to take the seat vacated by Pearl.

"Yeh're sittin' here carry'n on with some woman, not a care in the world." Kathleen gestured toward Pearl at the bar. "All the while I'm worried sick about yeh."

"You were worried about me?" Sage raised a quizzical eyebrow and smiled. "I'm flattered." Again he motioned to the chair.

This time Kathleen approached the table and plopped down. A cloud of dust rose around her.

"Not exactly worried." She lowered her head self-consciously and proceeded to address the felt table, running her finger randomly across its soft surface. "Angry with yeh is more like it. Yeh shoved me off that stage like a sack o'potatoes." She looked up accusingly. "Never carin' whether I was alive or dead!"

"As I remember, you were plenty alive, gesturing wildly and cursing me, last I saw you."

"But . . . but anything could have happened to me, on me

own in this town without a penny to me name."

"You're a pretty inventive woman. I figured you'd work it out."

"Work it out!"

"Well, did you? Work it out, that is?"

"I had to sell me beautiful wedding ring fer twenty dollars, that's what I had to do!" Kathleen held up her hand and shook it in front of Sage's face.

"Sorry, leprechaun." He was serious.

How could he take the wind out of her so easily? She was no longer angry.

"How come you didn't leave on the first train out of town?" Sage inquired.

"Because . . ." She hesitated to admit her foolishness. "Because . . ."

Almost on cue a train whistle interrupted them. It sounded as though the tracks ran behind the saloon. No doubt it was the train to San Francisco, the very one she should have been on.

"Because I was robbed of all me money," Kathleen blurted out.

"Robbed!" Sage rose angrily from his chair.

"Well, *lost* it, really." Kathleen added guiltily lowering her eyes.

"Lost it?" Sage ran a hand through his hair, then retook his seat, his eyes cloaked with suspicion. "How exactly did you lose it?"

"I was cheated in a poker game." She desperately needed a little sympathy right now. Maybe now he would console her.

Sage looked stunned. "A poker game?"

Kathleen nodded. She looked at him expectantly, her eyes widely innocent.

Sage began to laugh. He laughed so hard Kathleen thought he would fall off his chair. The bartender and Pearl looked over curiously. The color rose in Kathleen's cheeks, until she knew she was as red as the crimson drapes on the window behind her.

"Yeh uncaring fool. If yeh only knew the circumstances, yeh'd not be laughin' quite so hard."

"I can only imagine. Pity the poor men you played." Sage still continued to laugh. It irritated the daylights out of Kathleen. "I'm a good poker player. Me da taught me. I could beat any of the lot of 'em in Boston."

"Ah, so you've forgotten again. *This . . . is . . . not . . . Boston.*" Sage exaggerated each of the words as if she were a two-year-old.

"Stop it! Stop it now, I say!" Kathleen stomped her small feet under the table in a pique.

"You little Irish hellion, finally taken by someone more ornery than you, eh?"

He had breached her level of tolerance. She'd show him. "I was taken by someone ornery, indeed. Someone you know. I was taken by Morse Templeton. It was Morse Templeton cheated me out of me twenty dollars." As soon as anger drove the words from Kathleen, she knew it was a mistake. Sage stopped laughing. He grew very quiet.

Kathleen was scared. What had she done? She tried to take it back. "I don't know fer sure it was Templeton."

"Why did you say it then?"

"I just wanted to hurt you. I made it up, really I did." Kathleen tried to sound as truthful as possible, but she knew her continued high color gave her away.

"Where was the poker game?"

"I don't know."

"In a saloon?"

129

Kathleen just shrugged her shoulders. She couldn't look at him.

"Pearl." Sage turned his head and addressed the woman at the bar. "Where's the Golden Eagle?"

Kathleen rose. "No. Sage, please just stay here with me. Templeton left right after the game. I don't think he's even in town."

"If you hadn't gotten angry, would you have told me?" Sage asked.

Kathleen shook her bowed head and whispered, "no."

"Why?"

She looked up. "Because you're a stubborn, stupid man. Yeh're going to throw yer life away for revenge. It's stupid it is, stupid!" Kathleen was near tears.

Sage shared her frustration. "And what are you doing with your life, Kathleen Callahan? Chasing your husband across the West? Tell me what that is about!"

"It's none of yer business," Kathleen countered.

"Ah, there we have it. It's none of my business." He paused. "And Morse Templeton is none of your business." He pushed himself away from the table and rose. He shook his head at her. It was the worst condemnation Kathleen had ever felt. What had she said? What had she done?

Sage turned and strode out of the saloon. The racket of the swinging doors echoed his rage.

Kathleen stood stunned. How could she stop him? This wasn't at all what she wanted.

"Honey, take some advice from an old hand." Pearl had approached her. "I can tell you're a fighter. A real hellion. Anger can be a friend as well as an enemy. Put that temper to good use. If you love him, don't give him up without a fight."

If she loved him. Kathleen knew nothing of love. But certainly what she felt for Sage couldn't be love. She was just grateful to him for helping her. Concerned about him. It was her fault he was about to get himself killed. She didn't want his blood on her conscience.

She looked over at the blonde blankly. What could she possibly mean? Love him?

"Well," the woman asked, "are you going after him or not?"

Kathleen hiked up her torn skirts and made a dash for the swinging doors.

"Sage! Sage!" Kathleen ran as if she were possessed. Her torn green taffeta skirt and tattered petticoats flew out behind her. She almost tripped as she dropped off the end of the boardwalk into the dusty street. Her foot hit the ground at an odd angle. She gasped in pain before collapsing on the ground. Sage was a full block ahead, nearing the entrance to the Golden Eagle.

"Please stop! I should never have told you. Please!" She spoke the words to herself as much as to him.

Sage never slowed. He never looked back before he pushed open the doors to the Golden Eagle.

"Damn him." Struggling to her feet, she gingerly attempted to walk on the damaged ankle. She winced. It would support her weight, but only with a great deal of pain.

She held her breath and moved forward. She made it across the side street and put her good foot up on the boardwalk. Using the corner post as support she lifted her other foot up with its already swelling ankle.

At this rate, Sage would be dead before she ever reached him. She bit her lower lip and, throwing back her shoulders, she pushed herself to move faster. In the distance the train whistle blew again. She cursed under her breath.

Joan Avery

The ache in her ankle was dull compared to the ache in her heart. If she hadn't been so foolish, she could have been on that train. If she had wired Boston, she would have had enough money to get two tickets. Somehow she would have persuaded Sage to leave as well.

The thought of what might be happening in the Golden Eagle made Kathleen's stomach queasy. Sage didn't even have a gun. Templeton, she knew from personal experience, wore a well-used Colt. She had no doubt he would use it. With his henchmen to back him up, he would shoot Sage dead and collect the reward as his final insult.

Kathleen reached the swinging doors and hesitated. The taste of Morse Templeton's mouth on hers made the bile rise in her throat. She thought she was going to be ill. What would happen to her if Templeton killed Sage? Quickly she decided that it didn't matter and made her way through the swinging doors.

Sage stood at the bar. Kathleen scoured the room. There was no sign of Templeton or of the other two—Lonny and Harry. She felt her heartbeat return to normal.

The bartender nodded in her direction and Sage turned.

"What are you doing here?" he said sharply.

"I came to stop you."

"It seems you already have."

"What do you mean?" Kathleen was confused.

"It seems your little card game may have been more effective than you know. Templeton's friends indicated to the bartender here, that they were going to use the money to take the train west."

Kathleen put her hands on her temples. What was he saying? She shook her head in denial. Had she been the means of Templeton's escape? The irony of it would be too cruel. But at the same time a part of her wanted to cry with relief.

"But I didn't know." She shook her head, her green eyes pleading for forgiveness.

"And didn't care. You only think about yourself, don't you? A woman with any sense would have . . ." He never finished. Once again he just shook his head. Then he brushed past her and out the door.

Kathleen tried to run after him, but her ankle hurt too much. Instead she staggered to the exit. Once outside she saw Sage heading for the railroad station. A prayer slipped past her lips. "Jesus, Mary and Joseph let the train be gone, halfway to San Francisco if yeh please."

She hurried after Sage, her lopsided gait slowing her to half his speed.

She kept repeating her prayer. "Let it be gone. Please, let it be gone."

She rounded the end of the street past the telegraph office holding her breath. The train had left! She whispered her prayerful thanks.

Sage stood on the platform in the late afternoon sun. His grizzled beard and long hair caught the brilliance and gave off blue-black glints. His heavily tanned face showed lines she had not noticed before.

He looked tired. For the first time since she had met him he looked tired and defeated.

"Sage?"

He didn't turn around to face her. He stared down the westbound tracks, into the lowering sun.

"Sage?"

"What?" He spoke barely above a whisper. His flat tone gave her no clue as to whether he was still angry with her.

"I didn't mean . . . I was only trying to get some more money so that we . . ."

He turned accusingly. "So that *we?* When did you decide you and I were a *we?*" He shook his head and gave her a wilting look. "You have a husband, if I recall correctly, and I have an unfinished debt to repay. You and I are not a *we* and never will be. Can't you get that through your thick little head?"

Kathleen was suddenly embarrassed. And with her rising color came irritation. "I was just tryin' to help. If yeh want to go off and kill yerself that's none of my concern. Why should it be?"

Sage did not respond.

Kathleen blathered on. "Sure, go off and avenge yer brother. I'm sure Jimmy'll be at the pearly gates ready to greet yeh with open arms. Just what he wanted yeh to do, go and get yerself hanged for him."

"Shut up! You don't know him." He ran a hand through his disheveled hair, lowering his head as he did so, as if to avoid her words.

"No, but I know yeh." Kathleen wasn't going to let him off that easy. "And I know if 'twas tipsy-topsy and yeh were the one dead, yeh wouldn't want him to go and get himself killed, now would yeh?" She stared at him, daring him to contradict her.

"I'm his older brother. I'm responsible. If not for me, he'd still be safe in New York."

His real argument wasn't with her, she realized, but with himself, with his own guilt and anger.

"Yeh'd think the years would've given yeh more sense."

His eyes grew dark with anger.

Better anger than despair, Kathleen thought.

"You don't know what you're talking about," he said.

"You've lived a coddled life with more opinions than sense."

"I could get us both on the next train west," she bragged.

"Don't fool yourself."

"I told yeh I was good at poker. I am. If I had a stake I could get us both out of this place. You could go and happily get yerself killed."

"And what would you do?"

"I'd get on the next train to San Francisco, where I would quickly forget yeh and everything that's happened." She saw the sting of her words register. He was alive again. Hurting but alive.

"Ole 'Squirrel Tooth' seems to have risen from the ashes."

"Don't call me that."

"Why? The resemblance seems to be more than physical now. I think you may have sunk to her level of coldness."

"I don't know what yer talkin' about."

"It makes no never mind, 'Squirrel Tooth.' I'll be out of your hair as soon as I can figure out a way to earn enough for a train ticket."

"I told yeh I could get us tickets."

"In a poker game?" He laughed bitterly. "I don't think so."

"Yeh have no faith in me, do yeh?"

"No."

"That's sad. But yeh know what's sadder still? The fact that yeh have no faith in anyone or anything at all, do yeh?"

"It's none of your business. I've told you that before. My life is none of your business, and what you do with yours is none of mine. The sooner you accept that the better."

"Fine. If that's what yeh want, it's just dandy with me."

Sage did not respond. He stood staring at her for a moment longer, and then he strode past her and down the street.

Kathleen turned to watch him go. The late afternoon sun cast an unearthly golden glow over the entire town. A small swirl of dust trailed each of his steps. Her heart sank.

What had she done? She had only been trying to help . . . to make him see how foolish it all was. He would never forgive her this time. In the past she had always had hope. This time she knew she would never see him again.

Chapter Thirteen

Kathleen sat cross-legged on the train platform. She had lost track of the time. It must have been almost an hour since Sage had left. She was hungry and dejected. She stared at the stains that marred the small pool her skirt made in her lap. She pulled at a loose strand of lace only to have it come completely off in her hand. She found herself worrying the small strip as if it were a rosary.

She pondered some disturbing facts about her life. Somehow it had been turned upside down in just a matter of weeks. Somewhere along the way she had lost control of it. A wanted murderer had just stepped out of her life, and she wanted to scream and cry and throw a temper tantrum. In the past she might have, but even that had changed. It seemed so childish.

Avenging herself on Bret Merriweather didn't even have the attraction it once did. Life seemed more precious than it ever had been and spending time assuaging her wounded pride seemed suddenly a silly waste. Why? she wondered. What had changed?

She was too tired to think it through. Too drained to cry. She knew that eventually she would have to figure something out, how to get out of this godforsaken town. Money wouldn't just drop from the sky.

As if in answer to her thought, a shiny silver dollar tumbled into her skirt, followed by four others. They made a wonderful clinking sound as they landed. She stared at them incredulously. It was a miracle. She raised her head slightly. Two dirty-socked feet rested before her in the dust. She looked up further.

Sage!

He stood there for a long moment before he spoke. He rubbed his beard like a wizened seer. "You said I have no faith in anyone or anything. Prove me wrong 'Squirrel Tooth.' "

Kathleen was dumbfounded. "But your boots?"

"The man at the livery said I could buy them back any-time today." He shielded his eyes with a hand and looked to the setting sun. "But the day is fading fast. There's probably a game going on at Pearl's by now. Come on."

He turned and started to stroll down the street, his socks collecting more dirt with every step.

Kathleen carefully put the money in her skirt pocket and then tried to get to her feet to follow, but when she put her bad ankle under her for support, it gave way.

"Ooohhh!" She gasped as she crumpled back down onto the platform.

Sage turned, and rushed back. "What's the matter? Are you hurt?"

"I'm not really hurt. It's just me ankle, that's all. I twisted it before, and now it smarts a bit."

"Let me see." His face wrinkled with concern. He crouched down in front of her.

Slowly she untangled her legs from beneath her dress.

"Which ankle is it?" he inquired urgently.

"Me right one."

She watched as he tenderly ran his hands along her lower leg, feeling for breaks. She studied his bowed head. Funny, she could see his eyes clear and blue even when they weren't on her. She watched as he gently massaged the ankle. His touch gave her goose flesh.

Sage was back! And she didn't know if she should laugh or cry.

With him came so many memories. Laughter and tears. And something else, something electric that passed between them whenever they touched—something that lured her and frightened her all at the same time.

He prodded more forcefully.

"Ouch! What're yeh tryin' t'do, make it worse?"

"Well, it's swollen, but it seems there's nothing broken."

"Come on." He rose, swooping her up in his arms as he did.

From her high perch, Kathleen suddenly felt queen of the world.

Sage started down the dusty street, and she put her arms around his neck. As he walked she couldn't resist the opportunity to study his face. Why had she never noticed the lines of worry around his eyes?

There was a small scar just below his left eyebrow. She removed her right hand from around his neck and ran her thumb lightly over it. He turned to look at her and then looking back placed a soft kiss in the palm of her hand.

She took his encouragement and ran her hand along his beard.

It was soft. Much softer than she remembered from his last kiss. But that kiss had been rough, tinged with need. The thought of that kiss, of where it might have gone, made her tingle all over.

"I'm afraid, m'lady, 'tis not my best look."

Kathleen smiled. "I've never felt a man's beard before. It's very soft."

Now it was Sage who smiled. "As is your heart, Kathleen Callahan. No matter how hard you wish to be, you give yourself away. It's one of your more becoming traits."

"I didn't think I had any." Kathleen cocked her chin upward.

"If I told you about them, I'm afraid I would be doing you a disservice. Your head would be as big as your heart. That would be very dangerous indeed."

She playfully hit his chest. "To whom would it be dangerous?" She studied him carefully. What was it she wanted to hear?

He smiled. "To any man who came within a hundred yards of you."

She hit him gently again. "Yer daft man." But his answer warmed her heart.

Pearl looked up as the duo pushed through the doors of the saloon. She smiled. "So you've decided to return."

Sage cautiously set Kathleen in a chair at a table next to where Pearl stood at the bar. "We're looking for an honest poker game. Thought this would be the place." Sage moved to the bar, resting one elbow on it. "My friend here wants to play." He nodded toward Kathleen.

"I think we can work something out." Pearl nodded toward the bartender who slid two whiskeys down the glossy oak surface of the bar.

"What about your friend?" She nodded toward Kathleen.

Sage turned to Kathleen and held up his drink, offering it to her. Kathleen shook her head. "No, thank yeh."

Pearl nodded her approval. "There's not many'll pass up a free drink. A lady, eh?" Pearl toasted Sage. "To you and your friend."

Sage touched glasses with Pearl and then held his glass up to Kathleen. "To luck." Kathleen smiled, then turned away studying her possible opponents.

The saloon had taken on a warm glow as the last rays of the sun retreated through the windows. The bartender moved from gaslight to gaslight, and the warm amber of their flames touched Kathleen's cheeks and hair. She sat very calmly as if anticipating the challenge ahead of her. Even smudged and disheveled she was one of the most beautiful women Sage had ever seen.

He was reminded of the night by the fire when she thought she was dying. Of the kiss she had begged for, of the soft downiness of her skin, the silkiness of her hair against his callused hand, the warmth of her lips and then the quickness with which his kiss had put her to sleep. He smiled. She glanced back toward him, as if sensing his smile. For the first time since he had met the little hellion, she seemed reluctant to speak.

And she didn't have to. Her eyes spoke volumes. As green as the baize that covered the gaming table where she sat, as dewy as spring grass, they wanted something from him. Something that he knew he had no right to give her. Yet, something he wanted just as desperately himself.

The lull of conversation, the whiskey, all threatened his

equilibrium. He had to look away before she pulled him into her fantasy world.

He raised his eyes to study the room behind her. The red velvet drapes that covered the windows and flanked the small stage had soaked up the golden gaslight. Their crimson had mellowed to burgundy. The polished oak trim of the room appeared liquid with its heavily waxed surface. The baize that covered the gaming tables took on a life of its own. The delicate haze formed by cigarette and cigar smoke only added to the dreamlike scenario.

Loud laughter broke the moment. Sage pulled himself back to the more immediate problem.

"How about that game, Pearl."

"We don't have many women who join our games, but I think I can rustle something up for you."

Sage watched as Pearl sauntered over to a table nearer the stage. The woman worked the table, laughing and patting each man in turn until they would have given her every cent in their pockets if she had asked. She nodded in Kathleen's direction and the group grimly looked over. Once more Pearl was smiling and cajoling, teasing and urging. Finally with a great guffaw she signaled to Kathleen.

Kathleen almost panicked, all her bravado suddenly gone. She rose reluctantly and limped toward the table. What had she promised? To win back the money. What if she failed? What would happen then? She couldn't think about it now. She needed to regain her composure, use all the skills her da had taught her. Otherwise she would lose more than the money that jingled in her pocket as she moved toward the group of five men that awaited her curiously.

Pearl guided her to an empty chair. "Gentlemen, may I introduce you to . . ." She looked to Kathleen.

"Kathleen." She hesitated. "Kathleen Callahan."

". . . to Miss Kathleen Callahan." Pearl nodded toward Sage at the bar. "My friend there says she's a mighty fine poker player. She expects an honest game, as does my friend, who can be mighty ornery if he finds a man cheating. Are we clear then?"

A murmur of acceptance followed Pearl's question.

"Good luck then to you fellas, and to you, miss, as well."

"Thank you." Kathleen placed her hand on the woman's arm. "Thank you for everything." There was an understanding between the two women. Kathleen knew she did not have to say more.

It had been more than an hour since Kathleen had started playing. While the game had started off rather tentatively, the pace and skill of the play had increased as losers left to nurse their wounds and other more experienced players joined the small group.

Kathleen's skill had allowed her to hold her own in the group. The small pile of coins before her showed modest winnings.

Sage lounged against the bar, his eyes barely leaving Kathleen as he partook of Pearl's generous offer of drinks on the house. Kathleen had been right. She did know how to play poker. Now, if only her luck held, maybe they could get out of this town before the sheriff came sniffing around.

Sage finished off the last of his whiskey and quietly moved toward the game.

Kathleen looked at her hand—pair of fours. Not good enough, she realized. She laid her cards facedown. "Fold."

The two remaining players continued their betting. The call saw the pot collected by a balding, round-faced man who continuously smiled whether he was winning or losing. Kathleen shook her head as she watched ten dollars of her hard-earned winnings disappear.

The warmth of a hand on her shoulder startled her. She looked up. Sage stood behind her. "Thought you might need some moral support."

" 'Tis more than moral support I need. I could do with a wee bit more luck, I suspect."

"Perhaps I can bring it to you." Sage smiled.

"Aye, perhaps you already have." Kathleen placed her hand over his. "Now I don't want yer distraction. Stand over there if yeh must watch." Kathleen indicated the wall about four feet to her right.

Sage sidled over and leaned a shoulder against the wall.

The bald man to her left dealt. Kathleen picked up her cards. A two of diamonds. Five of spades. King of clubs. Ten of diamonds. And the three of clubs. Kathleen hadn't seen such a sorry excuse for a poker hand all evening. She smiled. Sometimes you had to make your own luck.

The betting started. Check. A four-dollar bid. Someone folded. An eight-dollar bid. By the time the betting reached Kathleen, she would have to ante up ten of her remaining thirty dollars to just stay in the game. It would claim most of her winnings. Any poker player worth his salt would have folded. But what had Sage said? Maybe he would bring her luck.

"I'll call." She pushed the precious ten dollars into the pot.

The dealer then folded. The next man, a thin pointy-nosed bank manager, fiddled with his shirt cuff before sliding six dollars toward the pot. "I'll call as well."

"Getting a little too rich for me." A tall man with a shock of white hair turned his cards down on the table. "Good evening, all." He rose, left the table and headed toward the bar.

The fourth man had a bulbous nose. He rubbed one of his rather large ears and called as well.

There were now three left in the game, including Kathleen.

The bank manager laid down two cards. "Give me two." He placed the cards at one end of his hand.

The man to his left, the ear-rubber discarded three. Kathleen watched him carefully as he picked up his cards. He placed one at the head and two at the end of his fanned hand. He did not touch his ears.

As for Kathleen, she discarded the king and ten, leaving her with the two of diamonds, three of clubs and five of spades. While a straight flush didn't seem likely it was worth a shot. She was committed now, whatever the outcome. She picked up the first of her newly dealt cards. The four of hearts! She held her breath as she slowly retrieved her last card. The two of clubs. Her heart sank. A pair of twos! How dismal! She had come so close. Still, the game wasn't over yet. She kept her expression noncommittal and studied her opponents.

The banker did not hesitate. "Ten dollars."

The ear-fiddler touched his ear before pushing a stack of coins forward. "I'll call." He pushed ten shiny silver dollars into the growing pile in the middle of the table.

Ten more dollars just to call! She couldn't give up now. She had never given up on anything in her life and she wasn't about to start now. It would be all or nothing.

"I'll see yer ten and raise yeh ten, gentlemen. I'm feelin' lucky tonight."

The banker hesitated. He toyed with the stack of coins before him. Then studied Kathleen.

She smiled at him sweetly as she prayed desperately. *Please Lord, don't let this fool of a man raise my bet. I promise I'll curb me tongue and say me rosary a hundred times.*

The man still hesitated. Kathleen folded her fanned cards and with steady hands calmly laid them facedown on the table.

The banker shook his head in disgust. "You're a damn good poker player, I'll say that, whatever your hand. I may be stupid, but I'm folding with three jacks. Can't afford to lose any more tonight. My wife will have my scalp if I do."

Stupid indeed, Kathleen thought. The man with the bulbous nose studied her, but she didn't flinch. Once more she just smiled sweetly.

Everyone's attention had turned to the remaining player. The man itched his reddened nose and pulled at an ear. He checked his cards again, then looked up to Kathleen.

"Hell, I'm folding too. My hand's not even close to Edgar's." He threw down a hand that held three of a kind.

"Thank yeh kindly, gentlemen. The evening's been a delight." Kathleen gathered in the seventy-dollar pot.

She looked over to Sage. He was smiling broadly.

"Do you mind us asking to see your hand, miss? We'd like to know whether we've been taken for fools or not."

Kathleen gave them a big smile. "I hate to pain yeh, but . . ." She turned over her cards displaying her pair of twos.

"Shit! I knew she was bluffing." The admiring compliment came from a bystander.

Kathleen was aglow. She turned once more to Sage. He suddenly seemed less than pleased. What had she done to aggravate him now?

He took three steps toward her and grabbing her by the arm dragged her out into the darkness.

Once outside he pulled her around to face him. "What the hell did you just do back there?"

"I jist got us train fare!" She jerked away from him. "Let go of me!"

"You almost lost everything on a pair of deuces!" He angrily hit the side of the saloon.

"But I didn't, did I?"

He sulkily refused to look at her.

"I said I was good. I am."

"You're good all right . . . good at risking my fate and my feet." He looked down at his filthy socks.

"Yer feet? Is that what yer so concerned about? Well, here. Here's your share of the winnings." She meticulously counted out half the coins. When he didn't hold out his hand she grabbed it and forced the money into his palm. "Take it. Buy back your darned boots and a ticket to hell as well."

Kathleen turned and stalked off toward the hotel. The insufferable man!

Chapter Fourteen

Kathleen stomped down the darkened street. It had to be almost eight o'clock. Many of the shops were closed. She headed for the Interocean Hotel. The elaborate gothic edifice stood back from the street near the train station. Gaslights and large potted shrubs marked its entrance. It seemed to be a haven of civility in the otherwise savage town. Light snuck out of its shuttered windows, teasing her with comforts she'd almost forgotten—a warm bath, hot food and a soft bed.

She was halfway to this haven when she passed the small dressmaker's shop. Through its window Kathleen could see a woman in a back room bent over a mass of gingham fabric diligently sewing by gaslight. Kathleen looked down and smoothed her ragged green dress. She had almost forgotten that she had nothing but the clothes on her back. She knocked on the door whose sign proclaimed it closed.

The Wild Irish West

A broad-faced woman with graying hair pulled back severely into a bun peered hesitantly out at her. Her gas lamp cast Kathleen in an eerie yellow glow.

Kathleen yelled through the door. "I'm sorry to disturb yeh, but I'm in dire need of some things." She smiled hopefully, although the woman's squinty eyes and severe countenance did little to encourage her.

The woman took in her disheveled state and looked as if she were about to turn and leave Kathleen standing there.

Kathleen reached into the pocket of her dress. "I've got money." She held up a silver dollar.

The woman took a moment to consider and then reluctantly unlocked the door.

"Come in then, but I've got little time to waste on you. I've got my sewing to finish."

"I'll just take a minute of yer time, Mrs. . . . ?"

"Jaeger's the name. Hilde Jaeger." The woman was stout and gruff, and Kathleen's opinion of her did not improve with their initial conversation.

"Mrs. Jaeger, I need but a new traveling dress and a practical night robe and I'll be on me way."

"I only sew custom orders. I've no time to be making things I can't sell." The woman shook her head in disgust. "What did you think you were going to find, a rack of dresses ready to wear? We don't do things that way in these parts."

"I thought only that you might have something that someone had ordered and not taken or some simple dresses, chemises or night robes from a catalog. Anything. I'll pay yeh well." Kathleen pulled a second dollar from the pocket of her dress and held it out with the first one in the palm of her dirty hand.

"You're nothing but a twit of a thing. Not got much for so

149

small a woman." She shook her graying head and eyed Kathleen suspiciously once more.

Once again Kathleen reached into her pocket. This time she pulled out several dollars. "And I've more if yeh have somethin' that might do me well."

The money seemed to have the desired effect on the woman. "I think I may have something you could use."

The woman walked toward the back room, Kathleen followed in the pool of light that surrounded the woman. She looked around her. Bolts of gingham fabric lined the walls of the small store. Here and there a silk or satin caught the lamplight and shimmered pale blue or vibrant green. When they reached the back room she noticed a paper pattern laid out ready to be cut on a large table. The piece the woman had been working on was a girl's gown and matching bonnet. Kathleen had no idea what the woman had in mind. She hoped it wasn't a child's dress. She'd feel even more of a fool than she did in her current tattered taffeta.

"Come here and help me with this," the woman ordered. She was removing several paper-wrapped bolts of fabric from the top of a trunk. "If I remember rightly these should come near to fitting you. Help me pull this thing out into the room."

The two women tugged the heavy mahogany traveling chest into the lamplight. The seamstress used a scrap of fabric to wipe an accumulation of dust off the two-by-three-foot traveling case. To Kathleen's eye it looked as if it had been lightly used, if it had ever been used at all.

The woman folded back the brass clasps and lifted the heavy top. Carefully folded in tissue paper, lay what appeared to be a complete wardrobe. The woman took hold of the top piece and shook it out. It was a walking dress with an underskirt of green-and-white-striped silk and an overskirt the same green as the striping. The woman held it up to Kathleen. "It should do well enough, I think. She was a blonde, so the color suits you as well."

Kathleen fingered the fine fabric and couldn't resist asking. "Who was blond?"

"Mary Alice Bundy was her name. It's her trousseau you're looking at."

Mrs. Jaeger lay the beautiful garment on the small table and returned to the chest. She carefully lifted out a French chemise of fine muslin. Its bosom was trimmed with torchon lace, and a pale pink ribbon was intricately worked through beading. Beneath the chemise was a night robe with a pompadour yolk solidly and delicately embroidered.

The clothes were as elegant as they were expensive. Kathleen's interest was piqued.

"Why did she not use her trousseau?"

Mrs. Jaeger laid a pearl gray, watered-silk evening gown the color of a winter sky across the table. She paused. Kathleen saw her features soften.

"Died, poor girl. Just a week before she was to marry Jacob Newirth. Her intended bought all these things as a wedding gift. Once she was gone, he couldn't bear to see any of 'em. Never collected 'em when he left town. Let's see, it must be over two years now since Jacob left."

"But I would feel badly takin' such as these." However great Kathleen's need, the story had upset her. A young girl dying just before her wedding. It somehow made Kathleen's own self-absorption with Bret Merriweather seem petty. But Kathleen didn't care to dwell on it, not now.

"Nonsense, my dear."

Was that a tear that Mrs. Jaeger wiped aside with the back of her sleeve?

"Mary Alice was my niece, you see. Guess I'm as good a

151

Joan Avery

one as any to say whether these things stay or go. The moths will be in 'em soon enough. Better someone should get some use out of them."

"If yeh think it proper then." Kathleen hesitated. "Would this be enough do yeh think? Besides this, I've barely enough for a room at the hotel and me train fare."

Mrs. Jaeger looked down at the coins in Kathleen's hand. Then up at her face. She studied her for a moment. "Tell me you're a good girl, not one to whore or carry on and they're yours. I want no payment for them."

"I am good." Kathleen insisted despite even her own misgivings. Then she added sincerely. "I will look after them well, Mrs. Jaeger."

The old woman nodded, looking suddenly very tired. "Shall I send them on to the hotel then?"

"If I could take but one or two things with me."

"Yes, yes of course. I can see your need." Kathleen pointed to the chemise and shook out a pair of drawers and a simple blue cotton dress. Hilde Jaeger turned and carefully began to wrap the garments in brown paper and twine. "I'll send my Jacob to the hotel with the trunk and the remainder of the things as soon as he returns from his dinner."

"Please, there's no need for you to send the trunk." Kathleen wasn't sure she was deserving of such a generous offer. After all, it was only her pride that kept her from telegraphing home for money.

"Makes no never mind." Hilde Jaeger continued with a wave of the hand. "No one here's going to use it. You might as well have it."

Mrs. Jaeger handed Kathleen the paper-wrapped items.

"Thank yeh. 'Tis kind of yeh, Mrs. Jaeger." Kathleen blushed, humbled by the woman's generosity. She made her way slowly through the dimly lit front of the store—her

152

thoughts on Mary Alice Bundy who never lived to see her wedding day.

"Come back for your boots?" The stable owner lowered his lantern and stared at Sage's filthy socks. A smile crossed his face.

"Yep." Sage returned the smile.

"Thought you might." The man was tall and lanky with red hair and a long red mustache. He seemed the kind of man who would take good care of your horse or anything else of value. He nodded to Sage then turned and walked back into the darkened stable. He stepped into an unused stall and reappeared with the finely tooled black leather boots. He set them on the ground and extended a hand. "Ian McBain's the name."

Sage extended his own. "Thanks for safeguarding them for me."

"Not a problem. Much as I would've loved to keep 'em, I'm just as happy to return them to their rightful owner."

Sage pulled out a handful of change including a twenty-dollar gold double eagle to pay the man.

"Pretty lucky at the cards tonight, I'd say." The man nodded at the wealth of coins.

Sage had the good sense to feel guilty. "Yes, I was very lucky."

"Never had much luck myself. Promised my wife years ago to stay clear of the tables." The man indicated a hay bale across from where he stood.

Sage sat and pulled on one of the Mexican boots. He stomped the boot down settling his foot and reached for the second one.

"Sheriff was here this afternoon shortly after you left."

Sage paused with the second boot midway to his foot. He waited warily for the man to continue.

"Told him about you and the description of 'Squirrel Tooth' Sally you gave me. You having seen her personally and all."

Sage searched for the best escape route. The man blocked the door.

He stomped on the other foot settling the second boot.

Unexpectedly, the stable owner lowered himself on an adjacent hay bale and set the lantern down on the dirt floor. He leaned back on his elbows. "He said to thank you kindly if I saw you again."

Sage exhaled, only now aware that he had been holding his breath.

Ian McBain seemed not to notice Sage's unease, but chatted on, "He said the two of them outlaws would be a pair of idiots if they stuck around here. They must know the sheriff in Deadwood would telegraph Cheyenne. The sheriff already telegraphed Deadwood and told them if they wanted to find them two outlaws they'd better come down here themselves and have a look,'cause he had better things to do with his time."

McBain pulled a pouch of tobacco out of his pocket and began rolling himself a cigarette as he continued. "Surely they ain't gonna walk in here and ask for a horse to make their escape." He laughed and gave his head a shake, pleased with his wit.

He held out the pouch and a paper to Sage.

"Thanks." Sage took the cigarette makings and began to roll himself a smoke. Suddenly, he needed it. His nerves were still rattled.

The stable owner was right. It would take bloomin' idiots

to hang around a town when they thought they were in imminent danger of discovery and capture.

Done with the tobacco, he handed the pouch back. "You're right, a man wouldn't be too bright, hanging around a town like this with the sheriff on his tail."

The other man shook his head still pondering the situation. "Still, you got to remember he's with a woman. It's the kind of thing a woman makes a man do. Stupid thing." He took a long drag on his cigarette. "Still miss the poker table myself. But. . . ." He shrugged his shoulder begrudgingly accepting his own fate.

Sage silently agreed. *The last few days* have *been the kind of thing a woman makes you do.*

He had never thought of himself as a stupid man, not until he met that Irish hellion. Now every time he turned around, he was doing some crazy thing or another, always against his better judgment. Before he met the green-eyed elf, his life was straightforward if unpromising. Hanging seemed a fairly reasonable end to his life.

Reasonable until she got hold of his head. What had she said to him? What would Jimmy want him to do?

Devil be hanged! He ran a hand through his hair and then rubbed his scraggly beard. This girl was definitely getting to him.

"The worse part is they make you feel guilty when it's them making all the outrageous demands." McBain's statement seemed to echo Sage's thoughts.

The guilt, in Sage's case, had started almost immediately. True, he had been too harsh with her. She had done what she said she would—gotten them both enough money to pursue their prey. So why did he feel so ornery. He should be happy. He was free of the Irish banshee and was once more on Morse Templeton's trail.

Kathleen Callahan. The Celtic Banshee. He smiled to himself.

"I know what you mean, McBain. We're always the guilty ones, and they're always the ones offended."

McBain nodded his agreement, and the two men sat in amicable silence.

Sage relaxed for the first time since he had reached Cheyenne. It sounded like they were both safe for the moment. He was happy for Kathleen, but where the hell was she? Left to her own devices, she undoubtedly would make a spectacle of herself and draw attention to them both. He wasn't about to let her draw him into danger again. Those days were in the past. What Kathleen Callahan needed most was to be protected from herself.

Well, he concluded begrudgingly, he'd better find her for her own good.

But first he had more pressing business.

Kathleen sighed with pleasure. She slipped under the warm water, soaking her hair. The sweet scent of the lavender soap gave her almost as much pleasure as anything had in recent memory.

Funny, she thought, how these little things had become important while major ones seemed to melt away just like the soap in the water. Even Bret Merriweather seemed a distant worry.

She studied the room. It was more luxurious than she had anticipated. A large four-poster bed dominated the small area. Made of pine, it was nicely turned with delicately carved pinecone finials topping each of its posts. Fine cambric draped the bed as well as the windows. Its sheerness added a feminine quality to the otherwise dark room. The walls were covered in a gold striped paper. Gold, she decided, gold and red she amended, seemed to decorate almost everything west of the Mississippi.

Next to the door stood a tall practical pine bureau. A folded piece of paper lay on the bureau where she had left it. The gentleman at the front desk had kindly helped her send off a telegram to her attorney in Boston. It was a noncommittal sort of missive, assuring her lawyer that everything was fine and that she would be heading to San Francisco the next day. She had asked him to hire a Pinkerton man to track down Bret and his mistress when they reached the city. She had not expected an immediate reply, but one had indeed come. It had been delivered just before the bathwater had arrived. She had read it more than once.

Miss Kathleen Callahan.
   Interocean Hotel.
   Cheyenne, Wyoming
   Relieved to hear from you.... *stop*...
Have hired Pinkerton man.... *stop*... Good
news.... *stop*... Annulment   granted....
***stop*... No need for you to worry further....**
***stop*... Forget   this   silliness.... *stop*...**
Come home.

At first she had been furious. Silliness. Is that what the imbecile lawyer thought of her desire for justice? Well, it wasn't silliness. Annulment or not, she was determined to make Bret pay for his thievery. No one seemed to understand that it was more than the money. It was a personal insult that needed a personal response. She wouldn't rest until she had exacted her revenge.

Thinking about the telegram, she lost all the tranquility

the bath had restored. She wouldn't let the odious message do that. She lathered up her hair and slipped low in the water once more. She continued her study of the furnishings.

Across from the foot of the bed, a low table held a porcelain pitcher and basin. Two straight-backed chairs flanked the small table.

The oak floor was highly polished. It reflected the lamplight and gave the whole room an enticing warmth. She dunked her head again and rinsed the lavender soap out of her hair.

Her hair done, she splashed water on her face and began to wash it with the fragrant soap. It was a simple act, something she had repeated thousands of times in her life, but as she ran her fingers over her slick face and lips, down her throat, and across her breasts her body seemed suddenly alive. Dangerously alive.

She was aware of the feelings Sage Duross's touch had drawn from her. She ran a finger over her top lip and back along her bottom one. His kiss still lingered there—on her lips and elsewhere.

It was an unsettling feeling. She scrubbed furiously, hoping to rub away his indelible mark. The pleasure of his lips on hers, the softness of his beard against her cheek, the caress of his hands down her back.

It should have been easy to dismiss these feelings. Yet it was easier to dismiss her long harbored hatred for Bret Merriweather.

It made no sense. She had nothing in common with the vulgar cowboy. The way he had looked, scraggly and unkempt—no decent woman would have given him a second thought, let alone . . . Kathleen thought of the liberties she had allowed him. She must have been mad. Now that she had reached civilization again, she was bound to see things in a much clearer light. Her brain had been addled by the strain of the last few days.

No doubt this was also the cause of the silly notion she had gotten in her head that Sage had cared for her. Certainly she didn't care if he cared. It had all been a great folly for him no doubt.

He was just a man who had taken advantage of an extremely naive girl. What else could it be? After all, once he had gotten his darned boots, he had abandoned her.

The whole thing was thankfully over. As if to force the conviction on herself, she dunked completely under water once more and stayed until her lungs were ready to explode.

She burst out of the water sputtering and gasping, but at least she no longer felt his touch on her bare skin. She stood up and shook her head to rid it of the remaining water. She burnished the wavy red strands with a linen towel until they began to regain a life of their own.

She stepped out of the tub. Taking a fresh towel she scoured her skin of every drop of water. The harsh rubbing made her pink all over. She slipped into the linen camisole and drawers she had brought with her from Hilde Jaeger's, but the brush of the fabric against her overheated flesh rekindled some of the feelings she had struggled to overcome.

She looked at the simple blue muslin dress she had selected.

Somehow being rid of Sage Duross was worthy of a celebration.

Kathleen looked down at the mahogany trunk that had been delivered shortly after she arrived. She couldn't help herself. She picked up the gray watered silk evening gown.

It was beautiful even by Boston standards. She laid it carefully on the chintz-covered bed, and smoothing her hand over it one more time, rang to have the bath removed.

She shook her wet head and made her way to the dressing table that was comfortably situated between the two gingham-covered windows that faced the street. She had found an ivory-backed brush in the trunk. Now she rubbed her head briskly with a towel again and began the long and arduous task of sorting out her tangled mass of red curls.

Kathleen smiled. She felt like a new woman. She was wrapped in a fine cambric peignoir trimmed in Medici lace. Except for the noisy western street outside the windows, she could have been comfortably situated in Boston. All the luxury and a good half an hour brushing her hair had finally left her feeling relaxed. She had been behaving like a madwoman this past week. Once again she was in control of her life. It was a good feeling.

The brushing had done its job. A corona of curls the color of the setting sun framed her face. She rose and approached the bed. Dinner would be arriving shortly. She had ordered it to be brought to her room at nine-thirty. She should dress. She took off the lace-trimmed peignoir and picked up a gray coutil corset trimmed with small pink ribbons. She put it on and fastened the front hooks.

The gray evening gown lay temptingly on the bed. It was much too formal to wear for dinner in one's room, but it would be appropriate for the private celebration she had in mind. After spending the last few days traipsing around the wilderness, it was a luxury she felt she deserved.

She slipped the pale fabric over her head. The gown flowed down over her full breasts and settled around her slender waist and hips. It fit beautifully! She worked diligently with the small pearl buttons that closed the front of the bodice. By the time she had finished she had a real crick in her neck. She bent over and worked her head around in a circle before righting herself with a shake of her head that added still more fullness to her hair and a glow to her cheeks.

She walked over to the mirror above the dressing table. The dress was perfect! The gown's neckline was low and straight baring her white shoulders. Blond ruching set off the neckline and trimmed the puffed three-quarter sleeves. The bodice was French seamed and drew the exquisite fabric tightly under her bosom further lifting it and rounding each pale mound. The skirt was full without overwhelming Kathleen's petite figure. French seams continued down the front of the dress making her actually appear taller. It was very simple and yet very sophisticated.

Kathleen recognized that it was far more becoming than anything she had ever chosen for herself. She fingered the small gold Celtic cross that lay nestled at the base of her throat, and thought of her poor da. If he could only see her now.

Kathleen smiled at her shimmering reflection and then suddenly, unfettered by worry, began to waltz, her hands offered to an imaginary partner. Her reverie was stopped short by a knock on the door.

Dinner! And she was famished.

Chapter Fifteen

Katherine took the arm of her imaginary escort. They made
their way to the door where she nodded her thanks before
opening the door.

"Your dinner, madame."

Kathleen's heart almost stopped. Sage Duross stood at the
door, tray in hand. He looked different, very different than
when she had last seen him.

"You!"

"Surprised to see me, 'Squirrel Tooth'?" Sage cocked his
head and lifted an eyebrow inquisitively. It was maddening.
Kathleen hated it when he teased. But she couldn't deny
that a wave of relief washed over her at the sight of the
newly washed and brushed Sage Duross.

He had not abandoned his beard but trimmed it closely.
His dark hair had been cut at least three inches and was
still damp from recent washing. It had been combed back

so that it curled behind his ears and lay over his shirt collar. Wet, it was sleek and the blackest of blacks. It posed an amazing contrast to his pale blue eyes.

His shirt was new. Nothing expensive. A light blue gabardine with metal buttons, but it fit more closely than the flannel shirt he had worn since she first saw him. He had on black twill pants, riveted at the pockets. These too fit more tightly than his previous pair. His whole body seemed more defined than she remembered, or was it her imagination?

She couldn't help noticing that the black boots were back on his feet. She prayed that he had also decided to change his socks and anything else he might have on that she couldn't see, and blushed at the impropriety of her thought.

"Happy to see me?" Sage grinned.

"Happy? I should be happy to see the means of me torture for the past few days? Yer daft man." Kathleen couldn't help but smile even if her words were less than welcoming.

She berated herself for the smile. She was only encouraging the man. He was the last thing she needed back in her life right now. Still, for some mysterious reason, her heart always lightened when she saw him.

"May I bring in your dinner, madame? I've taken the liberty to include a bottle of wine as well as my personal services for the evening."

Kathleen blushed deeply.

Shit! Sage thought. It hadn't been what he intended to say. She'd never let him in now. The remark had nothing to do with what she thought; he wasn't about to try and seduce her . . . or at least he didn't think he was.

Still, from the moment she had opened the door he was dumbstruck. He could barely speak in coherent sentences.

Joan Avery

She was the loveliest thing he had ever seen.

For days he had been badgered by a trouble-making, disheveled elf in a garish green dress. The creature who stood before him was no elf, no sprite. She was not even a girl. She was a woman with a waist that begged to be encircled by a man's hands, and breasts, wonderful pale breasts and shoulders, that begged to be kissed.

He wondered where she had gotten the magnificent gown. It was the color of old silver with the same subtleties and elegance. It was the perfect counterpoint for the crown of bewitching curls that framed her face.

His thoughts drifted back to the night by the campfire. Her pale back exposed to the firelight. His hands smoothing on the fluid jewelweed. The whisper of her breasts along his fingertips.

He tried to shake himself loose from these dangerous thoughts. He had to retrieve her good opinion. He didn't want the door slammed in his face. He wasn't sure why. He just needed to see her again, to talk to her.

"I've taken a room for myself down the hall," he assured her, nodding in the direction of his room. "I just thought you might like some company for dinner."

"But how did you know where I was?" Kathleen still eyed him suspiciously.

"I ran into the girl who was emptying your bath. A few inquiries and presto! Dinner for two and a bottle of fairly decent wine if I remember correctly." He held out the tray for her perusal. "Just dinner, that's all." He assured her again. "To celebrate our recent escape and a return to civilization."

"Just dinner?"

"Yes, just dinner." Sage made a solemn promise to himself. It would be just dinner. Anything else would be the height of foolishness. He had to forget the curve of her neck as it met her lovely shoulders and the small indentation at the base of her throat that lovingly cradled an Irish cross. He had to forget it all.

"Come in then, though I know I'll live to rue the day."

"Don't say that, leprechaun. We've made a pretty good team these past few days." Sage sought to reestablish the casual banter that had more or less successfully kept them at arm's length. He could just have dinner with her. It *was* possible, he assured himself.

Kathleen felt gooseflesh rise on her arms and bare shoulders as Sage brushed past her on his way to the small table that held the wash basin and pitcher. What was wrong with her? She was acting like a ninny. She had just spent four days in the wilderness with the man. Why was she suddenly so skittish when there were plenty of people around to protect her from any unwanted advances? And they would be unwanted. There was no question about it.

She closed the door and turned her back to him. She could hear him as he busied himself removing the basin and pitcher and laying out the contents of the tray on the table. She rested a hand on the bureau next to the door and steadied herself. She had to get hold of herself. It was a moment before she felt more in control.

Then she saw it. The telegram lay half-folded on the bureau where she had set it earlier. It sent a jolt through her. She grabbed it as if it were contraband. Her heart was beating much too rapidly again. She hid it with her body from Sage. Quietly, she unfolded it and reread the message. Two words jumped out at her.

Annulment granted.

She was no longer a married woman. She had never been

165

a married woman. She had been relieved when she had first read the message. Now it instilled something other than relief in her.

She folded the note quickly and tucked it into the pocket of her dress as she would a forbidden sweet. Out of sight, out of mind her da had always said. But she couldn't get it out of her mind. She felt suddenly unprotected. A safety barrier she had counted on had been torn down. She felt exposed and vulnerable. Uncertainty coursed through her in the form of a shiver.

"Are you cold?" She could feel the warmth of his body suddenly behind her and much too close for her liking.

"No. 'Tis nothin'."

He placed his hands on her shoulders. She stopped breathing. She felt his thumbs caress the fine hairs at the nape of her neck. She needed to breathe.

"Please . . ." It was an entreaty.

He moved his hands but only to slide them down her arms to the top of her puffed sleeves. She shivered again.

"Are you sure you're not cold? I can get you something."

"I'm sure." She shook off his hands and fled to the center of the room. She couldn't turn to face him. "I'm just hungry and tired. That's all."

"Then come eat." His voice behind her was deep and low. It was an invitation. She felt it caress her skin and then invade her pores until it reached her heart. Once there it activated a response in her that was more instinctual than any she had ever felt. A fire drove down the center of her from her heart to other places until they felt hot and moist.

She heard Sage return to the small table and withdraw one of the chairs for her. She braced herself and turned. She felt like a Christian entering the Coliseum. She was deathly afraid she was about to be devoured, if not by Sage then by her own feelings for him.

She thought it strange that she never considered not going to join him. Somehow that would be the equivalent of throwing herself into hell without any chance for heaven.

He did not touch her again, and she was grateful. He sat across from her and removed the silver covers from the dinner plates. She was not surprised to see a steak on the plate with fall squash. It had all been arranged rather elegantly. The steak was not seared to blackness, the usual preparation out West, and the squash had been attractively sliced. She was hungrier than she imagined. She took a bite of the vegetables. They had been glazed with maple syrup and were quite delicious.

Sage opened the wine and poured a small amount into her glass.

"Taste it, 'Squirrel Tooth.' Tell me what you think." He smiled slowly, an elbow on the table and his head perched on the open palm of his hand. She hated being under his scrutiny.

She turned her attentions to the wine. She raised the crystal glass and watched its ruby contents vibrate in the candlelight. She was still shaking. But she was sure she wasn't cold. She sipped the bloodred nectar. It warmed her throat as it slid down and settled in her belly, where it helped calm her nearly shattered nerves.

" 'Tis very nice." She looked back up at him. He hadn't moved. He studied her as if he had never seen her before and yet knew her intimately.

She had seen lust in his eyes, but this was more than lust. No man had ever looked at her this way. It demanded more than a physical response from her. It frightened her. She had to break his spell.

167

"So I assume yeh're still intent upon gettin' yerself killed?" Her voice was not as steady as she would have liked, but it did the trick. He glanced away and poured himself a glass of wine before he refilled her glass. Kathleen cut a piece of steak and shoved it in her mouth so she wouldn't have to say another word.

"That's my plan. Why do you ask? It shouldn't matter to you one way or the other."

He was irritated. This was good. This was safe.

It shouldn't matter to her what he did, but suddenly she knew it did. She knew it with her head and her heart and her body. But there was nothing to be done about it, not if he were hellbent on getting himself killed.

"I was just wonderin' if I should pick up a black dress before I leave town. I wouldn't want to attend yer hangin' without having somethin' proper to wear." She picked up her fork and fiddled with the steak in front of her.

"Always the proper one, so proper you married a man you didn't love."

Kathleen blushed. "Yeh've no right to say that." She blurted out. Then inhaled and choked.

"Here drink something." Sage offered her the wine but did nothing else to help her.

Kathleen gulped down the liquid. Her choking subsided to a cough.

"What do yeh care why I married? 'Twas as good a reason as any."

"Status, I take it, was the driving force behind the relationship?"

"And what if it was? Yeh don't know what it's like to have everyone and their uncle lookin' down their blue-blooded nose at yeh as if yer money was a different color than their money." She thought he'd understand—surely he was as poor as a church mouse himself—but strangely he said nothing.

They ate in angry silence, as the candle flickered and burned, casting ominous shadows on the striped walls. When the candle had shrunk to nearly half of its original size, the silence became unbearable.

Sage drank. Kathleen drank.

Neither spoke. Neither made any effort to leave. It was a standoff of the most combustible kind.

Finally, Kathleen could bear it no longer. She folded her napkin and laid it on the table. She thought she would burst from frustration. "Is this how it's to be then?"

She was losing control. The stubborn, stubborn man. "We're not to speak or see one another ever again?"

Sage fingered his empty wineglass. He did not answer her. He seemed moody, indifferent to what she was saying.

"If that's how 'tis to be, then go. I c'not stand it anymore." She pushed back from the table, her anger turning to despair. She could no longer hold back the tears. Ashamed, she turned away and fled to the bed, throwing herself on it.

"Kathleen, please." Her name on his lips was like magic, but at this moment it only intensified her pain.

"Don't tell me how reasonable we're to be! How it's all for the best." The words came out awash in tears. She no longer cared about her pride. "But most of all don't tell me I don't care!"

"Kathleen." His voice was tinged with regret. She did not hear him approach. She only knew he was there when she felt the weight of his body on the bed beside her. She didn't want him this close. If he didn't care, then let him go and not torment her.

"If yeh care jist a little about me, yeh'll go now and save me from more misery."

"Kathleen," he pleaded again. His hand was on her shoulder caressing it.

"And stop sayin' me name. Yer drivin' me mad."

She flipped herself over to free herself from his touch. She knew it was a mistake as soon as she looked in his eyes. She lost herself then in their crystal blue stillness. They spoke to her, telling her all the things she desperately wanted to hear.

She raised a hand and placed it gently over his mouth. She didn't want him to speak the words out loud and then leave her. It would be unbearable. His warm hand covered hers. He slid her hand from his lips up across his cheek and then turned and pressed an urgent kiss into her palm. Kathleen brought her other hand up to capture his face and slowly drew him toward her. She kissed him then. Hesitantly.

When she pulled away, his eyes held a warning that there would be no stopping once she chose this path. She didn't hesitate.

He kissed her then, at first softly and then with an increasing urgency. She opened to his urging and felt his tongue searching inside her. It electrified her. For long tender moments he explored the corners of her mouth and then he delved once more inside her. She reveled in the feel and the heady excitement it drew from her. When he withdrew, she felt spent. He kissed her eyelids and the corners of her mouth once again. He nuzzled her neck, and she found herself coaxing him back up to her lips.

His arms pushed her sleeves down trailing them with kisses as soft as a butterfly's wings. The warmth of his hands trailed back up until he cradled her face.

He said nothing. But there was nothing to say. Everything

they needed to communicate was in the air, palpable and undeniable. He kissed her again urging her response with teasing preludes that sought first the edges of her mouth and then her top and bottom lips. She smiled. She pulled him to her and explored his mouth in turn. She began tentatively and then gained confidence until she had encouraged him on. He stopped her play and deepened his kiss, meanwhile she felt his hand on the bodice of her dress.

She took his head and made him stop his kiss. She sat up and began to deal with the buttons herself. He moved behind her to cradle her, his arms securely around her. He smoothed kisses along the nape of her neck and her shoulders. She leaned back into him. She couldn't get out of her gown fast enough.

She bent again mentally cursing the buttons' delicate size. He pushed the mass of her hair to one side and nuzzled her neck and ears. At one point she had to pause, too distracted to continue. Finally, she released the last of the fastenings. He pushed down the bodice of her dress and reached around her to unhook her corset. She leaned back, pushing her breasts upward, desperate to escape the confines of the boned undergarment. She gasped when he finally freed her of it. His lips teased behind her ear as his hands came up to cup her breasts. She thought she would die from the pleasure of it, it was so sweet.

She felt his thumbs tease her hardened nipples through her chemise and the pleasure became excruciating. She pushed his hands away and he laid her back down on the bed. She watched, fascinated, as he untied her skirt and foulard petticoat. Then she closed her eyes. She could feel his spread fingers glide over her buttocks and hips. He moved tantalizingly slow. The thin muslin of her drawers proved an irritating barrier. He ran down the outside of her

Joan Avery

legs caressing them as he pulled the petticoat and skirt off. She felt him slip off her gray calf pumps.

The warmth of his hands as they made their way back up her legs to the top of her hose sent an unheralded shiver through her. She wanted to urge him on faster, but at the same time she was reluctant to abandon one moment of the pleasure that was his gift to her. The back of his hand brushed the inside of her thigh as he began to roll down one of the fine lisle hose. He repeated the act, again letting his hand rest against the inside of her thigh.

She opened her eyes. He was watching her as if expecting her to stop him at any moment. She patted the bed next to her and he came to her. She sat up and began to unbutton his blue shirt. Once done, she ran her hands inside letting her thumbs circle the areolas and then brush his nipples. She understood now the intensity of feeling this simple exploration called forth. She heard him take in his breath and she knelt before him. She bent and let her tongue repeat the act, licking and suckling until his nipples were erect.

He cradled her head and kissed the top of it and she knew she had pleased him. She continued to fondle him, licking and kissing until he drew her up before him. He kissed her then with all the force of a sudden summer storm until her spine became soft and her arms limp.

He laid her back and slid his hands down her throat and across her shoulders pushing down the lace straps of her chemise until the garment itself was to her waist. He held her then in a gentle trap, a hand on each of her upper arms, as his kisses first found her lips, then the indentation at the base of her neck and finally the soft mounds of her breasts. She groaned in pleasure. Rising to him, seeking something, she knew not what.

His tongue found the indentation on her belly and then

172

licked up her damp skin until his mouth captured the sweet flesh of her nipple and suckled there causing her to writhe with pleasure. She was hot—hot and wet. Wet in places that she had forbidden herself to think about. Places *he* always made her think of.

She pulled him to her, and she reveled in the feel of his bare chest touching her stomach and breasts. She reached for his belt buckle eager to extend the sensation along her entire length.

He sat up and began to remove his boots. She rose on her knees behind him and encircled him with her arms. She was an ardent student. Now she repeated her well-taught lessons raining kisses down behind his ears at the nape of his neck and across his shoulders. One boot off, he turned to steal a kiss. He removed his other boot and stood. She watched as he unbuttoned the black twill pants. He let them fall to the floor. She smiled. Clean gray merino drawers.

"What are you smiling at 'Squirrel Tooth'?" She knew by his lifted eyebrow he was teasing.

"You." She rose on her knees and kissed him, opening her mouth to him to let him explore at his leisure and then allowing her the same opportunity.

He picked her up and gently laid her back on the bed, covering her with his body.

"I want to see you, feel you—everywhere." Her eyes looked for an answer in his.

He rolled to his side and pulled her camisole up over her head. Then slowly he slid down her drawers letting his hand caress her belly and brush the fine hairs. In the low lamplight she saw the pleasure in his eyes.

"Well?" she asked.

"Well what?" His hand ran along her cheek.

"Figure it out, man. Figure it out." She laughed then and

173

pressed a kiss into his hand. He stood and took off the wool underwear. Kathleen's heart jumped. She had never seen a naked man before. But the sight of Sage didn't frighten her. His arousal seemed only to fire her own. She opened her arms to him and he covered her with his body. His kisses fell over her like a light summer rain giving delight wherever they landed—her breasts, her belly. Only when he moved lower to the soft downiness at the apex of her legs did she tense. He stopped his exploration and rose to an elbow. He crooked an eyebrow.

She smiled and shook her head in abandon. She would trust him with her life. She could not refuse him when he gave her that teasing look. She relaxed and wallowed in the new sensations he drew from her. And when she could stand it no more she reached down and drew him up once more along the length of her, relishing the taut planes and angles of his body. She drew him up until his manhood pressed against her seeking entrance. He paused once again searching her face for encouragement.

She reached out to his buttocks and drew him toward his final goal. She gasped as he entered her, and the gasp was smothered by his kiss.

Chapter Sixteen

Sage awoke lazily. The soft bed, the warm crescent of a woman molded to him lulled him for a moment. He looked at Kathleen still sleeping.

What the hell had she been thinking? Once again she had rattled his brain. Suddenly adultery paled in comparison to deflowering a virgin. Why hadn't she told him? And what kind of man was he, sleeping with another man's wife?

It was the first part that irked him the most. It was bad enough he had seduced another man's wife—although, truth be told, she did contribute to the event—but why the hell was she still a virgin?

He slowly separated from her and pulled the covers up around her, then quickly dressed. The best thing for her was for him to leave her alone.

*   *   *

Kathleen awoke with a start. She was naked. She was alone. Where had Sage gone? She sat up holding the linens to her bare breasts. His clothes were gone.

She had never felt so vulnerable in her entire life. This was worse than being alone.

What had she done? She rose from the bed and pulled on her peignoir. The remains of their dinner were on the small table. She crouched down and filled the basin with water. She gasped as the shocking cold hit her face. She didn't have time to waste. Her fingers fumbled as she urged them on faster. She pulled on her underwear and, wasting no time with a corset, pulled on the simple blue cotton dress she had considered last night. She pulled her hair up high on her head and secured it with several tortoiseshell pins.

She opened the door to her room and looked in both directions. There was no one in sight. She scurried into the hall. Sage had indicated his room was down the hall past her room. A window at the end lit the wood floor with the morning sun. Two doors glared at each other like stiff opponents across the hall. She cautiously approached the door on the left. She listened intently hoping to gain some information on its occupants.

Only silence greeted her. She knocked once, lightly. There was no answer. She knocked again harder. A door opened, but it wasn't the one before her. She whipped around.

"So yeh're still here?" It came out before she had a chance to think.

"Yes, I'm still here." Sage turned and walked into his room. Kathleen trailed after him, oblivious to propriety.

"Why did yeh leave?"

"Why didn't you tell me you'd never slept with a man?"

"Why did yeh need to know?"

"Don't answer a question with a question, Kathleen. It's not polite." There was a cold irony in his voice that sent a chill down Kathleen's spine.

"It made no never mind t'yeh that I was married." Kathleen charged, knowing it wasn't exactly the truth.

"Well maybe now you know what kind of man I am," he spit out in return. "A man who deflowers other men's virginal wives!" He turned, stalked over to the small table in the room and picked up a holster and a gun.

When Kathleen saw the gun she felt as if she had been hit in the face. A gun! Lord in heaven, what was he going to do with a gun? "I'm sorry, Sage, I did'na mean to say that."

"Perhaps not, but it's what you thought. Do you ever think of anyone but yourself? What if you have a child? What about that child? Do you even care? I believe it will be fairly hard to foist him off on your husband unless you hurry to his bed."

He was being intentionally cruel. She didn't deserve it.

"I have no intention of going to anyone else's bed." She spoke calmly, assuredly.

"Then, congratulations. We may have created another bastard for the world!"

"He doesn't have to be." Kathleen wanted desperately to explain.

"Lying doesn't become you 'Squirrel Tooth.' So I'd stop while you're ahead." He bolted out the door before she could get another word of explanation out.

Kathleen wandered back to her room in a daze after Sage walked out. His harsh words had blunted her sensibilities. She gathered her things and began to pack without any sense of what she was doing. She couldn't cry. She couldn't summon anger. She was drained of all emotion. She had never known it hurt to love someone. She had never anticipated the pain. It had shot through her like buckshot tearing through her belly, heart and lungs. She was without organs left to feel. An empty shell.

She closed the trunk and sat down on the bed still fragrant with their lovemaking.

Perhaps she would be all the wiser for her sorrow. San Francisco awaited and so did Bret Merriweather. But even her avowed revenge seemed trivial. Foolishness, her attorney had said. Perhaps all of it was foolishness, she thought.

Damn her! She had done it again. The Irish hellion had pulled him into her little scheme, whatever it was. Sage strode toward the train station. The thought that he might have given her a child haunted him. A child was the one thing he and Victoria had always wanted but never managed to conceive. It would be just his luck that he finally managed to beget one with this chit. Maybe that was her plan all along. Father a child and claim it as her husband's. Maybe the man was impotent.

Even as he concocted the justifications for his own behavior, he knew it was a useless exercise. Something had happened between them last night that went deeper than the physical. With every kiss, every caress had come a loving care he hadn't known these past two years. Even as the reality of this seeped into his consciousness, guilt and uncertainty joined it. What about her marriage was she not telling him? More importantly, why wasn't she telling him?

He had to laugh at himself. Why should she? What had he ever offered her? His future, or rather lack of one, was nothing to share with a woman you loved. She'd be better off without him. What had she said last night? If he cared for her, he would leave. He hadn't left. Instead he had badly abused her trust.

Even as he reached the station platform he knew what he had to do.

"I'd like a ticket to San Francisco, if yeh please." Kathleen plunked the twenty-dollar gold piece down.

"Yes, ma'am."

The smile on the clerk's face and his polite demeanor irked Kathleen to no end. Funny what a little money and a new wardrobe did to improve your treatment. That's what life was about. Power and money.

She looked around her. The platform held but a handful of passengers waiting for the three o'clock train. Sage was not one of them.

She had chosen the green walking dress from the trunk of clothes. It was the color of a shadowed forest. With its underskirt of green and white stripes and small green hat with a bow in the same striped fabric, it was the height of style. It reminded Kathleen of the green taffeta she had left crumpled in a corner of the hotel room; yet it was different. Even to her untrained eye, its fit and color was much more refined, much more elegant than the one she had worn so confidently into Deadwood only days earlier. What had Sage said? Dressed like she was, it was no wonder she was mistaken for 'Squirrel Tooth Sally.'

Was that what all of Boston society had thought of her as well? Someone without class, without taste? She felt her cheeks warm with color. She stood a little taller. She remembered the way she had felt last night in the beautiful gray watered silk. She remembered the look in Sage's eyes when he first saw her.

"Don't go there, yeh twit. Yeh're darn stupider than yeh

179

thought if yeh go there," she reprimanded herself.

"I'm sorry, ma'am, I didn't hear you."

Kathleen looked up at the clerk who had returned with her ticket. " 'Twas nothin', nothin' at all." And she wished that she believed it.

"All aboard! All aboard!"

Kate returned to her trunk and gave the tow-headed boy who had carried it for her an additional quarter to put it on the train for her. Kathleen did not immediately follow the boy. She stood on the platform, willing herself onto the train but unable to go just yet. Around her people laughed and cried and kissed goodbye. The train belched steam.

She was running out of time. She looked down the street. Not a soul moved toward the station. In the afternoon heat, the town was quiet. Almost deserted. The platform was now emptied of passengers.

"Miss, you'd better get on board now. The train will be pulling out." The conductor's touch made her jump.

"Yes, yes of course. I'll be gettin' on, I was jist . . ." Just what? she asked herself. Waiting for yet another man who had abandoned her? She gave the train station one last futile glance. He was nowhere in sight.

So be it.

"Thank yeh, sir. Yeh're most kind." The conductor lent her a hand to climb the two stairs to the platform between the train cars. She did not look back. She couldn't bear to.

"I've taken the liberty of stowing your trunk in the forward car, ma'am. Dining car is to the rear." The conductor touched his hat and hurried off. Kathleen had to steady herself as the train began to move. She stood there staring at nothing in particular. Paralyzed by fear and sorrow.

With effort she moved into the second-class Pullman car. While not luxurious, it appeared comfortable. She was pleased. She had been unwilling to pay the extra five dollars out of her meager winnings to travel first class.

She took in her surroundings. The benches that lay on either side of the narrow aisle were well padded and covered with fabric. Overhead open wooden bins held belongings. Suitcases and baskets. Hats and coats. She noticed that her trunk had found its way into a small open closet to her left. The car was only about one-third full. It meant there would be room to move about on the three-day trip. Maybe even space to stretch out and sleep. For a moment, she regretted not getting a berth in the sleeper car. Then she smiled. She had just spent the last few days sleeping on the ground and in caves. She could stand the softly padded seats for two nights.

The train whistle sounded a final farewell to Cheyenne. The next stop would be Ogden, then on to San Francisco.

Kathleen found a seat next to the window toward the front of the car. She sat and watched the trees as they passed. They had an almost hypnotizing effect. Within minutes she was asleep.

She was in Boston. In her own home and her da was alive and well and laughing. "Oi'm tellin' yeh girl. It'll take some man t'tame yeh, that it will. Yeh're so hellbent and stubborn, yeh'll run ramshod over any but the most ornery man. And Oi'll not have yeh wast'n yer loife with a brute."

He was sitting in his favorite leather chair by the fire in the card room. She could hear the flames crackling and smell the lemon wax that anointed the ornate furniture her da had had shipped all the way from England. Cigar smoke wafted through the room carried by the heat from the fireplace.

Despite his familiar tirade, she was happy. She was loved

and protected, warm and cosseted, buffered from society and all its prejudices.

"Oh, Da, am I so impossible?" She walked to where he sat, and he held open his arms. She plopped down on his lap.

"No, me darlin' girl, yeh're very good about wrappin' men around yer little finger." He held up his pinky finger to illustrate. Kathleen could see the huge gold ring emblazoned with a bear, the symbol of the Hibernia Society. "Jist see what yeh've done t'me all these years since yer dear mother died."

Kathleen laughed and lay her head against his shoulder. She would have been content to stay there for all eternity. But fate hadn't been that kind.

She could hear crying. Her da was in his big bed, in terrible pain. In her mind he had always been a large robust man. Now he lay dwarfed by the linens, wizened to half his former size.

"Da, please don't leave me. I've naught but you. What will I do without yeh?"

Again she could hear the crying, and now she was crying herself.

Her father reached out and patted her head. "Look at me, girl."

Kathleen looked up. He was fading. He was leaving her.

"Remember this, girl, Oi'll not leave yeh poor, but yeh must promise me yeh'll not d'anything but improve yer station. Promise me this, girl."

She had shaken her head eager to please.

"There's plenty out there who'd look down their snooty noses at yeh. Pick yer husband wisely, and yer children and yer children's children willn'a know the pain we've known."

"Oh, Da."

Kathleen awoke with a start, her heart in her throat. She realized the crying wasn't in her dream. Somewhere a baby was crying. She took a moment to get her bearings. Opening her small reticule she removed a fine linen handkerchief. The pale blue entwined letters M and N graced a corner. Kathleen stared at them.

Funny how death had a way of intervening and changing life. Mary Alice Bundy had thought she would be Mary Newirth. Instead, she had died and her trousseau had been given to a stranger.

Kathleen had always assumed her da would walk her down the aisle on her wedding day. Instead she had been alone. She had thought she was doing what her da had wanted her to do, but she had failed miserably. She couldn't even do that right.

Again the baby cried. She wiped her eyes. There was nothing to be accomplished feeling sorry for herself. She rose to stretch her legs.

The sun was setting. She had slept longer than she imagined. She made her way down the aisle. About halfway through the car she came upon the crying baby. She had never seen a child so young. The baby whimpered and occasionally made a sound that reminded Kathleen of an unhappy cat. Still pink from exertion, little fists pummeling the air, the child was anything but attractive.

Kathleen stopped, fascinated by the tiny thing. "She's but a wee one." She smiled sympathetically at the young couple who still handled the squirming baby awkwardly.

"I hope she's not been disturbin' you, ma'am." The young father's freckled face looked so distraught that Kathleen could only lie.

"No, no. Not at all."

The young man rose, pushing back a clump of tawny hair

as he did. "It's just that the babe was born a bit too early, and she's just gettin' adjusted to things."

The man extended his hand. "Wayne Rowe's my name. And this here is my wife, Eleanor."

"And the babe?" Kathleen took the man's hand.

"The baby we named Cora Mae after Eleanor's ma. We're sorry about the ruckus, ma'am. We're still a bit raw at this."

Kathleen looked again at the infant who seemed to have fallen to sleep. Asleep, the baby seemed different. Almost angelic. "How old is she?"

"She'll be four months tomorrow."

Kathleen's hand went to her stomach. What had Sage yelled? What if there were a child? A bastard. The irony was not lost on her. If she were pregnant, she would have sealed the child's fate and her own. If there was a child, not even money could protect them.

"Do you mind?" Eleanor Rowe had risen with the sleeping baby and now held it out to Kathleen. Kathleen took a step back.

"I've got to go take care of some things." She nodded toward the small privy room at the back of the car. "And Wayne, here, is still a little uncomfortable with the baby."

And she wouldn't be? Was this woman mad? Did this woman think that because she was a female she was born with some sense about children?

"I'm really not . . ."

"I really wouldn't impose but . . ." The woman walked toward her and held out the infant pressing it against Kathleen. Kathleen's arms rose reluctantly, afraid the baby would fall. Too late she realized the mother would never have let go without her arms there. She had sealed her fate.

She was startled. The child weighed next to nothing even bundled in blankets.

"Here, sit here while we wait for Eleanor." Wayne Rowe signaled to the seat recently vacated by his wife. "See, you have a real knack. If'n I had taken her, she'd be yowlin' something fierce by now."

A real knack? Kathleen's heart was beating so fast she could hear it in her ears. *Dear Lord, don't let this wee thing wake up,* she prayed. She was afraid to move, to settle herself more comfortably, for fear of waking the sleeping child.

"You don't sound like you're from around these parts, miss."

"No, I'm from Boston."

"And before that Ireland I'll bet." Wayne smiled and he seemed not much more than a child himself.

"Me father was from Ireland. I was a wee one meself when I left."

"That's good."

She smiled back. Wayne Rowe was the first person in a long time to think that being from Ireland was a good thing. She knew she was going to like Wayne and Eleanor Rowe. The baby in her arms stirred. She raised a hand to soothe its cheek and something tugged deep inside of her.

Chapter Seventeen

He knew she was on the train. He had watched her board. The train had already been moving when he fled his hiding place and climbed on himself.

Things between them couldn't be left the way they were. The look of hurt in her eyes the last time he had seen her had forced him to flee from his own savage words. He was angry with himself and he had taken it out on her.

As he worked his way through the train, he was on edge. His palms sweaty, his breathing shallow, he was prepared to be upbraided and attacked.

Only God knew how the little she-devil would react. Sage smiled. He probably deserved every ounce of trouble he was about to get.

He pulled open the door to the Pullman car and looked up. The train suddenly lurched in a weaving motion. He reached out to steady himself, but it was as much from shock as from the movement of the car. He had expected to find her feisty and rambunctious. Morose perhaps, angry more probably.

Instead, she was as calm as he'd ever seen her—serene almost. He would never have thought it possible.

She sat quite still, her head bowed over an infant. She was singing quietly. An Irish lullaby, he thought. The late evening light gave the still life a soft, muted appearance, as if it had been drawn in pastels.

Kathleen Callahan had never looked more beautiful. Her skin was moist alabaster, as unblemished as the child's she cradled.

The setting sun burnished her red hair. In its golden rays, the strands became the colors of autumn—burnt sienna and plum, magenta and wine.

The receding light played with the scene like a Flemish master, changing it with every moment that passed. He drank in the beauty of it.

She looked up. He had expected to see anger in her eyes, but what he saw cut him deeper than her anger could have. He saw relief. He saw need.

He saw her love.

And he knew he didn't deserve it.

The young man with her caught her glance. He turned to look in Sage's direction.

Then he turned back to the radiant Kathleen. "You shoulda mentioned your husband was on the train, ma'am. Why don't you and him join Eleanor and me? It would make the trip a might shorter, I'll bet."

Kathleen looked startled for a moment. She gazed at Wayne Rowe dumbstruck. Sage smiled. He would never have guessed the Irish hellion capable of either serenity or silence. She was full of surprises.

He waited curiously to hear her reply.

She looked back at him. His smile seemed to change everything. And not for the better. There was a familiar glint in her eye, a challenge to him.

"I must be losin' me manners." She smiled sweetly. Too sweetly for Sage's liking.

"Wayne Rowe . . . this is me husband, Sage."

"Mr. Callahan, this is a surprise." Wayne Rowe rose to greet him.

"I assure you, Mr. Rowe, not as much as it is to me." Sage glanced suspiciously at Kathleen. What was the sprite up to now?

"Me and the missus would be pleased if you and Mrs. Callahan would join us for the trip. There's nothing like good company to make the time fly."

Sage cocked an eyebrow toward Kathleen as he stepped forward to take the eager young man's hand. He felt like he was walking naked into a nest of hornets. What was she doing now, the little chit?

"Me and the *missus* would be proud to join you." Sage gave Wayne Rowe's hand a hearty shake.

The gauntlet had been thrown, and Sage was not one to pass on a challenge. He could play her little game whatever it was.

"Ain't that right, *darlin'?*" Sage plopped himself down next to Kathleen and put a protective arm around her.

"That baby's the sweetest thing I've ever seen." Sage reached out and tousled the baby's head, waking her.

Kathleen glared at him. "Now see what yeh've gone and done, yeh big lout." The baby had begun to cry and Kathleen had a panicked look in her eye that belied her previous serenity.

"My sweetie here has been countin' the days 'til she has

one of her own. We figured on eight maybe ten. Ain't that right, honey?" Sage's smile turned into a grimace as Kathleen's heel found his shin.

"She gets a little out a sorts when it's her time of the month, if you get my drift?"

The look on Kathleen's face was priceless. Revenge was definitely sweet.

Kathleen opened her mouth but before she could speak she was interrupted.

"Oh, has the baby been peevish for you? I'm so sorry." Eleanor Rowe held out her arms for her daughter.

Kathleen leaned across Sage and dropped the baby into Eleanor's outstretched arms as if she were a hot poker.

Sage placed a kiss on Kathleen's cheek as she did so. "Ready, sweet thing?" He gave Kathleen a look that would have wilted most women. It only seemed to raise Kathleen's ire to new heights. He thought she was going to burst.

He turned his back on her and addressed Wayne Rowe, "I promised my wife dinner in the Pullman car tonight, and I wouldn't want to disappoint the little lady." He rose, his hand firmly on Kathleen's elbow. "So if you'll excuse us for a while."

"We didn't mean to impose on you all. Because of the baby, me and Eleanor packed us some provisions." Wayne picked up a large wicker basket and placed it on his lap. A loaf of bread jutted out of one side. "You all go and enjoy yourselves. Sounds like the time will come when a little one may keep ya from it." He smiled.

Sage moved into the aisle, Kathleen in tow. When they had left the car and entered the dining car Kathleen snapped, "Let go of me you brute!"

"A brute, am I? You've displayed poor judgment in picking a brute for a husband, I'd say."

"Stop it!" Kathleen was as red as he'd ever seen her. She shook herself free from his grasp.

"What the hell was that all about back there?" he demanded.

Suddenly, she looked properly contrite. "I was only trying to save yeh."

"Save me, eh? From what, or dare I ask?"

Kathleen brushed at her dress, refusing to look up at him. She spoke quietly to her shoes. "I believe the law is still on yer tail, if I'm not mistaken?"

She glanced up then, daring him to contradict. "I jist thought I'd save yeh from hangin' 'til yeh found Morse Templeton."

"How nice of you to think of me." He regarded her suspiciously.

"But I think yeh've taken it a wee bit far." She added self-righteously.

"I thought you've always wanted me to talk like a cowboy. Or are you ashamed to be married to a plain cowpoke?" He rubbed his beard.

"No, 'tis not that. It's jist . . ." She studied her shoes again.

"Spit it out woman. What is it *jist?*"

She looked up defiantly and colored for a moment. "It's jist, I like the way yeh talk. Like a gentleman. A real proper gentleman."

"Even if I'm not one?" he teased.

She grew serious suddenly and put a gloved finger to his lips to silence him. She didn't speak for a long moment and when she did she was as ardent as he'd ever seen her. "Don't say yeh're not a gentleman. Yeh're more of a gentleman than half the swells in Boston. More of a gentleman than any man I know."

She had done it again.

Stripped him of his defenses.

He covered her hand with his and turning it palm up placed a soft kiss there. He offered her his arm. "Madame, if you'd care to join me for dinner, I'd be honored."

His reward for this simple courtesy was a smile that would have lit up half of Boston.

Kathleen studied Sage. The soft candlelight of the dining car softened his features, and she resisted the urge to smooth away the furrows that marred his forehead. Throughout dinner, at her prodding, he had talked of cattle drives and the beauty of the West. He had told her of places so strange and beautiful that she longed to see them herself.

She had watched his face find new life as he recounted his adventures.

"Ah, Kathleen, you should see the hot springs and the geysers west of Cody. Congress made the area a national park a few years ago. You've never seen anything like it. . . ."

She knew he left out the painful events, but the stories he did tell were fascinating.

"In southern Colorado there's a place they call the Garden of the Gods. It's as if a giant hand had come and placed these immense red rocks at every angle towering over you. They're shaped like the most amazing things. There's one that looks like a camel and another that looks like giant. . . ."

He had laughed.

She had laughed.

It had all become comfortable. Too comfortable.

Now, in the afterglow of the meal, reality began to eat its way back into the dream.

"What will yeh do?" She sipped at her coffee.

"About what?" He genuinely looked puzzled. He lifted his wineglass and took a sip.

191

"About Morse Templeton."

He stopped middrink and abruptly set the glass back down on the table, where its contents sloshed and spilled onto the white linen.

She dropped her head, regretting how she had broken the warm mood that had developed between them. The ruby wine spread around the base of the glass like blood on sand.

She looked back up, willing him to say what she wanted to hear. But when he spoke she felt what little hope she had had dissipate.

"I'll find him and kill him." His expression dared her to challenge him.

She was not deterred. "Could yeh not turn him into the authorities? Surely they would listen to yeh?"

"Listen to me?" He laughed cynically, shaking his head back and forth. "Wasn't it you who said I needed protecting from the authorities? Wasn't that your whole point about this little ruse you've concocted about us being husband and wife?"

No, she wanted to say. *That was only part of it.* The other part she couldn't or wouldn't put into words.

She couldn't let it drop. "I'm not savin' yeh from one sheriff only to see yeh die at the hands of another. Do yeh think that's what I want?" She worried the linen napkin in her lap.

"What *is* it you want, Kathleen? What keeps you here with me?"

"I'm not here with yeh. I'm jist here. But while I'm here I hate to see a man, any man do somethin' foolish, somethin' he'll regret later." She wanted to throttle him. Jump over the table and choke him until he saw reason.

"And you think I'll regret killing Morse Templeton?" He

placed his elbows on the table and rested his chin on his hands.

He was the most irritating man she had ever known, but she would tell him what he should know. What he didn't want to hear. "Yes, yes I do. And for the rest of yer life."

"So now you're my conscience?" He was angry. He sat back upright.

She didn't want to fight anymore. It was late, and she just wanted to have him tell her more stories and watch him laugh. But she had spoiled all that.

"No, but I'm yer wife, last I checked." She tilted her head and smiled. She waited.

She saw it in his eyes before she saw it on his lips. A smile. His smile—the one thing that restored her equilibrium— made her feel safe.

"Reminding me that people think you're my wife is not a good way to ask for a truce."

"D'yeh still think me a poor choice for a wife, then?" Her mouth made a little moue.

"You would make a man a fine wife, but damned if I know anyone that would have you."

"He'd have to be a sorry lot, eh?"

"A sorry lot, indeed." Sage reached across the table and took her hands in his.

She felt the warmth of his flesh pressed over hers. She couldn't look at him. It suddenly wasn't a joke any longer. She looked out the window, past their reflection.

She spoke into the darkness.

"He was."

Sage brushed a strand of hair away from Kathleen's face. She lay with her head in his lap. When she could no longer hold her head upright from fatigue, he had insisted upon it.

Several rows behind them the Rowes slept with their baby daughter. It seemed everyone in the car was now asleep.

But he couldn't sleep—couldn't stop thinking. No matter how hard he tried, his mind churned on and kept him awake. The sound of the rails should have had a soothing effect on his nerves. Instead, they seemed to beat out the time until all this would end. He looked down at Kathleen again.

What was he going to do with her?

How was it that she could break his heart with a look?

Stifle his anger with a glance?

Excite him with a touch?

They had known each other such a short period and yet it seemed an eternity. She had turned his world upside down and for the first time made him question his path. She had somehow seduced him with the offer of a world bright with possibilities.

He wasn't even sure if she knew how much power she had over him.

He closed his eyes and spoke to the dead. He begged for guidance. He begged for wisdom, but most of all he begged for forgiveness.

A vision of Victoria, dying, rose in his head.

"Edward, my love . . ." He could hear her voice, raspy from the disease that racked her body and drained it of strength. ". . . do not blame yourself."

"But it's my fault." In his vision, he bent over her, his head on her chest. He could hear her labored breath. She was losing the struggle to live.

"It's no one's fault, my dearest."

She caressed his hair, and he fought to keep his voice steady. "If I hadn't dragged you out to this godforsaken place you wouldn't be . . ." He shook his head violently. This couldn't be happening. It was so unfair.

"Shhh." She took his head in her hands and drew it up until she could see him. "Do you think it is impossible to die in New York?"

"No. But I would have had the money to find the best doctors, the best hospital. We would have had a chance. . . ."

"We've had our happiness, my love. And I wouldn't have traded it for all the doctors in New York."

"It's my fault." He protested again.

"Do not blame yourself. Life can be cruel at times, but do not take it upon yourself." Her voice dropped to a barely audible whisper. "It is not fair to you, my love. Your love has been the most cherished thing in my life. Your dreams have been my dreams. Your life has been my life. I have no regrets, and neither should you."

He was about to protest, but with great effort she shook her head slightly to silence him.

"Promise me that you'll go on with your life."

He shook his head in protest. "How can I go on without you?"

"Promise me." She could barely form the words.

"How can you ask that of me?" The agony was so consuming he did not think it possible to go on.

"Promise me," she repeated with effort.

He shook his head, tears streaming down his face. He could barely see her. He could barely breathe.

"Then kiss me," she struggled to speak. "It will be your promise."

He could not refuse her the kiss. He took her in his arms and kissed her, willing life back into her.

He drew back, his face drenched in tears, sobs racking his body.

He did not need to see her lifeless face to know he had failed yet again.

Chapter Eighteen

Kathleen opened her eyes. Around her she could hear the early morning stirring of the other passengers in the car. Above her Sage still slept. He looked tired, worn.

He was breaking her heart. She didn't think anyone capable of doing that after the debacle with Bret Merriweather. She had thought herself hardened to anything, any feelings beyond revenge. She had berated him for seeking revenge, and yet that was her mission as well.

They were two of a kind, she and Sage.

She rose carefully and made her way past the Rowes as she went to the privy in the rear of the car. Eleanor Rowe nodded an acknowledgment. She had the baby at her breast. Kathleen couldn't help herself. She stopped and watched for a moment. She could feel each tug of the baby's mouth on her own breast. And the feeling ran through her to other more private parts of her body. She fought the memory of Sage tight within her, arched above her, his mouth suckling her breasts.

That night in the hotel in Cheyenne had been a mistake. It had taught her about feelings and emotions that she would have been better off never knowing.

Every inch of her skin rubbed against the clothing she wore.

She remembered what it was like to be naked in his arms—to have his hands running over her, his mouth laving her, his manhood filling her. She remembered arching toward him, begging him for more.

Yes, it had been a mistake. A tragic mistake. It was only a matter of time before he got himself killed. She felt tears of frustration and rubbed her eyes with the back of her hand.

"You'll have your own soon enough, I'll wager on it." Eleanor Rowe had seen her pain.

Little Cora Mae had fallen asleep. Eleanor Rowe patted the seat next to her and Kathleen sat down suddenly exhausted. Eleanor handed her the sleeping baby and then busied herself refastening her dress.

Kathleen looked down at the sleeping child. She softly touched the child's cheek. The baby yawned and nestled into Kathleen. Kathleen had always thought of children as a commodity. She would bear them and then they would be turned over to the care of nannies and governesses. It was the way things were done in Boston Society. The same Boston Society that had once meant so much to her. But now, with the warmth of a child pressed into her, it seemed different.

For the first time in her life she wanted a child. Sage's child. What cruel words had he thrown at her in Cheyenne? What if you're pregnant?

What if she was pregnant? Forget the practicality of bearing the child alone. At least she would have a part of him. A part of him to keep forever, long after he had abandoned her. A part of him to remind her what it was to love someone and be loved in return.

He loved her. Of that she was sure.

He just didn't love her enough.

"You'll make a fine mother. There's no need to worry. Sometimes these things take time to work out between a man and a woman." Eleanor reached out and patted Kathleen's arm before holding out her own arms for her child.

Time, Kathleen thought sadly, was the one thing of which she and Sage had very little.

Kathleen released the child reluctantly. She felt the cool air rush against her thin dress where the baby had snuggled, and she shivered.

"It's about time yeh got yerself up. Yeh've been sleepin' like a man of means."

Sage opened his eyes to find Kathleen sitting across from him. He stretched lazily.

"Is my darling wife in need of something?" He narrowed his eyes and waited.

"I'm starvin' if yeh'd like to know."

"And you need me to eat? It's really not all that difficult. Fork." He held up a hand grasping the invisible utensil. "Knife." He held up his other hand and proceeded to mime the procedure.

"Yeh're daft, yeh know?" She was trying to keep a stern face, but he could see the hint of a smile.

"So you've reminded me more than once." He worked the kinks out of his neck and shoulders.

"I've been sittin' here for over an hour watchin' yeh snore yer head off."

"As I remember, I'm not the only one who snores, 'Squirrel Tooth.' "

"I don't snore," she protested.

He closed his eyes and took in two short breaths before he let out a short snort followed by a light snore.

"Stop it!" She was smiling now. "Stop it."

He opened one eye.

"I'm hungry I'm tellin' yeh." She faked anger.

He still only stared with a single eye, over which he now cocked the eyebrow. "And you didn't go to breakfast, because . . . ?"

She lowered her voice conspiratorially. "Because I thought it would look peculiar—a wife eating without her husband."

Sage returned her smile. "I've been meaning to ask you what privileges come with this little charade. Breakfast is fine, but I was thinking more along the lines of . . ."

"Stop it!" This time she blushed.

And he did. But not before a vision of Kathleen Callahan naked in his arms conjured itself up in his mind. The thought made him hard. It was time to move.

"Well, by all means, I will happily perform my husbandly duties." He rose and offered her his arm.

"Oh look!" Kathleen had spent the past hour staring out the train window at the most amazing sight she had ever seen while Sage dozed across from her in the Pullman car. But as the train started a long climb into the mountains she had to share the beauty of it.

Sage opened his eyes.

" 'Tis so beautiful. Yeh must come and look. There's a stream rushin' way down there in the gully."

He moved across to her seat. She was pressed against the window. He braced a hand on either side of her and leaned forward until his head was next to hers at the window.

He knew exactly what he was doing even as he reprimanded himself for doing it. Ever since this morning he had wanted to touch her. Now he was so close he realized his mistake. He could smell her—soap and lilacs.

He pressed farther forward until her hair brushed his face. He closed his eyes.

"Is it not beautiful?" she asked, her enthusiasm somewhat ebbing.

"Yes, it's very beautiful." He pressed closer until his chest lay against her back. He could feel her breathing. It was becoming shorter and shallower.

"Very beautiful, indeed," he repeated.

Tempted beyond endurance, he pressed a kiss behind her ear. He felt her sigh and lean back into him. He cocooned her with his body. His broad back gave them some privacy from the others in the car.

"Sage, please . . ." she whispered, her voice breathy with emotion.

"Please what?" He nibbled at her ear, the view long forgotten.

"Please don't." Even as she pleaded with him to stop, she pressed further into him.

"Don't what?" he teased as he nuzzled her hair.

"Don't do this."

He didn't care what she said. Her body spoke for her. He removed his left hand where it was braced against the car and let it drop to her waist brushing her breasts in its descent.

He heard her sharp intake of breath. Once more he was hard. And it was more tantalizing because they were not alone.

He laid his hand on her belly and thought again of their lovemaking and the possibility of a child from it. A child. Their child. He didn't want to leave her with a child. That would be unfair. But the possibility of a child by this spirited woman brought a smile to his lips.

He pressed her into him, his hand splayed across her belly. He ached to have her.

They had stopped talking. Stopped feigning interest in the passing scenery. Both had closed their eyes long ago. They had entered a world of their own.

The slightest touch, the slightest movement left them breathless. Only the faint murmur of the other passengers kept them in check. He let the back of his hand brush her cheek and then the thin muslin of her dress over her breasts. She reached up to him to caress his cheek and he captured one of her fingers in his mouth and suckled it. He felt her body tense.

He kissed her hair and bent to tease her ear with his tongue until he heard her moan softly. Her ardor only increased his. He was losing control.

Suddenly, somewhere behind them, glass shattered with a terrifying blast. Someone screamed in agony.

In a split second Sage was on his feet, his hand on his gun. There was no mistaking the sound. A shotgun blast.

He turned back to check on Kathleen. "Get down. Below the windows."

Neither one of them had noticed that the train had slowed. Now, it was almost stopped. The mountains around them soared above the small valley they were in. Sage crouched and moved to the opposite side of the car. The shattered window was near the rear of the car. Glass covered the seats and floor. The man who had screamed lay bleeding, his body wedged between the seats in an ungainly fashion. On his belly, Sage worked his way back toward the man.

Sage struggled to free the wounded man, but his bulk resisted Sage's initial efforts. A rifle shot pierced the window next to where he worked.

"Everyone get down! If you've got a weapon get it now, and any extra ammunition you might have," he yelled.

Several men in the car made their way to the front, where they reclaimed rifles they had stowed for the trip. One or two attempted to reach the overhead racks where they had left their handguns. Gunfire drove them back down.

Sage managed to free the bleeding man who was still alive but badly cut about the face and hands. With the help of another passenger he pulled the injured man forward until he could be tended by one of the women.

Everyone crouched low. Sage moved to a window and looked out. There were four men, bandanas covering their faces.

"There's four of them."

"Injuns?" someone shouted.

"No," Sage replied, almost wishing they were. There was something very familiar about the man who obviously led them.

He couldn't think about that now. "They must have put something on the rails to stop the train. We've got to hold them off until the rails are clear. Another bullet pierced a window catching a man in the shoulder. His rifle fell to the floor.

There were only five men left and four women, including Kathleen and Eleanor Rowe.

"Wayne, can you grab that rifle?"

Wayne Rowe had gotten his own rifle and now crouched protectively over Eleanor and Cora Mae. He nodded and began to move toward the fallen weapon.

"No! I'll get it." Kathleen had crawled into the aisle on her hands and knees and had almost reached the rifle. Once she had it in her hand she crawled toward Wayne.

They could hear gunfire directed at other cars and the engine.

Sage spoke to Kathleen. "I've got to go see if I can help clear the tracks. It's our best chance."

She shook her head in acknowledgment.

"Stay here and help if you can."

Again she nodded. He could see fear in her eyes, but she was fighting it. "I'll be back," he assured her.

Sage carefully proceeded to the back of the train car and let himself out the far side away from the gunmen.

Kathleen had never been so frightened in her life. Dime novels had never prepared her for the horror of bleeding men. With Sage's departure, the gunfire had begun in earnest. Whether they were trying to hit Sage or simply kill the passengers, it didn't matter. Bullets peppered the car one after the other in quick succession.

"Mrs. Callahan, can you load the extra rifle for me?" It was Wayne Rowe who made the request.

Kathleen looked down at the rifle still in her hands. It was the first time she had ever touched a gun in her life. She didn't have a clue as to what to do. The look of bewilderment on her face must have given her away.

Eleanor Rowe laid a hand over hers. "That's all right. I

can do it. If you'd just watch Cora Mae for me."

Kathleen wanted to refuse. How could she be responsible for this woman's child? But she knew she couldn't refuse, not when she was useless otherwise.

She sat, bracing herself in the aisle. She bent over the baby trying to protect it as best she could. The baby had begun to whimper.

"Jesus, Mary and Joseph," she prayed, "don't let harm befall this wee one."

Her prayer was drowned out by the sound of shots reverberating within the train as the remaining men returned the gunfire.

Sage made his way toward the engine. He didn't have to go far to see what had stopped the train. A large tree had been felled across the tracks. They would have to work fast.

Several men from other cars had followed his lead and now stood behind him. Sage took command. "Someone go back and tell the men to increase their fire. We'll need to keep them pinned down until we can move this." He nodded toward the tree trunk.

One of the men toward the rear of the small group broke off and, crouching low, went back along the tracks stopping at each car.

Sage waited until gunfire held off the thieves, pinning them behind rocks on the far side of the train, before he signaled the others. The tree was almost two feet in diameter. Luckily its branches hung over a small gully leaving only the trunk on the tracks.

"We'll have to try and roll it off. We'll never lift it." The six other men who bent over the tree nodded.

"One, two, three." The men strained and the tree gave

slightly. Suddenly, they were no longer unobserved. A bullet whizzed past Sage's ear.

"They've seen us," said a man with a thin mustache.

"Then we better do this now." Sage bent over the trunk once more. "On my count."

This time the men had more success. The tree rolled about three feet. They had almost freed the tracks.

"Again. We need to do it again," Sage urged.

Several shots hit the engine with a metallic ping. One of the men moaned as a ricocheting bullet found his leg. He fell back, grabbing his calf. Blood poured out between his fingers.

The incident only added to the urgency. "On three."

Again they strained, and this time the tree found its own momentum and rolled off into the gully.

Kathleen looked up. Sweat beaded Wayne Rowe's brow as he concentrated on firing the rifle at the gunmen, who were now largely unseen behind rocks.

They worked well together, Wayne and Eleanor Rowe. Kathleen admired their courage. Then, for one brief moment, the couple exchanged a glance that Kathleen felt awkward to witness. In an instant, without words, they revealed the deepness of their love and their greatest fear. It cut Kathleen to the core.

Eleanor continued to work, crouching next to her. As quickly as Wayne could empty the rifle he would offer it back without turning. Eleanor would take the empty and place a freshly loaded one in its place.

Only occasionally would Eleanor spare a tense glance over to her baby, who now screamed in terror. Again and again the rifles were loaded and fired. The roar they made in the small confined space only added to the din.

Kathleen struggled to calm the crying child.

Cora Mae would not stop crying.

Then a train whistle tore through the noise of the battle.

Sage took two strides up onto the back platform of the Pullman car just as the train began to move. As if on cue, the gunfire died. Sage moved forward. The four armed bandits, who had taken shelter behind rocks fifty or so yards away, could be seen remounting their horses. All four moved brazenly out from behind cover.

The man who seemed to be their leader rode forward. He reared his horse in defiance and pulled down the kerchief that hid his features.

A smirk crossed Morse Templeton's face. "Thought you were dead, Duross. Maybe next time, I'll be able to finish my job and you in the same breath. "Until then . . ." He pulled his horse around and fired once toward the train, missing Sage by several feet before galloping off into the hills.

Sage fired back, his Colt no match for the distance now between them. Once more Templeton had slipped through his grasp, but seeing him again, hearing him again reminded him of what he must do, and reaffirmed his commitment to do it.

A baby's cry cut into his thoughts.

Kathleen!

He rushed inside the car. No one spoke in the small compartment. Only two things marred the stillness—Cora Mae's plaintive cries and the lifeless body of her mother sprawled across the aisle, a bullet hole in her forehead.

Chapter Nineteen

Kathleen's eyes were wide with terror and disbelief. She did not move, did not react to the crying baby in her arms. She simply stared at Eleanor Rowe's unblinking face.

Wayne Rowe stood over his wife, frozen in place.

Sage moved toward them.

"Wayne . . ." Sage got no response from the man whose horror left him numb. He approached, closer. He had to step over Eleanor's lifeless body to get to the young man. Sage put his arm around Wayne's shoulders. It broke his silence.

"Oh God, Eleanor! Eleanor!" The young man dropped the rifle in his hand and sank to the floor beside his dead wife.

"Oh God, Eleanor!" He cradled her lifeless body in his arms and began to rock. His body shook with sobs. His agony found escape in his wailing. It had begun softly, but now it echoed throughout the car and raised gooseflesh on those who heard.

He rocked forward and back, forward and back. "Shhh . . . shhh . . ." He seemed to be trying to calm his own keening.

"Shhh . . . shhhh. . . ."

The attempt only lasted for a moment.

"Dear God, no! Not Eleanor!" He looked up, his eyes glazed with disbelief. He searched the faces of those around him seeking denial. His piercing look dropped the heads of those it found.

"Wayne, you've got to think of the baby now." Sage tried to draw the man out from his agony. He knew only too well his anguish. But Wayne Rowe was lost in the tragedy of the moment. And Sage fought not to get lost in it as well.

"Kathleen, take the baby to the next car." Kathleen had not said a word since Sage had reentered the train carriage.

"Kathleen," he repeated more forcefully. She looked up. "Take Cora Mae to the next car. I need to help Wayne with Eleanor." He waited for some acknowledgment, but none came.

"Do you understand, Kathleen? I need you to do this. *Eleanor* needs you to do this."

This time Kathleen nodded. She looked down at Eleanor Rowe's lifeless hand on her lap. Slowly she inched away, horrified.

"Kathleen, you have to get up." Sage bent and helped Kathleen to her feet. As if mimicking the silence in the car, the crying baby had quieted. Kathleen began to sing and rock the child. The words were Gaelic, but Sage recognized the cadence. It was a dirge.

*   *   *

Kathleen studied the sleeping child in her arms. After she left Wayne Rowe and the others, Cora Mae had begun to cry again and Kathleen had joined in her tears. They had both cried until neither had any tears left.

"Jesus, Mary and Joseph, protect this wee one from any more pain in her life. Keep her safe and protected. And take care of her dear dead mother until they can be together again." The whispered prayer helped somehow. It was as if she had turned part of her responsibility over to those she trusted implicitly.

She had never felt this kind of grief before. Even her father's death was not this gut-wrenching, faith-shaking tragedy. Her father had been old. Eleanor Rowe had not been much older than Kathleen herself.

Slowly her mind moved out of the fog. Her thoughts flew to Wayne, to his loss.

She bent over the baby and placed a soft kiss on her sleeping forehead. "You'll be your da's salvation. He'll need yeh now more than ever."

She heard the compartment door open and looked up. Sage stood above her. Something had changed in him. She could see it in his eyes.

She had finally had a taste of what his pain must have been like. But what else had happened? It wasn't just the memories of his own tragedies that she saw in his eyes. It was something else. And it frightened her.

"How is he?" she asked.

"He needs some time. Can you watch Cora Mae until we reach Ogden tomorrow?" Sage seemed distracted. It wasn't Eleanor Rowe's death and its repercussions that occupied him. Kathleen felt a new fear growing in her.

"How are *you*?" Kathleen asked.

He studied her a long moment. "Why do you ask?"

" 'Twas nothin'." Kathleen shook her head to dismiss it. She was unwilling to pursue it now. There were too many other things to do.

"I've got to go back." He nodded in the direction from which he had come.

"Yes, yes of course." She turned to look out the window.

He did not move immediately. Kathleen thought he might speak of what remained unsaid between them, but after a moment he turned and left.

Sage and the others in the car wrapped Eleanor Rowe's body in a clean quilt. One of the women in the car had been bringing it as a wedding gift for her niece in San Francisco. Together they carried the body forward to the luggage car. There they lay it respectfully on two trunks. Sage had left Wayne in a silent vigil over his wife.

Now, he stood on the platform between cars. The late fall air had a nip to it, but he relished it. He breathed in deeply to clear his lungs and his head.

Morse Templeton's smirking face had been etched in his mind since their confrontation. It had pulled him away from the last few days and focused him. He had been foolish to think he could go on with his life with Templeton still alive.

Templeton's continued existence was an abomination, an affront to justice. First his brother and now Eleanor Rowe. The man was scum.

He knew now what he had to do. He tried not to think of Kathleen. He could no longer afford to think of her. They had no future together. Morse Templeton was his future.

Kathleen looked around her. There were no women in the car she now occupied. The baby had started to stir again. She began to panic. She bobbed the child up and down

211

and patted her behind. The later only managed to leave her gloves uncomfortably damp.

"All the saints, what does he expect me t'do with yeh, darling?" She looked down at Cora Mae, who looked back expectantly. When nothing was forthcoming, the baby started to cry again.

"Shhh . . ." Kathleen bounced the child harder, her face reddening as the baby's cries grew louder and louder.

"Shhh . . ." Kathleen implored, helpless as to what to do.

Kathleen's lap was wet and a certain odor had begun to emanate from Cora Mae. The child, as well as Kathleen, needed fresh clothes and some nourishment. The first Kathleen could do something about. The second she would worry about later. She rose from her seat and fumbled with the door to the compartment. She backed her way out closing the door behind her. She turned to find herself face to face with Sage.

"The baby . . . I . . . we need some fresh things," She mumbled self-consciously. "I thought maybe I could. . . ."

Sage looked her up and down, taking in more of the situation than Kathleen would have liked. "Well, 'Squirrel Tooth,' it looks like you've met your match."

"Well, yeh could help instead of standin' there." Kathleen feigned irritation.

"You've taken on a new fragrance as well, I see. Not one I can say would attract many men of my acquaintance."

"Yeh've a wide circle of friends then. I wouldn't o'thought." She shrugged. The baby continued to wail, but Sage's teasing helped restore her equilibrium.

"Are yeh goin' t'help then, or are yeh goin' t'let this poor child continue to cry?"

"Help, of course." Sage opened the door into the adjoining car. Kathleen bustled past.

For all her bravado, Kathleen had little knowledge. She prayed she wouldn't embarrass herself. She moved through the car to where Wayne and Eleanor had sat. A basket and a small suitcase still sat on one of the seats. Kathleen poked around the best she could with one free hand.

"Here, give her to me. You're not about to accomplish much with one hand."

Kathleen started to offer the wailing infant, but Sage stopped her. "I think you'd better hand me that blanket first." He nodded to a pink cotton covering that had fallen to the floor. Kathleen crouched and retrieved it. She watched as Sage folded it several times before laying it across his arms.

"Now." He held out the blanket. Kathleen lay the fussing infant onto the small comforter. She looked down on the front of her skirt. It was dark from the wet baby.

Kathleen searched for something to change the little girl. She found a clean soft cambric gown and matching shawl and an interesting button-front garment that resembled short pants. She held up the latter for Sage's perusal.

He nodded his approval. "I believe that's what you want."

"Put her here then." Kathleen patted the seat across from her. Sage laid the squirming baby down. Kathleen hesitated.

She looked up at Sage. He seemed to offer no help at all.

Kathleen began to unbutton the front of the baby's soiled gown. It wasn't long before she discovered the cause of the unpleasant odor.

Every button, every fastener seemed to be a challenge, but she struggled on, determined to set the child to rights. Every now and then she'd steal a glance at Sage, who seemed as amazed and intrigued as she.

At one point, Kathleen sent Sage to wet some clean rags she had found. It took her several tries to figure out the configuration of the buttons on the diaper but once she did she moved ahead with more assurance. By the end of the process she looked up quite pleased with her accomplishments.

The baby had quieted at her ministrations, happy no doubt to be out of the wet clothes.

"Yeh see,'twasn't that hard after all."

Sage looked over at the baby whose silence was clearly coming to an end.

"My hat's off to you. And what will you do for an encore?" Sage lifted an eyebrow.

Kathleen looked puzzled until she heard Cora Mae begin to wind herself up again. Kathleen took the child in her arms and began to bounce her.

"You're going to jostle the poor child's brains right out of her head. Give her to me," Sage ordered.

Kathleen felt her womanhood challenged. "I know exactly what I'm doin'."

Sage laughed. "Kathleen, you stubborn elf, you don't have any more idea of what you're doing than I do."

"I do, too. I do."

"Give her to me," Sage demanded.

Reluctantly Kathleen handed the squirming baby to Sage.

"See if you can find the sugar tit I saw Eleanor using earlier." He nodded back toward the small suitcase.

Kathleen colored. She didn't exactly know what a sugar tit was, but she surely knew what a tit was. And it wasn't a word a gentleman would use.

"For god's sake woman," he said, "it's a small cloth tied around a lump of sugar. It should keep her quiet until I can figure something else out."

Kathleen rustled around in the bag once again. She pulled out the article in question and offered it to Sage. He, in turn, offered it to Cora Mae, who calmed almost immediately.

"She's going to find out soon enough that it's not the real thing." Sage looked thoughtful for a moment.

"Do you have any unused gloves? Kid gloves?"

"I think I saw some in the trunk." Kathleen offered with a puzzled look.

"Go and fetch them. I'll take care of the baby."

Kathleen did as he requested, returning with a clean pair of soft leather gloves.

"Here take Cora Mae."

Kathleen watched fascinated as Sage pulled a knife from his pocket and worked on the glove.

"That should do it." He held the glove up, pleased with himself.

"I don't understand?" Kathleen stared first at the glove then at Sage.

"You can fill it with milk and use it to feed the baby. I saw several cows in the cattle car, second from last." He handed her the glove. "Just tie off the finger loosely until it's full. I'm going to check on Wayne."

Sage rose, the baby still in his arms and headed forward to the baggage car leaving Kathleen staring at the glove in her hand.

Kathleen had been gone a long time. Too long for Sage's liking. It was time to start a search. He rose from where he sat next to Wayne Rowe. Wayne had taken his daughter at Sage's insistence and now father and daughter seemed to find comfort in one another.

"I'll be back, Wayne. I want to check on Kathleen. She went to get some milk for Cora Mae."

Wayne nodded.

Sage moved his way through the cars one after another, looking for any sign of Kathleen. He reached the cattle car without finding her.

The smell of fresh hay greeted him as he pushed open the door into the compartment. The car had been divided into several stalls just inside the door. To the rear a large open place held several dairy cows. Kathleen did not seem to be among them. He couldn't have missed her, he assured himself.

"Yeh're not bein' the least bit helpful, yeh know that, yeh dumb beast?"

Sage smiled. He knew the voice and the attitude. He took two steps into the car.

"Yeh've got to give me some milk. There's a wee one dependin' on yeh." Sage watched as Kathleen hesitantly moved a hand under the animal's belly. The creature shied away.

"I think I'd give up if I were you."

Kathleen looked up exasperated. "If yeh'll leave me t'me business. I'll do jist fine."

"Just fine, eh? You don't mind if I back up a little?" Sage took two exaggerated steps backward.

"Yeh're actin' a bit queer."

He smiled broadly. "You won't think it so queer in a minute."

"Yeh never say what yeh mean, man. Yer forever babblin' nonsense." She turned again to approach the animal. As she reached out the animal backed away, obviously disturbed.

"She's not likin' this one bit. I don't know why the poor thing is in such a tizzy."

"If I might make a suggestion?"

Kathleen's face scrunched up. Sage knew she hated admitting that she didn't have a clue as to what she was doing.

"Suggest away." She half swallowed the words, as she turned to once more reach out.

"More than likely you're about to get your teeth bashed in. It seems to me that he's been more than understanding."

"And what exactly d'yeh mean by that?"

"If I had a woman about to touch my privates, I might get a little excited too."

Kathleen turned bright red. Sage laughed.

"It's a steer, you Irish leprechaun. No matter how hard you try you're not about to get any milk from him."

He saw anger brighten her eyes. He had gone too far.

"Come." He held out a hand to her.

"Come on," he urged when she looked reluctant. "I'll help you."

She took his lead and followed him to the back of the car, where several cows stood contentedly. Sage pulled a milking stool and pail down off their pegs on the wall. Placing the bucket under a black-and-white Holstein, he turned to Kathleen. "Come here."

She approached him hesitantly, her eyes still alive with indignation. He motioned toward the stool beside the docile animal. "Sit down."

Once Kathleen was seated, he sat behind her on the small stool. He placed his hands over hers and guided them to the udder. Slowly he showed her how to apply just enough pressure to retrieve the precious white milk.

The movement gained a rhythm. They pulled down, then down again.

Down, then down again.

Kathleen had changed her dress. She smelled once again of lilacs. He pressed himself into the fragrance and away from the recent horrors. He buried his head in her hair. It was only when he felt her sob that he pulled back.

"Kathleen?" he whispered in her ear.

She didn't answer but withdrew her hands and let them fall to her lap.

"Kathleen?" Again he spoke to her back, anxious now for an answer.

She sobbed again.

He rose and pulled her up after him turning her until she faced him. He didn't have to ask her what was troubling her. The tragedy of the day was written across Kathleen's face as clearly as pen to paper.

"Will yeh hold me? Please hold me."

He folded her into his arms. She sobbed quietly. Neither spoke.

He kissed the top of her head and hushed her. He tightened his hold on her, driven by some inner need.

Slowly, she pushed away from him until she could see his face. But she didn't speak.

"What is it?"

Her eyes spoke first. He cradled her face in his hands. "No, Kathleen."

He waited. He did not think she would voice what he saw in her eyes. But he was wrong.

She would not be dissuaded. "Will yeh make love to me?"

He dropped his hands. "You don't know what you're saying."

Her eyes were awash in tears. "I need yeh to love me. Here . . . now."

He wanted to tell her she was crazy, but he couldn't. The same life forces that drove her were driving him as well. Forget the wisdom of it. He needed it as much as she did.

He lifted her in his arms and moved to the far side of the enclosure, where he lay her in the fresh hay. He kissed her gently at first, but she responded with desperate abandon and he found himself responding in kind. He pressed himself tightly into her, his tongue desperately dueling with hers. He clung to her. They clawed at each other, desperate to affirm the fact that they were alive. Desperate to perform an act of creation in the face of death.

Sage reached down and ran his hands up Kathleen's calves and thighs bringing her skirt with them. He sat back. Kathleen's eyes pleaded with him to hurry. They followed his hands as he unbuttoned his pants and released himself.

He felt her touch him. She guided him down until he was poised at her moist opening.

He drove into her then. Again and again. The act was rough and unforgiving. He heard her whimper and paused. Suddenly aware of his own fevered brutality.

"No!" she objected. She arched against him and he plunged into her again, desperate for release. He thrust into her, eager to lose himself in her, needing to spill himself into her.

Repeatedly she lifted herself to him, returning his thrust with her own. Their breathing became ragged.

Eyes closed, they urged each other on, oblivious to all but the act itself. Sage moaned and his rhythm sped up. Kathleen clawed at his back spurring him on.

Kathleen cried out. Sage shuddered. Both of them were momentarily satiated.

Chapter Twenty

Kathleen lay spent, stunned by what had just occurred. She had never known lovemaking could be this way. Frantic and furious. Raw and primal.

Strangely it had calmed her. But something troubled her as well. It was something about Sage. He had seemed distant and lost to her. It was the same something she had seen earlier in his face. She couldn't put her finger on what it was, but it was there. She was sure of it.

"Did I hurt you?" His voice was troubled. He lay with his head on her stomach. She caressed his hair reassuringly. Neither had spoken for a long time after their frenzied coupling.

"No, yeh did not hurt me." She smiled. Hurt her? He had saved her from despair.

"Are you sure?" He rose on an elbow and cupped her cheek in his hand.

"I'm sure."

"I'm sorry." He lowered his head. "I shouldn't have . . ."

She took his chin in her hand and raised his head back up. "D'yeh know how rare it is t'get yeh to do what I ask? Yeh're not about t'see me complainin'." She smiled again.

He bent over and kissed her bruised lips gently, then rolled over on his back beside her and buttoned his pants. When he was done, he came back up on an elbow and smoothed her skirts down for her.

"Much more respectable." He nodded.

"Respectable, am I?" Kathleen laughed. She could only imagine what the grande dames of Boston Society would think of her now, rolling around in the hay with a murderer.

Then, for the first time, she realized she no longer cared what they thought. She only cared about what Sage thought and that, she warned herself, was a sure sign that she was completely losing her wits.

"Am I so terrible?" she whispered, only half teasing.

"Terrible?" He laughed. "You are a walking catastrophe. A leprechaun from hell. An Irish elf sent to wreck havoc with men's lives." Propped up on an elbow, his face within inches of hers, he smiled, and it warmed her from head to toe.

"Don't yeh think yeh're bein' a wee bit harsh?" Again she laughed.

"Well, you don't expect me to tell you the truth, to expose my soft underbelly, do you?"

She nodded in the affirmative.

"But, you see, that would leave me at a terrible disadvantage." He closed the small distance between them and kissed her again lightly. "And I suspect that it would leave me completely under your control."

"Would that be so bad?" She lifted an eyebrow in inquiry.

"At another time, in another place that would be delightful." He didn't give her time to savor his answer. Instead, he rose and offered her his hand.

When she was back on her feet, he walked back to the cow. "Grab the glove."

Kathleen retrieved it from where it lay in the hay.

Lifting the pail Sage filled the fine leather with the fresh milk.

"We had better get back to the baby." He was brusque.

He turned and strode ahead purposefully. She wanted to stay just a moment longer. Talk just a little longer, but she suspected he knew this and moved ahead anyway, almost fleeing from her. And it hurt.

"That's what yeh've been wantin' isn't it?" Kathleen watched as Cora Mae suckled at the glove's leather finger. It seemed an awkward substitute for a mother's breast, but it was doing the trick.

She looked up as Sage, and Wayne Rowe entered the car. Wayne seemed a broken man. He had aged years in the past hours. He walked with his head bowed and shoulders stooped. Sage supported him with an arm across his back.

"I've convinced Wayne to get something to eat. I'll go with him." Sage spoke quietly to Kathleen as Wayne moved on toward the back of the car. Kathleen nodded.

"Will you be all right?" He still had a look of guilt about him that left Kathleen with a feeling of dread.

"I'll watch over her for you, Mr. Callahan." An older woman, maybe fifty or so with graying hair and stout build had risen from behind and approached them. She had earlier offered the quilt for Eleanor's body. "Name's Bertha, Bertha Stoller."

Her face was lined from hard work and deeply tanned

from many years on the prairie, but there was a softness to it as well. It came through her eyes. They were warm and inviting. Kind, nonjudging eyes, Kathleen thought.

"It does my heart good to see you with the baby." The woman situated her girth in the seat facing Kathleen's. She reached out and softly caressed the baby's bare head. "Such a tragedy. Lost my own husband nearly a year ago now." She looked up, tears beginning to form in her brown eyes. "Thought it would kill me. But it didn't."

Quickly she changed the subject, shaking off her own sorrows. "You'll make a wonderful mother someday. I can tell such things."

Kathleen blushed. "I'm afraid I know nothin' about wee ones."

"Ah, but you do. See how you've soothed her? It's something inside us that teaches us." She laid a hand on her ample bosom before continuing. "I had eight children myself. Two died when they was just babies." She shook her head sadly. "The others have made their mother proud as a peacock. I got ten grandbabies. The latest not much older than this dear one."

Once on a roll, Kathleen realized the conversation-starved woman was not going to stop any time soon.

"I heard your husband say you wanted a whole brood yourselves. I can't tell you how wonderful it is to have a home full of children. The noise and confusion! The laughter!" She raised her hands and slapped her lap to punctuate her point. She started to laugh at private memories. The woman's laughter became contagious and Kathleen found herself laughing as well. For a moment the baby stopped nursing and stared up at Kathleen.

"You think I'm a bit daft, d'yeh not?" Kathleen spoke to

Cora Mae, who responded to the inquiry with a curious look before she went back to suckling.

Bertha Stoller went on. "It's nice to see a young couple just starting out. So much in love. I've seen the way he looks at you, dearie. Ain't seen that kind of look in a man's eyes since my own sweet Henry, bless his soul, and me was courting. It won't be long before you'll have a bun in the warmer, that's for sure."

A bun in the warmer? What was the woman talking about? Suddenly Kathleen made the connection. Her hand went to her flat stomach.

"Betcha you might even have one warming up even as we speak." Bertha Stoller winked.

"Oh no, Mrs. Stoller. I don't think . . ." Kathleen stopped abruptly, suddenly aware that what the older woman said might be true.

What had she been thinking to ask Sage to make love to her again? If she ended up pregnant, the fault would be hers.

"You can't tell me you wouldn't be happy as a puppy with two tails to be carrying his child." Bertha smiled broadly. "I've seen the way you look at him as well." She winked again.

Kathleen wanted to deny it. But she couldn't.

The thought that she might be carrying Sage's child thrilled her even in the face of the social disaster it would be. No matter what else happened, she would have a part of him.

"Ah, to be young and in love again." Bertha Stoller droned on and Kathleen was lost in her own thoughts, reluctant to remove her hand from its protective place over her womb.

* * *

"It's all my fault." Wayne Rowe had barely touched his food. "It's all my fault."

He rested his elbows on the small dining car table. His face was twisted in agony, collapsing even as Sage watched.

"No, Wayne. It's not your fault." Sage reached over and touched the distraught man's arm.

"If I hadn't persuaded Eleanor to leave earlier than she planned . . ." Wayne rested his head in his hands and shook it from side to side.

"It still could have happened. You don't know."

"No, and I'll never know, will I? How can I live with that?"

"You can live with it. You must live with it for Cora Mae's sake."

"But how can I live with myself?"

Sage knew only too well the man's despair. Until that night in the cave with Kathleen he had known no peace. There had only been the unspeakable torture of knowing if he had done things differently . . .

If he had waited to send for Victoria.

If he had stayed in New York.

If . . .

And the ifs had nearly driven him mad.

Now he saw a man faced with similar agonies, and Sage's pain was fresh again.

He needed somehow to reach Wayne.

"I lost my wife—" Sage caught himself, "—my *first* wife to a tragic death. I blamed myself as well."

He had caught Wayne's attention. "I didn't know . . . I just assumed that Mrs. Callahan was . . ."

"No, my first wife's name was Victoria. She was my life. She would do anything I asked of her. I was cocky and shallow enough to ask for too much.

"I'd had a fight with my father . . . a stupid fight. The kind that only the conceit of youth can support. When my father wouldn't listen to my suggestion, follow my lead, I thought he was arrogant, but I couldn't have been more wrong. I was the arrogant one. I thought I knew it all."

Sage shook his head thinking back on it now. "I cut all ties with a man who had done nothing but love me all those years. I fled to the West. To dreams of the riches to be had there. I would make my own life . . . my own fortune. I begged Victoria to join me, and she did. Against her parents' wishes, against all good reason."

He had Wayne's undivided attention, and he prayed he could save this man from the misery he had endured.

"At first we lived on hope and endured the hardships. But it was the bone dry summer of '74. The crops were failing as we watched the skies and prayed for rain. It was July when I saw the dark cloud on the horizon. Rain, I finally thought. We were saved.

"But we weren't saved. We were lost . . . utterly and completely lost. I knew it when I heard them. I've never heard anything like it before or since, and pray I never will again.

"It started as a low hum, but as it grew closer it was like hell had opened up and the voices of the damned, millions of them, were whispering their agonies.

"The sound grew, and Victoria had become aware of it in the house. She came out to join me. We watched, mesmerized and horrified at the same time, as the black cloud covered the sun, pitching us into strange darkness.

"They hit like hail, living hail that ate everything around it. It was an Old Testament plague that even the Pharaoh couldn't withstand. Locusts . . . grasshoppers. We watched them for two days as they destroyed everything we had worked so hard for. They didn't even spare the onions and turnips. When they left, the ground was pocked with odd holes. The horizon was bare of anything green.

"That autumn we had little to eat. Victoria grew weaker and weaker, but she wouldn't let me send her home. I begged her, pleaded with her, offered to take her home myself. She said we couldn't give up the dream.

"And then winter moved in with all its force, and I couldn't get her out. She was too weak and a winter storm had trapped us in our home, miles from neighbors, a day's ride from the doctor.

"I watched her die, slowly and painfully and I knew it was my fault."

Sage had told his story with little emotion. Now he looked up at Wayne. "I lived with that for a long time, dead to everything. Berating myself every morning and every night and a hundred times in between.

"And then I met Kathleen." He smiled and shook his head. "And she told me to close my eyes and imagine Victoria as she was now. Safe from any harm. Happy and wishing more than anything else that I would be happy as well."

Wayne had started to shake his head. It was too soon for him to think ahead.

"I know you find this hard to accept now. But you have to remember that Eleanor is safe and happy, for it will be your salvation."

Wayne reached out and touched Sage's shirtsleeve. It was all he could manage at the moment to indicate that he had heard.

His touch gave Sage purpose. Sage knew what he had to do. Wayne's sorrow only intensified his own anger. He could no longer selfishly abandon his mission.

"I know who killed Eleanor."

Wayne Rowe's face showed surprise. "Who?"

"His name is Morse Templeton. Eleanor isn't the first innocent person he's killed. Back in Deadwood, he killed my brother as well."

"Your brother?"

"After Victoria died, my kid brother came out west. He was only sixteen, full of promise and the need for adventure. We drove cattle. I was ramrod for the outfit. We picked up Templeton on the last drive. He had too much attitude for me, but we had lost a couple of men in a stampede and I couldn't be choosy.

"Halfway through the drive he nearly beat a man to death over a card game. I let him go. When we reached Deadwood he sought his revenge. Templeton and a couple of his men lured my brother outside of town and beat him to death."

"I'm sorry. . . ." Wayne murmured, now staring at Sage with open surprise.

Sage had to do something. "Eleanor's death was no more your fault than my brother's was mine." Morse Templeton's leering face rose up before him. "But there will be no justice, there will be no peace until Templeton is dead."

Sage put his hand on Wayne's sleeve. "And I vow to you right here, that he will be dead within the week."

Chapter Twenty-one

"Dear friends, we are not here merely to mourn Eleanor Rowe's death, but we are here to pay tribute to her life. For however tragic her death is, it is in her life that we find meaning. It was her love for her husband, Wayne, and daughter, Cora Mae, that she showed us the love of the Lord Jesus Christ."

Kathleen stared down at the plain pine coffin. There was something particularly painful about burying Eleanor here, so far away from family and friends. Ogden, Utah, was where the golden spike had been driven to complete the railroad. It was a thriving town, but it was not a place to be buried. It was getting cold, and winter would soon visit this place leaving the grave vulnerable to snow and ice and predators. Kathleen shivered.

Sage put his arm around her. He played the dutiful husband still. But something had changed. Eleanor's death had a profound effect on him. Kathleen didn't know why. Though he stood inches from her, he was a million miles away. She looked up at him. He stared at the bare coffin, and she saw something in his face that caused her to shiver again.

"Are you cold?" he asked, looking down at her.

"No, not really."

She felt his arm flex unwillingly behind her back, and she looked up to see what had forced this reaction.

A man was approaching the small funeral party. A man with a badge.

"We can go," Kathleen whispered.

"No, that would draw suspicion. We'd better stay."

They both managed to talk without actually looking at one another. But the tension had mounted.

"It is in Jesus's name that we commend the body of Eleanor Rowe to the ground. May she find a sweet haven in the arms of her Savior." The minister nodded to Wayne Rowe, who held Cora Mae. He bent down, picked up a handful of the newly turned earth and threw it on the coffin. Bertha Stoller followed suit. The kind woman had stayed behind with them to see Eleanor safely interred. They would all catch tomorrow's train.

They would all catch tomorrow's train. Kathleen prayed that was true.

Sage bent down and took a handful of earth. Kathleen followed his lead. They both took a step forward. Sage scattered the dirt in his hand. It hit the cold wood with a dull thud.

Kathleen felt like a vice had been clamped on her heart. Her hand tightened around the earth in her hand. Suddenly, she didn't think she could do it. She stood frozen in place.

Unwilling to let go of the soil and add finality to Eleanor's death.

She felt Sage take her arm, offering support. She looked up.

"You can do it 'Squirrel Tooth,' " he whispered.

It was the shock she needed. She threw the dirt. She watched it fall onto the pine coffin like holy water. Then she looked back up, tears running down her face. She placed her hand over Sage's on her arm, and she prayed. Not just for Eleanor but for herself as well.

"Do you folks mind if I have a little word with you?"

Sage cursed to himself. He had been so lost in thought that he had forgotten about the sheriff. Now the lawman stood blocking their way back to town.

"No. No, of course not, sheriff. What can we do for you?" Sage answered. He felt Kathleen tense.

"I'd just like to find out a little more about what happened on the train."

"Of course, if we can be of any help in capturing the men who did this," Sage said.

"Why don't you folks follow me to the jail, if you don't mind. It would be a might more comfortable than talking out here."

"Sure, lead the way, sheriff." Sage nodded toward the town.

Kathleen resisted slightly. Sage gazed down at her and gave her a look that told her he wanted no trouble from her. She resembled a frightened doe.

He remembered her quick tongue. She could jeopardize everything if she opened her mouth.

Sage studied the lawman as they followed him. He was a big man, almost as tall as Sage and considerably broader.

He was not young, but neither was he so old that he could be overpowered easily. Although his hair was graying, he exuded strength and competency. More importantly, he wore a Colt strapped to his thigh. Sage's hand went to his own thigh. He had removed his gun out of respect before leaving for the funeral. He had left it back at the hotel.

The sheriff's office was near the church where they had held Eleanor's service. The office and its jail were in a weathered building. A board outside was posted with notices. On it, staring back at him, was his own face. WANTED FOR MURDER, it proclaimed.

Kathleen must have seen it as well, for he felt her arm tense beneath his fingers. She stopped dead in her tracks, her eyes riveted to the poster.

The sheriff must have sensed something. He turned.

"It's all right darling. I'm sure it won't take long. The sheriff is a sensitive man. I'm sure he's more than aware of how traumatic Eleanor's death was for you."

What Sage voiced and what he said with his eyes were two different things. If she had one of her fits he would personally throttle her. That's if he lived long enough to reach her.

The sheriff touched his hat. "I'm sorry ma'am. Don't mean to seem heartless, but me and a posse are going to be headin' out later to find the men who did this. We need to know as much as you can tell us."

Sage studied Kathleen. She didn't speak for a moment.

"Of course, sheriff. Me husband and me will do anythin' t'help catch the men." She looked up at Sage. "Not to worry, darlin', I'll be fine."

Sage let out the breath he had been holding.

The sheriff turned and entered the office. Sage and Kathleen followed.

A small well-used desk stood to the left as they entered. The sheriff pulled two straight-back chairs up in front of it before taking his own seat behind the desk.

The right wall was papered with additional wanted posters. The likenesses leered out at them. A quick scan assured Sage that his face was not among them. Two jail cells dominated the back of the small room.

"How many of 'em were there?"

"Three." Kathleen offered.

"Four, I think." Sage countered.

"Any women among 'em?" The sheriff made a note on a crumpled paper in front of him.

"Women?" Kathleen asked puzzled.

"Yes, ma'am. We got word 'Squirrel Tooth' Sally might have been headed in our direction. I understand she's real wicked, that one. Mean as sin and ugly as hell." He looked up and caught himself. "Sorry, ma'am. Didn't mean to offend with the language."

Sage smiled. Offend the little hellion. Not easy to do. "I saw 'Squirrel Tooth' myself once," he offered pleasantly. "She was built like a mule and was just about as attractive."

The sheriff laughed. Kathleen fumed. But the look on her face was worth the risk, Sage told himself. For the first time since Eleanor's death, Kathleen Callahan was in fighting humor. This was good, Sage told himself. She would need it soon.

"Getting back to your question, sheriff, they were all men," Sage contributed.

"Did ya get a good look at any of 'em?"

"They all wore bandanas over their faces." This time it was Kathleen who spoke up.

"Anything about them or their horses that might give us a clue as to their identities?"

233

Kathleen looked up questioningly at Sage. He said nothing, and she responded for both of them. "By all the saints that're holy, I wish there were. Me da used to say there was a special place in hell for their kind."

"I'm sure there is, Mrs. Callahan." The sheriff nodded. "I've talked with the train's crew. They gave me a good idea as to where to start lookin'. With any luck we'll be able to pick up a trail and find 'em."

The sheriff looked over to Sage. "You're most welcome to join us, Mr. Callahan."

"Thank you, sheriff. But my wife and I have obligations in San Francisco."

"Well, I'll let you two go then." The sheriff rose from behind his desk and extended his hand to Sage.

Sage took it. "Good luck, sheriff."

Kathleen struggled to keep up with Sage. "As attractive as a mule!" She cried.

"Well, 'Squirrel Tooth,' be grateful they didn't have a picture of the notorious woman robber on their wall. No doubt the resemblance would have been noticed immediately."

The nerve of the man. He could be absolutely infuriating.

Since he didn't offer her his arm, she had to favor her bad ankle as she stepped up onto the wood-planked sidewalk on the other side of the street. His lack of manners only irritated her more.

"I doubt they would see any resemblance between me and that . . . that other woman." She blurted out, "The sheriff was so thick he didn't even see yer smilin' face peerin' out from the front of his own jail."

"That's because I'm definitely much more attractive in person." Sage smoothed his beard as Kathleen hurried to keep up with him.

"Attractive? Is that what yeh think yeh are, eh? I've seen a man or two in me life, and believe me yeh're not the cat's meow."

"And I've seen a woman or two . . ."

"I'll bet yeh have."

He stopped and turned. She practically ran into him. Yet again, she was nose to chest with him.

"Your sarcasm wears a little thin after a while."

She looked up at him. "Sarcasm? Yeh think, *I'm* sarcastic? Yeh're not a wee bit overstatin' the matter? If I'm sarcastic, what pray tell me are yeh?"

"Competent, logical, sane."

"Sane?" she questioned. "D'yeh know how close yeh came to gettin' yerself caught back there with the sheriff?"

"You yourself said he didn't seem too observant."

"But yeh're the one who brought up 'Squirrel Tooth.' Yeh were beggin' him to make the connection."

"But he didn't, did he?"

They had reached the hotel.

"Yeh're the most infuriatin' man I know," Kathleen whispered angrily as Sage opened the door for her.

"And you are the most infuriating woman I know." He smiled and bowed slightly as she pushed past him into the lobby.

"Mrs. Callahan." Wayne Rowe looked up from the camel-hair sofa where he sat holding Cora Mae. He rose and walked to her. "I was hopin' you might watch Cora Mae for me. The sheriff asked if I could stop by and talk to him for a minute about . . ."

Kathleen stopped him. "Of course. Of course. Don't worry yerself. I'll watch the wee thing." Kathleen held out her arms and took the sleeping child from her father.

"I bought a few things for her at the mercantile. Bottles

and such. I was hoping that maybe you would help me with Cora Mae until we got to San Francisco. I've got a sister there."

Kathleen stroked the sleeping baby's brow. "I'd be pleased t'help. Yeh can count on me."

"Thank you, Mrs. Callahan."

"Please, yeh must call me Kathleen."

"It would be an honor." He touched his hat. Kathleen watched as the man closed the door behind him.

"I been prayin' fer him. 'Tis a hard thing to lose someone."

"Yes, it is."

Something in Sage's voice caused her to look up. She felt cold again, despite the warmth of the baby pressed against her chest.

"Let me take that for you." Sage took the bag with the baby's things. Slowly, he followed her up the stairs and to the room they had arranged. Kathleen sat down with the baby on the bed. She was lost in thought. She began singing. It was the same Irish lullaby he had heard her sing once before. He watched as she rocked the sleeping infant.

He realized it was all too much to hope for. It had been from the beginning. They had spent a lifetime together in the last week, but yesterday the dream had come crushingly to a halt.

Seeing her bent over a child, he knew she deserved much more than he could offer. With any luck he could get out of town before the sheriff made a connection between him and the wanted poster that stared out onto Ogden's main street.

It was just a matter of time. And the more he delayed, the more his chances of success diminished.

He emptied his pockets and counted the money that remained. He should have just enough to buy a horse and saddle and a few other things. He returned the money to his pocket, picked up his gun and strapped it on.

Grabbing the hat he had bought in Cheyenne, he turned back to Kathleen.

Her eyes were wide.

She knew.

He wanted to leave immediately before she could say anything. But he owed her more than that.

He watched as she set the baby on the bed. Denial was written across her face as she turned to face him.

"No." She shook her head from side to side. It was all she said.

"Kathleen . . ." he pleaded.

"No, yeh cannot do this."

"I have to."

"Yeh don't have to do anything."

"You don't understand." He dropped his head, unwilling to face her vulnerability.

"What is it I don't understand?"

"The men who tried to rob the train . . . the man who killed Eleanor . . ."

She shook her head, puzzled.

"It was Morse Templeton."

He watched as understanding washed over her features followed by a new terror.

"Don't you see?" He pleaded with her for understanding. "I have to go."

"Let the sheriff go!" she demanded. "We can continue on to San Francisco."

"And what? Live as husband and wife? Always afraid that someone will recognize me, or that your husband will come for you. Always afraid that our life together will be shattered. You deserve better than that, Kathleen."

"No!" She took a step toward him.

"Don't, Kathleen. It's for the best. I promised Wayne."

"Promised him what? That yeh'd get yerself killed? Shot down by Templeton or hanged by the sheriff?" She took another step forward. "Wayne wouldn't want that. Yer brother wouldn't want that."

He couldn't listen to her. He had to leave.

"Morse will only kill another innocent person if he gets away. Do you want another to die? And another after that . . . and another."

She shook her head.

"Then you have to understand. He has to be stopped."

"But it's not yer job."

"Whose job is it Kathleen? I know him better than the sheriff. I know how he thinks. Where he'll hide."

"Tell the sheriff then."

"And risk getting caught before I find Morse? I won't do that, Kathleen."

She didn't say anything for a long moment. Finally, she put words to her thoughts.

"If yeh love me, yeh'll tell him."

He saw her love brimming over in the tears that filled her beautiful green eyes. How could he explain to her? She was so young, so unfamiliar with the cruelties of the world.

Her pain was palpable.

How could he explain it? It was difficult to form the words that would crush all her dreams.

"Sometimes, Kathleen, love isn't enough."

He fingered the brim of his hat before putting it on.

"Sage, let me come with you," she pleaded.

He nodded toward the sleeping baby on the bed. "You're needed here."

He walked the several steps to the door and reached for the knob.

"Sage, please don't leave me," she whispered.

He turned the knob and let himself out.

Chapter Twenty-two

Sage kicked the large bay horse into a gallop. The Wasatch Mountains loomed before him. He had chosen the quarter horse for its strength. It was compact and heavily muscled. His mount would need to have heart and stamina to keep him ahead of the posse that was forming in Ogden.

It was late in the afternoon, and Sage hoped to be well into the mountains before night fell. He had learned the sheriff's name in his inquiries. It seemed Dwight Franklin was not as slow as he and Kathleen had thought. Sheriff Franklin had been making inquiries of his own about Sage.

The livery stable owner had been a wealth of information. The sheriff was putting together a posse. They were planning to leave at first light tomorrow heading east into the Wasatch Mountains to Morgan Valley.

It was a good thing he'd left when he did, Sage thought. Good for him and good for Kathleen.

Kathleen. It hurt still to think of her and the look on her face of betrayal and defeat. He had warned her. He had never lied to her about his plans. If she thought she had dissuaded him, she had deluded herself.

He kicked the horse again and picked up his pace.

He needed to cross the mountains to get to Morgan Valley, where Templeton and his men had attacked the train and where the sheriff assumed they were holed up. As he climbed higher, the air took on a chill. He stopped long enough to don the buffalo-skin jacket he had purchased before he left. It was his only luxury—that and a small amount of food and water. It was all he needed. He had no plans beyond killing Templeton. It would no longer matter if the sheriff caught him. Nothing would matter after that.

It was long past dusk before he built a small fire and stopped for the night. He tried to sleep, but sleep did not come easily.

Kathleen stared at the food on her plate. She had no appetite. She hadn't cried after he left. Now, she was too numb to cry.

Cora Mae had cried for her. Almost immediately after Sage had left, the baby had become fussy. Kathleen was exhausted from trying to calm the infant. It was hours before the child had returned to sleep.

Now, with Cora Mae safely down for the night in her father's room, Kathleen had a moment's respite. She had ordered dinner in her room, but the food seemed tasteless. She gagged as she tried to eat the sad gray peas that lay beside a well-charred piece of meat, and then, finally, she wept.

Tears filled her eyes and nose, and sobs heaved her chest and made a low guttural sound in her throat. She pushed back from the small table and threw herself on the bed.

She had never felt so abandoned. Not even when Bret Merriweather had left; that had been more a matter of pride. This, this was more a matter of . . .

Of what? she asked herself.

The answer was too painful to acknowledge.

The pain of his leaving made her body ache. She felt battered and bruised, yet her body was whole. It was as if he had taken her soul with him.

The tears came freely now. Tears for Eleanor and Wayne. Tears for Cora Mae. And most of all, tears for herself.

She had never been one for self-pity. Anger had always suited her better. But tonight, alone in this room, miles from where she had begun her journey she felt despair for the first time in her life. She cried with abandon. She cried without regard to how she must look. She cried with the belief that her life was, without a doubt, changed forever.

Within minutes, she had cried herself to sleep.

"Mrs. Callahan!" The pounding on the door awakened her. Disoriented, she had no idea how late it was. She sat up on the bed. Her hair was in disarray, and her eyes were puffy with crying.

"Who is it?" Her voice was hoarse.

"It's Sheriff Franklin, ma'am. I need to talk to you."

Kathleen's heart caught in her throat. Sage! Had he been caught?

The sheriff's voice sent her scurrying to the washbasin on the small pine bureau beside the window. "Just a minute, sheriff," she called over her shoulder.

She splashed her face with cold water, then looked at the small mirror above the bureau. The water had done little to disguise her recent crying. The small lavaliere watch on the bureau indicated it was only a few minutes past eight. She had been sleeping for less than half an hour.

She attempted to smooth her hair but only succeeded in making it worse. Finally, she pinned the wayward locks firmly at the base of her neck.

She walked as calmly as she could to the door and opened it.

The sheriff loomed large in the doorway.

"If I could talk to you briefly, Mrs. Callahan." He doffed his hat.

"Of course, sheriff. Why don't yeh join me in the lobby?"

"If it's just the same with you, ma'am. I'd like to talk with you up here. I'll leave the door open."

He took a step into the room, and Kathleen had to back up to keep from being stepped on. She watched as he took in every item in the room, from the rumpled bed to her trunk beside the bureau. She prayed he didn't notice the lack of men's clothing.

"Thought I might find your husband here."

"No, sheriff, he's not here." Kathleen fussed with her hair.

"When do you expect him back?"

"I'm afraid I don't know."

"Seems he was traveling light." The sheriff studied the room again.

"Me husband's not one to need a lot."

"Clem, down at the stable, said he sold a horse and a saddle to a man who resembled your husband this afternoon." The sheriff approached the bureau and opened the top drawer.

"I wouldn't know a thing about that. Maybe if yeh told me what yeh're lookin' for, sheriff, I could help."

"Where'd you and your husband come from?"

"Boston." Kathleen walked over and stood between the

243

sheriff and the small bureau preventing any further snoop-
ing.

"Boston?"

"Yes, yeh've heard of it no doubt." Her sarcasm was not
lost on the tall man. Kathleen suddenly realized that she
and Sage had underestimated the man. She found hope in
the fact that it was obvious to her now that the sheriff didn't
know much more about Sage's whereabouts than she did.

"How long have you two been married?"

"About two months now."

"Married in Boston?" He walked to the window his back
to her.

"Yes. What are yeh suggestin' by this line of questionin'?"
Kathleen was tired of the man's roundabout approach.

"Your husband bears a striking resemblance to a cowboy
wanted in Deadwood for murder."

Kathleen laughed. "Yeh've got to be talkin' blarney to
imagine me husband a criminal."

"What should I imagine, then?" Sheriff Franklin turned
back to study her.

Kathleen needed to come up with something. The man
wasn't a dolt.

"Me husband's left me, sheriff." Real tears welled up in
her eyes. "I was flattered when he courted me in Boston.
He was a real gentleman's gentleman." Kathleen's mind
flew back to the first few days she had known Bret Merriweather. How long ago it seemed now.

"A man of good breedin' and status, he was. Yeh can tell
I'm not quite of the same social class." Her distress was real.
" 'Twas every Irish girl's dream . . . to marry into a society
that scorned her.

"He offered me a place in society. I offered him money.
I am a woman of some means, yeh see." She pulled herself

to her full height. "I didn't know the money was all he loved."

The sheriff looked a little surprised. "I've seen a lot of couples in my day. I would have guessed you two loved each other. At least that's what it appeared to me."

"The last few days have been tryin' on us all. The truth is he's left me. You don't leave someone yeh love." A sob grabbed her throat. She stared at the sheriff willing him to deny it. "I don't know where he's gone. I don't expect ever to see him again, and the better off I am for it."

"Sorry to have bothered you, ma'am." The sheriff touched the wide brim of his Stetson. He seemed almost convinced.

She needed to avoid any more of his questions. "If yeh'll leave me then."

Again the sheriff touched the brim of his hat and walked to the door. He paused for a moment before shutting it quietly behind him.

Kathleen stared at the closed door. She told herself she had not lied. Somehow the two stories had become intertwined so that everything she said was the truth. Everything that is, except being better off without Sage Duross.

"Are you ready then?"

"Yes, thank yeh, Wayne." Kathleen nodded to the young boy who had come for her trunk. "Here let me take Cora Mae. Did she sleep through the night for yeh?"

"Yes, ma'am. She slept real well. I just wish it had been as easy for me." Wayne Rowe's eyes were circled by dark rings and tinged by inescapable sorrow.

Kathleen laid her hand on his arm. "It will get easier, Wayne. Pain fades with time."

"Do you think so?" Wayne looked at her hopefully.

"It has to, Wayne. It has to." Kathleen prayed she was

right, not just for Wayne Rowe's sake, but for her own as well.

"Where's Mr. Callahan?"

"He'll not be travelin' with us."

Wayne stopped at the top of the hotel stairs. "Not traveling with us? Where's he gone to?"

Kathleen couldn't relive the pain of last night. "He's gone with the posse to find the men who killed Eleanor," she lied.

"Oh shucks, ma'am. He was talking to me about the man last night at dinner, Morse Templeton he said his name was."

The name once more struck terror in Kathleen's heart.

"Morse Templeton," she repeated fearfully.

"Yes, ma'am. He told me how he killed his brother. I thought he was saying those things just to make me feel better. I didn't think he meant to go after him. I'm so sorry. If I had known I would have tried to stop him."

Kathleen simply stared at the distressed man. She pressed Cora Mae tighter to her breast.

Wayne went on, "I had no idea he'd go off to find 'em himself. Oh, ma'am, I'm so sorry. I don't want anyone else hurt. Least of all you."

"Don't blame yerself, Wayne." Kathleen spoke with little intonation, her mind working frantically.

"But it's for me and Cora Mae, he's doing it." Wayne ran a hand through his hair.

Kathleen tried to console him. "Yeh couldn't have stopped him any more than I could. D'yeh not see that? 'Tis somethin' he must work out for himself. There's none of us that can do it for him."

The man mumbled on, blaming himself.

"Wayne. Wayne." She shook the man's arm gently to pull him back to the task at hand. "We've got t'get to the station.

The train for San Francisco will be there shortly. Yeh must do it for Cora Mae."

Wayne nodded and took her elbow.

Kathleen sent a desperate prayer heavenward. *Jesus, Mary and Joseph, don't let Sage throw his life away.*

Sage awakened cold and stiff. He restoked the small fire and rubbed his chilled hands to warm them. He had ridden hard and made good time. By late afternoon he should reach the Morgan Valley. Morse Templeton's leering face haunted him still.

But his wasn't the only face that haunted him. *It's not what yer brother would want.* Kathleen's urgent appeal was as fresh in his mind as the day she had made it.

But the little chit knew nothing of loss, nothing of pain, nothing of guilt. He had to kill Morse Templeton as much for his own sake as his brother's. He rose and threw the saddle on the quarter horse's back. His mount neighed in response. He patted the tired animal's haunches. "Not too much longer." He bent to buckle the cinch. When he looked back up he noticed a cloud of dust on the plain where he had been yesterday. A group of horsemen, six maybe, were headed up toward him. The posse was making good time. He had better move.

He saw the smoke long before he saw the valley. It trailed up into the cloudless sky like a paper serpent. He had been riding most of the day. His information had been correct. He had little doubt that the smoke came from Templeton's hideout.

Morse Templeton, he concluded, was either fearless or stupid. The man was arrogant enough to assume that he could handle anyone who might come after him.

The bay picked its way down the far side of the Wasatch Mountains, down into the valley. Morgan Valley was nestled tightly into the massive Rockies. Sage could see the tracks of the Union Pacific on the north end. The smoke poured from a deserted mining camp on the far side. A cabin and several small dilapidated outbuildings, their wood gray with age, clung to the rocky hillside. He would have to ride farther south to avoid being seen.

It was late before he finally had worked his way within shooting distance of the small enclave. The smoke had stopped long ago. The cabin was quiet. He saw no signs of life. Not horses, not men. He worked his way still closer. There were some signs that the bandits were still nearby. A bunk roll was propped up against the rough wood, and a water bucket showed the dark stains of having been recently used.

He situated himself within easy rifle range behind a large grouping of boulders and dropped to his haunches to await their return.

"Shit, did you see their faces? They were so scared I thought they'd pee in their pants. Heehaww!"

Sage heard them before he saw them.

"Morse, I got to hand it to you. You got some balls hittin' the train twice in two days." The first rider rounded a softly grassed outcropping. He rode at a gallop with a burlap sack heavy with loot held high above his head.

"Glory Hallelujah! We're gonna see us some good times now. I know a sweet little whore in Cheyenne that's gonna see me done real fine. Real fine indeed."

Sage recognized the last speaker. He was the one they called Lonny.

He trailed the original rider by a few hundred feet. Sage

now recognized the first rider as well, Harry Slag.

"Shit, look at this." Harry dumped the sack out onto the top of an upturned wagon next to the shack. The jingle of coins and watches cut through the quiet evening.

"Hey, this one here's real purty. Think I'll keep it for myself." Lonny stuck the pocket watch into his filthy vest pocket.

"Leave it!"

The order cut through the good spirits of the two already on the ground. Morse Templeton brooked no argument. Lonny removed the pocket watch and placed it with the others on the wagon.

"I'll see who gets what." Templeton swung himself down off his horse. He nodded toward Lonny. "You," he ordered, "get some grub going."

"But boss . . ." Lonny whined.

A fourth man whom Sage didn't recognize dismounted behind Morse and joined the other three.

"You heard what the boss said."

Lonny stared defiantly at the newcomer.

Morse spoke again, "We need to get some rest and hightail it out of here. I don't think they're gonna let this one pass."

"Yeh, Harry, if you hadn't killed that bony-assed conductor, we might not've upset 'em so bad." Lonny laughed.

"I told him not to move the train 'til we were outta sight. Guess he was hard a hearin'." Harry laughed as well, and Lonny snorted a reply.

"If you two had followed orders . . ." the fourth man reprimanded, but he was silenced by Morse with a raised hand.

"The law will be on our tails by daylight. We'd better be ready to leave at daybreak."

Morse walked over to the wagon and looked at the afternoon's take.

"Not much from that cheap bunch. I think we better look into something a little more lucrative, boys."

He pulled out a small tobacco pouch and rolled himself a cigarette. He lit it and leaned up against the building.

Sage had a clear shot. He realized Morse didn't even know he had killed Eleanor yesterday. Not that it would have mattered. He knew Morse too well. One body more or less would not have made any difference.

In the sights of the rifle his features were clear. Sage quietly moved his finger over the trigger.

He remembered the vacant stare of Eleanor Rowe and the battered body of his brother. This is what he had set out to do, and now was the time to finish it once and for all.

Sage's finger pressed against the trigger. Finally it would be over.

Chapter Twenty-three

"There you are. I've been looking all over for you, dear." Bertha Stoller bustled up the aisle toward Kathleen and the baby.

"Mrs. Stoller, 'tis good t'see yeh." Something about the woman put Kathleen at ease. Kathleen had always wondered how it would feel to have a mother. Never having known her own, she had tried more than once to imagine what a mother might have been like.

Bertha Stoller, even without an Irish brogue, seemed to fit the bill. Kathleen thought how nice it would be to throw herself into this woman's arms and lay her head against her ample bosom and cry her eyes out.

"You look a bit peaked, my dear. Are you feeling well?"

"As well as anyone can, I suppose."

"Yes, yes. This tragedy with Eleanor is enough to turn a strong man ill. Look at poor Mr. Rowe." She nodded to the

Joan Avery

far side of the train where Wayne Rowe sat staring out at the passing countryside with glazed eyes.

"Let me take the baby from you and give you a little rest." She reached out toward Kathleen.

Kathleen had been clinging to Cora Mae, as if to a lifeline. Somehow the baby assured her that life went on even after tragedy. She was desperately in need of that reassurance now.

Reluctantly she handed the child over. Cool air rushed against the warm muslin of her dress where she had cradled the infant. She shivered. She felt the abandonment all over again.

Mrs. Stoller cooed over the infant and then looked up. As if sensing a problem, she inquired, "I've not seen Mr. Callahan since the train left Ogden."

Kathleen was gazing out the train window. She shook her head in the negative, unwilling to lie again.

Bertha Stoller probed further. "Is there a problem, my dear? I know there's Eleanor, but is there something else?" She waited a moment and when Kathleen didn't respond, she went on softly. "Surely you don't have to tell me, I'm nothing but an old busybody. But I've lived a long life. Not all of it filled with happiness. Perhaps I can help."

Again Kathleen shook her head. How could she tell this sweet well-meaning woman the sad story of her life? Kathleen found it unbelievable herself. To find sympathy for her foolishness would be too much to ask.

Moisture welled up in Kathleen eyes.

Bertha Stoller leaned forward and touched the sleeve of her dress. It was a connection that broke Kathleen's silence.

"He's not on the train."

If Bertha Stoller was surprised, she didn't show it. "I see."

"He's gone after the men who killed Eleanor." She finally

looked at Bertha Stoller, her eyes awash in tears.

"There's no need to be shamed by your fears, my dear. But it is an honorable thing he's doing. It's not a selfish act to track down men who gun down innocent women."

Kathleen wished it were that easy. She resisted the urge to scream out that it was the most selfish act she had ever seen. She wanted Eleanor's killer brought to justice as much as anyone. But Sage wasn't the one to do it. Somehow if he did it it wouldn't be an act of justice but rather one of revenge.

"I remember how devastated I was when my dear Henry left for the war. I knew what he was doing was the right thing, but I was filled with fear, fear so great I thought I would die. But I didn't die, my dear, and neither will you."

Maybe that was the biggest tragedy of all, Kathleen thought.

"Stop it, girl." The sharp reprimand startled Kathleen. Bertha Stoller must have read her mood. "You can't go on feelin' sorry for yourself. It accomplishes nothing. Men do what they have to do. They don't think of the ones who are left to worry and weep. He'll come back to you, that I know."

Kathleen's heart warmed at the reassurance. "But how d'yeh know fer sure?"

"Nothing is for sure, my dear. But the love I saw for you in his eyes will bring him back. Don't you worry about that."

"But what if somethin' happens to him?"

"A man like your husband has been around a bit. I think he'll come out all right."

Kathleen wished she could believe that.

Bertha fussed over the sleeping baby before she continued. "Do you know how much you love him?"

Kathleen looked at Bertha Stoller puzzled. It seemed a

strange question. She never had thought about loving him at all until . . . Until when?

"Sometimes it takes a parting to let us see what we couldn't have seen otherwise." Bertha Stoller brushed the baby's soft cheek before continuing. "A man and a woman find their love not in the good times, my dear, but in the bad times. Trust me on this."

She caught Kathleen's eyes and held them. Somehow she offered a hope that Kathleen hadn't thought possible.

"And on that bit of wisdom, I'm gonna leave you for a moment. Got to go take care of some things." She nodded toward the privy and laughed.

Her laughter brought a smile to Kathleen's face. Kathleen didn't know why she should believe this woman, but she did.

"Wayne, think of Cora Mae. Yeh have t'move on with yer life." It was Kathleen's turn to offer hope. Her conversation with Bertha Stoller had pulled her from her stupor and restored her to a semblance of her former self.

"I know. But I didn't know how much I loved her. I've an ache the size of a barn in my heart."

"Yeh're entitled to yer sorrow, but yeh've got to think of the wee one here."

Wayne looked up at his daughter.

"D'ye not think she's fattenin' up a bit?" Kathleen asked.

Wayne smiled at Kathleen's enthusiasm. "She does seem well."

"Well? She's fit as a fiddle, that she is. She'll grow up to be a woman that'll break a man's heart in a second.

"Look at her, lookin' at her da with such big blue eyes. D'yeh not think yeh'll have to beat 'em off with a stick?"

Wayne laughed and Kathleen was encouraged. It was time to celebrate life, not dwell on the past.

"She'll be a girl after me own heart, that she will." Kathleen offered the baby, who was awake and alert, to Wayne.

"Take her. She's been missin' her da."

Wayne took the child, and Kathleen saw that with Cora Mae in his arms he was a changed man. With his child he had hope, a reason to go on.

"Did I not tell yeh about the time Michael O'Rourke decided to shower me with his affections?" Kathleen fell comfortably into storytelling. "He was a ruddy lad with hair that looked like it had been plopped on his head by a windstorm. He might have won me over, 'cept that he smelled like a cat that's been crawlin' the alleys for more days than he should.

"There was this day when he came sniffin' 'round with some o'his friends. I think he wished to demonstrate his affections, but I would have none of it. He chased me 'round the house more than once before he cornered me in me neighbor's doorway. With his friends urgin' him on, he went for a kiss.

" 'Twas his biggest mistake of the day. I bit down on his lip so hard he screamed, and with a swift knee to some more private places, I left him considerin' his manhood a bit tarnished."

Wayne laughed as he rocked his daughter. The baby, concentrating on her father's face, smiled.

"Yeh see." Kathleen nodded to the baby. "I think she's a woman after me own heart."

"Thank you." Wayne smiled.

"Fer what?" Kathleen threw up her hands with a puzzled look.

"For making me see how precious and important this lit-tle one is."

"We're all precious in God's eyes. Me own da taught me that. He also taught me how to gamble like a fiend and throw a punch like a man."

Wayne shook his head dumbfounded. "I would never have thought you were . . ." He shook his head, still smiling.

"Such a wild one?" Kathleen winked.

"So full of life, so full of laughter," Wayne continued.

"Me father used to call me his 'curse.' Yeh had to see the smile on his face when he said it. It was broad as the sky and bright as a rainbow." She thought for a moment.

"He was the light o'me life, me da. Me mother died when I was but a wee one like Cora Mae. But me da never let me miss her. He talked of her constantly, but always with warm laughter.

"Me da was as Irish as a leprechaun and twice as mis-chievous. One day he and some fellas of his were bent on celebratin' St. Paddy's day. Me da had made a fortune in the meat packin' business. He had faced the snubs and taunts of Boston Society his entire life. At the same time he wanted t'be accepted.

"He decided it would be me comin' out party. He got a ballroom at the fanciest hotel in Boston. He hired the finest chef to prepare the food. He sent out invitations to all the fine folk of Boston. And they responded to the last of 'em. Out of curiosity, I'd wager."

Wayne nodded. "He must have loved you very much."

"That he did. I've no doubt about it. He ordered me gown from Worth's of London, and when it arrived I felt like a fairy princess. I'd dress up in it every day and swirl around with a fella me da had paid a pretty penny to teach me to dance. We'd twirl and sashay, and I thought meself the queen of the county."

She stopped for a moment, a ghost of a smile on her lips as she thought of the pure ecstasy of those days.

"Then the big day came. And me da and his friends began to celebrate St. Paddy's day a wee bit early. We got through the early part of the evening with flying colors. The Boston Brahmins were all duly impressed although a wee bit skeptical."

"It sounds like a lovely time, Kathleen." Wayne smiled.

"It was, for ever so long, then me da and Michael O'Shaunessy and Danny Horrigan and a few of the others who'd been tipplin' since the sun first shone over Boston harbor decided it was jig time.

"Danny grabbed a fiddle from the orchestra and began to play a jig. There's no finer fiddler in all of Ireland than Danny Horrigan.

"And me da dragged Mrs. Colby Bryant Phelps out onto the dance floor and before yeh knew it there was a full-blown Irish drunk goin' on."

Wayne Rowe laughed out loud.

"At the time I was duly humiliated. The guests left quickly, but me da and his friends never really noticed. I should have known then that I had no place in Boston Society."

A broad smile crossed her face. "What I really never realized until now was how me da had everything right. He cared naught about what the others thought. He lived life t'the fullest and gave as good as he got."

She shook her head and laughed. Bret Merriweather, in fact the whole lot of them, suddenly meant very little to her. So much had happened in the interim.

She no longer cared what the people of Boston felt about her or her da.

"Me father tried to teach me to embrace life, but I was embarrassed for him. Now I know he was right, and it was the best lesson he could have ever taught me."

She looked over to Wayne Rowe. His face had lost its pallor. A smile touched his eyes and his lips. Life was meant to be celebrated. She had forgotten her da had taught her that.

"If yeh'll excuse me, I think I'll get a breath of fresh air."

Wayne Rowe became earnest all of a sudden. "I wanted to thank you, Mrs. Callahan—" he caught himself. "—I mean, Kathleen, for all your help."

Kathleen tried to dismiss him but he wouldn't be quieted.

"I don't know what Cora Mae and me would have done without your help. I'm sure Eleanor is smilin' down on you right as we speak, sayin' 'I told you, Wayne, she was good people.' "

Kathleen was touched more than she thought possible. She nodded her thanks and rose.

"I'm sure sorry about your husband, I never wanted him to go. . . ."

This time Kathleen quieted him by interrupting, "We'll be all right, Wayne. Both of us."

Kathleen opened the door and stepped out onto the platform between cars. She pulled her shawl more tightly around her. The train was still in the mountains. The air bore the chill of approaching winter. She inhaled deeply and held the breath for a moment before exhaling.

We'll be all right. Both of us. She prayed she had not lied.

She raised her head toward the heavens. The sky was clear and a myriad of stars shone overhead. Sage was somewhere beneath this same beautiful canopy.

Bertha Stoller had asked her if she knew how much she loved him. She had not answered the kind woman.

Her answer should have been, *Not until now*.

Not until now did she realize how much she loved this funny, obstinate, troubled man. Not until now did she realize how much she had lost in losing him.

She had never thought about love. She remembered her father's face when he spoke of her mother. How infused it was with joy and sorrow. As a girl, the complexity of feelings that shadowed his face was lost to her. Only now did she begin to appreciate the nuances and depth of his emotions.

She smiled. She had been a girl when she had left Boston. A spoiled, obstinate, petulant child. When she thought back on it she could hardly believe her own behavior. She didn't feel like the same person any longer.

She wasn't the same person.

She had enjoyed cheering Wayne up. She had enjoyed spinning her yarns. But she was no longer that open, that simple. Her hopes, her dreams, her fears were no longer those of a child. She had tasted love and she was spoiled all over again.

She had so much more to offer a man than she'd had when she stood at the altar with Bret Merriweather.

Sadly, she perhaps had lost the man to whom she wanted to offer her new self. Why did one always learn too late?

She closed her eyes. "Keep him safe, Lord. I will n'ask for more. Yeh know I love him." She smiled and tears made the night stars twinkle. "I know 'twas wrong of me, a married woman an all. But I ask yer forgiveness and ask yeh to protect him and take the bitterness out o'him.

"He's a good man, Lord. He's suffered terribly. I know Yeh're takin' this into account." She was tempted to bargain but caught herself.

"Teach me to accept what I c'not change. To learn from me mistakes. To be forgivin' of that scoundrel that married me. Show me, Lord, what it is Yeh want of me an' I'll do me best.

"Just keep him safe. Keep him safe." She crossed herself, and pulling her shawl more tightly around her, stared into the blackness of what was behind them.

Chapter Twenty-four

Sage slowly squeezed the trigger. The report of the rifle echoed wildly in the small valley. The single shot accomplished its goal.

Raising the rifle, Sage signaled the posse below. Sheriff Franklin headed a small group of five men.

Sage still didn't know why he hadn't finished off Templeton when he'd had the chance. Leaving Templeton to go and find the sheriff was a stupid thing to do. He risked losing the man completely.

Somehow the decision had to do with the Irish sprite he had left back in Ogden. The look on her face when he left haunted him still.

Sage kicked the bay and made his way down to meet the approaching men.

* * *

"Mr. Callahan." Sheriff Franklin nodded but said nothing more.

"I've found them. Follow me." Sage pulled his horse around and headed back into the hills. He didn't want to risk a long conversation with the sheriff, and the man's face told him he had plenty of questions.

He had ridden out just before dawn and found the posse within a few hours. With any luck Templeton and his men would still be where he left them. They were drinking heavily when he left, and he hoped they were boozed up enough to sleep later than they had planned.

It took them a good two hours of hard riding to reach the spot where Sage had found the gang. On a ridge above the camp, Sage pulled up.

The sheriff pulled his horse up alongside.

"They were holed up in that mining camp last night, sheriff. Looks like they might have left before we got here."

The sheriff nodded. Signaling the others to spread out, they approached the camp cautiously.

"Lookey here, sheriff." One of the first men to reach the camp had dismounted and now stood poking at a fire that still smoldered.

"Couldn't be gone more than a half-hour, hour at the most."

"We'll rest for a few minutes, then head out." The sheriff dismounted and tied his horse to the upturned wagon.

Sage dismounted with some trepidation. He didn't want to spend any more time with the sheriff than was needed to catch Morse Templeton. Suddenly, the last thing he wanted to do was get himself hanged. He didn't know exactly when his feelings had changed, but he knew he had Kathleen Callahan to blame. If she were nearby he'd gladly strangle her for complicating his life.

"Appreciate your help, Mr. Callahan. I'm a little surprised to see you out here. Thought you'd be with your pretty bride on your way to San Francisco."

Sage knew this would need some explaining. "I promised Wayne Rowe I'd find Eleanor's killer."

"Surprised you didn't join up with the posse. We coulda used the extra man."

"As you said, sheriff, I'm eager to join my wife in San Francisco. Thought I could travel faster on my own."

The sheriff nodded, but Sage knew he didn't believe a word. "Well, glad to have you with us now." The sheriff turned. "Saddle up, men. We don't want too much time to get between us and these bastards."

There was a murmur of agreement from the others as they remounted.

"Take the lead, Mr. Callahan, since you seem to have a special interest in finding these men."

Sage moved out ahead. Templeton and the others had made no attempt to cover their trail. Evidently Templeton's ego had prevailed. It would be his downfall this time, Sage swore.

About a half-hour out, the sheriff rode up beside him. Sage had been uncomfortable enough with the man thirty feet or so behind; now his discomfort rose several notches.

"Where are you and the missus from, Mr. Callahan?"

Sage hesitated for a moment. This was a test of some kind. Had the man spoken to Kathleen? If so, he'd be comparing their stories. If not, then it wouldn't matter what he said.

"Boston, sheriff. We're from Boston."

"Seem mighty familiar with the West for a man brought up in the city."

"I met my wife in Boston, sheriff. I had returned there after spending some time in the West."

"Whereabouts would that be?"

"South of here. In cattle country. Texas and thereabouts."

"Your wife's a real purty thing. Must want to catch this guy real bad."

"I told you, I promised Wayne Rowe."

"Still, to leave your wife like that . . . Been married long?" The sheriff scratched the day's worth of dark beard that covered his face.

"Not long." Better not to be too specific, Sage decided. He purposely leaned forward and casually patted the big bay.

"She looks like she'd have a real temper, that one."

Sage smiled. "I think that would be an understatement, sheriff."

"A real hellion, eh?"

Sage took off his hat and wiped his brow with the back of his shirtsleeve. He could barely remember his life before Kathleen Callahan. "She's a very remarkable woman. Any man would be proud to have her as his wife."

"Then I guess you're a pretty lucky fella."

The sheriff spurred his horse ahead. Sage studied the man's back. Had the sheriff believed him? Or was he just biding his time?

They climbed farther into the hills. The trail was becoming increasingly difficult to follow. Sage began to curse himself for not shooting Templeton when he'd had the chance.

"Let's take a break, men." Sheriff Franklin held up his hand to stop the group. They were in a narrow gap between towering rocky sides. They had lost the trail sometime back and were proceeding on instinct alone.

They had thirty or forty feet of level ground before the grass gave way to rocks and began to climb on each side. Sage scanned the hills above them. They seemed quiet, undisturbed. It was unlikely that Morse would double back to check if they were being followed, but if he had, this was not the place to be.

"Sheriff . . ." Sage approached the sheriff.

"I know. I don't like it any better than you do, but the horses have to rest."

The sheriff scanned the heights as well. He removed his rifle from his saddlebag. He shouted back at the others. "Charlie, set two men as guards." A tall thin man with a deputy's badge nodded.

"You know this man? This Templeton?" The sheriff didn't mince words. He continued to scan the hills.

"Yes."

"Has he killed before?"

"Yes."

"Why didn't you kill him when you found him?"

"Two weeks ago, I would have."

"Somethin' change since then?" The sheriff glanced over.

Sage once more took off his hat and wiped his brow. He didn't dare glance at the sheriff. He looked once more up into the hills, but they were quiet still.

"Everything's changed since then."

He was grateful the sheriff didn't ask him to explain.

They hadn't seen any signs of Morse Templeton or his men for more than three hours. It was late afternoon, and the sun warmed their backs. They had climbed still farther into the mountains. Tracking had become almost impossible. The ground was rock-strewn and hard. It hadn't rained in more than a week, and the chance of them picking up the trail in what remained of the day seemed to diminish with every hour that passed. The men had begun to talk about turning back.

"Regrettin' you came back for us?" It was almost as if Sheriff Franklin had read his mind. They rode side-by-side at the head of the small group.

Sage shrugged. He had regretted it for the last ten miles, if not before. Morse Templeton would be dead if he'd only had the guts to shoot him when he had the chance.

"I'd say she's worth it. Can't live on regrets, ya know."

Sage looked over to the sheriff. The man knew more than he was letting on, but he couldn't worry about that now. He still needed to catch Morse Templeton.

The shots came suddenly, without warning. They ricocheted off the surrounding rocks, covering their own trajectories. Sage saw the sheriff wince and then blood stain the right shoulder of his shirt.

Sage threw himself from his horse, dragging the sheriff down with him. Together they crawled behind a large boulder.

They had been on the right trail all along. Templeton and his men had either slowed or finally had the sense to check behind them. Either way, it was Templeton now who had the advantage.

"Are you all right?" Sage watched as the sheriff pulled out a handkerchief and stuffed it into his shirt to help stanch the flow of blood.

"It takes more than a bullet in the shoulder to stop me." Finished with his wound, he pulled out his gun but had to shift it to his left hand.

"Always knew I shoulda practiced more with this hand." He held the gun up awkwardly with his left hand.

Sage smiled. "I'll get the rifles."

Crouching low he raced out from behind the rocky protection. Rifle fire increased both from Templeton and the men of the posse as they offered Sage protective fire. He reached the sheriff's horse. Withdrawing the Winchester he tossed it the twenty feet or so back to the sheriff. He then pulled out his own.

"I'm going to try and get above them."

The sheriff nodded. "Take Charlie and some of the men with you. Charlie'll know which ones."

Sage nodded back. He picked his way back to the rest of the men. The tall thin deputy named Charlie spoke up.

"Me an' Fred'll head up that a way." He nodded to a small rise just behind where they were. "We'll circle 'round an' meet ya up ahead."

He signaled to a boy of maybe eighteen or so. The boy crawled forward to where they were. "Take Jimmy here with you."

Jimmy, his brother's name. In some ways the kid's fresh face and eager eyes reminded him of his brother. With that reminder came a renewed vow to kill Morse Templeton.

Sage nodded, then offered covering fire as he watched the other two make it safely out of sight over the rise.

"Well, Jimmy, here we go." Sage took off for a large cluster of boulders high and to their left. Jimmy followed. When they reached the position, they were able to determine where the gunfire was coming from.

At least two of Templeton's group were three hundred feet dead ahead, holed up in some brush and small boulders. The other two were higher on a crag overlooking the sheriff. They had Sheriff Franklin pretty well pinned in place.

"I'm going to try and get behind them. You stay here and keep them in place."

"My pleasure." A smile crossed the young man's face. He brought his rifle up and, taking careful aim, began to fire at the two in the brush.

267

Sage moved off, finding cover where he could. It took him a good five minutes to work his way behind the two who continued to return Jimmy's fire.

Even from behind he couldn't tell whether he had cornered Templeton or two of the others. He took careful aim and fired toward a flash of white among the brush.

"Shit! Harry, I been hit."

Sage knew the voice . . . knew the man. Lonny. Not too bright, but mean as a rattler in the sun.

"Shut up, Lonny! You'll get us both killed."

"One of 'em has got behind us."

"I'll take care of that one. You just worry about the one down there in the rocks."

Sage worked himself down the embankment toward the scrub that hid the two. Harry was a good shot. Too good. Twice Sage felt the bullet as it whizzed past. He was now within forty feet of the two. He watched the brush move and took aim.

The shot slid silently into the brush but within seconds the scrub pines began to shudder. Harry stood up gun in hand.

"Hell, Lonny, I think I been hit." Harry saw Sage and tried to lift his rifle. He got it to his chest before his mouth went limp and his eyes glazed over.

Sage held his gun ready. There was no need to use it. The man fell backward into the brush. Sage approached cautiously. There was no more gunfire. He knew Lonny had been hit. The question was how badly?

He was within ten feet when Lonny lurched up, his left shoulder awash in blood. Before Sage could fire, a shot rang out. Lonny stood motionless. Blood appeared in the corner of his mouth. He pivoted and fell face first on top of Harry. A rifle bullet suddenly visible in the back of his head.

268

Sage looked up. Charlie's long stride carried him forward. The gaunt man nodded a greeting to Sage.

"Thanks." Sage touched the brim of his hat.

"Don't mention it."

"Did you see the other two?" Sage could think only of Templeton. Where had he gone?

"They moved out before we got there."

Moved out. But to where? Sage knew Morse Templeton too well. He was not one to run from a fight.

The sound of gunfire had died, but not Sage's fears.

"I'm going back to check on the sheriff. Take these two back with you."

Sage doubled back. He kept alert for any signs of Templeton and the other one. He saw nothing. Nothing that is until he was within a hundred feet of the sheriff. He had followed the path Charlie had taken and it brought him out over the rise slightly behind the sheriff.

A man stood over the sheriff. The sheriff's face was ashen. His weapon lay beside his limp hand. The man who hovered over him did not care. He held his gun two feet from the sheriff's head and cocked the trigger.

Sage's shot caught the man in the middle of his back throwing him forward over the boulder that had shielded the sheriff. Sage rushed forward and grabbing the man pulled him back until he lay on the ground faceup.

It wasn't Templeton.

He crouched down to check on the sheriff.

"I told you I wasn't done with you yet, didn't I Duross?"

Sage heard the revolver cock.

He rose and turned. Morse Templeton was an arm's length away, his Colt pointed at Sage's chest.

"Throw the rifle over there."

Sage tossed the gun in the direction Templeton indicated.

"Now take out the Colt real slow." Sage debated as to whether he could get a shot off before he was killed himself. The odds were not in his favor.

"I said to take the Colt out."

"What? So you can kill me in cold blood?"

"I'll kill you any way I please. You've been a thorn in my side for too long." Templeton sneered.

"You only kill men when they're unarmed?"

"I kill men I don't like. And I don't like you, Duross."

"And my brother?" Sage was stalling for time.

"Your brother was just for sport." Templeton smirked.

The act enraged Sage. Nothing mattered anymore. If he died, he died. But he wasn't going to die without taking Morse Templeton with him.

He reached for his gun.

The barrel of Sage's Colt had barely cleared the holster when the shot rang out. The smirk had not left Templeton's face.

Sage stood paralyzed waiting for the pain. Maybe there would be none. He raised his own gun.

Templeton's face was frozen in the smirk even as he pitched forward into Sage's arms.

At first Sage didn't know what had happened. It had taken only a fraction of a second. He pushed Templeton away. The body fell to the ground. Suddenly Sage saw what he had missed.

A bullet hole, smooth and sleek and bloodless had perforated Morse Templeton's forehead.

Sage turned.

Sheriff Franklin's Colt, freshly fired, was in his hand. It pointed at Sage's chest and did not waver. A grim expression held the sheriff's features motionless.

"Now, Mr. Callahan, *we* need to talk."

Chapter Twenty-five

Steam from the train rose around them like mist in a forest. Kathleen looked down at Cora Mae asleep in her arms. It was hard to give her up.

Kathleen knew that even when the child and her father were gone she would still have a need of her own. A need for a child. She had never known how much love it took to raise a child. How much pain and sorrow. Her father had grown in her eyes these last few days. He had been a remarkable man, her da.

She only wished she had known then what she did now. About love and about loss. Perhaps they could have formed an even stronger bond.

"Are ya sure ye'll be all right, Kathleen?" Wayne and his sister Amy stood on the hazy platform across from her. A beehive of activity swarmed around them. There were hugs and greetings, tears and laughter.

"Yes, I'm sure." She offered the baby to Wayne.

"You know, dear. You can always come with me. I'm sure my niece would be more than happy to have another guest at her wedding." Even Bertha Stoller's motherly presence couldn't assuage the loneliness that had washed over Kathleen like a tidal wave.

"Thank yeh kindly, Mrs. Stoller, but I'd best be on me way. I've a thing or two to do here in San Francisco. I've already got a room booked at the Palace Hotel."

"Well, if you're sure, dear." Mrs. Stoller put an ample arm around Kathleen's tiny shoulders and squeezed. "You're sure your husband will be along shortly?"

"Yes, yes 'twill not be a problem. He promised me no more than two days lookin' for the villain. Then he'd come regardless."

"All right then. I'd best be on my way." Bertha Stoller gave Kathleen a hug that nearly took her breath away and left her feet dangling just above the ground for a moment.

"You take care of that young'un Mr. Rowe. She's gonna grow up to be a real beauty and the apple of her father's eye." With this the large woman turned and, barking orders to the young man who guarded her luggage, strode down the platform.

Kathleen watched as the woman bustled away, giving directions to the harried baggage man the whole time. She smiled. She would miss Bertha Stoller.

She turned back to Wayne and his sister.

Wayne Rowe still looked hesitant about leaving her. He looked to his sister for encouragement, and the young woman nodded. "I know you expect Mr. Callahan shortly, but if there's anything that delays him and you're in need of a friend, you can always call us." He nodded to the quiet dark-haired woman by his side. "Amy has written down her address. Cora Mae and me will be stayin' with her until things get sorted out."

Kathleen took the small card from the woman. "Thank you."

She was afraid she was going to cry. The lie that she had been living threatened to suffocate her. All these kindnesses. All these good people only served to point out her own inadequacies. What would they think if they knew the truth about her and Sage Duross? She felt as if she had betrayed them.

Tears welled up in her eyes. She bent over Cora Mae and kissed her forehead. Rising up on her tiptoes she kissed Wayne's cheek. "Take care of yerself and the baby."

"I will. Don't you worry." Wayne still hesitated to go.

Kathleen had to end it. "There are me bags now." She indicated a porter. "Amy." She extended her hand to Wayne's sister. "It's been a pleasure, fer sure. Take good care of 'em."

"I will," the woman responded earnestly.

Kathleen forced herself to turn and walked with leaden legs to the porter. "I need to get to the Palace Hotel."

"Yes, ma'am. I'll call you a cab. This way." Kathleen followed the porter through the vaulted station and out through the front doors. A soft moist wind lifted her red curls as she stepped out the front.

Before and below her lay San Francisco Bay. Dark and churning, it matched her mood. Several merchant ships lay at anchor. Agitated by the winds, their masts shuttered. Kathleen felt a shiver run down her spine.

She had come to find Bret Merriweather. She would find him and deal with him, and then she would book passage on a clipper ship home to Boston. It would be the end of it. She no longer cared beyond that.

"Kathleen! Kathleen Callahan! Is that yeh, girl?"

Kathleen barely heard the shouted greeting. She turned. Kevin O'Leary, an old friend of her father's, was waving like a banshee at the far end of the platform. "Kathleen Callahan! The saints be praised! Mary Kathleen Callahan!"

He came at her full tilt, his bowed legs carrying him faster than Kathleen thought possible. The last time she had seen Kevin O'Leary was five years ago when he had left Boston to seek his fortune in San Francisco.

His bright red hair and freckled face made him appear much younger than his years. He had to be nearly her father's age and yet he moved with a distinctly youthful gait.

"Kathleen Callahan! In all me born days Oi'd not bet on seein' yeh again."

The man's enthusiasm as he approached brought a smile to Kathleen's lips. Always scheming and one step ahead of the creditor, Kevin O'Leary now looked a new man. He was dressed in a finely cut suit and silk cravat, neither of which could hide his bandy-legged walk.

"What are yeh doin' here, lass? And where's your da?" He looked around expectantly.

Kathleen went to speak, but the man interrupted. "Let me look at yeh, gal. Yeh've grown into a fine lookin' girl, that's fer sure."

"Mr. O'Leary . . ." Kathleen attempted to interject.

"Don't be callin' me Mr. O'Leary, gal. I'm Kevin. Yeh know that."

"Kevin—" she started.

"Your da's not with yeh then? Ah, yeh've gone and gotten yerself a husband, eh? Not about to be waitin' fer the O'Leary then? Don't blame yeh. Not one bit." Once more he searched the passengers for a likely candidate.

Exasperating as always, Kevin O'Leary had barely let her get a word in edgewise.

This time Kathleen drew up to her full four-foot-ten inches and nearly shouted the man's name. "Kevin!"

"Oi've been goin' on a bit, eh?" The man looked appropriately sheepish. He worked the beaver skin top hat in his hands.

Kathleen smiled. "A bit?"

"Well, it's just such a surprise, seein' yeh, lass. What is it lass, yer da or yer husband?" Once more Kevin surveyed the surrounding crowd.

"Neither, Kevin."

"Neither? Surely yer not travelin' alone, then?" Once again he searched.

"I'm alone, Kevin. And if yeh go blatherin' on about it anymore I'll turn around and leave yeh right now."

"Don't do that, lass. We've got plenty o' catchin' up t'do. How's your da?"

"He's dead, Kevin. He died last year. God bless his soul."

Kathleen had finally managed to silence the high-spirited Irishman. His stunned appearance made her regret her blunt announcement.

"Dead?" He shifted on his short legs and lowered his head.

"Yes." She looked at his bowed head and remembered the many nights her father and Kevin had spent at O'Doul's pub. She had always liked the lively man. His presence in San Francisco was as much a surprise to her as hers was to him.

"Oh, yeh poor girl. He was a good man, yer da." He shook his head from side to side before looking back up.

"Yes, he was." Once more she smiled and was rewarded by one of Kevin O'Leary's broad grins.

275

"But what brings yeh here, girl?"

"I've come on some business, Kevin."

"Business? That sounds serious, lass. Yeh'll have to tell me about it."

Kathleen wasn't too sure how much she wished to share with this gregarious man, however much she liked him.

"Where are yeh stayin' then, girl?"

"The Palace Hotel."

"Well, child, let me see yeh there then. 'Tis the least Oi can do. And yeh can tell me all about yerself on our way." Kevin O'Leary offered Kathleen his arm.

"As yeh can tell, Oi've had a bit o'success meself. Oi'll have to tell yeh how Oi've found the pot o' gold here in San Francisco. It was only a matter of time before a man o'my worth would discover his true callin'. Kathleen, me dear, Oi'm a man of some substance now. Substance and position." The little man puffed up with pride.

Kathleen laughed. "Well I will be sorely lackin' in funds meself, if I don't find a telegraph office and wire home."

"Not a problem, dear girl, we'll stop on our way to the Palace." Kevin O'Leary extended his arm, all the while babbling on. Kathleen smiled and took the arm he offered.

"Charlie! Where've you gotten yourself to? I want to send a telegram to Deadwood." Sheriff Franklin fought with the pen and ink. His right shoulder was heavily bandaged, and he moved his right hand only with a great deal of pain.

He sat at his desk in Ogden. Across from him, Sage stared at his hands. Retelling the story of his brother's death yet again had exhausted him and doomed him.

Morse Templeton was dead, his brother was dead, his wife was dead. Hanging had always seemed a grim conclusion to his less than illustrious life, he thought bitterly.

If he had a regret, it was Kathleen Callahan. He smiled just thinking of her. She was irritating and temperamental, but when he was with her he had felt alive for the first time since Victoria's death. He had allowed himself to dream and to think of the future.

She had found his weak spot, and he had succumbed. Now it was all over.

"I'd like to send a telegram as well, sheriff."

The sheriff looked up, curiously.

"It's just that . . ." How would he explain Kathleen to the man without destroying her reputation? "I need to send a telegram to my wife. She'll be worried."

He wondered grimly if Kathleen Callahan had given him another thought. He had been prepared to be roundly cursed out in her fine Irish brogue.

What disturbed him was that she hadn't cursed him, hadn't been angry when he left. What haunted him were her eyes. Her beautiful tear-filled eyes. He needed to finish it for her. To tell her he was to be hanged. To tell her it was over. He would end it for her and she could go on with her life. It was a kindness she deserved.

"I'd hold off on sendin' that telegram. There's no need to rush into breakin' that poor girl's heart." The sheriff tried once more to write.

"Charlie! For pete's sake where has he gotten to?" Sheriff Franklin shook his head. "He's a great deputy if you can find him." He leaned back in his chair and studied Sage.

"Do you love the girl?" It was a strange question for the sheriff to ask. Curiously he didn't question the true nature of their relationship. Something in the lanky man's tone suggested that wasn't really important.

When Sage didn't answer right away, Franklin pressed. "Do you?"

277

"Yes." Sage threw away the response and moved on to what was really important. "But she has nothing to do with this." He nodded to the wanted poster that no longer graced the front of the sheriff's office but sat instead on his desk.

"She knows nothing about it," Sage lied.

"Funny, I find that hard to believe." The sheriff didn't elaborate. Neither did he indicate what he might do if in fact Kathleen had known that Sage was a wanted man.

"Does it matter whether she knew or not?" Sage sat forward in his chair and challenged the sheriff. "We didn't meet until after I had killed the man in Deadwood. That's all you need to know."

"Aiding and abetting a known criminal is a serious offense."

Sage ran a hand through his hair. "But she had no choice. . . ."

"How do you mean?" Now it was the sheriff who leaned forward.

What could he tell the sheriff? Sage wondered. That she was handcuffed to him when he escaped from the Deadwood jail. That would just further complicate matters.

"Just believe me. She had no choice. She left me the first chance she had."

The sheriff rubbed his stubble. "Seems it was you who was doin' the leaving."

The sheriff was right. He had done the leaving. "It was the best thing I could have done for her." Sage dropped his head into his hands.

"Charlie!" The sheriff bellowed again, with still no sign of the deputy.

"The sheriff in Deadwood's a friend of mine. He doesn't make mistakes. If he arrests a man it's because the man is guilty as charged."

It seemed the sheriff was going to talk him to death. Well maybe a slow and painful death is what he deserved.

"Good men are hard to find. Charlie's a good man if sometimes a little misdirected if you know what I mean."

No, Sage had no clue as to what the man meant. The sheriff hadn't jailed him, hadn't even handcuffed him. The only acknowledgment he had made after hearing Sage's story was to ask for his gun and rifle. It was peculiar and yet offered little hope since he was ready to telegraph Dead-wood.

The sheriff leaned back into his chair once more and, crossing his legs, rested them on the desk's heavily marred surface.

"Doesn't look much like you." Sheriff Franklin nodded to the wanted poster that now lay under his boots.

Sage didn't answer. He hadn't a clue as to what the man was talking about.

"I've seen a lot of them in my day." He gestured to the wanted posters that papered the wall to his left.

"You don't seem to fit the bill. Don't know any of 'em that would risk their own hide to save a sheriff."

"I told you before, Templeton had gunned down a young woman. He needed to be killed."

"You could of killed him just as well after he'd finished me off."

"But I didn't."

"No, you didn't. And that's what got me to thinkin'. That and that pretty thing you had with you."

Sage bristled. "What does Kathleen have to do with any of this? I told you, she knows nothing."

The sheriff ignored Sage's outburst. Instead, he tinkered with the bandage on his arm, then continued as if Sage had never spoken.

"I seen the way she looked at you. Ain't many a man that

gets that kind of love from a woman." Once again he rubbed his stubble.

"So I asked myself what kind of man you'd have to be to get a woman like that to love you."

"You have to understand, sheriff. Kathleen is a crazy Irish woman. Daft as a cat on catnip." For the first time since his capture, Sage smiled. All he could think of was her antics of the past month.

Ole 'Squirrel Tooth' had nearly driven him mad.

A vision of Kathleen scratching herself madly from poison ivy came to mind.

Dying of snakebite. *Could yeh pretend yeh loved me and kiss me?* she had asked with such innocence that he had felt obliged to comply.

Angrily recovering. *'Twas not me that said it was a snake bite. Pucture wounds, yeh said. Poison. Fangs,* she had retorted, her fingers forming distinctively attractive fangs.

Kathleen—her mouth stuffed with biscuits defying him to take one.

Kathleen—bluffing her way through a high-stakes poker game.

Kathleen Callahan—the Irish banshee, the Celtic sprite.

Kathleen Callahan begging him not to go after Morse Templeton. Not to leave her.

"Charlie! Where has that deputy gone!"

Sheriff Franklin's shout brought Sage back to reality. He let his head sink once more into his hands. The sheriff rose. He went to the door. "Charlie!" he bellowed once more.

"Yes sir, sheriff. Sorry, I was down at the livery stable tending to the horses."

"I've been yellin' my head off for over fifteen minutes tryin' to raise you."

"Yes, sir." Charlie followed the sheriff back into the office. He looked curiously at Sage.

"I need you to send a telegraph to Sheriff Davis over in Deadwood."

"Yes, sir."

"Well sit down man and write what I've got to say."

"Yes, sir." The deputy grabbed the pen and paper and sat at the chair the sheriff had deserted.

"Bank robbers dead in gunfight in Wasatch Mountains. (STOP) Sage Duross . . ." The sheriff paused and studied Sage once more.

"Sage Duross among men killed. Sign it Sheriff Franklin, Ogden."

"Yes, sir. I'll run down to the telegraph station right away." Charlie slammed the door on his way out in his hurry to accomplish his mission.

Sheriff Franklin picked up the wanted poster on his desk and crumpled it in his hand. He threw into into a nearby basket.

"I think this is settled then."

Sage rose in disbelief.

"I like to think I can judge a man's character, Duross. Don't prove me wrong."

A train whistle cut through the air.

"I believe there's a very pretty Irish lass waiting for you in San Francisco."

Sage couldn't speak

The sheriff opened a drawer and pulled out Sage's Colt. "This is yours."

Sage took the Colt and strapped it on, still dumbfounded by his good luck and the kindness of this man.

"Thank you, sheriff." He extended his hand.

The sheriff took it in his own.

"Now, go on man. You've got a new life. There'll be no one looking for you after today."

Chapter Twenty-six

Kathleen stared at the small piece of paper in her hand. It had been delivered to her earlier that day. She had moved it from table to dresser to bed and back again throughout the day. Now she set it back on the high bureau near the door.

She knew the address by heart. Number ten Mission Street. The irony of the street name was not lost on her.

If she had had a mission these last weeks, it was to find Bret Merriweather. Now she had found him. What troubled her was that she no longer cared. She walked to the window of her hotel room and stared out into the bay and the island that sat in lonely isolation there.

The mist hung low, and only the top of the island was clearly visible. Somehow hovering above the clouds, detached, without roots, it seemed to symbolize her life at the moment.

The Pinkerton man who had delivered the note that morning had asked her if she needed his services any longer. She had said no. She wasn't sure what she was going to do with the information, but whatever it was she would do it herself.

It had been two days since she had arrived in San Francisco. In that time she had barely left her room. She was drained, completely drained. She knew she had to make some decisions, but she kept putting them off. Hoping that somehow . . .

Somehow what?

She wouldn't have to make the decisions?

She was as stupid and foolish as ever. If she thought for one moment that Sage Duross would come walking through the door and sweep her off her feet and they would live happily ever after . . .

It was lunacy. He had always told her she was daft. Perhaps she was.

She needed to book passage home on a clipper ship. *Home.* There wasn't much left in Boston to call it home. Humiliation and ruin were her legacy there. Still, it was the only place she had left to go.

Her thoughts flew back to the afternoon before. To Kevin O'Leary's enthusiastic portrayal of California and the life it offered.

"Kathleen, me dear, 'tis no place on earth like this. There's no care if yeh've got blue blood or no. They care only for yer talents and them'll get yeh riches beyond belief.

"Look at this place here, Kathleen." He had gestured broadly. They stood in the drawing room of a home that was luxurious even by Boston standards.

"Who'da thought ol' Kevin O'Leary would one day be the proud owner of such a princely home and a thrivin' cartage business as well?" He proudly strutted around the room like a bandy cock, his thumbs hooked in the arms of his silk striped vest.

"Yeh must come down to me offices as well, Kathleen. Yeh c'not be sulkin' in yer hotel room the whole time. Oi know yeh're down about the matter in Boston, but there's another world, lass. One that cares nought about yer family and whether it came by way of the Mayflower or cattle boat. It cares only fer hard work and brains." He tapped his temple.

"Who would o' thought Kevin O'Leary would be the toast of San Francisco, a man of means and influence?"

Kathleen smiled. At least around Kevin there was no need for her to talk. He talked enough for both of them. She had told him about her father's death, and he had been deeply moved. She had also told him about Bret Merriweather, and he had sworn and carried on. Only after much persuasion from Kathleen had he promised not to track the man down and run him out of town on a rail.

"Oi've a treat fer yeh, lass. There is a grand ball Saturday next. Oi have me invitation right here." He handed the beautiful vellum card to Kathleen.

"D'yeh see who it's from lass? From Charles Crocker, it is. Only the richest man in San Francisco. His home sits atop Nob Hill like a castle, girl. The finest of everything." He approached Kathleen.

"Oi want yeh to come with me and see it girl. It'll shake yeh from yer doldrums, there's no question of it, lass."

"Kevin, thank you but—"

"There'll be no buts about it, girl. In two days yeh'll find yerself the toast of San Francisco. There'll be no regrets, no tears then." He took her hand.

"Promise me yeh'll accompany this poor old Irishman."

Kathleen couldn't say no. Kevin O'Leary's bright face and cheery banter had been a lifeline.

"I'll go with yeh, Kevin. But then I must be back to Boston."

Now, standing in her room watching the setting sun send flares of red, blue and violet across the deepening sky she hoped she wouldn't regret her promise. It was time to make decisions and move on with life. Tomorrow she would deal with Bret Merriweather and book passage home.

Sage leapt from the train. Even with the threat of rain, San Francisco bore all the marks of a vibrant growing city. He had seen it as the train had approached. Sophisticated and bawdy all at the same time, the city promised wealth to the ambitious and status to the wealthy.

His spirits were high. He felt as if a heavy weight had been lifted off his shoulders. He had been granted a new life full of promise and hope. A life he didn't intend to live alone.

He had to find her. He didn't care that she was still married. Divorces weren't unheard of. He would wait. He didn't care what it took, he would find the Irish hellion. But first he had to have something to offer her. A future.

"Can you tell me where I could find a telegraph office?" He had approached a porter. The man pointed. "Down at the end of this street, mister. At Post Street."

Sage's long strides took him to the building indicated in no time. He approached the lone clerk. "I'd like to send a telegram."

"Yessir." The bespectacled clerk nodded and picked up a pen.

"To Edward Duross Sr., Duross and Company, Washington Square, New York, New York."

"And the message, sir?"

"Have business proposal for you. STOP Are you interested? STOP Telegraph response."

"And how would you like that signed, sir?"

"Sign it Edward Duross, Jr."

"Yes, sir."

"Where would you like the response sent?"

"I'll wait for a response." Sage looked around for a place to sit. A single straight-back chair sat against the front window. "There." He nodded toward the chair.

The clerk looked momentarily perplexed. "But, sir. It could be hours."

Sage nodded. "I know. Just the same, I'll wait."

The clerk sighed. "I'll send it right away."

"Thank you."

Sage read the telegram yet again. He couldn't believe his luck. His father was in San Francisco. After all this time that they should both be in the same city at the same time seemed a harbinger of good luck. He folded the paper and put it back in his pocket. Now all he had to do was find Kathleen.

He had tried several respectable hotels with little luck. He debated on whether he should move up or down the social ladder. What little she had told him about her husband led him to the Palace Hotel.

He looked down at his faded dungarees and dusty boots. He looked up at the gilt letters that spelled out the name of the hotel. He watched the doorman hold the beautiful Tiffany glass doors as two couples—the women in Worth gowns, the men in formal wear—made their way to an awaiting carriage. He ran a hand through his long hair and unkempt beard.

Damned if he was going to let himself be intimidated. It

had been years since he'd entered such an elegant establishment, but if there was one thing he'd learned since he left New York, it was that clothes did not make a man.

He dusted himself off once more and raised each boot in turn to rub it against the back of his pant leg in a valiant attempt to polish them. It was no use. They'd have to let him in just the way he was. He hadn't worried about how he was dressed since he had left New York five years ago. He wasn't about to start now.

He approached the door and for a moment he thought the doorman might block his progress. Instead the man opened the door with a skeptical look.

"Sir." He bowed slightly.

Sage acknowledged the man with a nod.

The inside was more elaborate than he imagined. Aubusson carpets, Tiffany glass, French furniture, elaborately carved ceilings. It reminded him of the marble-fronted Fifth Avenue Hotel on Broadway in New York.

He was aware of his dirty boots every step of the way across the cream and pastel carpet. If he drew attention, so be it. San Francisco still had enough of a rustic charm that his presence shouldn't be too much of a shock.

The man at the front desk seemed to have seen him coming. He tapped the desk impatiently with his fingers.

"Can I help you, sir?"

"I'm looking for a woman."

"With that, sir, I don't think we can help." The man cleared his throat as if to dismiss him.

"Her name is Kathleen Callahan."

"Yes, sir." The slight balding man with steel-rimmed glasses made no move.

"I thought perhaps you could check and see if she's a guest here."

"Our guests, sir, guard their privacy and we respect that."

"She's expecting me," Sage lied.

"In that case, sir, if you could write down your request perhaps we could check and see if Miss Callahan is one of our guests."

"Can't you just check the register?" Sage leaned forward to turn the large book in front of the irritating little man.

The man grabbed the book and pulled it behind the counter. He furtively glanced first to one side and then the other side of the lobby. Sage looked himself. Two burly men in cheap suits and bowler hats were slowly approaching, one from each side.

Sage reached over and grabbed the smug little man by his shirtfront, lifting him up until he balanced on his tiptoes.

"I want to know! And I want to know now! Is she here or not?"

A hush fell over the patrons in the lobby.

The burly security men quickened their pace.

"Well, is she here?" Sage bellowed in frustration.

Kathleen had dressed for dinner slowly and without much enthusiasm. She was forcing herself downstairs to the hotel's dining room. She couldn't stay a recluse. It wasn't her style, she decided. If she were going to be a spinster the rest of her life, she'd better start preparing now.

She closed the door to her room in the dim hallway and heard some kind of argument coming from the brilliantly lit lobby below. She walked toward the light and reached the top of the stairs.

She grabbed the oak railing to keep from fainting. Below her was a sight she never dreamed of in any of her scenarios. Sage Duross was in a shouting match with the desk clerk. She wanted to laugh. She wanted to cry. She wanted to throw herself in his arms.

Relief sucked the strength from her legs and drained the blood from her head.

And with the relief came another familiar emotion.

How dare he put her through this! She would gladly strangle him!

"Jesus, Mary and Joseph. Look at yeh. Yer makin' a scene and a half, Mr. Callahan. Yeh're in the big city now, yeh'd best be behavin' better."

Sage knew that voice. That irritating, sarcastic voice.

The desk clerk looked past Sage. "I'm sorry, Mrs. Callahan. I didn't know he was your husband. He never identified himself. Had he . . ."

"Had he, I'm sure yeh'd have treated him much more kindly."

Sage smiled. He knew the attitude.

The desk clerk was distraught now. "Why, yes ma'am," he blurted, "had we known . . ."

Sage turned. Kathleen stood halfway down the grand staircase, her red curls pulled up into a rioting mass on top of her head, her green taffeta dress setting off eyes that twinkled with devilment.

Sage couldn't take his gaze off Kathleen. She was in fighting form. She hadn't missed a beat.

Yet she was paler than he'd ever seen her, and she held the banister as if it were a lifeline. He'd seen her bluff before, but this was the best he'd ever seen. He smiled. There was something in her eyes that challenged him to play the game just one more time before they both capitulated.

" 'Squirrel Tooth,' it's great to see you again," Sage

shouted for all to hear. He had become quite astute at playing her game.

Kathleen turned a shade of red just deeper than her vibrant hair. He wanted to laugh but couldn't. He wanted to take her in his arms and hold her tightly, to shower her with kisses and promise her . . . He still couldn't promise her a thing. Maybe it was better this way for a while longer.

"Such sweet endearments me husband has for me, don't you think?" she asked the little man behind the big desk as she descended the stairway, her hand securely on the banister.

"Yes, ma'am," the bewildered clerk replied. "Would you like me to give your husband the adjoining room, Mrs. Callahan?"

Kathleen had sauntered over to stand beside Sage.

The bespectacled manager looked up at Sage and then down at Kathleen with a great deal of anxiety.

"I fear me husband is in need of a bath. Perhaps yeh could arrange fer it?"

"Yes, yes of course." The man was more than eager to please.

Kathleen turned. This close she was nose to chest with Sage. She looked up. " 'Tis good to see yeh again, Mr. Callahan. After yer bath, perhaps yeh'd care to join me for supper in the hotel dining room?"

Sage doffed his hat and made a small bow. "A pleasure, Mrs. Callahan, a pure pleasure, indeed."

Kathleen fidgeted. She finished off the remains of her sherry and signaled for another. She didn't know why she was so nervous. It was what she had hoped for, what she hadn't even dared pray for. He was alive! And he was here!

Now she was acting like a daft twit. Why hadn't she just

thrown herself in his arms and blurted it out—all of it? Why did he always have this effect on her? Rankling her until she made an even bigger idiot of herself.

Get hold of yerself, lass, she warned herself while her heart beat so wildly she looked around her to see if anyone in the elegant dining room heard it. The other diners seemed unaware of her plight.

The formally attired waiter arrived with her second drink on a silver tray. He turned to leave, and she took a long swig of the second sherry. Her head was feeling light, but it helped calm her nerves.

She heard a murmur behind her and turned. Sage stood at the entrance to the formal dining room. She had not expected him this soon. His hair and beard were still damp. He had rushed. She couldn't prevent a small smile from slipping into place.

"I see you've made good use of your time." Sage nodded to the sherry.

" 'Tis no business of yours what I drink."

"Ah, but Mrs. Callahan, a husband would always want his wife to act in a decorous manner."

It was a challenge, and Kathleen was up for it. "Like her husband, I suppose yeh're about to say. Caterwaulin' in the elegant lobby of this hotel."

"The man was less than cooperative, *'Squirrel Tooth.'*"

"Yeh took yer sweet time gettin' here. Are we to expect the authorities anytime soon?"

"Ah, 'Squirrel Tooth,' I hate to disappoint you, but it seems the man they are after for murder died in a shootout with the sheriff of Ogden. A shootout that also killed Morse Templeton and several of his men."

"I see. 'Tis good news."

"Good news, indeed. Would you like another glass of sherry?"

"No, I don't think it will be necessary." He was driving her crazy. He was playing her game better than he ever had. He was a stubborn man. Stubborn and annoying.

"Would you like to order dinner?"

She couldn't take her eyes off him. To see him again, alive and free.

"Would you like to order dinner?" he repeated.

She no longer wanted to play this game.

"No," she said, lost in studying every plane of his face, every nuance of his expression. He seemed more relaxed than ever. More confident. The pain that had always touched his eyes and mouth was gone, replaced by something else. Something that set her heart singing and her body tingling.

He had grown quiet. His teasing mood was gone. He simply studied her in return. And she relished it. She felt naked under his gaze. Naked and desired. She remembered their lovemaking. The first time soft and gentle, the second rough and demanding. Color rushed to her face. Could he tell what she was thinking? She watched him watching her.

She could hear his breathing ragged and shallow. Her own was not much better. She lost track of where they were. She was only aware of where she wished they were. She could not say the words she wanted to say without knowing what he was thinking. She wouldn't embarrass herself.

It was an idiotic standoff. Their eyes met and spoke volumes, yet neither put words to their desire. Each waited for the other to speak. Each, suddenly, peculiarly shy in each other's presence.

How did you ask a man to . . . ?

The answer, she knew, was that a lady didn't ask a man for such things.

"Sage . . . ?" she ventured, frustrated and on edge.

He waited expectantly, but she could say no more. She just shook her head.

She reached for her glass of sherry. Getting drunk seemed suddenly like a good option. Her da would approve, that's for sure.

His hand caught hers.

"Would you like to go back upstairs?" he asked quietly.

She looked back up at him.

"Yes," she whispered. "Yes."

Chapter Twenty-seven

Sage pushed open the door into Kathleen's room. She moved past him. He could smell her, fragrant with lilacs and chamomile soap. He had had no right to ask her. But she had come.

From the moment he saw her on the staircase he had fought not to touch her. At dinner he had lost the fight. But now, he hesitated. Nothing was settled between them. They should talk. She had a husband. And he had nothing to offer her but himself.

"Kathleen . . ." Her name slipped off his lips quietly.

"Shhh . . ." She turned and silenced him with a whisper.

In the soft glow of the lamp, her red curls were touched with ripples of light and her flesh was as pale as porcelain. He took a step toward her.

"Kathleen . . ." He reached out and cradled her cheek in his hand. The touch sent a shock through him. She turned and pressed a kiss into his palm. Soft and warm, the kiss assaulted all his senses. He was losing the will to think.

She pressed another kiss and then another. Excruciatingly slow, she drew his index finger into her mouth and suckled it before granting it release.

He sucked in his breath. He was hard. Harder than he ever remembered being.

"Kathleen . . ." His breath was ragged. This time her name hung in the air as a supplication.

She closed the space between them and slowly began to unbutton his shirt. With each button released, she pressed a kiss. And when she was done, she pushed it back from his shoulders and began to explore his chest with her tongue.

He reached out and cradled her face in his hands. He should stop her. But he couldn't. Instead his hands, still cradling her head, followed her every movement.

Down to his belly and back up to lave the dark rings of his nipples. She suckled there. Desire ran rampant within him. He resisted the urge to act on it, finding in her ministrations a pleasure so intense that it was almost painful.

Her hand ran up his back slowly as once again she pressed kisses to his belly and chest. He could feel her warmth against him. The lamplight flickered, and he closed his eyes. Her eyelashes grazed his flesh, burning into it delicate trails of her passion.

He moaned.

She hesitated.

He buried his hands into her flaming hair, and she began anew. Laving his nipples and suckling them. Pressing kisses across his chest and slowly down his belly. She pulled away.

He hesitated. Then he felt her hands working the buttons of his pants.

"Kathleen . . ." he entreated.

"Shhh . . ." she whispered. Her warm breath against his belly gave him gooseflesh. He felt his erection respond, tightening, hardening. When she finally finished with the buttons, he felt himself burst out into the cool air, only to be surrounded by the warm moistness of her mouth.

The agony was so sweet he groaned with pleasure and entwined his hands more tightly in her hair. But he didn't pull her away. However much he struggled with the urge he couldn't. Her mouth on him, her kisses covering him, were ecstasy. He silently begged for more, his hands holding her tight while she offered him delights he hadn't experienced in many years.

"Kathleen . . ." He finally exhaled in capitulation and felt the release he had desired.

She held him tightly, her arms wrapped around his waist, her head pressed against his belly. She could feel his breathing, ragged and heavy. She was pleased. She had given him something in return for all he had given her. The warmth of his hands entangled in her hair, the way they had held on to her for support told her she had pleased him as well.

She felt him remove his hands, and she was disappointed. But soon his hands were under her arms lifting her back to her feet.

She looked up, a smile softening the corners of her mouth.

"So are you pleased with yourself, you little leprechaun?" He acted stern, but she knew him too well.

" 'Twas nice?" she asked him impishly.

"Nice?" He laughed, shaking his head.

Her smile grew broader.

"You think you're safe now, 'Squirrel Tooth'?"

She studied him. The smoldering look in his eyes gave her such an intense response that she trembled.

"You will not get off easy for this indiscretion, you little hellion." He grabbed her by the shoulders. "I'll make you pay. I'll torture you until you scream for mercy."

"Will yeh?" she asked, suddenly breathless. She raised her hands until she could cup his face in them. " 'Twould be nice."

He turned and pressed an ardent kiss into her palm. Then with little effort lifted her up and carried her to the bed. He lay her softly down on it. But didn't follow himself.

"Don't move," he warned.

She studied him, fascinated as he finished undressing. Sitting beside her to remove his boots, then standing to strip off his pants that hung loosely around his hips.

He stood before her naked. In the soft flickering lamplight he was beautiful. His chest was wide and heavily muscled. She watched his even breathing move it slightly. A soft trace of curls ran across his chest and then down toward his waist, tapering into the curls that protected his manhood, now flaccid. He moved with a grace that had always attracted her. In the dirty cowboy clothes he had always seemed slightly out of place. Now, naked before her, he seemed at ease, comfortable in his body.

His arms exuded a strength that she had often experienced. Taught and sinewy, they had held her and caressed her and saved her more than once. But it was his hands that intrigued her. They were far too elegant for a cowboy. Even roughened and callused by labor, their long tapered fingers moved with a grace that had always mesmerized her.

She remembered his hands running along her skin and warmed at the thought.

"What're yeh gonna do?" She suddenly could hear her own heartbeat quicken with anticipation.

He sat beside her on the bed. "I'm going to teach you the penalty for trifling with a man's feelings."

"Is that what you call it? I trifled with yer feelings, did I?" She smiled even as her heart beat wildly at the sight of him.

He slowly began to unbutton her boots.

"Yes, you did, 'Squirrel Tooth,' and now I must trifle with yours."

Her heart leapt with pleasure.

He had loosened her boots and removed them. He took one of her feet and began to massage it. Kathleen sighed with pleasure. But her breath caught as his hands moved up her calf and then higher, searching for the top of her hose. She shut her eyes. He slid the palm of his hand up the inside of her thigh and, despite its warmth, she shivered with delight. He began to roll the fine cotton lisle down with his palms. His fingers trailed behind, teasing her soft flesh. When he was done, he once again massaged her foot. She purred with pleasure.

He repeated the ritual on her other foot. Again the furtive movement of his hands up her leg left her wallowing in pleasure. She remembered the first time he had removed her hose. High in the mountains. She had suspected he had done it many times before. Now, she was grateful for his expertise. He was as sure in his lovemaking as he had been in so many other things.

"Roll over," he commanded.

She widened her eyes.

"Does you no good to plead innocence with me, you little elf, not after that performance earlier."

She smiled. He thought her skilled at lovemaking. That was good. But she had so much to learn. So much to be taught.

He began to unbutton the bodice of her dress, then her skirt and petticoats.

He rolled her back to her front. He rose and grasping the waist of her skirt began to pull it down over her buttocks. He paused for a moment, and she could feel his warm hands lingering for a moment.

She looked up to him.

"Patience, elf. Patience."

Finally she was free of the skirt and petticoats. He leaned forward and caressed her face. Slowly he ran his hands down her neck and across her shoulders. He brought the bodice of her dress with him as his hands slid down her arms leaving a trail of warmth in their wake.

She lay in her thin cambric chemise. But even it seemed a heavy barrier to what she wanted.

He let his hand run over her breast. The fine fabric only served to tease her flesh.

"You are very beautiful, sprite." He let his hand wander over her other breast, then down across her taut belly. "Do you know that?"

"As long as I am beautiful in yer eyes. 'Tis all I want."

He untied the ribbon at her throat and rose to remove her chemise. As he stood, she realized he was no longer flaccid. The sight of him hard and upright made her desperate to shed this last thin layer that stood between them.

He removed the chemise and with care laid it at the foot of the bed.

"Sage?" Anticipation made her moist and full.

He watched her with hooded eyes. "What, sprite?"

She held out her hand and he came to her, covering her with his body.

The feel of him stretched over her length caused her to tremble.

"Are you cold?" he whispered into her ear as he kissed it and caressed it with his tongue.

"No." She whispered her reply, burying her face in his long hair.

"Good." He slipped down to find her lips with his. Teasing first the corners, then the top, then the bottom, and finally he covered her mouth with his and let his tongue explore its depths. Urgently, fervently he paid homage. With kisses and small bites, his lips and tongue moved slowly downward. To her throat and then shoulder.

She buried her hands in his hair as he found the soft mounds of her breasts. He scooped the warm flesh with a hand and then suckled it and laved it. Her body tingled with pleasure, and her need grew, leaving the nave between her legs hot and wet.

She fought the urge to push him lower. She was wallowing in the pleasure he was giving her. Lost in his attentions. An urgency grew in her.

"Sage . . ." she whispered in need.

His answer was to move lower. To spread kisses across her belly and at the apex of red curls that led to her womanhood.

He played there for an eternity teasing her with the slightest downward movement.

"Sage!" she gasped. "Please." She implored, unsure of what it was she wanted.

He was between her legs, his head buried where they joined, his tongue finding entrance to the warmth of her womanhood.

She gasped, then moaned. It was ecstasy. It was torture. It was heaven. It was hell.

He increased his attentions, and she writhed in happy agony.

She twined her fingers more tightly into his hair, urging him on.

Her response only served to increase his fervor.

She opened her legs wider and groaned. She arched against him and her body convulsed, openly declaring her passion.

He moved up and lay his head on her belly.

He pressed a kiss once more against her hot flesh.

He came to his elbow and slid up her.

His face was still dark with passion. He rested on his hands and pulled his loins up. She could feel him between her legs, at the entrance of her womanhood. He was hard and throbbing.

Neither spoke. They were caught up in a passion that took them out of themselves and entwined them forever.

Kathleen felt like she was about to fall into an abyss. Yet she did not want to stop herself from leaping. She reached out and, grabbing his buttocks, urged him on.

He entered her. The feel of him within her made her gasp. He had stretched her wide and left her full. She reached out to touch his face. He drew one of her fingers into his mouth and suckled. She arched against him and he began to move within her, thrusting and then withdrawing.

She moaned and he bent over her and covered her mouth with his own. He thrust upward again.

Their mouths dueled even as their bodies sought union.

Kathleen arched again, and Sage drove himself into her. She felt as if she would be rent in two and wanted nothing less.

She clawed at his back, and he responded by increasing his rhythm. They no longer kissed, too distracted by the primal urges. Sage let out small guttural sounds and Kathleen shuddered, then convulsed.

Sage was still shaking his head, still whispering his satisfaction.

Finally he collapsed on her.

Slowly, both their bodies softened and relaxed.

"Kathleen, oh God, Kathleen, I'm sorry." His voice was still husky with passion or tears, she couldn't tell.

Tears welled up in her own eyes, threatening to spill over.

"Shhh, my darlin', 'tis nothin' to be sorry for."

She kissed the top of his head, and together they drifted off to sleep.

Chapter Twenty-eight

In the early light of dawn Kathleen reached out. He was still there. Warm and real.

She said a prayer of thanksgiving.

She rose from the bed and shivered in the cool morning air. She retrieved her peignoir from the wardrobe and covered her nakedness. She walked over to the bureau.

There was one thing she had to do. One thing that would free her from her past. One thing that would free her for Sage. She owed him that.

Hurriedly she dressed. Sage slept soundly, no doubt exhausted by the last few days. When she was ready, she walked over to the bed and gently kissed him. He stirred only slightly before he fell back into a steady pattern of breathing.

"Sleep well, me love. Sleep well."

* * *

"I'd like a cab, if yeh please."

"Yes, ma'am." The top-hatted doorman flagged down a hansom cab and helped her in.

"Tell the gentleman I'd like to be taken to 10 Mission Street, if yeh please."

The doorman touched the brim of his hat.

"Yes, ma'am."

Kathleen heard the man give directions to the cabbie. She sat back thoughtfully as the carriage moved forward.

It was funny how life changed.

"Ah, Da, forgive me. He's not rich and he has no claim to status, but I love him." She closed her eyes to speak to her father.

"Yeh made me promise that I'd only improve me station in life, Da. I tried t'do what yeh asked and failed miserably." She hung her head in shame. Then she approached her da in prayer the same way she had in life. Her da never had a chance against her.

"But there's more than one way to improve yer lot. I love him, Da, and he loves me the way yeh used to tell me yeh loved me ma. Surely yeh cannot find fault with that?"

She sat in silence, her eyes still closed. She waited for a response, sure that one would come.

As if on cue, the clouds broke and a warming ray of sun shone down on Kathleen. She smiled. "Thank yeh, Da. I love yeh, too."

The ray of light penetrated the lace curtains at the window and hit Sage square in the face. He rose up on an elbow. "Kathleen?"

When there was no response he scanned the room and called again. "Kathleen?"

With still no response, he threw his legs over the side of

the bed and pulled on his pants. He studied the room. The green dress had been hung carefully in the wardrobe. The room had been straightened, but there was no doubt that Kathleen was gone.

Had she gone down to breakfast? He walked over to a chair by the door. His shirt lay neatly draped over its back. He picked it up and started to button it.

A piece of paper on the bureau beside him caught his attention. He picked it up. It bore the printed address of the local Pinkerton office. His curiosity piqued.

The hand-written letter was short and businesslike.

Dear Mrs. Merriweather,
We are pleased to inform you that we have located your husband. Mr. Bret Merriweather is currently residing at 10 Mission Street.
If we can be of any further service, please do not hesitate to call on us.

Sincerely,
Arnold Beavy
The Pinkerton Agency

Bret Merriweather. He had chosen to forget about Merriweather. Obviously Kathleen had not.

He crushed the paper in his hand. What was the little hellion up to now? Was this all a game for her? Had she used him? Was she now going to reconcile with her husband? It wouldn't be the first time a man was blind to the sweet ploys of a woman. He dropped the crumpled missive on the floor, plopped onto the bed and angrily pulled on his boots.

After he left the room, the door reverberated behind him with the force of the slam.

"Yes, sir?" The front desk clerk looked up.

"I'm looking for my wife. Kathleen Callahan?"

"Yes, sir. I saw her earlier this morning. She asked if we could hail a cab for her. I believe she said she wanted to go to Mission Street. I directed her to the doorman." He nodded toward the elaborate front entry.

"Thank you."

"Woi yeh slimy bit o'scum. So yeh're the one that's hurt me darlin' Kathleen. Oi been wantin' t'meet yeh, yeh dirty piece of horse shit."

Sage whirled around to face a bandy-legged Irishman in a bowler hat with a face as red as his silk cravat.

"Oi've a bone to pick with yeh."

Were all the Irish in the country demented? Sage wondered as he stared at the complete stranger.

He had little time to ponder. The little Irishman threw a punch to his midsection that nearly doubled him over. Seeing the lunatic about to strike again, Sage delivered a blow of his own that sent the diminutive figure flying across the floor. The man lay momentarily dazed and confused.

Sage let out an oath. God save him from any more Irish!

Kathleen stepped down off the cab with the help of the cabman. "Could yeh wait? I don't expect to be long at all." She opened her reticule and offered the man a silver dollar.

The man tipped his hat. "Wait all day fer ya, ma'am, if ya'd like."

"Thank yeh kindly." Kathleen smiled.

The man tipped his hat again. "If I might offer ya a word. This here part of town ain't the nicest. I'd be careful if I was you, ma'am."

"Thank yeh again."

Number 10 Mission Street was a room over a saloon.

Hardly the place Kathleen would have expected to find Bret Merriweather. He had always stayed at the best places in town. Kathleen saw it as a bad omen.

She crossed herself. "Jesus, Mary and Joseph, give me strength." She entered the darkened hallway. A steep stairwell rose into the gloom. She could hear movement above. It was still very early. She had hoped to catch them before they went out for the day and she had.

She had little doubt that she would find Elizabeth Milgrim with him. She sometimes suspected that the woman was the one behind the scheme. Kathleen would happily strangle both her husband and his mistress, but that wasn't why she had come. She had come to get her money and to tell the lowlife she had married, Bret Merriweather, that it was over. The marriage had been annulled and that she never wanted to see him again.

She knocked on the door. There was a scurry of activity behind the door, and then she heard the lock pulled back.

She had not thought about what she might see when the door opened, but she was not prepared for the sight before her.

Bret Merriweather was a shadow of his former self. His eyes sunken, a filthy silk robe pulled around his thin body, he looked like a banshee from days of old.

"Kathleen, my dear. I knew you wouldn't give up until you found us." A smirk twisted his lips. "Please come in, dear wife." He stepped back and gestured toward the filthy room behind him.

Kathleen stepped in until she had cleared the threshold. Bret closed the door behind her.

"Make yourself at home, my dear." He moved toward a well-worn settee whose mohair stuffing could be seen in several places. "If you won't sit, I'm sure you won't mind if I do."

He sat and reached for a glass. The amber liquid suggested it wasn't any of the usual morning beverages.

What had she ever seen in the man? she wondered. His light hair was greasy and matted. Without the trappings of wealth he was a sad sight of a man.

"I've come for the money." It was the first thing she had said since seeing him. "If yeh'll give me the money, I'll not prosecute yeh. Yeh can go your own way without fear from me."

He did not answer her. He swirled the contents of his glass and took a large gulp.

A door opened to one side of the room. Kathleen barely recognized Elizabeth Milgrim. She stood bleary eyed in only a dirty nightgown. She had lost her health as well. The thin fabric of her gown clung to sunken breasts and a wraithlike frame.

Her hair, once thick and shiny, lay limp and stringy around her thin face.

"What have we here?" She snorted. "The dutiful wife?"

"Shut up!" Bret finally spoke again.

"Don't ever tell me to shut up!" Elizabeth Milgrim snapped.

"I'll tell you to shut up anytime I feel like it!" Bret got to his feet and turned to face his mistress. "You've got nothing, no one but me, and I demand that you give me respect."

"Respect?" Elizabeth Milgrim chortled. "You want respect?"

She turned on Kathleen, "You're the cause of all of this, you little Irish whore. If he hadn't gotten the urge to get into your tight little knickers we'd be living comfortably in Boston right now."

She turned back to her lover. "I'll marry her, you said!

309

We'll have enough money to live in luxury the rest of our days!" She slammed her fist against the doorjamb. "More the fool I, for believing you. I was as naïve as that one." She nodded in Kathleen's direction. "But even then we could have lived comfortably."

"Don't say it!" Bret warned his mistress.

"You!" She screamed shrilly at him. "You couldn't live with only the hundred thousand!"

"Shut up, Elizabeth!" Bret covered his ears.

Elizabeth only screamed louder. "You greedy bastard! You had to have more, didn't you? I told you they would take you for everything. You don't have the common sense of a jackass."

She turned toward Kathleen. "Take him if you want him. He's penniless, of course. He lost every cent he stole from you on a mining scheme in Deadwood."

She sneered. "But then you were always more concerned with status than money. Maybe you can reform him and drag him back to your precious Boston Society."

She turned and went back to the room she had come from, slamming the door behind her.

Bret was slumped once more on the settee. He took another swig from the glass. "There you have it, my dear."

His endearments made Kathleen's skin crawl.

"You see, I've lost all your money. Gone." As he held up his hands, the remaining liquid in the glass sloshed over the side. He looked at it as if he hadn't seen it before and finished off the remaining spirits.

"Where are my manners?" he said. He rose and moved to a small table in front of the dirty window that faced the street. He picked up a bottle of whiskey and refilled his glass. "Would you like a bit, darling wife? I believe I have another glass somewhere." He almost stumbled as he turned. His speech had grown slurred.

"I'm not yer wife, Bret. I asked for an annulment and received word it was granted."

"Tsk, tsk, tsk." Bret picked his way slowly back over to the small sofa. "You hurt my feelings, dearest." He beat on his chest in a mocking motion. "It hurts me to think you no longer want me."

Kathleen watched him, stunned by the changes in him, appalled by the life he and his mistress were living.

Kathleen was no longer angry with this sad man. She felt only disgust and pity.

"I'll not send the authorities after yeh. It was as much my greed as yers that brought us both here. Perhaps I should even thank yeh."

She had caught his interest now.

"Thank me, dearest? How so?"

"Yeh taught me how shallow me motives were. Yeh taught me what it means to marry without love. No amount of riches or status can compare to a man that loves yeh."

Glass to lips, he paused. "You talk like a woman who knows such a man, sweet Kathleen." He eyed her with a knowing look.

"Perhaps I do." She held her chin high.

Bret raised his glass to salute her. "To Kathleen Callahan," he intoned, "and the man who loves her, whoever he is. May they live a long and healthy life."

"Thank yeh, Bret, I'll believe that yeh mean it."

She turned to go. With her hand on the door she heard him mumble drunkenly, "May you both rot in hell."

"Ah, there ya are ma'am. Got a little worried." The cabbie climbed down and offered Kathleen a hand. "Did your errand go well?"

311

"Yes, thank yeh." Kathleen climbed up and settled herself in.

"Back to the hotel, then?"

She was distracted by her own thoughts.

"The hotel, ma'am?"

She looked up finally hearing the man. "Please."

The ride back to the hotel was filled with remorse and self-recrimination for Kathleen, but it was also one of new hope and determination.

Pride had never let her tell Sage about her humiliation in Boston. She had kept the truth well hidden from him. He had shared himself with her, flaws and all. She wondered what he would think of her after she told him about her sham marriage and her shallow reasons for it. Could he still love her?

The cabbie pulled up the horses in front of the hotel. Kathleen stepped down with the help of the doorman. She entered and crossed the marble lobby.

"Mrs. Callahan!" She barely heard her name.

"Mrs. Callahan." She looked up. The man at the front desk gestured. She crossed the floor to him.

"Ah, Mrs. Callahan, I'm so glad I caught you. Your husband was looking for you earlier. I told him you had caught a cab to Mission Street. He seemed upset. I hope I did nothing wrong."

Kathleen felt her heart rise to her throat. She didn't answer the man. Instead, she ran toward the staircase. She held up her skirts and mounted the steps as quickly as she could. The hallway to her room seemed interminably long. She reached the door.

"Sage!" she called.

She fumbled in her reticule for a key. "Sage!"

She fought the door lock. "Sage!"

The door opened to an empty room. She tried the door to the adjoining room. It wasn't locked. That room too was empty. She prayed then. Her heart beat so loudly in her ears she wanted to scream. She turned and walked slowly back into her own quarters.

That's when she saw it.

"Sage," she whispered despondently.

The Pinkerton letter lay crumpled on the floor, a sad testimony to her pride.

What a fool she had been not to explain.

Chapter Twenty-nine

Sage rubbed his clean-shaven chin and ran a hand through his freshly cut hair. It was a small concession to the world he had left so long ago. He had washed his shirt and dungarees. Nearly penniless it would have to do.

He knocked on the heavy oak door. He shifted uncomfortably, the only indication of his anxiety. The door opened.

"Yes, sir. May I help you?"

"Yes, I understand I might find Mr. Edward Duross here." Sage studied the butler. Impeccably dressed. English. Discrete. He was everything his father would expect.

"Yes, sir. This is his residence." The man was too well trained to show either curiosity or disdain.

"I wish to see him." The words made Sage's chest tighten. What kind of reception would he get from the old man?

When they had parted it had been in anger. Each irate, convinced of their own rectitude.

"Yes, sir." The butler stepped back from the doorway to allow Sage to enter. The massive marble-floored hallway was glistening with highly waxed mahogany walls. An exquisite eighteenth-century French bureau sat against the right wall. A small Limoges porcelain plate held the calling cards of San Francisco notables.

He stood there for a moment overwhelmed by his past. Daunted by the world he had happily abandoned. He fought the urge to turn and leave. But if he left, he would have abandoned his best chance of providing for Kathleen. He wouldn't risk losing her the way he had lost Victoria.

He had been stubborn and arrogant once. The last few years had beaten pride out of him, but Kathleen Callahan had restored it in a new way. She had restored his belief in himself. She loved him flaws and all. He didn't have to pretend with her.

Facing his father would be difficult, but he owed Kathleen this much.

He now knew why she had fled Boston.

"Oi'll see yeh hanged and quartered, Mr. Bret Merriweather. That Oi will. 'Tis a duty and a privilege to defend me sweet Kathleen's honor." Kevin O'Leary's unexpected flight across the hotel lobby floor had only silenced him momentarily. Before he was on his feet he was repeating his diatribe.

Sage had picked the man up by his cravat and half-carried, half-dragged the little Irishman up the stairs to the privacy of Kathleen's room.

"My name is not Bret Merriweather." He pinned the bandy-legged leprechaun to the back of the door.

"It's Sage Duross. What do you know about Kathleen Callahan? Who are you?"

"Oi thought yeh was her husband, yeh see. The other one." Kevin O'Leary was clearly confused but not put off. "Yeh said yeh were lookin' for your wife, Kathleen Callahan, did yeh not?"

Sage was not about to jeopardize Kathleen's reputation by responding.

"Who the hell are you?" he demanded with a shake that sent the Irishman's head banging against the door.

"Me name's O'Leary, sir. Kevin O'Leary that is. Cartage is me game."

"How do you know Kathleen?" Sage released his grip enough that Kevin O'Leary's feet could once more touch the ground.

"I'm a dear and lovin' friend of 'er father, God rest his soul." O'Leary signed himself.

"The poor lass told me 'er sorry tale. She's been done dirty, that she has. And I intend to see right by 'er."

"What has she told you about me?"

"Naught about you. 'Twas the other one that broke her heart."

Broke her heart? What was the man babbling on about? Was it true then? Did she still love her husband? The gutwrenching thought nearly paralyzed him.

"I want to know everything you know. Everything. Do you understand me?"

Half an hour later Sage knew all about Kathleen's catastrophic marriage and the subsequent annulment. He wanted to throttle her and console her all at once. But before he could do either he needed to see his father.

If she had gone after Bret Merriweather she was only going to be hurt more. He had a chance to offer her a new

316

and better life and he would do anything to secure it.

"Sir."

Sage barely heard the man.

"Sir?" the butler repeated.

"Yes?"

"Who may I say is calling?"

"Tell Mr. Duross it's an old friend."

"Yes, sir." The man nodded and proceeded down the hall to a double set of doors on the right. Opening them, he disappeared inside.

He was gone for what seemed an eternity. When he reappeared he showed no sign of what had transpired inside the room.

"You may go in." The butler nodded to the half-open door of the room he had just left, then discretely disappeared.

Sage walked slowly toward the door. He couldn't see anyone in the room. He pushed the door open farther and stepped in.

His father stood with his back toward him behind a large ornately carved desk. He was reading something in the light of the window before him. His hair was whiter than when Sage had last seen him. His broad shoulders were unbowed by age. The fabric and fine cut of his jacket suggested he was still favoring his London tailor.

Sage was shaken more than he had thought possible. He stood quietly, unwilling to disturb the moment.

It was a few more moments until his father had finished his reading. He turned slowly, his eyes still on a telegram in his hands. Finally, he looked up.

His face was more lined, his eyes more sunken.

He opened his mouth to speak. At first there was nothing. Then Sage heard his father's familiar voice, heavy with emotion. "They telegraphed that you were trying to find me."

The telegram in his father's hands slipped away and floated down to the floor. "I didn't want to believe it." His father's eyes glistened, his voice when he spoke again broke. "False hope is an old man's downfall."

"I'm sorry to cause you pain, Father."

"Pain? When have you ever caused me pain?" The father searched his son's face.

"We argued. We both said things we wish we hadn't." Sage shook his head. He couldn't look at his father. Emotions were too close to the surface, threatening his equilibrium.

"An ardent exchange of ideas . . . I never expected that you would leave, that. . . ." His father's voice broke. Sage looked up. Tears ran down the older man's cheeks.

"I never thought . . ." His father tried again to speak, again without success.

He took a moment to pull himself together. Stepping out from behind the desk, he cleared his throat.

"You look well, son." His father attempted to smile, but it was strained. Other emotions seemed to be overwhelming him.

His father stood but a few feet away now. He waited.

"Father, I'm sorry."

"No . . . no . . . don't say that. There is nothing to be sorry about." His father closed the two paces between them and embraced him.

Sage returned the embrace. His father's body shook with his tears. Sage held the older man closely and shut his own eyes tightly. God help him. He had been a fool to remain estranged all these years. Why had he thought his father wouldn't forgive him?

His anger with himself had led him to believe that no one

could love him. First Kathleen had proved him wrong, and now his father.

"The men who killed Jimmy are dead," he offered, patting his father's back. The older man drew up and back.

"You would have been welcome back without that."

"I know that now. It was just something I had to see to, for Jimmy."

"Did you kill them?"

"No." Sage told only part of the truth. "A sheriff's posse out of Ogden killed them."

"I'm glad it wasn't you." His father had removed a handkerchief and dabbed at his eyes.

"Father, I have a favor to ask of you."

"What is it, son?" The older man looked back at his offspring.

"I need a job. I thought maybe I could work in one of your warehouses or at the docks."

"No!" His father responded angrily shaking his head.

Sage was taken aback by the forceful response. He turned and walked toward bookcases on the far side of the room. "I'm sorry. I shouldn't have asked. It just that there's someone . . ." He let the sentence trail off. Surely after that heated response his father wouldn't want to hear about anyone he loved.

"I won't give you a job in the warehouse or on the docks! You have the brightest mind of anyone I know. I won't waste it on some menial work!"

Sage turned around. He had misunderstood. His father's face was alight with excitement. "Did they tell you why I was here?" he demanded.

Sage shook his head puzzled. "No, why?"

"You remember what we fought about? About your great

319

scheme to tap into the agricultural resources of California's central valley?"

It had been a long time, but the argument was as fresh in Sage's mind as if it had been yesterday.

"That's why I've been here these last few months," his father continued. "It was a good idea, a valid one. I was just too stubborn to see it. I think I let my pride get in the way of good thinking. After you left, I blamed myself and my pride for driving you away."

His father ran a hand through his hair in a familiar manner. "I left your idea in limbo until last year. I made some contacts here in California. I ran your idea by them. Making it work seemed suddenly viable. Within a few months we could be shipping the finest fresh grain and produce to the East Coast." He paused a moment to let Sage absorb all the information.

"I need your assistance, son. There are people here who can help us make it work. Once it's up and running, someone will have to supervise the entire operation from Sacramento. I thought perhaps that someone could be you."

Sacramento, Sage thought. The train had made a stop there on the way to San Francisco. He remembered the lushness of the valley and the beauty of the surrounding mountains. It had made an impression on him. It had made him think of Kathleen. It was the kind of place a man could raise a family.

"You have to come to Charles Crocker's tomorrow night. Made his money in the railroads. I've already talked to him about using his trains to move our goods east. Several other influential men who might prove helpful in our project will be there as well. In fact, I hear that there is an heiress to a meat-packing fortune from Boston just arrived in town. Crocker has arranged for her to come. Might be a good contact for the future. She's a feisty one I've heard. Irish you know. Seems she married badly and has chased her husband clear across the country seeking some sort of redress. Nothing you can't handle though. You were always good with the ladies. Will you come then, son?"

Sage smiled. "I'll attend with pleasure, Father. With pleasure."

Kathleen's despondency had turned to efficiency. She had booked her passage home on a clipper ship leaving for Boston the following week. In the meantime she had gone out and made some purchases. She had lived without luxuries for so long it seemed almost decadent to spend money on the fine soaps and perfumes she had been accustomed to in Boston. She had found solace in shopping. She stopped at the best dressmakers in town and ordered several new dresses to take home with her. She visited parks and galleries with Kevin O'Leary. She did everything she could to keep from thinking—to keep from hoping.

"Well, lass are yeh goin' or not?" Kevin O'Leary asked as he sat across from her in the small tea shop.

"I told yeh I'd go, Kevin, yeh daft Irishman. And I'll keep me word on it."

"Fine. Fine. It's just that yeh've been so jumpy lately. Oi thought yeh might have changed yehr mind."

"No, I haven't changed me mind."

"What's a troublin' yeh then, lass?"

Kathleen threw up her hands. The man wouldn't leave her alone.

"Kevin, 'tis nothin', nothin' at all."

"Oi likes t'think o'meself as your da now that he's gone, bless his soul." Kevin crossed himself for the tenth time since they'd been out.

Joan Avery

Kathleen wanted to scream. But she told herself the little Irishman only meant well. At least his constant talking left her with no requirement to speak.

"Who is this man, this Charles Crocker?"

"Who is he? Lass, he's only the richest man in San Francisco. Made a fortune in the railroads."

"Yeh know Kevin, those things once impressed me, but no longer."

"But yeh must, think o'your father's business now. Yer sudden loss of capital—" he cleared his throat diplomatically, "—means yeh must make some new contacts."

"Yes, yeh're right, Kevin." She studied her hands. Why couldn't this all be behind her? Why couldn't she be on board a ship back to Boston? A long sea voyage was just what she needed to clear her head and forget.

Her greatest fear was that she might never forget. Never forget the weeks that she spent chasing her husband across the better part of the West. The weeks she had spent finding out what it meant to love and be loved.

He hadn't returned. It had been two days, and he hadn't come back. She tried not to think about him, but every moment that ticked by sealed her fate. He was never returning.

It was time to start thinking of the future. Of her da's business. She looked up at a silenced Kevin O'Leary. "I've bought a new gown for the ball, Kevin. I didn't want t'embarrass yeh."

The Irishman brightened. "Yeh'd never embarrass me, girl. Can't think of any man that'd be ashamed t'have yeh for a wife."

"I'm not what yeh think."

"Yeh're talkin' blarney now, girl."

"I've been small-minded and vengeful and proud, Kevin."

322

"What're yeh goin' on about, gal?"

"I don't think there's a soul alive who would want me." Kathleen stared out of the lace-covered window in the small teashop.

"He would be a sorry lot, indeed."

Outside, rain had begun to fall.

Chapter Thirty

"Oi'm not goin' t'let yeh back out now, lass." Kevin O'Leary's bowlegged gait swung him from side to side as they crossed the marble floor of the hotel lobby. "Yeh've just picked up yer dress." Kevin held up the ribboned box in his hands. "And yeh've naught to do tonight."

"I have a headache, Kevin." Kathleen placed a gloved hand to her temple, hoping the little man would leave her alone.

"Oi've seen yeh pull that little trick on your da. Oi'll not let yeh give me some sorry excuse, girl. Oi've made promises."

Kathleen turned on the Irishman, her dander up. "What kind of promises Kevin?"

Kevin O'Leary had the good sense to color. "There's some men who want t'meet yeh, girl. That's all. No harm intended."

Kevin hadn't changed a bit, Kathleen thought. Always scheming, always dealing. "What kind of men?" she demanded.

"Businessmen." Kevin O'Leary brightened. "Important men from New York. They're into shipping. 'Tis on a much grander scale than mine. They're looking t'start shipping East from the valley."

"What valley?" Kathleen was growing tired and impatient.

"The Sacramento Valley. East of here. Surely yeh remember passing through on yer way."

Kathleen thought back to the blur that was the trip from Ogden. Yes, she did remember. It was the one thing she did remember. The lushness of it, the green. She had remembered her da speaking of Ireland. "Yeh've not seen anything like it, girl. So many colors of green yeh'll think yeh've shrunk to the top of a shamrock."

But Ireland had not been fertile. It was what had driven her father to America. The Sacramento Valley, on the other hand, was fecund. Fresh produce of every kind had been visible from the tracks as they made their way across the large valley.

It was the kind of place that you could raise a family.

Her mind betrayed her then. All the feelings she had stifled, all the hurt she had denied came rushing upward.

She felt it wash over her, drowning her. She gasped for breath.

"Are yeh all right lass? Yeh look like yeh've seen a ghost?"

She shook her head, unable to speak.

"Sit, girl. I'll get yeh some sherry." He guided her to a brocade loveseat beside a potted palm. Several people in the lobby stared. She would not cry. She would not embarrass herself further.

325

If she could only stop thinking. Why couldn't she just stop thinking?

Memories ran rampant. The touch of his hands on her arms, his infectious laugh, the softness of his beard and the twinkle in his eye when he teased. The way it felt to be enveloped in his shirt and the smell of him. The look in his eye when she had given him pleasure. How safe she had felt in his arms. How desolate she had felt when he had gone.

In the time it took Kevin to get the sherry, she had relived every one of the emotions she had felt in the past six weeks. Each one was more intense than anything she had known before she had met him. The thought of never feeling anything so deeply again left her despondent.

"Here yeh are, lass." Kevin offered her the glass of sherry.

Kathleen took a sip. The warmth slid down her throat and dulled the pain.

"Oi'm sorry t'upset yeh. Oi was only thinkin', what with losin' quite a bit o'yer capital, yeh might be of a mind to improve your situation. Oi felt Oi owed it t'yer da."

Kevin couldn't have said anything better to drag her from her doldrums. Her marriage to Bret Merriweather and the loss of the hundred thousand dollars had jeopardized the business that her father had worked all his life to build. In the midst of her own selfishness she had forgotten that. She owed it to her da to keep the business going. A business deal, especially one that offered substantial benefit was not to be slighted at this point.

"Yeh're right Kevin. I was just being foolish for a moment. I'll go with yeh tonight."

Kevin looked relieved. "Yeh'll not regret it, lass. Oi know that."

Kathleen smiled at the anxious little man. She hoped he was right.

Sage stared at himself in the long mirror. He barely recognized himself. After five years, it felt peculiar donning the finely cut evening suit. He rubbed his clean-shaven face, then ran a hand through his short hair. He became thoughtful.

He was not the man who stared back at him from the mirror. But neither was he Sage Duross any longer. He was someone new, someone who wanted to keep the best of both worlds, but live in neither.

He knew there was only one woman who could understand this need. His conversation with the little Irishman who had attacked him in the hotel lobby had changed his world.

Kevin O'Leary had been a wealth of information. Finally, Sage knew what drove Kathleen Callahan. For the first time in their relationship, he had the upper hand. And he was bound and determined to make the most of it. A broad smile crossed his face. He hadn't known whether he wanted to console her for her unfortunate marriage or throttle her for not telling him. Tonight, with any luck he would do both.

If Kevin O'Leary did his part, he was about to one-up Kathleen Callahan at her own game.

Kathleen stared at the beautiful dress laid out on the bed. The richness of the nun's veiling and Egyptian lace, the vibrancy of the shade of azure would have left any woman breathless. Its décolletage, fashionably low, would definitely impress the gentlemen she was to meet.

She fingered the fine fabric, then turned and walked to the mirror above the low dresser. She looked well despite the strain of the past few days. In the soft lamplight, her pale coloring and flaming hair, the high color of her cheeks and bright green eyes left her looking fit as a fiddle, she thought. It seemed even God did not commiserate with her self-indulgent misery. Well, so be it.

She pulled her red curls up and fastened the ostrich-plume headdress that had come with the gown. She shook her head; the feather bobbed and swayed. It was foolish, she decided.

Before she left Boston, she would have been delighted with the ensemble. Tonight it seemed fanciful and extravagant. It might have been what she would have selected not so long ago, but no longer. She no longer had to impress people. That need had grown from desperation. It had sprung from a girl who had no sense of her own worth.

She was no longer that girl.

She walked slowly to the wardrobe and opened the elegant mahogany doors. She reached in and extracted the dress she would wear.

It was Mary Alice Bundy's dress. The young woman who had never lived to see her wedding day. The woman who had known love but never enjoyed its fullness.

Kathleen held it up to the soft light. The watered-silk pearl gray gown was still beautiful. The color of a winter sky, the gray was dark one moment, light the next. Subtle and fluid, it reflected the complexity of Kathleen's life of the past weeks. Simple and yet elegant, it marked the new confidence she had gained through the turmoil.

She lay the dress over the back of the chair and withdrew the elaborate feathered concoction from her hair. If she were to survive, it would have to be as a woman who was now well versed in the reality of life, including both its joy and pain.

Life would go on. She would not shrivel up and die, no matter how much she would like to. There was her father's business to maintain. She would return to Boston and ignore the society that had thought her tragedy a comedy.

She slipped out of her robe and into the dress. She smoothed the close-fitting fabric and felt a strange calmness.

A knock on the door disturbed her meditation.

"Are yeh ready, gal?"

Kathleen smiled. Her escort had arrived. She opened the door to see Kevin O'Leary's ever-cheerful face.

"Yeh look a sight, me dear Kathleen. A truly beautiful sight. But yeh're not wearin' the dress yeh bought."

"This one is better, I think, Kevin."

"Makes no never mind. Yeh'd be as beautiful as an angel in a flour sack."

Kathleen laughed. Kevin's compliments had a way of running amuck.

"D'yeh have a wrap, dear girl?"

Kathleen nodded.

"Well grab it up and let's be on our way then."

Kevin clicked his heels together and for a moment Kathleen thought he might disappear like a leprechaun. But the little bowlegged man in the expensive evening suit and top hat stayed put.

She grabbed a gray mohair shawl and took the arm he offered.

"To a productive evening, lass. May the saints smile down on our endeavors."

"Amen," Kathleen murmured.

Charles Crocker's home on Nob Hill was as finely appointed as any in Boston or New York. Lamplight from within and flaming torches without gave it the appearance of some fairy castle. All carriages that night seemed to be headed toward the elaborate railroad baron's home.

Kathleen had anticipated a much smaller event. A stab of anxiety found the pit of her stomach. "Kevin, I don't think I feel well enough for such an elaborate affair."

"Shush, now." He patted her hand. "Yeh'll be fine, lass."

The carriage crawled forward in the throng. The light blazing from the windows lit the inside of the vehicle. Kevin O'Leary seemed pleased as punch with himself, Kathleen thought. She couldn't help wondering if there was anything in the proposed deal for him. But it was a mean-spirited thought, she concluded, acknowledging the help he had offered her these past days. Still, he seemed to be fidgety and anxious.

"Good evening, sir. Madame." A liveried servant opened the door of the carriage and offered a hand to Kathleen. She stepped down and became suddenly aware of the luxurious gowns on the women that surrounded her. She smoothed the gray silk and stood up to all her four-foot-ten-inch height. Kathleen Callahan was not easily intimidated.

They entered by the beautiful beveled glass double doors into an entryway twice the dimensions of Kathleen's parlor in Boston. A crystal chandelier the size of a small horse was ablaze with candles overhead. Heavy baroque furniture lined the walls. She could hear the strains of a waltz floating down from a ballroom somewhere above them.

"Your hat, sir?" Kevin gave his hat to another liveried manservant. Kathleen felt like she was in a fairyland where anything was possible. A frisson of excitement shuddered through her.

"Are yeh ready then, lass?" Kevin offered his arm and Kathleen took it. Her anxiousness seemed to fade away.

Confidence returned. She could do this. She would bargain with the devil himself if it meant she could keep her da's business going.

The ballroom took her breath away. California's wealth had found expression in the gilt room. While ornate, it was done with an elegance that left Kathleen dreaming of the great palaces of Europe. For a moment she felt like a princess about to meet a prince.

"Kevin. My God man, didn't think you'd come for sure. And who is this lovely thing?"

Charles Crocker was a man of considerable girth, balding and flushed. He chomped on a large cigar as he spoke. Kathleen smiled. So much for Prince Charming.

"This is the dear daughter of a life-long friend. Kathleen Callahan, may Oi present Charles Crocker."

Kathleen extended her hand, and the man took out his cigar long enough to kiss her gloved hand. "You're the one then Kevin touts so. I can see your beauty, and I have no doubt as to your brains."

"Yeh're too kind, sir."

"I don't think so, my dear. I don't think so at all."

Kathleen felt that his peculiar statement was based on some knowledge blurted out by the ever-chattering leprechaun at her side. She would happily kill Kevin O'Leary if the night turned out ill.

"Well, get yourself a drink and take a spin on the dance floor. We'll talk business later."

"A pleasure, sir. A pleasure indeed." Kevin nodded, very pleased with himself.

He pulled Kathleen toward the tables replete with silver and snacks and an ice-sculpted swan almost as large as Kathleen herself.

"A glass of yer best whiskey if yeh please." The music

started, and the dance floor was once more filled with whirling couples. It resembled Boston and yet somehow was different. People like Kevin were somehow at home here as well. What had he said about California? That it cared little for where you were born and who you knew?

"Would yeh like some punch lass?"

"No, Kevin. Thank yeh, though." Kathleen studied the crowded room.

She couldn't help wondering if Sage would have been comfortable in this world. She had accused him of not being a cowboy, yet she had difficulty picturing him in this elaborate ballroom.

It was a foolish thought she told herself. She was doing herself no good by dwelling on the past.

"Come on girl, let's take a swing at it."

Kevin had grabbed her arm and pulled her out onto the dance floor before she could object. His exuberance and ungainly stride left her breathless within moments. But instead of being embarrassed, she began to laugh. She twirled with abandon, not caring about what others thought. This was who she was. Irish. Poor born. Proud. They could take it or leave it.

The light danced across the other dancers as Kevin twirled her one last time before the music stopped. She doubled over with laughter and fought to regain her breath.

"Ah, lass, yeh're a dream of a partner. That yeh are."

"Mr. O'Leary. Can you and Miss Callahan join us?"

Kathleen pulled up, still short of breath, to see Charles Crocker signaling to them to join the group of men he was with.

"Are yeh ready then, Kathleen?"

"As ready as I'll ever be, Kevin." She pushed a stray curl

back from her face and smiled. Her color was high and her mood carefree for the first time in weeks.

"Miss Callahan, some of my friends have shown an interest in doing business with your company in Boston. If you knew me better, you'd know I never let pleasure interfere with business." Charles Crocker slipped a hand behind her and guided her toward the small group of formally attired men who were deep in conversation at one end of the large room.

"Gentlemen, may I present Miss Kathleen Callahan."

"Miss Callahan, I've heard so much about you." An elegant white-haired man took her hand and delivered a kiss, drawing her into the little group.

"I'm sure anything you heard was exaggerated, Mr. . . . ?"

The older man ignored her prompt and continued. "My son rarely exaggerates, Miss Callahan. But where has he gone to?"

"I understand that yeh wish to discuss a business arrangement, sir."

"He said you had a brogue." The white-haired man smiled. "It's quite charming."

Kathleen was losing patience. Who had been talking about her, and what else had they said? Was she once more to be the laughingstock of the city? "I don't know what yeh've been told. But I know me business and I can cut a deal as good as any man."

"I've no doubt about that, Miss Callahan."

Well, whoever had been talking about her at least got her name right. She wouldn't have to lie about a husband.

"Ah, here's my son now."

A man approached from across the room. Tall and dark, for a moment Kathleen had a flash of déjà vu. She was being silly, she told herself. This man was undeniably at home in his surroundings. Clean-shaven with short hair and wearing the finest cut evening suit, he was, without a doubt, "to the manor born."

"Get hold of yerself, girl," she mumbled. "Yer beginnin' to hallucinate." Madness, she determined, was not a promising future.

She looked down for a moment to clear her thoughts. She needed to appear sane even if she doubted her own sanity at the moment. When she looked up she could only see the starched white shirt of the man she was to do business with.

The man bent over her hand. She stared at his black hair and smelled his cologne and something else, something terribly familiar. Her heart began to beat faster, and she still didn't know why. He straightened and still she stared at the man. He was devastatingly handsome, but that was not what disturbed Kathleen. It was something else.

"Is your husband joining us tonight, 'Squirrel Tooth'?" The inquiry seemed almost bitter.

Kathleen's legs almost buckled beneath her. It seemed a lifetime ago when an unshorn murderer had bent over her hand the same way.

It couldn't be. She studied him, all the time struggling to make sense of it all. He was angry, angry and bitter. She could see it in his eyes. Why hadn't she told him? Why couldn't she forget her pride? She had been a fool, and it appeared she would pay dearly for her foolishness.

How could she explain to him about her husband? He hated her. It was clear in the icy stare he gave her.

For the first time in her life, Kathleen was afraid to speak. Afraid to drive him away still further.

"Ah, I see you have already met the younger Edward Du-ross. He and his father have proposed what I think will be a mutually beneficial agreement. But I will not give it away." Charles Crocker had come up behind her. "Let us leave the young ones to work out the details, shall we gentlemen?"

Kathleen was only vaguely aware of the others leaving. She was paralyzed. Unable to speak, unable to move.

Sage. His name formed on her lips without finding a voice.

He seemed hardened. Oblivious to her pain. How would she make him understand?

"I didn't mean t'hurt yeh," she pleaded desperately.

"And you think running off to see your husband would what . . . ? Endear yourself to me?"

She had to make him understand. It was her last hope. Her pride had always prevented her from saying what needed to be said between them.

She had no pride left. She had only a desperate driving love that gave her the strength to say anything.

"I did not run off to be with me husband." She searched his face for any softening, any hope. " 'Twas him who did the runnin'."

An arched eyebrow was the only sign he was listening.

"Me husband left me on our wedding night. He stole over one hundred thousand dollars of me money and with his mistress headed west. He made me the laughingstock of Boston. I was a stubborn, vengeful girl. I chased them across the West like a madwoman, vowing to find them and see them pay."

"And you found them?"

The question was cold. She had not reached him with her explanation.

"I found them. But they were in their own hell, whereas I . . ." Her voice shook with emotion. "I'd had a glimpse of heaven."

She waited for a response. Somewhere in the background there was a disturbance, the music had stopped, the crowd had hushed. She didn't really care. She cared only about one thing—that he would forgive her, that he would . . .

Sage's glance left hers and she followed it. A constable had entered the ballroom. He was approaching them. She fought the urge to flee.

The man nodded to Sage. "This is her then?"

"Yes, constable."

"You're under arrest ma'am."

"Under arrest?" She looked back incredulously at Sage. His face showed no emotion whatever.

"Arrest for what?" she demanded of the uniformed police officer.

"Bank robbery. You've been identified as one 'Squirrel Tooth' Sally by this here gentleman."

She turned away from the constable. What was going on? He couldn't be this cruel. Did he hate her that much?

"Please, Sage, don't let them do this," she begged.

Sage nodded to the constable. Kathleen felt the cold metal of the handcuff encircle her wrist.

"Sage! You can't let them do this!" She was angry now.

"Do what, my Irish sprite?" A smile lit his face. "This?"

He held out his hand and the officer clamped on the other cuff.

Kathleen tugged at the cuff angrily.

"How dare you!"

Sage scooped her up in his arms. "How dare I what?"

Kathleen was within a breath of his face. "Scare me half to death." She pummeled his chest with her free hand.

"Calm down, you little hellion," Sage advised.

"I thought . . ." Kathleen couldn't finish. Tears welled up in her eyes and her throat. She suddenly became aware of the staring crowd around them. "Put me down. Everyone is looking," she whispered.

"Then we shall give them something to look at." His kiss when it came drove away the crowd and the stares. Drove away the doubts and the fears. Drove away the girl and restored the woman.

"We have a business deal to discuss, do we not?"

She shook her head affirmatively, a mischievous smile on her face.

"I think that would better be done in a more private setting. Don't you?"

Again she shook her head in agreement.

With her still in his arms, Edward "Sage" Duross strode across the ballroom and down the stairs to the privacy of his carriage. Once there he placed her on his lap and kissed her soundly again.

"Happy?" he questioned as the carriage pulled away.

She pulled a hairpin from her curls and, holding up her shackled wrist, offered it to him.

"I believe I will be very, very, shortly."

Epilogue

Kathleen Callahan stood on the wide, covered porch and admired the beautiful green valley before her. *Like being shrunk down to the top of a shamrock,* as Kevin O'Leary had said. It seemed equally true of what lay before her. The valley held every shade of green, from the palest yellow-tinged sprouts of new growth to the deep emerald of the towering trees. And in between there were enough shades to challenge even Ireland.

She took two steps forward until the April sun washed over her. The earth smelled wonderful. Pungent and fertile. She let a hand pass over her protruding belly and smiled. It wasn't just the valley that had proved fertile.

The land around her reflected her own state. It too burgeoned with new life. It too basked in the sun and awaited

338

the fruits of careful tending. She never knew she could be so content.

"Oi'll be off now. Tell the mister Oi said goodbye." Kevin O'Leary appeared at the door of the sprawling Victorian home, traveling bag in hand.

Kathleen turned and smiled. "Goodbye, Kevin. Don't stay away so long next time." She walked forward to embrace the bandy-legged little Irishman.

"Oi'll be back fer the baby's baptism, which from the looks of it, will not be long."

Kathleen rubbed her stomach. "I think yeh may be right."

"Until then, lass." He offered her a peck on the cheek. She watched as he toddled off toward town and the train back to San Francisco.

It was good to have friends visit, but it was equally nice sometimes when they left, she thought. Then she reprimanded herself. She turned to go back into the house when a scurry of activity distracted her.

"Papa, Papa!" Four-year-old Devin and two-year-old Maeve came careening around the corner of the house. The towheads were trailed by their nursemaid.

Kathleen looked in the direction they ran.

"Papa . . . Papa!" Once more their screams of delight pierced the warm air. Kathleen smiled broadly.

She watched the tall dark-haired man scoop up a child in each arm. He offered a nuzzling kiss to each of the fidgeting children and was rewarded with giggles of delight.

"I think it's time for you two to eat if I'm not mistaken. Go with Bridget now and have your lunch." He set the two children down and sent them off with a kiss on the forehead. He looked up.

It was the same every time he looked at her the way he did now. She felt awash in his love, reborn in his smile.

How could she have guessed that, more now than ever, her world was only complete when he was in it.

He strode up the gravel walk until he stood on the first step of the porch.

He put out his hand and let it rest on Kathleen's belly. "Tired?" He kissed her cheek lingering there longer than necessary.

"A little."

"Well then, 'Squirrel Tooth,' I think it's time you got some rest." He scooped her up and carried her into the house and up the stairs. The wood floors shone with polished wax, and the sun pierced the wide windows to reflect on the burnished surface and reverberate throughout the comfortably furnished rooms. He strode up the wide staircase two steps at a time. Placing her on a beautifully carved four-poster bed in their bedroom, he lay down beside her.

For a long time, they lay quietly, face to face, neither feeling they had to speak. It was an unbelievably beautiful feeling, Kathleen realized, to be so at ease that speaking wasn't necessary.

"What are you thinking, 'Squirrel Tooth'?"

She smiled. "I'm thinkin' yeh're gonna have the divil of a time explainin' to the children why yeh insist on callin' me 'Squirrel Tooth.' "

Sage smiled back. "When we are old and gray and we gather our ten children around us . . ."

"Ten? Did I hear yeh say ten? Are yeh daft, man?" She slapped his shirtfront.

Sage Duross looked offended. "I guess I am daft or I would never have married such an ornery woman."

"Ornery? I thought I had become quite the model of decorum."

Sage's smile returned broader than ever. "I hope not,

'Squirrel Tooth.' " He rose on one elbow and cradled her cheek with his hand. He leaned in and kissed her then. "I certainly hope not."

It was a magical kiss. A kiss that carried the weight of the years they had shared, the hopes they had dreamed, and the love and laughter that had miraculously brought them together. Kathleen Callahan closed her eyes and whispered the prayer that had crossed her lips every day for the past four years. "Thank yeh, Lord. Yeh have been mighty kind. That yeh have."

HANNAH'S HALF-BREED
HEIDI BETTS

Wounded and in desperate need of help, David Walker has survived the treacherous journey to reach the blue-eyed, blond-haired girl of his memories. And in Hannah's arms he discovers Heaven. But torn between the white man's world and his Indian heritage, David wonders if he's been saved or damned.

The man who calls himself Spirit Walker bears little resemblance to the boy who comforted Hannah during her darkest hours at the orphanage. There is nothing safe about the powerful half-breed who needs her assistance. Still, the schoolteacher will risk everything to save him, for their love is strong enough to overcome any challenge.

Winnie Griggs

What Matters Most

Reed Wilder journeys to Far Enough, Texas, in search of a fallen woman. He finds an angel. Barely reaching five feet two inches, the petite brunette helps to defend him against two ruffians and then treats his wounds with a gentleness that makes him long to uncover all her secrets. But she only has to reveal her name and he knows his lovely rescuer is not an innocent woman, but the deceitful opportunist who preyed on his brother. Reed prides himself on his logic and control, but both desert him when he gazes into Lucy's warm brown eyes. He has only one option: to discover the truth behind those enticing lips he longs to sample.

_4829-9 $4.99 US/$5.99 CAN

Dorchester Publishing Co., Inc.
P.O. Box 6640
Wayne, PA 19087-8640

Please add $2.50 for shipping and handling for the first book and $.75 for each book thereafter. NY and PA residents, please add appropriate sales tax. No cash, stamps, or C.O.D.s. All orders shipped within 6 weeks via postal service book rate.
Canadian orders require $2.00 extra postage and must be paid in
U.S. dollars through a U.S. banking facility.

Name_____
Address_____
City_____ State_____ Zip_____
I have enclosed $_____ in payment for the checked book(s).
Payment <u>must</u> accompany all orders. ☐ Please send a free catalog.
CHECK OUT OUR WEBSITE! www.dorchesterpub.com